"Mia Long died under sus[...] told me that you knew the victim. Sergeant Murdock and the county Crime Scene Unit will be arriving shortly. They're going to cordon off the bakeshop and conduct a thorough investigation of the premises, gathering any evidence that might be pertinent to this case. In the meantime, I'm going to ask you to come down to the station with me for further questioning."

"What?" I cried, feeling a welling of outrage. I wasn't even at half-blown New Yorker and the poor man flinched. Rory, Kennedy, and Dylan were staring at me, urging me with their eyes to tone it down. The young officer, after all, was only doing his duty. Still, it rankled. "But I've already told you everything!"

McAllister's gold-dusted brows furrowed, causing his handsome, boyish features to look either displeased or embarrassed, it was hard to tell which. "I'm sorry, Ms. Bakewell, I truly am, but you didn't tell us that Mia Long was having an affair with your fiancé, Jeffery Plank."

"Ex-fiancé," I corrected.

McAllister cleared his throat. "Right. I understand that you caught them in the act, so to speak. She died on your property, Ms. Bakewell. Mia Long ate one of your donuts. You have motive and opportunity. Do you see how this might look bad for you?"

Unfortunately, I did. And, unbelievably, my day had just gone from bad to a whole new level of horrible . . .

Murder at the Beacon Bakeshop

Darci Hannah

KENSINGTON
PUBLISHING CORP.

www.kensingtonbooks.com

KENSINGTON BOOKS are published by

Kensington Publishing Corp.
119 West 40th Street
New York, NY 10018

Copyright © 2021 by Darci Hannah

All rights reserved. No part of this book may be reproduced in any form or by any means without the prior written consent of the Publisher, excepting brief quotes used in reviews.

To the extent that the image or images on the cover of this book depict a person or persons, such person or persons are merely models, and are not intended to portray any character or characters featured in the book.

This book is a work of fiction. Names, characters, businesses, organizations, places, events, and incidents either are the product of the author's imagination or are used fictitiously. Any resemblance to actual persons, living or dead, events, or locales is entirely coincidental

If you purchased this book without a cover you should be aware that this book is stolen property. It was reported as "unsold and destroyed" to the Publisher and neither the Author nor the Publisher has received any payment for this "stripped book."

All Kensington titles, imprints, and distributed lines are available at special quantity discounts for bulk purchases for sales promotion, premiums, fund-raising, educational, or institutional use.

Special book excerpts or customized printings can also be created to fit specific needs. For details, write or phone the office of the Kensington Sales Manager: Attn.: Sales Department. Kensington Publishing Corp., 119 West 40th Street, New York, NY 10018. Phone: 1-800-221-2647.

The Kensington logo is a trademark of Kensington Publishing Corp.

First Printing: March 2021
ISBN-13: 978-1-4967-3172-2
ISBN-10: 1-4967-3172-7

ISBN-13: 978-1-4967-3175-3 (ebook)
ISBN-10: 1-4967-3175-1 (ebook)

10 9 8 7 6 5 4 3 2

Printed in the United States of America

CHAPTER 1

I stared out the window, my stomach churning with remorse as I gazed upon what was undoubtedly the worst financial decision I'd ever made. My trembling hands were another sign that my good judgment was slipping. What was I thinking? Had I gone mad? Had I been drunk when I pulled the trigger on my successful Wall Street career? Obviously, I mused, unable to help a dramatic eye roll. But why . . . WHY had I thought this would be a good idea? I was still trying to figure it out when I caught the driver's amused gaze in the rearview mirror.

I cleared my throat.

The beastly man smiled wider.

"Mike, is it?" I said, addressing his reflection in a no-nonsense tone. Mike had been waiting ten minutes for me to exit his car. If he wanted a good tip, he'd continue to wait. If he wanted an even better tip, he'd wipe that idiot grin off his face. "Again, I apologize. It's just that . . . it looked different on the internet."

A burst of ill-concealed mirth rumbled from the front seat. "And that's a surprise?" Driver Mike was wheezing, he thought it so funny. Then, adding insult to injury, he said, "I thought all you New Yorkers were supposed to be *street-smart* and *savvy*. Guess I've been driving around the exception."

That last remark threw my sarcasm meter into the red zone. I could dish it as good as I got, and often did. However, the amount of attitude coming from this man, this utter stranger, was irksome. I had just possibly made a terrible life decision—a terribly expensive terrible life decision—and he thought it was funny? It wasn't funny. And it hadn't been funny when I'd been expecting a limo to pick me up at the tiny Cherry Capital Airport in Traverse City and got a sarcastic, squatchy-looking Midwestern Uber driver instead. After a quick call to Betty Vanhoosen, my Realtor and the person who insisted on handling my transportation needs from the airport, I was told that Mike not only had a GMC Yukon, but a five-star rating as well. He was obviously related to her or had pictures of her in a compromising position. The Yukon, aside from the prevailing smell of corned beef and wet wool, wasn't bad; the five-star rating, however, I was beginning to question. I locked eyes with Mike in the mirror and gave him my best *don't-mess-with-me* face.

"I have exceptional taste in clothing and a knack for making money. Those are *my* New Yorker qualities, Mike. And here's another. I don't like to be deceived. I distinctly remember reading the word *renovated* in the Realtor's description."

"Wow!" he said and commenced another bout of laughing. "Are you sure you're from New York? Did you grow up under a rock or something?" Before I could reply, he mocked, "Hello! It's the internet. Pigs fly on the internet, Ms. Bakewell. Literally. Nothing's real on the internet."

"I know that," I snapped. "But you can't use the word *renovated* in a real estate ad if the property wasn't renovated! That's misrepresentation!"

Mike stopped laughing. "Well, don't get your panties all in a bunch just yet. The old girl *was* renovated . . . in the nineteen-seventies. That's when they shored up the indoor plumbing. Then there's our Michigan winters. Takes a toll on everything around here. How old do you think I am?"

He turned and smiled at me from the front seat. His cheap haircut and full, untrimmed beard were light brown, his eyes a twinkling blue. As far as I could see there wasn't a gray hair on his head or a wrinkle on his cheeks.

"Fifty," I said, aiming to insult. "Sixty, perhaps? I can't tell with that beard."

My bitch-tastic powers were useless on him. Mike grinned. "Thirty!" he exclaimed as if it was a wonder. "It's our Michigan winters." He beamed with pride.

"I have a good moisturizer. I think I'll be just fine." I waved at him to turn back around, then scanned the cold, frozen bay once again, shaking my head in dismay. A lighthouse? Correction, an old, run-down lighthouse on the shores of Lake Michigan. What had I been thinking?

I pulled out my iPhone and stared at the picture on the internet. The image before me depicted a large, historic, two-story brick house built on rolling sand dunes and perched on the shores of Lake Michigan. Sun glinted off the windows and white-painted brick. The entire structure was surrounded by cream-colored sand, flowering azaleas, and pink rugosa roses. The long, gabled roof, with not a shingle out of place, had been painted bright red. It was a striking contrast to the magnificent cylindrical light tower attached to the side of the house. Although the thirty-eight feet of brick had been painted to match the house, the cast-iron gallery and decagonal lantern room were matte black. It looked to be the perfect spot to watch a sunset or count the sails on the horizon. The image was not only a vision of tranquility, it was fodder for my dreams. No wonder I had been sucked in.

The lighthouse out the window, however, was another matter. The white paint, or what was left of it, had been sand-blasted away by harsh winds, revealing large splotches of dingy brick. The trim and most of the gutters had fallen off, and the roof was missing a quarter of its shingles. One of the two chimneys had crumbled away, exposing a rusty vent pipe, and the other was badly in need of tuck-pointing. The light tower was also in need of fresh paint and a new set of windows. But that was only half of it. The real gut-clencher was the fact that the entire building was caked in snow and covered in layers of dripping lake ice. It looked like something straight out of the animated movie *Frozen*, only without the talking snowman and catchy show tunes. My stomach gave another painful lurch, thinking that I had traded civilized luxury for this. Clearly the photo on the internet had been Photoshopped.

"Can't slap enough moisturizer on that old thing to save it."

Thank goodness he pointed at the lighthouse and not me.

"However, once the snow melts, a good coat of paint should help. Pity they were going to knock the old relic down and sell the land. I'm told your generous offer saved it."

Saved it? Oh, he definitely had an in with Betty Vanhoosen! The moment I made an offer on the historic landmark, I learned that I had entered into a bidding war against a developer. He was planning on turning the prime lighthouse real estate into high-end lakefront condos. Knowing a thing or two about investments, his proposal was obviously the more lucrative choice. However, I wanted the old lighthouse. And I got it.

Running a critical eye over all the costly work yet to be done, I said, "I'm not so sure it should have been saved."

Mike chuckled, thinking I was joking. For once he was correct.

Buying the old lighthouse sight unseen was a leap of faith. One that I needed to make. There was something about the old relic that had spoken to me. Perhaps it was just the fact that ordinary people don't generally get to own lighthouses. The notion was as romantic as the thought of a fresh start, for us both.

"Old Beacon Point Lighthouse is a landmark around here," driver Mike continued. "Did you know that at one point, Michigan had nearly two hundred and fifty lighthouses around its coast? The number's dwindled to around a hundred and twenty-four since then. This old thing didn't make the cut. Ironically, it was one of the last lighthouses to be tended by a real keeper. Another irony? Some say the first keeper never left." Mike turned back at me and gave his eyebrows a menacing wiggle.

I smiled, refusing to take the bait. "Wow. You're a font of Michigan lighthouse knowledge. I'm impressed. What else can you tell me about Beacon Point?"

"Coast Guard had it for a while. In the seventies the town purchased it, hoping preservation enthusiasts would keep it running. They fixed the plumbing, gave it a coat of paint, and restored the old Fresnel lens. But the old-timers are dying off, and our generation," he said, lumping me into that category, "is too busy to care. Pity they had to sell it, but I'm glad it's going to a hot chick with cash and not some greasy developer."

I made the mistake of looking at the mirror. Dear Lord, had he actually winked at me? Yes. Yes, he had. And due to his suggestive look, he thought he had a chance. Must be those Michigan winters, I mused. Harsh conditions forced men to take risks. Fortunately, untrimmed beards and the smell of corned beef did nothing for me.

The truth was, I'd been blessed with good genetics. Mom had been a fashion model in the late seventies and eighties, and Dad a Wall Street hedge fund manager. Doesn't take a genius to do the math there. Thank goodness I'd gotten my light green eyes, high cheekbones, and ash-blond hair from Mom and Dad's affinity for numbers. Had fate not been so kind I'd have a receding hairline with a bad comb-over and a compulsion to wear matching designer outfits with my dog.

"But I have to warn you," Mike continued, realizing I wasn't taking the bait. "Not everyone's happy that the light is moving into private hands. Truth is, the folks of Beacon Harbor don't much like change. I certainly hope your *knack for making money* has followed you from the Big Apple, or else it's going to be one long summer for you."

The mention of summer reminded me that there was another season in Michigan other than arctic. It was early March, and snow was still falling. At Betty's suggestion I had hired an interior designer and her contractor to spruce up my living quarters in the keeper's house, making sure the plumbing, electric, and gas were up to code. Hopefully, the weather would cooperate for the other renovations yet to be started. I smiled at Mike's reflection. "Never hope when there's money to be made, Mike. It's all hard work and meticulous planning."

"Well, well, look at you, Big Town. Coming to our little corner of the world to show us how it's done. So, what are you waiting for?"

What *was* I waiting for?

Chapter 2

Four months ago, I'd been perfectly happy with my life in New York City until the night I walked into my fiancé's trendy Midtown restaurant and found him with that tart-of-a-pastry-chef of his in his office. He'd been covered in icing sugar and chocolate curls. She'd been sitting on a slab of Himalayan sea salt. And all I could think to say was, "I hope you're not planning on cooking my birthday dinner on that . . . that thing!" I was pointing at the pricey slab of imported sea salt under Mia Long. He thought I was pointing at Mia. He also thought, albeit wrongly, that cheating fiancés were to be forgiven.

After keying the Jaguar I'd bought him for his forty-fifth birthday, I went home and anger-baked six dozen of the most decadent cupcakes on the planet—cupcakes the likes of Mia Long could only dream about baking, the tart!

My dirty little secret was that I'd always had a passion for baking. But I had pushed that passion aside to pursue a lucrative career in investment banking. I baked pastries and cakes for my friends, who thought it both ironic and hilarious that my last name was Bakewell. Three years ago, they had all pitched in and got me private lessons with a renowned chef. That's how I'd met my ex-fiancé, Jeffery Plank, a rising celebrity chef on the verge of his first cookbook deal, the cheating pig!

Jeffery may have further inspired my passion for baking, but the talent was all mine, and it showed on all the intricately decorated, decadently rich cupcakes I'd made. I ate one, threw a half dozen at his picture, and gave the rest to the doorman. Mr. Rosenstein, used to my baking outbursts, kept a dozen for his kids and gave the rest away to my neighbors. The next evening, Martha Durand, a former Miss America turned America's favorite morning talk show host, came pounding on my door.

"Did you bake this?" Martha was holding one of my cupcakes as if it was a Golden Globe. "Girl, we need to talk. This, Lindsey Bakewell, is your destiny."

Martha had gushed about my cupcakes and my talent for baking. I told her about my cheating fiancé and my looming depression. She then bolstered me up with a heartfelt speech on passion, and dreams, and how important it was to embrace the one and follow the other. I had a job I was good at, I reasoned, but admitted that finance had never been my passion. Opening my own bakery, as Martha kept hinting I should do, had never crossed my mind. That was because I had spent years and years carefully laying all the track needed to chug away on a safe and successful life. I never thought of jumping them and branching out in a totally different direction. Then again, I never thought Jeffery would be such an idiot.

Growth, Martha had said, didn't come from complacency, but from living on the outer edge of one's abilities and constantly pushing into the unknown.

"Bake, Lindsey Bakewell. That is your destiny."

It was. Martha had made me believe it. She'd started the wheels turning. A broken heart, an empty apartment, and a bottle of wine did the rest. I opened my laptop, typed a few key words into Google, and began searching. When the old lighthouse filled my screen, everything clicked. I thought it was destiny. Now I wasn't so sure.

An earsplitting howl from the third-row seating brought me back to the problem at hand—my cold feet, both literally and figuratively.

"Wellington!" My two-year-old Newfoundland had finally shaken off the heavy dose of travel sedation.

"Looks like that bear of a dog of yours is finally awake."

He was. A drool-covered tongue licking my cheek was proof of that. I hadn't known about the drool when I'd fallen in love with the pudgy little ball of black fur. I liked to joke that Wellington was the first financial blunder I'd ever made. He wasn't exactly a good fit for New York City apartment living. He ate a lot, chewed a lot, pooped a lot, and required a team of groomers, trainers, and walkers. However, his unconditional love and companionship more than made up for it. And, if truth be told, he was part of the reason I'd made the risky internet purchase to begin with.

"What do you think, Welly?"

He pressed his wet nose to the window.

"That's our new home." I looked in the backseat and

saw that his tail was working double-time. Wellington was ready to begin our new adventure. I took that as a good sign.

"Well, as they say, in for a penny, in for a pound," I remarked and opened the door.

"Welcome to Beacon Harbor, Ms. Bakewell. I'll get the luggage."

"Whoa! Now this *is* a shocker." Mike dropped the first load of luggage inside the doorway and stared in wonder. "Looks like somebody blew their entire renno budget on the interior. I thought you said you were going to open a bakery or something?"

"Bakeshop café," I replied, ignoring his budget remark. "It had to be livable."

It was more than livable. It was, quite frankly, perfect. Although only part of the keeper's house had been renovated (most of the main floor being reserved for the industrial kitchen, bakery counter, and café), what had been set aside for my private use had been transformed into a thing of wonder. The interior designer and her team had outdone themselves, fusing old lighthouse charm with clean, modern living. The original hardwood floors had been beautifully restored. The plaster walls had been replaced with a tasteful mix of shiplap and drywall. The entire living quarters dazzled the senses in a palate of airy blues, sea foam greens, and clean whites. The wooden rocking chair by the fireplace was original, as was the antique table beside it; the hand-woven rug, white wingback chair with footstool, and the two-piece sectional in berry-red leather were new. A bouquet of red and white roses sat on a rustic white-painted coffee table with four sets of keys neatly laid beside it along with a note of welcome from the design company. It was a nice touch. I'd have to call Betty and thank her for the suggestion.

"These are for the lighthouse," Mike informed me, picking up a set of keys. "Those are a duplicate set. And those," he added, pointing to the other two sets, each on a Jeep key ring, "are for your sweet ride. Betty said it was delivered Thursday and is now in the old boathouse, which is like a garage, only bigger." Mike grinned. "I had you pictured as more of a Range Rover type of gal. The white Jeep Rubicon threw me, but it's a fine car for these parts."

"So, you've seen it." Why did this surprise me? Mike grinned, affirming that he had.

"I haven't owned a car in years. Didn't need to. And, financially speaking, you get more bang for your buck with the Jeep. Besides, it's Wellington's favorite vehicle. Every time he sees one with the top off and a dog buckled into the passenger seat with the wind ruffling its fur, he perks up and barks with joy."

He looked at me as if I were crazy. "You bought a Jeep for your dog? Well, it'll be a few more months before you can take the top off that thing."

I smiled at Mike. "Thanks for reminding me. You can leave the bags there." A look behind him out the door told me that Wellington was still bounding around in the snow, eating half of it and pleased as punch with his new home. And he had plenty of room to run. Although the little town of Beacon Harbor sat just across the road, the lighthouse grounds were extensive. Once again, I was overcome by the thought of how perfect it was going to be for outdoor seating and a beachside pup café. Perhaps down the road it might even serve as a romantic light-house wedding venue. I could now see that the possibilities were endless.

The lighthouse itself was a large two-story brick structure designed for the keeper and his family. The front of the house faced the public beach and had two main entrances. The entrance on the lakeside required a little set of steps to enter and was closest to the light tower. This was the entrance Wellington and I would use for access to our living quarters, consisting of a cozy parlor with a fireplace, the original kitchen, now remodeled into a quaint workspace that even Joanna Gaines would approve of, a small dining area, a powder room, and access to the entire second floor. Not as spacious as my New York penthouse, but the views were spectacular.

The second main door was on the other end of the house and had a short set of wide steps flanked by wrought-iron railings. This entrance had better access to parking and was at one time the assistant keeper's apartment. The spacious rooms on this side would soon be converted to a bakery café.

In a few weeks' time, the wind-battered brick would be tuck-pointed and given a fresh coat of white, the gabled roof and dormers re-shingled in bright red. The bakeshop door would be refitted with a glass-and-wood one, with a sign above it, welcoming hungry customers to *The Beacon Bakeshop & Café*. Large picture windows would be reset into the brick. Above the windows there'd be a charming red awning with scalloped edges. I had envisioned it all and had meticulously planned it out to the last detail. Excitement coursed through me. It was going to be the business I had dreamed of owning. Yet as heady as my dream bakery was, the three-story light tower over-looking Lake Michigan was the real showstopper. I couldn't wait to climb up there and have a look.

By the time I had coerced Welly inside, Mike had un-loaded all our luggage.

"Okay, well, I'll leave you to it, then."

I handed him a sizeable tip and sent him on his way. He was about to walk out the door when he suddenly stopped.

"You're opening up a bakery, right?"

"That's the plan."

"I have a cousin," he said. "She lives in town and used to work for the old Downtown Bakery until they went out of business. For the last two years she's been cleaning cottages and baking for private events. If you're looking to hire some experienced help, she'd be a great choice."

I watched as Mike scribbled a name and phone number on the back of his business card. Apparently, Mike had a day job. "*Beacon Harbor Fishing Charters and Boat Tours*, by Captain Mike Skinner," I read aloud. "Captain Mike Skinner? Sounds like you're living the dream as well."

"You're not the only one with a knack for making money. Not quite Wall Street here, but you'd be surprised at what tourists will pay for a day out on the lake. With any luck they'll have enough left over to buy some of your big city baked goods too."

"I hope so."

"Call Dylan when you're ready. If you want to know anything about Beacon Harbor, she's the one to ask. See ya later, Ms. Bakewell."

"Lindsey," I said. "Call me Lindsey."

CHAPTER 3

The arctic winds whipping off the lake were brutal, but even they were no match for a full-scale construction crew wreaking havoc on the lighthouse. Construction on the bakery started the day after I arrived. That's the day I learned that planning a renovation was a lot more fun than living through one. Before the kitchen could be set up and the display cases brought in, the building had to be configured to house everything I needed. Financing, my specialty, hadn't been a problem. Getting the right permits proved a little more difficult, but not impossible. What was impossible was trying to concentrate with the sound of table saws screaming, drills whining, and nail guns popping throughout every fiber of the building.

"That's sure to wake the dead."

I was in my private lighthouse kitchen. The quaint

room, bedecked with fresh white upper cabinets, navy-blue lower cabinets, and pristine white granite counter-tops, was the place I'd spent most of my time since arriving in Beacon Harbor. I'd been in the kitchen all morning, trying to perfect a new donut recipe for our beach-day launch on Memorial Day weekend. Although I planned to have the shelves filled with all kinds of sweet rolls, coffee cakes, muffins, croissants, and a list of rotating delights, there was just something about a freshly made donut. Not only were they delicious, but they were the perfect treat for a celebration. Oversized specialty donuts were even better. Besides, they looked like mini inner tubes, the filled ones like flattened beach balls. My plan was to have fun with the beachy theme and offer shoppers and beach frolickers alike a feast for the senses. The unfamiliar voice had broken my concentration. For the last two weeks stragglers kept making the same mistake, confusing my private entrance with the one for the construction site. Without turning to look at the speaker, I said, "Construction entrance is through the other door."

"I'm not here to work. I'm here because of this."

There was just enough annoyance in the male voice to grab my full attention. I stopped kneading my second batch of dough and turned to the doorway.

My jaw dropped. This was definitely not one of the construction workers I was familiar with. Nope, the man staring at me with extreme displeasure was a real Northwoods vision, a well-built, black-haired, blue-eyed hunk-a-licious Paul Bunyan, swaddled in hunter-green Carhartt. Due to his impressively good posture, thick neck, and smartly cut hair, I suspected some military training as well. Whatever the case, he was a welcome vision. I hadn't looked at another man since my breakup with Jeffery, partly because I was so fed up with men in general, but mostly because of the bakeshop. But this man? He could distract me any day of the week.

"Ahem," Hunky Woodsman cleared his throat, bringing me back to my senses. That's when I noticed the thin rope dangling from his hand. The sight of the mangled fish hanging from it made me recoil.

"I'm sorry, and you're here why?"

"I'm here because of this!" He pointed at the disgusting fish.

Not only was I miffed, I was confused. What person in their right mind would bring a smelly, mangled fish into my private kitchen? The nerve! The germs! Then, chancing another look at the man, I was struck with a sinking feeling. This was the village idiot. He had to be. There was no other explanation for it. What he lacked in brains, he more than made up for in looks, and he was clearly a menace to fish. But just as I was staring at the mangled remains of the poor fish, another troubling thought struck. What if it wasn't just fish? Dear Lord, no one would hear me scream over the sound of hammers and saws.

Whenever I was approached by crazy in NYC, I just threw up a stern hand and continued walking. But I was in my own kitchen now. Paul Bunyan and his rotting fish filled the entire door frame. Being rude to this beast of a man was not an option. On my life I would not be strangled in my own kitchen with a rope smeared with fish guts! Time for option number two. Blind him with kindness. I smiled, wiped my flour-dusted hands on my apron, and asked very slowly, "Do you want me to buy your fish?"

His dark brows furrowed. "What?"

"Your fishy thing," I repeated. "Isn't that why you've come?"

The look he gave me this time confirmed that he was not the village idiot. In fact, if I was reading him correctly, he thought that title belonged to me. "No, I don't want you to buy it," he snapped, turning an alarming shade of red. "This was my dinner!"

"Oh. Well, thank you for sharing that with me. I'm making donuts. Would you like to try one?" I held up a tray of the first batch I'd been testing. They were a lighter-than-air yeast donut, infused with pure maple syrup, dipped in maple frosting, and sprinkled with thick-cut, naturally cured, hickory-smoked bacon. "I call these Hog Heaven."

Hunky Woodsman was drawn to the donuts like a moth to a flame. Good, I thought, urging him on with my smile. Good. Good boy. Take a donut.

His large hand reached out. He was just about to grab a warm donut off the tray when his hand suddenly jerked away—as if he'd been slapped.

"No! I mean, I'm not here for a donut. I'm here because your dog ate my fish!"

"What?" It was my turn to be shocked and offended. "Well, that's ridiculous." I retracted the donut tray. "My dog doesn't even know where you live."

"I'm your neighbor!" he stated with a touch of annoyance, as if I should have known. "I waved to you the other day. I live right over there!" He pointed to the wall.

I honestly doubted he'd waved at me. I mean, I'd remember if I'd seen this man before.

"I was in the black pickup truck?" He was trying to jog my memory. Unfortunately, I'd seen more black pickup trucks in the last two weeks than I had in my entire life. "I passed you on the road, driving to my cottage on the other side of the point?"

"Oh?" I said, recalling that I had waved at somebody. It suddenly dawned on me that he was the owner of the charming little log home, tucked into a thick scree of pines with a private stretch of beachfront. It was one of the little treasures that had caught my eye when I had climbed the lighthouse tower. So, this gorgeous man was my neighbor. Still, the thought that he had the nerve to barge into my kitchen and blame the mangled fish on Wellington annoyed me. My inner New Yorker flared.

"So, we're neighbors. That still doesn't give you the right to blame my dog for that." I pointed an angry finger at his fish. "You don't have any proof. My dog doesn't know you, and I assure you, he doesn't eat fish on a string. He eats Blue Nature. It's the best dog food money can buy."

"Well, now he eats fish on a string!" Apparently, I'd gotten under his skin. Hunky Woodsman turned abruptly and left the kitchen. Good riddance, I thought, until a moment later when he returned with yet another rope. He glared at me and gave it a good tug.

On the other end was a sullen Wellington, looking like a prisoner waddling to the gallows.

"Welly!" I cried, shocked to see my dog. I thought he was curled up before the fireplace in the parlor. I dropped to my knees, untied the rope, and forced the droopy brown eyes to mine. They were riddled with guilt.

"Caught him red-handed," the man continued. "I had five fish on here this morning, fresh from the lake. This is all I have left!"

I took a closer look at the fish, and my heart sank. Wellington had definitely made a visit to this man's cottage. Not only had the lower half of the fish been chewed clean off, but it was covered in drool. There was even a long black hair or two tangled in the innards, leaving no doubt as to who had done the deed. I looked up at the man. "I'm sorry. He must have gotten out when I wasn't looking. It's the construction. The poor thing can't stand it."

"I can't either," he said plainly. "Used to be so quiet and peaceful around here before you moved in. Can't concentrate on anything now with that racket." He made a gesture to the other side of the house. "Thought I could get out on the lake far enough to escape it, but you'd be amazed at how sound carries across the ice. I only wonder what it's doing to the Captain."

"The Captain?" I repeated, wondering who that character was.

"Yeah, the Captain. Don't tell me that you don't know about the Captain?" There was something cryptic in the way he said this. Once he realized that I had no idea what he was talking about, he quickly changed the subject. "I'll have that donut now." He forced a smile and plucked one off the tray.

His first bite was aggressive, as if he wanted to hate it. But no man I knew could hate bacon, especially when liberally sprinkled on a maple-flavored, lighter-than-air donut. I watched as his eyes rolled back in his head. He then made a sound that made me go weak in the knees. I nearly dropped the pan.

"Oh my God, these are good!"

"Heavenly, even?" It was shameless of me, but thanks to my ex-fiancé I was totally turned on by good-looking men who moaned while eating my baked goods.

"Yes," he uttered, shoving the rest of the first donut in his mouth. "Definitely heavenly. Sorry," he mumbled.

"Rory Campbell." He wiped a few remaining crumbs on his pants, then stuck out his hand. "I may have come off a bit gruff."

"Lindsey Bakewell," I said, taking it. I offered him another donut. "No problem. You were probably just hungry. Happens all the time. And I am truly sorry about your fish. Can I make it up to you? Can I pay for them? What's the market price on . . . ?" I had no idea what kind of fish they were.

"I'm good," he said. "But I'll take another one of these." He helped himself to another donut. "And dinner tonight."

"You . . . want me to buy you dinner?" The thought never crossed my mind, but I didn't hate it. In fact, I rather liked the idea. Why not go out with this man? He was my neighbor, after all. The fact that Wellington was sitting at his feet, leaning against his leg while being fondly petted was also an indication that he wasn't a half-bad guy. Wellington might have stolen the man's fish, but he was also an excellent judge of character.

"Actually, I want to buy *you* dinner." His vibrant blue eyes, fringed with thick black lashes, suddenly turned playful. "Pick you up at seven, Lindsey Bakewell." He grabbed another donut, gave Welly another pat on the head, and walked out the door.

All my life I'd considered myself to be a savvy New Yorker, but I got the feeling that I'd just been played by Mr. Rory Campbell—and my own dog.

CHAPTER 4

People were staring. Had they never seen Chanel before? Obviously not, I thought, looking at the enormous pair of antlers dangling on the wall above me. I'd never seen so much pine paneling in a room, or so many heads of dead animals. I supposed that's what one gets when one dines at The Moose.

"It's a local favorite," Rory explained, picking up his menu. Although camo and Carhartt seemed to be the fashion of choice, Rory had dressed up his jeans and light gray sweater with a tweed blazer in dark navy. He looked good, so good, in fact, that I didn't even mind that my black Chanel pencil dress and houndstooth bolero jacket stood out like a sore thumb. At least Mom would have been proud. Having Ellie Montague-Bakewell for a mother, one was taught early that there was no such thing as being too stylish. Rory grinned and closed his menu.

"Don't need to look at that. I brought you here because of the perch. If you can't pull it out of the lake yourself, you come here instead."

"I don't fish, so I guess I'll be coming here then. It smells delicious." And it really did. I wasn't one to hunt down my meat, but I always appreciated great food. If I was being totally honest, it was part of the appeal of dating a celebrity chef. Baking was my domain; cooking had been Jeffery's. His restaurant, Sizzle, specialized in fine cuts of meat seared to perfection on exotic surfaces, like slabs of exotic salts, heated rocks, and smoked woods. His New York strip on Himalayan sea salt was to die for— until a few months ago. Now the thought repulsed me.

The Moose might not have been a swanky Midtown restaurant, but there was something surprisingly comfortable about it, just like the man across from me. Perhaps it was the fact that on the ride over he'd admitted that Wellington had been coming to his house every morning for the last two weeks. The first time Wellington had walked onto his front deck and pressed his nose to the window, Rory thought he was a bear. Then he saw the bushy tail. He was immediately let in and given a breakfast sausage. And once a person slipped Welly a treat, they were friends for life.

"I thought it was the beginning of a beautiful friendship," Rory said, "until I ran out of breakfast sausage. He must have thought I hung the fish out for him." Thankfully there were no hard feelings.

After we ordered, Rory leaned across the table. "So, why does a nice Wall Street banker like you purchase an old lighthouse in Beacon Harbor and plan to start a bakery?"

"You know I'm a banker?" I found that surprising.

"It's a small town, Lindsey. Word travels fast. In fact, the moment the papers were electronically signed, Betty came pounding on my door to tell me the news."

"Betty Vanhoosen?" I asked. "The real estate agent?"

Rory nodded. "Yep. Bought my cottage from her as well. She's also a member of the town council, the development board, and the Chamber of Commerce. Nothing happens in Beacon Harbor without her knowing about it. So, why a bakery and why Beacon Harbor?" He was persistent.

"A change of scenery," I said, which wasn't a lie. "I was tired of the city. I've worked my tookus off; I've clawed my way up the ladder. I have a portfolio that would be the envy of any thirty-five-year-old. Why not start a bakery?"

Rory smiled. I found it enchanting. "I'm not exactly following the logic there, but I know you can bake." He smiled at me, then addressed the waitress who'd come to take our order.

Karen, our slightly frazzled middle-aged waitress, had come with a frothy mug of beer in her hand and a basket of warm rolls. They were on a first-name basis, which I found charming, until she said, "You must be his agent," giving me the once-over.

"His neighbor, I'm afraid. I'll have a glass of Chablis."

"Oh, sorry. I just assumed you weren't from these parts on account that there's a foot of snow outside and you're in a dress and heels. Oh!" Another terrible thought struck her. "You're on a date!" She turned and ran for the Chablis before Rory had a chance to correct her.

"Is it that obvious I'm not from *these parts*?" I asked him, grinning.

"The lack of camo must have tipped her off." His lovely

blue eyes were sparkling with mirth. "But don't change a thing. The moment you walked in, this tired old lodge got an injection of class."

I blushed. "I guess I need to watch a YouTube video on how to dress for success in Beacon Harbor. I don't suppose they have a video for that yet?"

Rory chuckled. The sound of it was highly seductive. "You could make one, but don't bother. Here's a little tip. Get yourself some jeans, a good pair of boots, and a nice warm jacket for the winter. In the summer all you need is a thong bikini, the smaller the better."

I stared a moment, then burst out in giggles. "I nearly believed you."

"You're more gullible than I thought," he teased. "What gave me away?"

"You went too far. You should have stopped at 'nice warm jacket.' Also, I'm well-versed in all the health codes. Serving bakery goods in a bikini will get me shut down. Beacon Harbor isn't ready for that."

"Pity," he teased. Then, looking more serious, he asked again, "But why Beacon Harbor? Why not the Florida Keys or Hawaii or some place with better weather?"

I leaned on my elbows. "Oh, you want a real answer, do you? Well, here it is. I used to come here every summer when I was a child." This, I was happy to see, surprised him. "It's true," I said. "My dad grew up in Traverse City. His parents owned a bakery there. Every summer Mom and Dad would send me to my grandparents' house for three weeks while they flitted across Europe." I made a flittering motion with my fingers. It was then that I noticed a glass of Chablis had magically appeared near my elbow. I waved at Karen and took a sip.

"You weren't angry that you weren't flitting around

Europe with them?" Apparently, Rory would have been furious with his parents if the tables were turned.

"No. I loved spending time with my grandparents. Nothing in New York City or Paris smelled as good as their bakery. My grandmother used to let me help her bake. Everything that came out of her oven tasted amazing. On warm summer days they'd close the bakery at noon and take me to Beacon Harbor. Although they were closer to Grand Traverse Bay, Beacon Harbor was their secret lakeside retreat. Gran loved the little shops, and Gramps kept his boat at the marina. Some of my best childhood memories happened in this town. I remember the year Grandma and Gramps retired to Florida. That was the year I was sent away to boarding school."

I frowned at the memory. I missed my grandparents; I was sad at their passing—sad that I never got the chance to share my plans with them for my own bakery in Beacon Harbor. I finished my Chablis and placed the empty glass on the table. "I nearly forgot about this place until the old lighthouse popped up one day in a Google search. I'd been toying with the idea of opening a bakery. The moment I saw the Beacon Harbor Lighthouse, a light went off, and I thought how awesome it would be to have a bakery in an old lighthouse that's a stone's throw from the beach." I strategically left out the part about catching my fiancé in the act, or that'd I'd been a bit tipsy when I made an offer on the lighthouse.

"And you just had to buy it," Rory remarked, looking impressed.

"I did."

"Must be nice," he said, buttering a roll. "Everything you desire at the swipe of a charge card." He smiled ironically and took a bite.

"It's not that easy," I told him, having dealt with peoples' assumptions my entire career. "Wealth requires discipline. And never use a charge card unless you can pay off the balance. I'm lucky, yes. But I've also worked hard and invested wisely." I went to take a sip of wine, but realized my glass was empty. Rory motioned to our waitress to bring another round. "Okay," I confided, leaning forward. "Buying an old lighthouse wasn't the wisest decision I've ever made. Probably would have never made it if not for a cheating jerk of a fiancé. But I did, and I'm glad."

"I knew it!" he said, and raised his glass. "Had to be a jerk in there somewhere. Beautiful women don't buy lighthouses in Beacon Harbor."

"That's because there's only one lighthouse in Beacon Harbor, and I beat them to it."

Karen set down two plates heaping with lightly breaded, golden-fried perch, perfectly baked potatoes, coleslaw, tartar sauce, and a wedge of fresh lemon. My mouth was watering just looking at it. The moment Karen left, Rory smiled and picked up his fork. "Well, I know two things for sure. Beacon Harbor is the perfect place for a fresh start, and you won't get a better plate of perch than here."

CHAPTER 5

I was smitten with Rory Campbell. There was just something about the man I found compelling. Maybe it was the fact that he was so different from Jeffery, whose subtle arrogance and carefully manufactured metrosexual looks had sucked me right in. Jeffery was big city swank, Rory was ex–Navy SEAL, which explained a lot. He oozed competence and masculinity with just a hint of danger, and I'm sorry to admit that I found it refreshingly sexy. Rory had admitted to me, while savoring his fried perch, that he would have spent the rest of his life in the navy, if it wasn't for his dad's failing health.

Unfortunately, Rory's dad passed away two months before his last tour of duty had ended. His mom had been gone a while. Settling his parents' estate had been a horrible experience, but it had gotten him thinking. He had a sudden desire to put down roots somewhere. He was still in the long process of grieving when he bought the log cabin in Beacon Harbor. He moved up after selling his childhood home in Grand Rapids, which, according to Rory, was two hours south. All his life he had vacationed in the area, but he admitted to a soft spot for Beacon Harbor. He had come in search of solitude and almost had it until Welly and I moved in. Rory Campbell was trying to write a book.

"I'll tell you what," I said as his big pickup truck pulled up the lighthouse drive. "Welly and I will try to be good neighbors. I'll do my best to keep the noise and commotion to a minimum, and Welly will try to not eat your fish. All you have to do in return is to sample my baked goods from time to time and offer your honest opinion."

"Sounds like I'm getting the better end of the deal. How about I sample your baked goods and you go out for dinner with me from time to time?"

"I think that can be arranged," I said, schooling my careening emotions enough to offer a coy smile. On the inside I was cheering like a schoolgirl.

"And Wellington's welcome at my place any time. He's the best kind of neighbor: giant, fluffy, and silent. Besides, I've developed a real soft spot for him."

"He'll be glad to hear it," I said, hoping Rory hadn't noticed the copious amounts of drool Wellington produced. He might retract his offer. As for Wellington, a few hours away from the hammers and saws would do him good. "Thank you." I was just about to open the door when Rory's words stopped me.

"Say goodnight to the Captain for me."

"The Captain?" I turned back and looked at him. "This is the second time you've mentioned him. Should I know him? Where does he live? Is he close by?" I looked across the lighthouse grounds to the cluster of distant lights on the hillside, twinkling through the woods. "Does he live in one of those homes over there? I suppose I should apologize to all my neighbors for the noise."

"Actually, he lives in the lighthouse."

"Funny," I said as the hair on the back of my neck prickled. "Because last time I checked, I live in the lighthouse. Just Wellington and me."

Rory, who'd been grinning, suddenly looked very serious. "Captain Willy Riggs lives here too, or so legend has it. He was the first keeper of Beacon Harbor Lighthouse, Lindsey, manning the station from eighteen-seventy-seven to eighteen-ninety-two. That's when he died. The town of Beacon Harbor was a big shipping port back then, and Captain Willy, ever vigilant, saw something one night that got him killed. All that's known was that he left the lighthouse one night and walked down the beach to confront an unknown party. Captain Willy was shot in the altercation, yet he managed to make it back to the lighthouse, where he climbed the lighthouse stairs for the last time. They found him two days later, dead in the lantern room."

"What?" I shot him a troubled look. "That's a terrible thing to tell me. Are you insinuating that my lighthouse is haunted?"

"I'm not insinuating. I'm telling you. It's common knowledge around here. Haven't you heard anything since you've moved in?" he prodded. "Anything strange?"

"No, I haven't heard anything strange! I live in a drafty old lighthouse on Lake Michigan. All the rattling and creaking I hear I attribute to the arctic winds, which is what us sane people do."

"Right. Okay." Rory suddenly looked contrite.

"Oh, sure, I've seen the old rocking chair by the fireplace rock from time to time, but that I attribute to Wellington's tail. He's always whacking things with his tail. And maybe sometimes I hear footsteps, but then I realize it's just one of the workmen, or my dog."

"Yeah, that makes sense." After dropping his little bombshell on me about some ghostly captain haunting my lighthouse, he was awfully quick to back down. I found it a bit patronizing. I found it a little infuriating. In fact, I found it downright disturbing. I mean, what if he was correct?

"Okay," I said. "Let's say Captain Willy Riggs is still here. What should I do?"

"Nothing," he said plainly.

"But how do I get rid of him?"

"You don't. He's a ghost, Lindsey. And in my opinion, a good one to have around. He's not going to hurt you or Wellington. He's simply still here, doing his job, which is to keep a vigilant eye out for danger. In fact, Betty told me the day I was moving in that people have reported seeing a strange light blinking in the light room. The old Fresnel lens was removed years ago, and as far as I know the electric one's been disconnected. But that strange light, Lindsey, folks around here say it's a portent of danger."

"What?" I'm sorry to say that my inner New Yorker flared. "Betty Vanhoosen? That bubbly, little pink-clad busybody knew the place was haunted and didn't say anything to me about it? She knew my grandparents. She used to go to their bakery, or so she told me. So much for full disclosure." I glared at him and shook my head. "And here I thought you Midwesterners were supposed to be friendly and honest!"

"Betty is friendly," he stated. "And I'm honest." Rory, damn him, was grinning at my little tirade. "Listen, Lindsey, don't let it bother you. It probably slipped her mind. You have a beautiful place here, a real piece of Michigan history. And it's going to make one heck of a bakery. Just stay focused on that. You want me to do a walk-through to make sure everything's okay?"

"A walk-through? You just told me that the ghost of some old dead captain lives here. I don't need a walk-through, Rory, I need a ghost hunter!"

"Relax, Lindsey." He took hold of my hand. His own was large, warm, and very capable. "It's just legend. Shouldn't think a legend was any match for a New Yorker." He smiled.

"You're right," I agreed and removed my hand. This was my new life, and I was determined to make the most of it. Beacon Lighthouse wasn't haunted, and on the off chance that it was, Welly and I would just have to cross that bridge when we came to it.

"Okay. Well, thanks for coming to dinner with me. You've got my number if you need me. And regarding the Captain, Google him. See what you can find out. I think you'll feel better once you've read a little bit about him."

"Good advice," I said and shut the truck door. For the second time since arriving in Beacon Harbor, I was filled with a whole new wave of trepidation.

CHAPTER 6

I might have wanted to Google Captain Willy Riggs, but I didn't. In fact, I refrained from giving in to my fears, or to any thoughts of ghosts, and pushed on ahead with all my new plans. If I was being totally honest, living in the lighthouse was wonderfully freeing. Any creaking or rattling I heard was easily dismissed as wind, because there was plenty of that. And even if the Captain did still reside in the old lighthouse, he never made his presence known to me. I didn't take that as an insult. On the contrary, I found that more than considerate. Rory, who made good on his promise to sample my baked goods, never mentioned him again, for which I was grateful.

Every evening after cleaning the kitchen and locking up after the construction crew, I took a glass of wine with me up the winding steps of the light tower to the lantern room. Wellington wasn't a fan of the light tower. There were too many steps for his taste, and they were too steep, so he stayed below by the hearth. Once in the lantern room, however, the unobstructed view was spectacular. It was so vastly different from living in a high-rise penthouse apartment in the city. It was peaceful, serene, and enchanting. I kept a pair of binoculars up there and a flashlight, and had even hauled up an extra chair so that Rory could join me. The evenings we sat in the light room side by side were the ones I liked most.

Rory was still much of an enigma to me, disappearing for days at a time only to reappear on my doorstep with a case of beer, or deer sausage and crackers, or a fresh-caught fish. He was definitely the hottest man around, probably a player as well. I never pried. I didn't feel I had the right to. And if I wasn't so exhausted preparing for the bakery's opening day, I might have tried harder to seduce him. My powers were failing me. I chalked it up to bad juju still lingering from Jeffery Plank. Since my move to Beacon Harbor, Jeffery began calling me again. Mia had probably found him out for the arrogant pig he was. I didn't care, and I wasn't going to answer his calls. It got so bad that I finally had to block his number.

Thankfully, my days at the lighthouse were busy from sunup to sundown, giving me little time to worry about Jeffery. However, there was always time for a phone call from Mom. Every morning my phone would buzz, displaying her old *Vogue* cover. Mom was barely more than a teen when she did that cover, and it always made me smile. However, after the first month of living at the lighthouse, I began to dread that photo.

"Hi, Linds. Just checking to make sure you haven't gone stir-crazy yet." It was her opening line. At first it was funny, but with each passing day, the humor began to fade.

"Not yet," I'd tell her, then fill her in on the progress I was making. I loved my mom, but she still couldn't fathom why I had thrown my uber-lucrative career away to start a bakery in the wilds of Michigan. Mom loved hearing about my adventures at the lighthouse and of the friends I was making in the town, but she had never liked bakeries. I guess when one was always dieting, bakeries were a constant torment.

Dad, on the other hand, understood my career change a little better. He'd grown up in a bakery but had wanted to stretch his wings and make his own mark on the world. He had wanted to prove that Bakewells could hold their own on Wall Street as well as on Main Street. I was a Wall Street Bakewell and couldn't resist the pull of my ironic name. Most of my New York friends were still laughing about it. But I strongly felt that stretching my own wings and owning my own business was the right thing to do.

My best friend, Kennedy Kapoor, who both laughed at and applauded my decision, called nearly every day as well. Of all my old friends in the city, Kennedy was the person I missed most. We'd met during our freshman year at Columbia where Kennedy had *crossed the pond*, so to speak, to study journalism. The daughter of an English baroness and an attorney of Indian descent, Kennedy not only had an exotic look to her, but a killer English accent as well. And she'd been positively obsessed by the fact that my mom had once been a fashion model.

"Ellie Montague's your mother?" she had cried the day my parents came to visit me at school. Kennedy was angry I'd never told her. Honestly, it had never occurred to me.

"Good gracious, wasn't she, like, *Vogue*'s model of the year?"

"Twice," I had told her. "In the eighties. Clearly she's hoping for a third cover." This I remarked noting Mom's perfectly airbrushed makeup, her high-collar button-down designer blouse opened to her cleavage, and her long, billowy Ralph Lauren skirt. Normal parents didn't dress like my mom. Both Kennedy and I burst out laughing. However, neither Kennedy nor I were laughing seven years later when she came to me, admitting that she had a shopping addiction.

Kennedy was a struggling journalist who liked to shop and dress like a supermodel. She had ten credit cards, all of which were maxed out. That was the night Kennedy and I had a little heart-to-heart. I gave her a lecture, made her a spreadsheet, and held a Cutting of the Credit Cards ceremony for her. Then, after she purged her wallet, I convinced her to let me manage her financial affairs.

Keeping Kennedy on a budget had put quite a strain on our friendship. We struggled through a few hard years, but it was all worth it. Kennedy was now a highly sought-after celebrity publicist and influence blogger with a killer financial portfolio. Her conversations were always hilarious and enlightening. Every week Kennedy was dating someone new. Surprisingly, she never mentioned Jeffery Plank, or his tart of a girlfriend, Mia Long.

As the snow and ice melted, exposing a landscape of rolling sand dunes, greening hills, budding trees, and early spring flowers, the Beacon Bakeshop was coming together.

The industrial kitchen with its stainless-steel counters, industrial mixers, freezer, fridge, proofing oven, cutting board, bakery racks, trays, stove, and double ovens was up and running. The display cases and open shelving were put in, as was the coffee counter and espresso machine. The cute black-topped tables and red-backed chairs would be arriving soon, and the red awning was yet to be installed. My dream was coming together, and it looked marvelous.

Betty Vanhoosen dropped by every week to see how things were progressing. Betty, a sixty-year-old real estate diva and town gossip, was not opposed to dragging a friend or two from the town along with her. The phrase, "Oooo, I smell something good," always preceded her as she rounded the bakery counter and popped into the kitchen. Wellington, who was banned from the kitchen for sanitary reasons, seldom barked when Betty and her friends came. He loved the attention, and I found that I liked Betty's company as well. Besides, Betty and whoever accompanied her that day were always willing to sample my latest pastry. I was still working out my menu.

"These lemon tarts are delicious. I think the bakeshop looks fabulous, dear. I heard you hired Mike Skinner's cousin. I'm glad you're giving her a chance. When does Dylan start? When are you planning on training the staff? Don't wait too long. Opening day is just around the corner."

Betty always shot out six or seven questions at a time. Once, after having learned from Rory that the lighthouse was supposedly haunted, I tried to get Betty to admit what she knew.

"Haunted, you say?" Her face blanched. "Oh, that's an old wives' tale. Isn't that right, Ginger?"

The Ginger she was addressing was Ginger Brooks, a

friendly, capable woman in her early forties who owned Harbor Scoops, the town's famous ice cream shop. At the mention of my haunted lighthouse, Ginger's eyes went wide as she gave a slight shiver. Betty, noticing it, waved it off as a head freeze. "That'll be from all the ice cream," she informed me. "Ginger's been trying out new flavors all morning." Then, before Ginger could answer, Betty launched in with, "You don't really believe in ghosts, do you? Rory's a strange sort. What do you suppose he's getting up to in that cabin of his? Don't you find it odd that he just disappears? He's the ghost, if you ask me. Hey, are you planning on serving milk shakes too? I thought I saw the Oberland Dairy truck here this morning. They've the best ice cream, isn't that right, Ginger?"

Ginger nodded, raising a brow as she did so. "Oberland ice cream is the secret to my success. Been ordering from them for years. Please don't tell me you're going to sell ice cream as well?" Her pleasantness deflated with the possibility.

I was quick to assure her that I wasn't, but I would have a few flavors on hand for the occasional pie à la mode request.

Betty, thinking otherwise, added, "Last summer I was addicted to Ginger's peanut butter cup overload. So yummy! Nobody could fault you for serving up a scoop every now and then. That's a good move for a beachside café. You'd be amazed at what I can see from my office window."

And that's how that conversation went. Betty Vanhoosen, plump, platinum blond, and wrapped from head to toe in cotton candy colors, was an expert at deflection. It was probably why she was such a successful real estate agent.

As much as I hated to admit it, one of the best decisions I'd made was taking Uber driver Mike's advice. At the end of April, I'd given his cousin a call and hired her on the spot. Dylan Dykstra was a five-foot-two powerfully built force of nature. Her exterior was tough—from the boots on her feet, to her ripped jeans and pink camo T-shirt, to the piercings on her ears and nose—but I found her to be confident and friendly. Sure, she was sassy, a bit edgy as well, but her *take-on-the-world-or-be-damned* attitude was just the thing I needed. Dylan had rich brown hair that fell below her shoulders and soulful brown eyes. However, it was her passion for baking that sealed the deal. Dylan was full of great ideas, and her previous baking experience was a welcome bonus.

Dylan had been helping me ready the bakery and peruse through a stack of applications when I got a call from Kennedy. It wasn't even noon yet.

"Guess what?" she said the moment I answered the phone. I had no idea what had her so excited at eleven thirty in the morning. "I'm coming to Beacon Harbor for your grand opening!"

"What? You're carving time out of your busy schedule for me?" I was joking.

"I wouldn't miss your opening day for the world, Linds. Besides, as your friend, I've put myself in charge of publicity. I've already contacted all the local radio stations, papers, and dining guides. I've just launched your website last night, though I'll need more photos once you're up and running. And I've been blogging about *The Beacon Bakeshop & Café* nonstop. I'm creating quite the buzz, and not only in Michigan."

"That's amazing!" I said, and flashed Dylan a thumbs-up. "However, we might be a little short staffed. If you're here, I'm going to put you to work. Would you rather bus tables or work the register?"

"Definitely the register. I may not have your knack for numbers, but I can swipe a charge card faster than a bored mommy with a trust fund."

CHAPTER 7

Things were moving fast. Our menu was nearly finalized, boxes and bags ordered, and additional help hired. Opening day was swiftly approaching. I didn't think anything could dampen Kennedy's good news, until Wellington started barking out the window.

"Oh, God. Brace yourself," Dylan warned, staring over the empty display case she'd been cleaning. I was at the espresso machine trying to master a latte.

"That's Fiona Dickel," she said, pointing with her rag. "Town downer and proverbial turd in the punch bowl. Fiona winters in Arizona. That's why we love winter. She must have finally read the paper."

I looked out the window and spied a wild-haired redhead in her late fifties wearing a billowing plaid cape and mud-splattered knee-boots. She was hiking up the walkway. I took Wellington by the collar and escorted him through the door to our living quarters. "Dang, you're harsh," I remarked, grinning. Dylan was no pushover.

"Well, I'm not the newcomer, am I?" She set down her rag, took her latte, and smiled at the lopsided heart in the froth. "Getting better. It actually resembles a heart and not a weird blob. A few more lattes and you'll be a pro. Hey, bet you a fiver you'll be loving winter too when that witch makes her way up here. By the way, did you remember to lock the door?"

I hadn't. No sooner had Dylan asked the question when the door burst open, welcoming a gust of wind and a riled-looking woman.

Dylan, obviously familiar with the intruder, addressed the woman as she stormed up to the counter. "Here for a job, Fiona? Sorry. All our positions have been filled. But you can leave your application with us." Dylan's smile was sarcastic.

"I'm not here for a job, you . . . insufferable ingrate! Did you have something to do with this . . . this travesty?" She glared at Dylan, oozing hatred. "How fitting you'd wheedle your way in here."

"Excuse me?" I walked to the counter, placing myself between the two women. Dylan, carrying a bit of a chip on her shoulder, was like a territorial pit bull. She was a dream in the kitchen, but I had the feeling she'd defend the bakery with her life. Fiona was purely obnoxious, but I was used to dealing with unpleasant people. The first rule was to hold your position and offer kindness. Although I could feel my inner New Yorker rearing her ugly head, I held her down and forced a smile. "If you have a complaint, it should be addressed to me, not my assistant baker."

The cold, rust-colored eyes shot to me. "Oh, I have a complaint."

"We're not even open," I reminded her. "And before you judge us, why don't you try one of our donuts? It's one of our opening day specials. We call it our Traverse City Cherry Delight."

"I'm not here for a G-damn donut!" she cried, turning as red as her hair. "I'm here because you've debased my lighthouse! You've turned it into a . . . a horror show!" Her finger pointed at me.

Down, down, girl, I told my inner New Yorker. But what did she mean by *her* lighthouse? I looked at the woman. "Sorry? *Your lighthouse*?"

"It's a historical landmark!" Her red cheeks quivered as she talked. "Nobody should own a historical landmark. I'm president of the Beacon Point Lighthouse Preservation Society."

"Which is basically just you now, right, Fi?" Dylan smirked at the woman and took another sip of her latte.

"There's seven of us and we're growing every day, thank you very much. When the government decided to sell the lighthouse, we had no idea it was going to be cheapened with your disgusting donuts and garish awning!"

"'Disgusting?'" Now the woman was just asking for it. "I'm sorry, but I bought this lighthouse with cash. The contract was legitimate, and I have all the proper permits." I forced a smile and held out a small tray of freshly made donuts filled with a combo of tart cherry jelly and light butter cream. They were topped with a delicious cherry glaze. "Why don't you try one of these before you insult it?"

It was a small batch. There were only a dozen of our

latest cherry delights on the tray, which Dylan's cousin, Mike (who now spent most of his time at the marina), and her boyfriend, Carl, were coming over to sample. I was planning on taking a few over to Rory as well. Fiona, clearly torn, reached across the counter and took one. She sniffed it, made a face, and then threw it at the bakery case with surprising violence. "This is my official warning, ladies. I'm here to make sure this . . . this bakery of yours doesn't succeed."

I could handle a lot of things, but smashing a beautifully prepared, fresh-out-of-the-fryer donut wasn't one of them. My patience with this woman had just run out.

"Oh, great!" I cried. "Is that supposed to be a shot across our bow?" I was glaring at her, my full-blown Lindsey-tude rearing her ugly head. "Well, you've come to the wrong lighthouse for a fight, missy. It's going to take a hell of a lot more than a . . . a delicious donut smashed against my bakery case to get me to tuck tail and run. I've invested six months of my life into this bakery. I've made incredible improvements here, more than you and your friends ever did. I love this lighthouse. I can't wait to share it with the public—not as a crumbling old relic from the past, but as a vibrant destination—a place to come, eat good food, and celebrate life. Yes, I've turned it in to a bakery café, but that's a heck of a better transition for a lighthouse than demolition and condos. Like it or not, I'm here, and I'm staying."

"We'll see about that!" Fiona huffed, spat on my polished floor, then turned on her heels and marched out the door.

"And good riddance to you, Dickel," Dylan called after her.

I reached into my pocket, pulled out a five-dollar bill, and slapped it on top of the defiled bakery case. "I now see why winters are so attractive. That was a perfectly good donut." I shook my head in dismay, picked up a rag, and walked around the counter.

Poor Fiona, I thought, gingerly wiping up the remains of the donut. I respected her anger, but she was a day late and a dollar short. And now she was up against the influence of Kennedy Kapoor.

And Kennedy Kapoor had ten million followers on YouTube.

CHAPTER 8

Kennedy, having created quite a buzz about my light-house bakery, swept into town five days before our grand opening on a wave of expensive perfume and un-flappable optimism. Dylan and I had been in the kitchen as usual, this time making bread dough like two mad-women.

I had decided early on that the Beacon Bakeshop would open at 7 a.m. offering specialty coffee drinks, freshly made donuts, sweet rolls, muffins, a coffee cake of the day or two, and a few varieties of mini quiches. Those would fill out our bakery cases. Any extra baking would be reserved for special orders. After the breakfast rush, we'd restock the cases with lunch fare. I planned on having a variety of premade sandwiches available for the panini grill as well as a standard list of deli sandwiches made on one of our homemade breads. Each sandwich would come with a side of potato salad or fresh veggies and dill dip, with a choice of cookie or brownie. On the sweeter side, along with the morning leftovers, cookies, and brownies, there'd be a couple of fresh-baked pies and two varieties of cake, all to be sold by the slice for afternoon tea or coffee on the beach. The bakery would close at three in the afternoon.

Since the donuts and sweet rolls needed to be made fresh each morning, Dylan had talked me into par-baking our bread for the week. Par-baking was a method where the bread would be made, proofed, and baked as normal. However, just before the crust started turning golden brown the loaves would be pulled from the oven. They'd be cooled, wrapped in an airtight container, and frozen. All we would need do when a loaf was needed was to remove it from the freezer, thaw it, and bake in the oven at the normal temperature for about fifteen minutes, giving it a fresh-baked taste and a golden-brown finish. The last bakery Dylan had worked for had gotten all their frozen par-baked bread from a supplier. She swore the result was just as good as the original method, plus it cut down on waste and production time. I'd give it a try.

Therefore, when Kennedy burst into the bakeshop, Dylan and I were in the back, our hands sticky with bread dough.

"Linds, darling, I'm here!" At the sound of her melodic English lilt, Wellington popped up beside the decorative lighthouse in the café (his new favorite place to sleep) and could be heard howling and grunting with excitement. "Welly!" Kennedy cried, greeting her old friend. She then exclaimed, "Oh, Linds! This place is *fabulous*!"

I pulled Dylan with me from the kitchen to meet her. After a round of hugs, squeals, and introductions, Kennedy took a step back. "You're wearing a pink camo T-shirt?" Her pretty face pinched into a frown.

It was a bit of a joke. Dylan had bought it for me after I had admired hers. The swirling shades of pink on our women's-cut V-neck tee were supposed to mimic jungle camo. I think they looked cute and were now our unofficial baking uniform.

"It's my lucky baking shirt," I told Kennedy. "Dylan and I wear them when we want to hide out in the kitchen and power-bake."

Kennedy laughed. "I suppose you blend right in with all the pink frosting. However, out here in the bakery you'd stand out like a pig in a dog pound. So posh! I love all the red diner wear on the open shelving, and the lighthouse motif is spot-on. Your customers are going to love it. The six-foot lighthouse next to the bakery counter is genius." She couldn't resist touching the eye-catching piece.

"That's our mascot," I said, admiring our wooden lighthouse. "Mr. Beacon. He draws the eye the moment you walk through the door."

"No," she said, shaking her head, her sleek, long black hair echoing the motion. Kennedy looked nothing short of spectacular in her butter-yellow sundress and cute strappy sandals. It complemented her flawless, light mocha skin. "No," she said again. "Wellington is your mascot. Mr. Beacon, or whatever you call it, is a posh accent piece. Tomorrow I'm going to be taking some shots of the lighthouse and café for the website and your social media pages. I want to do an entire spread on Wellington. People just adore Welly."

"Knock yourself out," I told her, giving Wellington a loving pat on the head. I then talked her through all the old Beacon Point Lighthouse memorabilia hanging on the white-painted shiplap wall. The white walls, the polished oak floor, and the black marble countertops made the remarkable nautical history of the old lighthouse stand out. The bright red dishes and bakery boxes brought a contrasting splash of color.

After Kennedy was settled in one of the lighthouse guestrooms, Dylan and I brought her up to the lantern room, where we all shared a bottle of wine over a spectacular Lake Michigan sunset.

"Seriously," Kennedy remarked for the fifth time, "this place is magical. I thought you'd gone batty, cashing it all in for an old lighthouse on the edge of nowhere, but I must say, you've got vision."

"She does," Dylan said, grinning. "This is hands-down the coolest bakery I've ever worked in. Hey," she said, refilling our glasses, "I'd like to make a toast. Here's to a successful grand opening."

"Hear, hear!" Kennedy and I chimed in, and clanked our glasses. Thanks to the wine and the company of good friends, Fiona Dickel and her warning never crossed my mind.

CHAPTER 9

The next few days, Kennedy, with Wellington in tow, flitted around the charming town of Beacon Harbor, snapping pictures, introducing herself to the other shop owners, and promoting the bakery's grand opening. Although I was just beginning to really feel a part of the town and loved perusing the shops, I stayed closer to home, calming my nerves in the bakery kitchen. I was mixing pounds of butter and loads of sugar in the industrial-size blender for cookie dough when I heard the telltale, "Oooo, something smells good!" I turned off the mixer as Betty Vanhoosen popped into the kitchen.

"Have a cookie," I said, handing her one from my first batch. It was an oatmeal-based dough stuffed with dried tart cherries, white chocolate, and toasted pecans, with a touch of vanilla and a hint of cinnamon for good measure. The cherries were from an orchard in Traverse City.

They were my favorite go-to. I'd given Rory a dozen earlier with a thermos of coffee to take out on his fishing boat. Hopefully they were bringing him luck.

"Heavenly," Betty murmured, chewing. "This is going to be the best Memorial Day ever! I don't know what your friend has been saying, but whatever it is, it's working. I just got a call from the Harbor Hotel. They're all booked up for the weekend. Same with the Lakeshore Inn. It appears that lighthouse enthusiasts from all over the state can't wait to step inside your renovated lighthouse bakeshop. And just wait until they taste one of these. You will be serving these, won't you, dear?" She held up her half-eaten cookie. I assured her that I'd stock dozens of them.

"Excellent! There is one small blight on the face of all this good news, I'm afraid." Betty paused and helped herself to a cup of coffee. I always had a pot brewing when I baked.

While she took a sip, I offered, "You wouldn't be referring to Fiona Dickel, by any chance?"

"The very same." Betty gave a disparaging shake of her head, sending her platinum-blond bob jiggling. "That Dickel woman and her friends stormed into my office yesterday. I was about to close on a large lake house for a Bloomfield Hills couple. That crazy woman stomped into my office with her grungy followers and threatened to have my real estate license revoked. She really can't, but her anger scared off my clients! They just picked up and left. Can you believe the nerve of her? Fiona thinks I've done something wrong by selling you this lighthouse. It was becoming an eyesore. Every year people would try to break in to it. It was a real liability. Anyhow, as the real estate agent on the project, I was representing the town.

Beacon Harbor got the money for it. Fiona and her followers are just angry. Still, she had no right storming into my office like that. And poor Paige."

Paige was Betty's office assistant, a bright young woman in her late twenties who was not only kind but capable. I liked Paige.

"It's not like she's a Millennial," Betty continued. "You know, with an axe to grind against the man. Fiona and her followers are grown-ups who should know better. Anyhow, I just came to warn you. They're planning on creating a ruckus on your opening day."

I shook my head at the thought. "Don't they have other hobbies to pursue rather than harassing me?"

"This old lighthouse was her passion project." Betty pursed her pink lips, then helped herself to another cookie. "The trouble is"—she paused to take a bite—"Fiona's militant mission and grating personality prevented many from donating to her lighthouse preservation fund. Now she's taking her failure out on us."

"I'm sorry to hear it," I said, cracking eggs into my butter-sugar mix. "But don't worry. Fiona's already lost the battle. If she does anything too crazy, I won't hesitate to call the authorities."

It was the night before the grand opening, and I was frantic as I rapped on Rory's door.

"I'm sorry," I said the moment he opened it. Although he was barefoot and wearing pajama pants, I knew he wasn't asleep. His lights had been on.

Rory looked at both Wellington and me.

"I know it's late," I apologized, "but I need to ask you a huge favor."

I had just finished making cookie dough for the three types of cookies I planned to serve on opening day, my dried cherry, white chocolate, and toasted pecan; a killer chocolate chip; and a lemon sugar cookie with a raspberry-piped lighthouse on a background of white icing. Things like cookie dough, piecrusts, fillings, cake batter, and icings could be refrigerated overnight. The donuts, cinnamon rolls, and yeast breads would have to be made fresh in the morning. And since donuts were our opening theme, we were planning on making a splash with our delicious varieties.

All the prepwork had been done, the four young people I'd hired to work the bakery counter and cash register had been trained and scheduled. However, my experienced barista, Mark, a college senior home for the summer, had just called from the emergency room. He'd broken his arm skateboarding.

Rory, standing in the doorway, grinned. "No baked goods to sample?"

"Oh, there are plenty of those," I assured him, marveling at how he could sample so many and stay so fit. "You can have whatever you like at the bakery tomorrow. It's opening day and I have no barista. Can you brew coffee and work an espresso machine?"

"You've tasted my coffee," he reminded me with a self-effacing grin. I had and had loved it, although in retrospect it probably had nothing to do with the actual taste of the coffee itself but the company. "As for espresso," he continued, "you might have to give me a refresher on the machine and a cheat sheet. I take it you're asking me to work tomorrow?"

"Yes . . . if you can. I know this is a huge favor to ask. Honestly, I would never ask you if I wasn't in a bind."

"No problem," he said. "I was planning on spending most of my day over there anyway. Betty told me that Fiona Dickel is threatening to ruin your grand opening. You've worked too hard for that. So, I guess I'll be over there trying to make fancy coffee drinks while I keep an eye on things."

"Oh, thank you!" I cried and kissed him full on the mouth. It was impulsive. We'd gone for dinner a dozen times, but I had never kissed him. I was now, and he wasn't in any hurry to pull away. Truthfully, neither was I.

"I . . . I . . ." I stammered, coming up for air. I was certain I was red as a cherry, "I have to get to bed. Big day tomorrow. Can't oversleep."

"No," he said, grinning at my discomfort. "Would never do to sleep in your first day on the job."

Why was he staring at me like that? And why was I finding it so hard to leave? Then, however, his smile faded.

"Lindsey, is someone up in the light tower?"

"No," I said. "It's late. Kennedy's asleep, and I've just come from the bakery with Wellington. Why?"

"Because there's an odd sort of light glowing up there. Look."

I was afraid to turn around, but I had no choice. "Oh my God," I breathed, spying the odd yellow light up in the lantern room. "What on earth is that?" The hair on the back of my neck prickled, and I had to look away.

The grim look on Rory's face softened as he looked at me. "Probably nothing. Trick of the light or an odd reflection." He offered a kind smile as if it was nothing, then, glancing at the light room once again, he grimaced. "Just to be sure, I'm going to check it out."

As Rory disappeared back into his house to slip on some shoes and grab a light jacket, I couldn't shake the troubled look on his face. Because we both knew what the odd light meant. I didn't believe in ghosts, but I was beginning to believe in them now. According to legend, Captain Willy Riggs was sending us a warning. Like black clouds heralding a coming storm, I looked at the light and felt my skin prickle uncomfortably. Could it really mean something bad was about to happen? For the sake of my bakeshop, I acknowledged the light and the fact that Captain Willy Riggs had lingered a bit longer than I had hoped. Beyond that, however, I wasn't willing to give it another thought.

CHAPTER 10

"All clear," Rory said, clomping down the last few steps of the light tower.

Wellington, parked at the bottom and growling softly, had been agitated the moment we stepped into the light-house. I had volunteered to stay below with him, giving Rory the ostensible reason that Welly was scared. Yes, my giant, loveable Newfie was a great big chicken, but so was I. I had grown to love the old lighthouse. I didn't know how I'd feel if I came face-to-face with the ghost of the old keeper, Captain Willy Riggs.

Rory appeared with my laptop. The sight of it sent a wave of relief washing through me. I had taken it up there after dinner to do a little work while watching the sunset and must have left it. If it was open, that might explain the odd light we had seen.

"I forgot I left this up there. Thanks," I said, as he handed me the laptop. "Was this it, or did you see anything else?"

"Just a couple of empty wine bottles and a half-eaten box of Triscuits." He raised an insinuating brow.

"I wonder how those got up there?" I feigned innocence and directed his attention to my laptop. "So, was this the culprit?"

His open gaze darkened a measure. "It wasn't open, if that's what you're asking. You do have a flashlight up there, however. Maybe your friend Kennedy went up there in search of more wine and turned it on?"

"Not out of the realm of possibilities," I agreed. The truth was, I'd been so busy prepping for my grand opening that I'd left her on her own these last few days.

"Look, Lindsey, there's nothing to worry about. The lighthouse is safe and secure. Just lock the doors after I leave and get some sleep."

"Okay." I nodded, then was seized by a troubling thought. "But . . . what if it was the Captain?" I chanced a glance at the darkened spiral steps ascending into more darkness. "What if it was him up there, giving us a warning?"

The lighting was dim at best in the tower stairwell, but I could still detect a ripple of trouble on Rory's strong, handsome face. "Look, all that about the ghost light, it was just a story, Lindsey, a morbid old legend. I told it to you to scare you."

"What?" My sudden outburst caused Wellington to whine. "Well, that's a terrible thing to do!"

"True," he admitted. "And the only explanation I can give you is this: I thought you'd call me more if you were scared. But you're a tough cookie, Bakewell. You're a hard one to scare." Was he joking? From all appearances it looked like this was the story he was sticking with.

"I was busy!" I snapped, growing a bit defensive. "I'm renovating a lighthouse! I'm opening a bakeshop café! And, for your information, I would have called you more if you had made it clear that you wanted me to call you. I didn't want to bother you while you were writing, or fishing, or whatever it is you do over there all day. Why couldn't you just say, 'Hey, Lindsey, call me?' Why are all you men so damn complicated all the time?"

Rory was grinning. "Oh, Lindsey, we men can't hold a candle to you women. Anyhow, now you know." Then, before I could make sense of his grin, he kissed me.

I was so angry with him and his ghost story that I should have slapped him away. But I didn't, because I was battling an even greater urge to throw my arms around him and beg him to stay. Thanks to Wellington's impatient whining, I was brought to my senses. Welly was tired, and I had a bakery to launch in less than eight hours.

"Alright," I began, suppressing a smile. "I'll call you more."

"I look forward to it. Good night, Lindsey Bakewell," Rory said, and slipped out the door.

It wasn't until I dragged Wellington up the stairs, gave him his night-night cookie, and tucked him into his bed at the foot of mine, that I realized Rory Campbell was a big fat liar. I should have been asleep the moment my head hit the pillow, but I wasn't, because I had picked up my laptop and began reading about Captain Willy Riggs and the ghost lights of Beacon Harbor.

CHAPTER 11

The best thing about having a bakery below your bedroom was the commute. After a restless few hours of sleep, I got out of bed, took a cool shower, then stumbled downstairs to work. Unfortunately, my head was still filled with the information I had stumbled upon last night, namely the legends surrounding the first lightkeeper and the fact that he had died in the lantern room of my lighthouse. I still didn't fully believe in ghosts, but it was hard to dismiss such legends, especially since I now lived and worked in the lighthouse where they all began. It was new territory for me.

As I kept my hands busy making twenty dozen extra-large gourmet donuts, I couldn't help myself from continuing my research. As I worked the tender yeast dough, letting it rise in batches, turning each onto a floured surface to be rolled out, cut into donuts, and placed in the proofer for the second rise, I listened to a podcast devoted to ghost stories. Admittedly, it probably wasn't the smartest thing to be listening to on my opening day, but there was something very compelling about the haunted stories. In fact, I'd been so focused on baking and the dulcet voice calmly explaining his hair-raising encounter that I never heard Dylan enter the bakery. With a filled bakery tray ready to go into the proofer, I spun around, saw Dylan, and screamed.

"Ahhh!" she screamed as well and grabbed the tray before I dropped it. Steadying her nerves, she said, "Didn't mean to scare you, boss. Carl dropped me off." Carl was Dylan's boyfriend. He worked with Mike on his charter fishing boat. "What the heck are you listening to?" Focusing on the voice, she shot me an admonishing look. "No more spooky stuff. It's our grand opening. We need some baking jams."

I was glad to have Dylan in the kitchen with me. As she worked on the donuts, frying them, cooling them on trays, filling them with our homemade, piquant jellies, and dipping them into our flavored frostings, I began making the coffee cakes.

Dylan and I worked together in the kitchen like finely choreographed dancers. As I pulled trays of giant muffins and mini quiches from the oven, I went down my list, checking things off as they entered the bakery cases. Before long they were filling up. Dylan continued to work in the back while I set up the register and checked the supply of bakery bags and boxes. I started the coffee, brewing three pots at a time of different grinds. The moment the coffee was started, the girls, Elizabeth and Wendy, arrived.

Elizabeth and Wendy were recent high school grads

with excellent customer service skills. They were also best friends. As the girls put on their aprons and began wiping down the inside tables, Rory appeared. He looked absolutely hunky in his form-fitting black T-shirt and jeans. I consciously stilled my careening heart and threw him an apron.

"You're a big fat liar," I hiss-whispered as we stood by the espresso machine.

"Don't tell me you finally Googled the Captain?" He grinned. "It's opening day. Forget about last night. Dear God, look at that crowd out there. Early morning beach-walkers, commuters, a good many business owners, and cops. Unfortunately, my special ops training hasn't pre-pared me for the caffeine-deprived frenzy that's about to descend on us."

"You'll be fine," I assured him. "And thank you for lying."

Kennedy swept into the café five minutes before the doors opened with Wellington prancing beside her on a white leash. My big dog had been washed, deodorized, and brushed to a glistening black sheen. He looked like the ultimate fashion accessory next to Kennedy. She had even tied a blue-and-white-striped, sailor-inspired scarf around his thick neck.

"Ready, Linds?" she asked, brushing flour off my left cheek. She straightened my apron, refreshed my lipstick, and tucked a rogue lock of my hair back into my ponytail. Once I met with her approval, she handed me Welling-ton's leash, told everyone to smile, and unlocked the door.

We were open for business.

CHAPTER 12

After greeting the first rush of customers, I handed Welly off to Kennedy and jumped behind the counter. Kennedy took Welly outside and proceeded to greet people as they came through the lighthouse doors.

There was a mad rush for pastries. The girls smiled and filled orders, placing giant glazed donuts on red plates or in bakery bags. Rory and I manned the coffee station, making lattes, macchiatos, and Americanas as fast as we could, coming up for air every now and then for coffee purists who preferred their morning joe brewed. I chatted away, answered questions, and welcomed every guest.

The morning was flying by. Dylan, working her magic in the back, kept resupplying the bakery cases, which were swiftly emptying. I was putting in a new tray of our Traverse City Cherry Delight donuts when I saw Betty

Vanhoosen push through the doors, looking like the real estate diva she was. Amazingly, she'd brought nearly every shop owner with her. Only in a town like Beacon Harbor, I mused, could there be such a show of local support, and quite frankly, it had me choked up to see them all there.

Ginger, from Harbor Scoops, waved with excitement from behind Betty. Ali and Jack Johnson, a retired couple with an adorable golden retriever, owned the Book Nook, the town's vibrant little bookstore. They grinned like kids in a candy shop as they eyed my bakery cases. Zoey and Zack Bannon, the young couple who owned the historic Beacon Theater, had also come. In their late twenties and fashionably hip, I knew they had come for the coffee. When I had met them and told them I was getting an espresso machine, they had cheered with excitement. Behind Zoey and Zack was Betty's good friend, Carol Hoggins, from You Had Me In Stitches, quilt shop and stitchery, and the perpetually cheerful Felicity Stewart, an attractive woman in her early forties who owned the Tannenbaum Shoppe, a year-round Christmas boutique at the other end of town. Her good friend and fellow shop owner, Christy Parks, was also there. Christy owned Bayside Boutiques & Interiors. Her eye-catching windows were filled with furniture, art, and accent pieces that were irresistible to tourists and townies alike. Bill Morgan brought up the rear. Bill, a local retiree, was a fixture in the town and a font of maritime knowledge. Welly and I had met him and his dog, Dan, on the beach this spring. Bill, like Betty, had been excited by the prospect of the lighthouse becoming the crowning jewel of the town once again.

"Lindsey!" Betty cried, marching up to the counter in

her light-blue high heels. Somehow they complemented her bright pink dress. Then, spying Rory at the espresso machine, she cried, "Oh, Rory! I thought you were working on a novel?"

"I've got a case of writer's block. Lindsey's helping me work it out by making me pull shots of espresso."

"Clever girl," she said, and grinned. "The bakery looks amazing, dear, and smells heavenly too."

"It sure does," Ali agreed, her cornflower-blue eyes twinkling. Jack gave me a thumbs-up.

"We've all come to celebrate your opening day," Betty informed me. "And, of course, we've been dying to sample all of your baked goods."

"This is wonderful," I told them all, tears welling in my eyes. Moving to Beacon Harbor had been a leap of faith, but today, with my doors finally opened, I really felt like I belonged.

"This," began Betty with a giant grin, "is how we welcome a new business to our town. Also, I've been raving about your Traverse City Cherry Delight donuts," she confided. "I hope you still have some left."

As if on cue, Dylan came bursting out of the kitchen door with a tray of fresh donuts. She faltered slightly when she saw the size of the crowd.

"Dylan, there you are!" Betty pressed forward. "You made all those? I'm glad to see you finally putting your talents to good use."

"I'm trying, Betty. But you know me." Dylan shot her a sardonic grin.

"Don't let her fool you," I added. "She's a baking goddess."

Dylan might have wanted to dash back to the safety of the kitchen, but we were slammed. Instead, she jumped right in, helping Elizabeth and Wendy fill orders while Rory and I worked on the coffee drinks.

Betty, lingering at the counter, dropped her voice to a whisper. "Your friend Kennedy has just met Fiona. I didn't want to say anything, dear, but Fiona and her lot are out on the sidewalk, parading up and down carrying signs protesting your bakery. Can you believe it? The nerve! I've already called the police. The Beacon Harbor Police don't suffer trash on the beach."

"Thank you," I said, genuinely touched that Betty had my back. "But you don't need to call the police. Fiona is free to protest."

"Maybe. But when that bus pulled up with all the tourists, I thought your friend was going to come to blows."

"What bus?" I shot her a look. Fear gripped me at the thought of another crowd descending on my already crowded café. I craned my neck to see over the press of heads. It was useless. I then glanced at the bakery cases. My heart dropped into the pit of my stomach. They were emptying as fast as we could fill them.

"You know," Betty pressed on, "the bus with all the wealthy New Yorkers?" She pointed to the door. Trouble was, I couldn't see out the dang thing.

As Betty spoke, Rory looked up from his espresso machine. Holding back a grin, he admonished, "A bus full of wealthy New Yorkers?"

"Well, they sound like they're from New York," she informed him self-righteously. "Besides, it's true. I saw them last night when they arrived. All in limos, they were. Must be a wedding or something."

"Limos?" I shot her an accusatory look. "When I arrived at the airport last March, you told me there weren't any limos that serviced this area."

"Well, Mike has a Yukon and a cousin who's a baker. It all worked out in the end." Her wink was pure cheek. "But I'm afraid your Kennedy is fit to be tied. I think she's put Wellington in the house. He wasn't too fond of New Yorkers."

"I can't believe Kennedy is getting into a fight with Fiona. That doesn't sound like her. She's a professional. She keeps her fights strictly to social media."

"No, dear. Not Fiona. I meant the New Yorkers . . . or at least one of them."

"Fiona is fighting with the group from the tour bus?" I asked.

"Not a tour bus, dear." She flashed me a pitying look, as if I was simple. "It's a hotel bus, one of those short ones. And it's not Fiona who's fighting the wealthy New Yorkers, it's your friend Kennedy. Oooo, looks like the New Yorkers won because here they come."

Rory flashed me a look, uttered the word "crazy," and rolled his eyes at Betty. I was just about to plate up a Traverse City Cherry Delight donut as well as a Hog Heaven for her when a familiar voice in a distinct Asian accent stopped me in my tracks.

"Lindsey Bakewell. I hear you opened a bakery. This is a very bad location for a bakery."

The crowd parted to reveal a short, attractive, glammed-up fashionista who oozed a curious mashup of both skank and diva in her chunky high heels, sleeveless designer top, flared short skirt, and large-framed sunglasses. The tips of her shoulder-length black hair were tinted electric pink.

My jaw dropped. I had to do a double take it was so unbelievable. It was Mia Long. She'd been wearing a good deal less the last time I'd seen her. Because of her, I'd never look at a slab of sea salt the same way again. I shook the image from my head and whispered to Betty, "I can't believe this."

"Mia!" I said, addressing the woman. I was still shocked as heck to see her in Beacon Harbor. She was standing at the head of what looked to be either her enthused book club or her entourage. Seriously? She had brought all these women to Michigan to confront me? Last time I checked, Mia had slighted me by stealing Jeffery. What the heck had I done to her?

I was trying to process the image before me, feeling trapped in some crazy, surreal standoff, when Kennedy burst through the door, panting.

"I'm sorry!" she blurted as Fiona pushed past her, the older woman's bright red hair fluttering like a warning flag in a rogue gust of wind. Fiona wasn't alone. Seven grungy protesters crammed into the café behind her, and there was no mistaking these newcomers for book club members. A skunky smell preceded them as they elbowed their way up to the counter, crying their baseless complaints about my lighthouse. Then, as if things could possibly get any worse, Jeffery Plank appeared. My heart gave a painful lurch. The look in his eyes was pure justified revenge. Kennedy, spying him as well, made her way toward him.

"What the hell is going on here?" Rory asked, looking up from the espresso machine. He was steaming milk for one of the many lattes Betty and the other merchants had ordered.

I shook my head as Mia clip-clopped toward me. "I honestly haven't a clue."

The jostling between Fiona and the merchants stopped.

The entire café fell silent as Mia confronted me, her posse fanning out behind her like the train of a wedding gown.

"Give me these donuts," she ordered, waving her long, vibrant pink nail at an entire bakery tray. "All of these for my friends. You," she said, pointing at Rory. "Give me a latte. Now!"

A steely look came over Rory. I was grateful that he wasn't the type of man to be pushed around by a rude little diva. "I'm sorry, but you're going to have to wait your turn like everyone else."

Elizabeth and Wendy, frightened by the little woman and her colossal attitude, were plucking donuts off trays as fast as their arms could move. Dylan, Rory, and I were frantically trying to fill the huge coffee order placed by Betty and the merchants, calling out names and placing the cups on the counter. A press of hands reached for the cups.

Betty pushed Mia aside. "What a rude woman you are!"

"What a fool of a woman you are!" Mia snapped back, and stole a donut off Betty's plate before the older woman could stop her.

Fiona cheered and thrust her hand over Betty's shoulder, reaching for the counter as well. Yet instead of grabbing one of the lattes, she purposely slapped it, knocking it over and spilling it everywhere. Her followers cheered as the hot milky mess gushed to the floor. It was utter madness.

"These are terrible donuts!" Mia cried, her shrill voice echoing though the café like nails on a chalkboard. She shook the Hog Heaven donut in my face, launching succulent bits of bacon. They were covered in maple frosting and stuck to my skin. "So dry! Terrible flavor. This bacon is so fatty and tough!" She went to grab the remaining cup of coffee out of Rory's hand, but he lifted it out of her reach. Mia snarled and grabbed the one in Betty's hand instead. Before Betty could snatch it back, Mia dunked her donut into it, spilling half on the floor.

Betty shrieked in outrage. Her friends were aghast. Fiona, finding a kindred spirit, cheered Mia on like a bully in a bar fight.

"Eat these terrible donuts and see for yourself!" Mia called out. She shoved the soggy donut into her mouth and followed it with a swig of coffee. She made a face. "This latte is putrid, like sour milk over tar water. What kind is it? Does it come in a can and say Maxwell?" Her friends laughed. "Dry donut, terrible coffee. You should be shut down!"

"Shut her down! Shut her down!" Fiona chanted and, not to be outdone by Mia, threw a donut at the bakery case. Apparently, it was her signature move. Unfortunately, others just had to try it too.

When I had envisioned my opening day at the bakery, this scenario had never entered my mind. And why would it? I thought, as a donut sailed over my head. Mia and Jeffery had been out of my life for over six months. That they had come here on my opening day was enough to unleash my inner New Yorker. However, adding insult to injury, my inner New Yorker was too stunned to move.

Rory, sensing that I was on the verge of a breakdown, jumped over the counter and grabbed hold of Mia. Kennedy jumped in and helped him drag her out the door. Mike and Carl, having arrived at some point, stepped up and began clearing the café. The sound of fake-choking continued out the door and onto the lawn, thanks to Mia and her posse. Jeffery, I noticed, was standing alone in a corner, inspecting a generous slice of blueberry coffee cake. The cheating pig! Fury hit me then. It was just the thing I needed to keep from collapsing in tears. I stormed around the counter and was just about to confront him when someone outside screamed.

I looked at Jeffery. We both ran for the door.

Outside, just beyond the café tables, a press of people had gathered around a spot on the lawn. There was no sign of Mia. Great, I thought. What now? A fake claim of food poisoning? It would be a fitting end to her pitiful performance. However, once she was finished making her point, I could finally get an answer as to why she and Jeffery had traveled all the way to Beacon Harbor to ruin my bakery. I deserved at least that much.

"What's going on?" I asked, running to where everybody stood.

"Lindsey, call an ambulance. Quick!"

"What?" I looked at Rory. He was kneeling on the ground beside a prone body. It was Mia. I shook my head in disgust. "Don't be fooled. This is the final scene of her act. Bad donut plus bad coffee equals food poisoning."

"Lindsey, I'm not joking. She's not breathing!" He looked truly shaken. It scared me. I had never seen Rory look anything but completely confident. One sweep of the sober crowd and I knew something had gone terribly wrong.

"Start CPR!" I cried and ran for the phone.

CHAPTER 13

I called an ambulance, then calmed down Elizabeth and Wendy. Both girls were understandably shaken by the morning's events. Wendy was slumped on the floor behind the counter in tears. Elizabeth was standing beside her looking lost and confused. Dylan, who had worked just as hard as I had getting the bakeshop ready for the grand opening, was in front of the counter busying herself with the Herculean task of trying to clean up the café. Seeing the state of my bakery and my three employees made me want to fall on the floor and cry too. We'd been open less than four hours and the café looked like the scene of an unsupervised preschool lunch. The floor was littered with smooshed donuts and spilt coffee. The bakery cases were empty on the inside. On the outside they were covered in jelly, powdered sugar, and fudgy fingerprints. Instead of breaking down in tears, however, I called Dylan to my side as I ushered both girls into the safety of the kitchen. Once there, I pulled out a carton of eggs, butter, a variety of cheeses, and precut veggies. "You girls need something healthy to eat. Dylan will make you an omelet."

"I will?" she asked, looking partially terrified.

"Don't you know how?"

"Of course I know how to make an omelet," she said, looking slightly frustrated. "It's just that . . . well, it's a war zone out there. The bakery's in shambles. I want to clean it up."

"There'll be time for that later. For now, just stay right here. Take a break and don't worry. Everything's going to be alright. I promise."

In retrospect, promising wasn't a good idea. In fact, I was in no position to make such promises when I was assailed by near-paralyzing doubt as well. However, as I've learned in business, confidence wins the day, and if one isn't feeling confident, pretending to be is the next best thing.

By the time I returned to the lawn, I was relieved to find that the cops had already arrived, well, one cop at least. A few of the town's police officers had come by the bakeshop early this morning. The man on the ground helping Rory perform CPR was a young officer named Tuck McAllister. There were two reasons I remembered his name during the whirlwind morning I had. The first was because Officer Tuck McAllister was the youngest person on the Beacon Harbor Police Force by at least two decades. The second was because Officer Tuck McAllister was a total cutie pie. Just my luck that both men were bent over Mia, pumping her chest and breathing life into her lungs. I hoped she was enjoying the attention. I pushed my way through the crowd of gawkers. "Ambulance is on its way," I informed everyone with authority.

Carl and Mike were on crowd control, holding the onlookers back from falling on Mia and the two men trying to keep her alive. I had to admit, she wasn't looking good. In fact, I was so nervous that it wasn't until I heard the blaring of sirens racing down Main Street that I remembered to breathe.

"Are you okay, dear?" I realized Betty was beside me. Her face looked ashen. "It's such a shame. All the work you put into that bakeshop. You were off to a darn good start too." She sounded as if I was about to lose everything. A donut-dunking diva had collapsed. It was a minor setback. At the hospital they'd pump her stomach and discover she'd overdosed on diet pills or something. Hopefully, in a year or two I'd be able to laugh about it. However, I certainly wasn't laughing now.

"I'm so sorry, Linds." Kennedy was standing on my other side, looking nearly as pale as Betty. "I tried to stop her. I mean, I had no idea she and Jeffery would come all this way." She shot a look at the man in question, who was standing across from us. Mia's friends were scared, tearful, and pointing accusatory fingers in my direction. Fiona had picked up one of her Beacon Bakeshop protest signs and held it aloft, looking more smug than frightened. Honestly, the sign was nothing to be proud of. It was a rough drawing of the Beacon Bakeshop with a giant donut around it and a line slashed through the middle. The general message was no lighthouse bakeries. As far as I knew, mine was the only one. Disgusted with Fiona and Mia's friends, I turned my attention to Jeffery Plank.

Again, I asked myself, why the heck was he here?

Why go to such lengths to sabotage my business on opening day? After all, it was Jeffery who had ruined our engagement. He was the one having the affair. Dear heavens, could all this really be about the dang Jag? I looked at him again, at the hooded eyes behind the trendy black-rimmed glasses, the flaring nostrils on an otherwise straight nose, the arrogant lips resting at neutral as if they were above expressing worry. Yeah, I thought, definitely still mad that I keyed his Jag. And yet he was oddly catatonic regarding his collapsed pastry chef lover on the ground. Was it shock? Apathy? Arrogance? A sugar coma? Whatever it was, he hadn't moved a muscle to help.

"Let's back up, people," I cried, pushing the circle of gawkers wider. The ambulance had arrived with two more squad cars. "Let's give them some space." I walked around, grabbed hold of Jeffery, and pulled him aside. My grip on his arm woke him from his stupor. He yanked his arm away and glared at me.

"You and Mia came here to cause trouble," I hissed. "Why?"

"Why? It should be obvious why," he snapped. "Revenge."

"It was just a flipping car!" I seethed. "It was nothing compared to what you did . . . and on my birthday, no less!"

This made his lips pucker. "Look, I'm not perfect, but you had no right—" Jeffery didn't have time to finish that thought. Mia was being whisked into the back of the ambulance. He ran after her and climbed aboard as well, but not before shooting a murderous look at me. I deserved a lot of things, but not that look. It chilled me to the bone.

It was only a moment before I realized that Rory was beside me. He looked worried and exhausted.

"It's a nightmare," I told him, feeling all my hopes and dreams being trampled into the floor with my donuts. "The Captain, he was trying to warn us last night, wasn't he? What if I really had something to do with her collapse and didn't even know it? What if this place is cursed? What if I bought a cursed lighthouse?" I could hear the escalating panic in my own voice, which made me panic even more.

Rory gripped my hand, his bright eyes darkening like the sky before a storm. "Forget about the Captain," he said. He was about to say something else but couldn't, because Officer McAllister was nearly upon us.

"Ms. Bakewell?" The young officer nodded a greeting while pulling a notepad from his top pocket. In fact, in broad daylight he looked fresh-out-of-the-academy young, which did nothing for my nerves. "We met earlier. Officer Tuck McAllister. There was a report of a disturbance at your bakeshop. I had no idea I'd be helping Mr. Campbell here perform CPR on one of your customers."

"Believe me, none of us had any plans of performing CPR this morning. However, I thank you for your quick action. I'm sure Rory thanks you as well." I looked at Rory, suddenly grateful he'd taken matters into his own hands and had known what to do. I doubted that Mark, the young barista I'd hired, would have been so quick to act had he been here this morning and not Rory. I didn't even want to think about that now. Instead, I told the officer, "There was a disturbance here. As you can see, it ended badly."

"I'm sorry to hear it. You gave me a free donut earlier. I've been thinking about it ever since. Haven't tasted anything that good since my granny died."

I cringed. "Thank you, I think?"

He smiled shyly. "It's a compliment. Would you mind walking me through the events of the morning?"

"Not at all," I said, and began describing as best as I could the chaos that had erupted when Fiona Dickel, Betty Vanhoosen, and Mia Long had descended on the bakeshop counter at once. Rory, standing beside me, helped flesh out the picture for the young officer.

Scribbling notes as fast as he could, Officer McAllister suddenly looked up from his notepad. "So, when did Ms. Long collapse?"

"The moment I brought her to the lawn," Rory answered. "She was dragging her feet. I thought it was all part of her refusal to leave the bakeshop."

"You mentioned that everyone was making choking noises. Was Ms. Long, in fact, choking?"

Rory shook his head. "I left her on the lawn and was heading back up the steps when I heard her friends scream. That's when I noticed Ms. Long was unconscious. At first, due to her earlier performance, I thought she was just acting, you know, to make her point. Two of her friends were on the ground beside her, shaking her. However, there was something about her face. She looked flushed, her body limp. She was rolling like a rag doll as her friends shook her. When I realized she had no pulse, I told Lindsey to call an ambulance, then started CPR."

"Any sign of a donut in her mouth?"

Rory flashed me a sideways look and nodded. "Yeah, she had a whole wad of donut in her mouth. I cleared her airway before starting CPR."

"So, she hadn't choked on the donut?"

Rory shrugged. "She was pretending to choke on the donut, I think. I don't know why she stopped breathing."

Officer McAllister nodded. He was just about to close his notebook when he thought to ask, "Do you recall what kind of donut it was?"

"Is that relevant?" I asked a little defensively. "I mean, does it really matter? The woman was causing a scene, grabbing donuts off paying customers' plates and shoving them in her mouth only to spit them back out again. She came here to ruin me. I'm sure in a few hours you'll be able to ask her yourself what kind of donut she was 'fake' choking on."

Without flinching or a single blink of an eye, McAllister shifted his wide blue gaze to Rory. "It may be important, sir."

While the older officers were taking statements, and Fiona Dickel was pointing her finger at me, yelling, "She did it! She murdered the lighthouse and that woman!" I watched as young McAllister opened a ziplock baggie and scooped a glob of masticated donut off the lawn. I suddenly went cold.

My donut was now evidence. Dear heavens, why did that thought terrify me so?

CHAPTER 14

The crowds on the patio and front lawn were beginning to disperse as Rory, Kennedy, and I walked back inside the bakeshop. To my surprise, I found that the floor had already been mopped, the counters wiped down, the coffee bar straightened, and the outsides of the bakery cases cleaned. The place sparkled once again. Dylan, I silently mused and shook my head. I had told her to hang out in the kitchen and take a break. She must have continued to clean after making the girls a hearty meal. She was not only a great baker but a model employee. I felt an instant welling of gratitude that I had found her and that she had come to work for me.

"Dylan," I said aloud. "She's worked a miracle here. Only now the place looks so empty. I'm not sure what the proper protocol is when a customer's collapsed. Do I keep baking? Yes," I answered my own question, thinking it was still my grand opening. "I probably should."

"What?" Rory looked unnerved. "I just got done trying to breathe life into a woman who, for the most part, was dead after fake-choking on one of your donuts."

"But she . . . wasn't really dead, was she?"

Rory's vibrant eyes were reduced to mere slivers of glassy blue as he looked at me. "Look, I'm not a doctor, but I have seen my share of trauma. The woman collapsed. Her heart had stopped, and she wasn't breathing. That doesn't happen from a donut."

His intense look frightened me.

"Not a donut, Rory dear, probably something much stronger." Kennedy, in her breezy manner and patronizing English accent, swooped in. "I have no doubt you brawny army men have seen some pretty terrifying things on the battlefield, but you have absolutely no idea what the New York City food scene is all about. It's fast-paced and competitive, not to mention the ungodly pressure in those hot kitchens. The poor thing was probably chock-full of stimulants. One sip of Lindsey's rich coffee and *Ka-bloowie!* The old ticker goes out and she goes down. Happens all the time. You valiantly kept her heart pumping. The professionals will do the rest."

"I hope you're right." Rory glared at her, unable to hide his skepticism.

"I do too."

"Linds." Kennedy's voice softened as she looked at me. "I think you should keep things going. Aside from a crazy woman protesting the bakeshop and a spiteful diva collapsing—none of which was your fault—the morning's been a huge success. The bakery cases are all empty, and now the whole town's buzzing about the Beacon Bakeshop. Screaming sirens? Police *and* an ambulance? This is a small town. It's also Memorial Day weekend. There's been a whole lot of action here, and everyone's going to want to stop in for a nibble and the latest gossip. I'm not saying it's ideal PR, but it's happening. You should put on a brave face and capitalize on this tragedy while you can."

Rory, all six foot, four inches of him, glared down at Kennedy and uttered, "*Who are you?*"

"Only the best PR money can buy, darling." Kennedy winked and headed toward the door to my private living quarters. "I'm going to get Welly. Had to lock the poor thing up, he was so upset by that woman." She pointed down Main Street, in the general direction the ambulance had taken. "It's gorgeous outside, and the beach is teeming with potential customers. Welly and I are going to take a little stroll on the sand and chat up the Beacon Bakeshop. My advice? Fill those gorgeous cases as fast as you can, darlings."

"Is she serious?" Rory asked the moment Kennedy was out of view. When Rory first met Kennedy, he genuinely liked her. Kennedy was not only exotically beautiful, smart, and exquisitely dressed, her English accent had the power to draw men in like hipsters to a coffee bar. Now, however, he was looking at my friend as if she was patient zero for a new, more virulent form of plague.

"She's just nervous," I told him. "And so am I. We both need to keep busy and focus our attention elsewhere. Kennedy is a PR machine. She can't turn it off. I'm a number-cruncher but have rolled all my energy, nervous or otherwise, into baking. Regardless of whether we open or not, I need to work. And you look like you could use a cold drink and something to eat. Come on," I said, pulling him to the kitchen with me. As much as I wanted to jump right in and start loading the cases with cakes, cookies, pies, brownies, and premade sandwiches, I refrained. We had all worked hard this morning and deserved a little reprieve before we reopened for business.

"What's the news, Lindsey?" Dylan, looking worried, stood up from her stool. She had made the girls delicious-looking omelets and buttered toast. Amazingly, she had read my mind and was already working on our prebaked loaves of bread. Half a dozen loaves of white bread were already cooling on the butcher-block counter; others were in the oven browning. Although the café had been the scene of utter chaos, thanks to Dylan the kitchen had remained orderly and kept its wonderful smell. The entire bakeshop was filled with the heavenly scent of baking bread. To a foodie the smell was as intoxicating as a bouquet of fragrant roses to a romantic. Part of me wanted to stay in the safety of the kitchen all day, whipping up batches of cookies, delicate pastries, and more loaves of bread. Instead I turned to Rory.

"Fancy an omelet? I can make you a sandwich if you'd rather."

"It's still before noon," he noted. "I'm a breakfast man. An omelet sounds perfect." He took a seat at the long stainless-steel counter beside Wendy. The girls looked much better after having eaten a fortifying meal.

It felt good to all be in the kitchen together after the hectic morning. Rory chatted with Dylan and the girls as I turned on a gas burner and placed a small sauté pan over the flames. As the pan heated, I chopped up an Italian sausage and added it to the pan. While the sausage cooked, I cracked three eggs into a bowl, added a dash of milk, a dash of salt and pepper, and a pinch of freshly chopped basil. I liked putting fresh spices directly into the egg mixture. A light basil flavor would infuse the eggs for my Italian-inspired omelet, while the salt and pepper would be evenly dispersed. It also saved time from having to add spices later.

I whisked the egg mixture until everything was nicely blended together. When the sausage was done, I removed it from the pan, wiped out the grease, and placed the pan back over the burner. The first thing that went into the pan was a dash of butter. Butter was the key to flaky baked goods. It was also the key to making fabulous eggs.

I kept the conversation going as I continued to cook. The moment the butter melted, I added the egg mixture. While the eggs cooked, I chopped up a fresh tomato and grated both provolone and Parmesan cheeses. I then flipped the eggs and topped it with the cooked sausage, the two cheeses, and diced fresh tomato. As the omelet cooked, the entire kitchen smelled divine. I gave it a minute before folding half the eggs on top of the savory filling. Then I turned off the burner and covered the pan to let the cheese melt. While my omelet was resting, I toasted two slices of fresh-baked white bread. It came out lightly browned on the outside and warm and soft in the middle. I slathered on more butter and plated it next to the Italian omelet.

"Here you go," I said, placing a fork in Rory's hand.

"Heavenly," he said, breathing in the warm essence of the omelet. "Which is appropriate after the little slice of hell we've been through. Thanks, Lindsey. This looks delicious." He dug right in, cutting a man-sized chunk. Strings of molten cheese and bits of tomato oozed out the sides. "I've never had an Italian omelet before, but I have to warn you, this little beauty has ruined all other omelets for me."

As Rory ate his omelet, I proceeded to make a second one for me, while toasting up more bread for Elizabeth and Wendy. Our conversation in the kitchen had helped the girls. The angry protesters had set them on edge, but the thought of death had really spooked them. They were both bright, hardworking kids. It would be horrible if both girls quit on opening day. Rory, in his deep voice and calming tone, had done wonders explaining to the girls how he had performed CPR, and how Mia was going to be just fine now that she was in the hands of doctors.

Dylan had been worried as well. Like me, however, she had channeled her nervous energy. She not only had cleaned the café, but she had taken command of the kitchen. While I made omelets, Dylan pulled loaves of bread from the oven and scooped generous mounds of chocolate-chip cookie dough onto parchment-lined baking sheets. The cookies were ready to go into the oven.

I had just taken my omelet out of the pan and was carrying my plate to the counter when a loud thump directed my attention to the swinging door. The moment I looked, the door flew back and Welly came bounding in, his leash dragging behind him like a rubber snake.

Wellington wasn't allowed in the kitchen, and he knew it. Something must have spooked him. His wild eyes locked on me just before he leapt. Wellington was not a lapdog. But in that moment he had channeled his inner terrier and, no doubt, hoped for the best.

"WELLINGTON!" I cried. The giant paws struck my chest with the force of a micro-car. I half-expected airbags to deploy as I hit the floor. They didn't, of course.

It was up to my own padding, which, for a baker, wasn't very impressive. "Ouch!" I cried, watching my omelet crash to the floor beside me.

"Whoa, boy," Rory commanded, jumping to my rescue. He grabbed hold of Wellington's collar and pulled the dog off me before helping me to my feet. "You okay, Lindsey?"

"Yes," I said, rubbing my rear while giving Welly a stern look. "Naughty dog!" Wellington dropped to the floor and buried his fluffy head between his paws.

"Where's Kennedy?" Rory asked.

That question was answered a moment later when Kennedy burst through the door with a look in her deep brown eyes to match Wellington's.

"Linds! My God, I'm so sorry! I need to tell you something. I think . . . I think I've made a terrible mistake."

I was stunned. "Not your fault," I said, picking up Wellington's leash. "He knows he's not supposed to be in the kitchen." Wellington, like all opportunistic creatures, was gobbling up my omelet with the speed of one who knows he's about to be dragged out the door.

Kennedy's eyes flashed wide. "No, not that. I mean, yeah. Sorry he got away from me." She fake-smiled at Rory, then asked, "Can we talk?"

"I'll take him, Ms. Bakewell." Wendy, ready to get back to work, took Wellington's leash. Elizabeth got up as well. Both girls adored my dog. They were just about to take him through the door when it swung open again, this time revealing Officer McAllister.

The girls stopped. Wellington let out a mournful whine. Kennedy inhaled sharply. The troubled look on McAllister's face made him seem far older than his twenty-something years.

"Ms. Bakewell, sorry to barge in, but I have some bad news. Mia Long has been pronounced dead on arrival. The medical examiner has asked for an investigation into the matter of her death. I'm afraid, ma'am, that your bakeshop is now a crime scene."

"Dead?" Wendy uttered. Her eyes rolled back in her head as her knees buckled beneath her. Wellington, having finished my omelet, was there to break her fall.

CHAPTER 15

The words *Mia's dead* rang through my head as I jumped to Wendy's aid. Wellington, confused and unhappy, was nervously licking the poor girl's face. I pulled him away and saw that his gooey licks had worked. Wendy was starting to move.

"Wendy! What happened?" I was on my knees beside her. "Are you okay?"

Elizabeth, who was also by her side, answered for her friend. "She'll be okay. She has a fainting condition. Too much empathy, or something. When she sees something gross or hears something really disturbing, she passes out. Once, when we were in health class, we had to watch a video about childbirth. It was one of those tame instructional videos, but it really triggered Wendy. When the woman was about to give birth, Wendy turned white and toppled off her stool."

My hand flew to my mouth. Rory, Kennedy, and Officer McAllister looked troubled. Dylan, however, was on the verge of giggles.

"It's true," Wendy said, struggling to sit up. She was still a little wobbly and was holding on to Welly for support. My giant dog was happy to be of service. He was in the forbidden kitchen playing the hero. I wasn't about to throw him out, and he knew it. As Rory handed Wendy a glass of water, she continued, "It's called vasovagal syncope, and it's a total bummer. I've been to the emergency room so many times." She rolled her eyes as she said this. "Please don't send me there now. I'm fine. I probably should have told you about it, but really, who'd have thought a bakery would have so much drama?"

She was right. A bakery shouldn't have this much drama. What the heck had happened? A woman had died on the lawn outside my bakery. The knowledge had not only triggered Wendy's bizarre fainting illness, but I was feeling ill as well. Fighting to maintain my composure, I asked Officer McAllister to wait a moment while I sent the girls home. There was no need for them to stay and listen to the gory details of Mia's death.

Elizabeth agreed to drive Wendy to her house, but not before I sent each girl home with a loaf of fresh-baked bread and a dozen chocolate-chip cookies. I told them I'd call tomorrow and give them an update on the state of the bakeshop.

As the girls left, I wondered how the day could possibly get any worse. My bakery had been set upon by angry divas, a young woman had died, and my eighteen-year-old employee had just collapsed on the kitchen floor because she had some disease that caused her to pass out when confronted with emotionally distressing situations, namely death. If that wasn't the mark of an ill-fated grand opening, the look on my best friend's face was enough to hammer the message home.

I recalled how Kennedy had rushed into the kitchen in a panic. Yet the moment McAllister appeared, all her previous urgency and excitement had melted away, replaced by professional composure and mild surprise. It dawned on me then what Kennedy had come to tell me. The very thought of her involvement in Mia's death sent my heart tripping away like the misguided beak of a woodpecker on a tin roof. I felt faint.

"Ms. Bakewell?"

"*Yes?*" I snapped. It was a moment before I realized Officer McAllister was speaking to me.

"Do you understand what I'm saying?"

I shook my head and stared at him.

"Mia Long died under suspicious circumstances. You told me that you knew the victim. Sergeant Murdock and the county crime scene unit will be arriving shortly. They're going to cordon off the bakeshop and conduct a thorough investigation of the premises, gathering any evidence that might be pertinent to this case. In the meantime, I'm going to ask you to come down to the station with me for further questioning."

"What?" I cried, feeling a welling of outrage. I wasn't even at half-blown New Yorker and the poor man flinched. Rory, Kennedy, and Dylan were staring at me, urging me with their eyes to tone it down. The young officer, after all, was only doing his duty. Still, it rankled. "But I've already told you everything!"

McAllister's gold-dusted brows furrowed, causing his handsome, boyish features to look either displeased or embarrassed, it was hard to tell which. "I'm sorry, Ms.

Bakewell, I truly am, but you didn't tell us that Mia Long was having an affair with your fiancé, Jeffery Plank."

"Ex-fiancé," I corrected.

McAllister cleared his throat. "Right. I understand that you caught them in the act, so to speak. She died on your property, Ms. Bakewell. Mia Long ate one of your donuts. You have motive and opportunity. Do you see how this might look bad for you?"

Unfortunately, I did. And, unbelievably, my day had just gone from bad to a whole new level of horrible.

I didn't love being a suspect in Mia's death, but I respected the process. The Beacon Harbor Police Station was less than a mile away from the bakeshop, which, under normal circumstances, was a comfort. It was a relatively modern building sitting at the end of Waterfront Drive, just off Main Street. And the officer questioning me wasn't hard on the eyes at all, either. Tuck—that's what he asked me to call him—was only trying to do his job. Surprisingly, he'd been on the force for five years, was twenty-eight (pushing the boundaries of my creeper zone but not entirely out of the question), loved water sports, snow skiing, and baked goods, and had never dealt with a suspected homicide before. I told him I hadn't either, right after I told him that I didn't kill Mia Long. In fact, after a bout of small talk, I answered all the young officer's questions. I had also made it quite clear that Mia and Jeffery were a big part of the reason I had left a successful career in New York to come to Beacon Harbor. I had never wanted to see Jeffery or Mia again. When they had shown up at my bakeshop during the grand opening, I had gotten the shock of my life.

"I expect that's so," Tuck said. He sat back and took a sip of his coffee. I'd been offered coffee as well but was already buzzing with caffeine and nerves. I felt that if I had one more sip I'd explode with a full-blown case of the jitters. Trembling hands during questioning might give the wrong impression. "So," he began, looking adorably perplexed with his furrowed brow and his slightly parted lips. What the heck was wrong with me? The guy was still in his twenties . . . and trying to puzzle out whether or not I'd just murdered Jeffery's lover. My God, maybe I had? She'd been in my shop eating one of my donuts! I took a deep breath and tried to smile. My mother could smile and look sexy on command. It wasn't a skill I'd inherited. From all accounts, my fake smile was making him even more suspicious. I bit my lip instead.

Tuck, blowing a hard breath, leaned on his elbows. "Why were they at your bakery?"

That *was* the question. I honestly had no idea and told him as much. "Look," I said, "as far as I know, I've done nothing to upset them. Jeffery had Mia, his restaurant, and the sweet red Jaguar F-Type convertible I'd given him for his fortieth birthday."

"What?" Officer Cutie Pie nearly choked on his coffee. "You gave that dude an F-Type convertible?" He gave me a wide, blue-eyed stare. "That's, like, a super-expensive car."

"I thought I was in love," I explained. "And Jeffery had always wanted that car. I was fortunate enough to be able to give it to him. Even when I called off our engagement, I let him keep the car. I think I just wanted a clean break, you know?"

"Sweet merciful Jesus." Cutie Pie's eyes were as wide

as pop cans. "I heard you had money, but how much money can a baker make?"

"I'm not sure yet," I told him honestly. "But I'll tell you one thing. I'm not doing this for the money. It's my dream. It came bubbling to the surface the moment I broke it off with Jeffery. By the way, did Jeffery say why he and Mia were here in the first place?"

Tuck shrugged. "I haven't spoken with Mr. Plank. The Sarge talked with him at the hospital. Sergeant Murdock's the one who wanted you brought in for further questioning. My understanding is that Mr. Plank is very shaken up by the death of Mia Long. He's also claiming that you had something to do with it."

"Oh well, he can just stand in line then, because Fiona Dickel is claiming I murdered the Beacon Harbor Lighthouse! Great," I said. "Everyone's pointing a finger at me, simply because I converted an old lighthouse into a bakeshop and sell donuts and baked goods. I don't mean to sound insensitive, but everyone was eating my donuts. Mia's the only person, as far as I know, who actually died. Spoiler alert," I said, my voice escalating, "it's not from eating one of my donuts!"

Officer Tuck McAllister, having been blessed with the same fair skin as me, turned the color of a beet. "I know," he uttered, looking at his hands. "But . . . the woman died all the same."

I lowered my voice and reminded myself to remain calm. "She was a pastry chef who was no stranger to eating baked goods, so we can rule out allergies and anaphylactic shock. Do we know if she had a medical condition? Did anyone ask Jeffery if she was taking any drugs?"

Officer Tuck shook his head. "I honestly don't know the answers to those questions. However, I have been told that the medical examiner's ordered a full toxicology report. We'll have to wait until that comes back before we know what, if anything, Ms. Long was taking. However, the ER doctor has been interviewed. He's told us that he believes Ms. Long's death is linked to acute cyanide poisoning."

"What?" I had never expected to hear that. "But that's impossible. I don't own cyanide, nor would I have it anywhere near my bakery. Look, I made all the dough for those donuts. I made all the frostings, and fillings, and hand-filled each one of them. I can assure you, with absolute certainty, that there isn't a speck of cyanide in my baked goods!"

He blushed. "Of course. I had one of your donuts. But still, according to the ER doctor she had all the signs. The autopsy is expected to confirm the ER doctor's report. I'm sorry, Lindsey, but she died from something she ate. And she was eating your donuts."

CHAPTER 16

I left the police station with my heart pounding in my ears and my head swirling with the possibility that Mia had been poisoned by eating one of my donuts. I had refused Tuck's offer to drive me back to the lighthouse. I wanted to walk. I needed to feel the warm air on my face. I needed to feel the welcoming rays of the sun. I needed to walk on sidewalks teeming with humanity and clear my head.

It sounded odd, counterintuitive even, but for a city girl the deepest solitude can often be found walking in the press of a rush hour crowd. So many bodies moving in the same direction instilled a primal sense of belonging, and yet the mere fact that everyone moving around you is a stranger provides an oddly comforting form of isolation. There was never a lack of humanity filling the streets and sidewalks of New York City. The same could never be said of Beacon Harbor. However, the summer tourists had finally arrived, and although it wasn't exactly a rush hour crowd, the town had come to life with fresh, happy faces. Those tourists who weren't at the beach worshiping the warm sun were in town, strolling up and down the sidewalks with a definite lack of purpose. No one was in a hurry, and that was just fine with me. It was exactly what the merchants of Beacon Harbor had been waiting for all winter.

I was seeking solace in anonymity, but Beacon Harbor was a small town, and a nosy one. When I passed by Harbor Scoops, Ginger Brooks popped out, her face contorted in a look of concern.

"Lindsey, are you okay? I've been so worried. Is that woman going to be alright?"

I didn't know what to say. I just shook my head and kept walking, noting with dismay that some of the tourists were still carrying the flyers that Kennedy had passed around.

"Hey!" A young man in form-fitting shorts and a souvenir T-shirt raised his arm in greeting as I came around a corner. The lighthouse was in sight, but little good it did me. My solitude had been shattered by a friendly couple. "Heard someone went into a sugar coma on your lawn," he said, and smiled at his girlfriend. She was wearing a short, flouncy sundress making my flour-dusted jeans and frosting-smudged shirt feel old and dirty by comparison.

I must have stared at them too long without answering. The woman, being a bit more tactful, asked, "Did you make the blueberry coffee cake? It was delicious. I'm still thinking about it."

"Thank you," I said, relieved to be focusing on something other than death. "Tomorrow I'm making a cherry pecan coffee cake. I think you'll like that one too."

The man frowned. "Ma'am, I don't think you're going to be open tomorrow. Your bakery's been roped off with crime scene tape. The lady from the Book Nook said she heard that the cops are closing you down."

"What? That's . . ." I was going to say ridiculous but peered around the man instead. Sure enough, across the street and down past the public beach was my newly remodeled lighthouse, blocked off from the public by a perimeter of cop cars and yellow crime scene tape. I swore under my breath.

"I guess that's a pass on cherry coffee cake tomorrow," the man remarked as I stormed off.

I had every intention of returning to the lighthouse, until I came upon the Harbor Realty building. Was I even allowed back on the premises if it was a crime scene? I didn't know. I didn't know what to do, but hopefully Betty would.

Betty Vanhoosen's building was an impressively remodeled turn-of-the-century, two-story storefront now serving as the town's largest, and only, real estate office. Like Betty, the furnishings were bright and cheerful. The pale-yellow walls were full of colorful pictures of the town's most prestigious lakefront dwellings. The couch in the waiting room was large and floral. I walked over to the cottage-white desk and asked Paige if her boss was in.

"Heard what happened this morning at the bakeshop. Can't believe that Dickel woman was protesting your bakery and throwing donuts! I used to think she was funny, but now it's just sad. Betty was supposed to bring me a donut, but never got the chance. If I ever see Fiona in here again, I'm giving her a piece of my mind!" Paige, a very competent young woman in her midtwenties, made a menacing face before dialing Betty's extension. "Mrs. Vanhoosen, Lindsey Bakewell's here to see you." She replaced the receiver and added, "I was going to trot on over for lunch, purely to see Beacon Harbor's favorite mystery man making coffee. Is Rory one of your employees now?" She obviously thought it amusing.

"I wish," I said, and attempted a grin, though I wasn't really feeling it. "He'll deny it, but the man does know his way around an espresso machine. He's just helping out for the day. Sorry you missed him."

Betty's office took up the entire second floor. It was a welcoming space with a smattering of comfortable seating for tired clients, a box of toys for fidgety kids, and a small table to have a snack on, or sign contracts. Betty's large desk faced the room and was adjacent to a wall of windows that overlooked the harbor. It was a spectacular view, of which Betty was fully aware.

"Lindsey, my goodness! Come in! Come in!" Betty shot around her desk and pulled me to a chair. "I've been watching the events since I got here. I saw young McAllister whisk you away to the police station and now they've cordoned off your bakeshop! What's happened?"

"You saw all that from here?" I glanced out the window. No wonder Betty knew everything and everybody. She not only had an unobstructed view of the harbor, including my lighthouse at the far end of the public beach, but also much of the town as well.

"After the commotion at your bakeshop, the rest of my day's been boring by comparison." She gave a careless wave of her hand. "The moment they whisked that rude little woman off in the ambulance, I was questioned by the police. Me! As if I had anything to do with it! I told the officer that everything was going just fine until that woman and her friends showed up and started stealing donuts off people's plates. The nerve!"

"It was odd behavior," I agreed, and sat back in the comfy chair. "I never expected it. I don't know why she came all the way to Beacon Harbor, and worse yet—"

"Oooo, don't tell me!" Betty's normally pleasant, round face took on the troubling taint of dark satisfaction. "She's dead, isn't she?"

"How . . . how do you know that?"

"Why else would McAllister take you down to the station for questioning? I don't mean to speak ill of the dead, dear, but she had it coming. This is Beacon Harbor. We don't suffer fools or outright malicious behavior. Serves her right if she choked on one of the donuts she stole. You've worked so hard on that old lighthouse. She and her friends had no right to make a scene like that."

"Yes, but Betty, she's dead." I gave her a hard, face-slapping look and repeated, "Dead! And worst of all, they think I had something to do with it."

My look and words were enough to rattle her mother-hen emotions. "What?" she said, wrinkling her pert little nose in distaste. "They think you murdered that woman? You were behind the counter the whole time. Did you tell McAllister that?"

"That's the trouble. Officer McAllister said they think Mia died from eating something poisonous, but the only thing she ate were my donuts."

Betty frowned. "Well, we all ate your donuts . . . except for Fiona. She was throwing them. She was also questioned by the police. You don't suppose she had anything to do with that woman's death, do you?"

"It makes no sense. Fiona didn't know Mia. Besides,

they were virtually on the same team, both having wanted to close me down, which, by the way, they have." I looked at Betty and suddenly felt the impending weight I'd been holding at bay all morning crumble. It was oppressive. My eyes stung with the threat of tears. Embarrassed, I covered my face with my hands. "Oh, why did I have to throw away a fabulous career and open an ill-fated bakery? Why couldn't I have just stayed in New York City and concentrated on making money, like normal people do?"

Betty, who was the age of my mother yet had the comforting roundness of my grandmother, sat beside me and removed my hands. "Because, dear, you're needed here in Beacon Harbor. Did you ever think of that? That old lighthouse needed you. That poor place sat empty for years, rotting on the beach like an abandoned boat. And look at it now! It's the jewel on the lake it was always meant to be. And, better yet, it's now the home of your scrumptious baked goods. You cannot deny that your wonderful donuts and baked goods made a lot of people happy this morning. Why, the whole town is abuzz about how yummy everything tasted. Also—and here's another important point—you gave Dylan another chance to use her talent."

It was kind of Betty to say so, but I couldn't take all the credit. "Dylan could get a job anywhere . . . with her talent." I hiccoughed.

Betty offered a kind smile and leaned across her desk. "She doesn't like to talk about it, but Dylan has had her challenges. Her parents were alcoholics, she struggled with depression, and she was quite the wild child in her teens. She even dropped out of high school."

"What? I didn't know that." I sniffled. "I guess I never

asked, and she never offered. But it hardly makes a difference now."

Betty smiled and patted my hand. "You're giving her a chance. You're making a difference in her life because you can. Her cousin, Mike, needed a leg up too. Money can be so tight around here in the off-season. He works several jobs to make ends meet."

I took a tissue from her desk and wiped my nose. "Uber driver being one of them?"

"Indeed. He's our local jack-of-all-trades. But my point is, when the Village Bakery went out of business, that poor girl was cleaning hotel rooms and cottages until you came along. You made her a baker once again."

"I . . . I did do that," I said, and dried my eyes.

"And what about Rory Campbell?" she continued. "He barely said boo to anyone until you and Wellington moved next door. So handsome, and so reclusive. You had him working at your bakeshop this morning making lattes! If that isn't a miracle, I don't know what is."

The thought of Rory working like a fiend and pulling shots of espresso made me smile.

Betty cocked her head. "Dear, I don't mean to be pesky, but when was the last time you've eaten? You look a bit pale and gaunt. Don't tell me that you've forgotten to eat?"

"I tried to eat," I protested, remembering the delicious plate of eggs I'd made and lost to Wellington.

"You know what the trouble is with your generation?"

I shrugged. "We worry too much?"

"No. Yoga pants. They're mainstream fashion. You have to be a thin little twig to wear them. It promotes unhealthy eating habits, like skipping meals." As Betty talked, she picked up the phone. "Harbor Hoagies is just across the street. You must try their tuna salad sub with extra black olives. I won't hear no for an answer." Before I could protest, Paige was out the door heading for the sub shop to pick up Betty's order.

Honestly, it felt good to have a quiet place to think while the lighthouse grounds teemed with police and crime scene investigators. It was also a relief to be in the company of a new friend who had my best interest in mind.

Lunch ended when a middle-aged couple came in, asking about available beachfront properties. I thanked Betty for the sandwich and left her office, feeling much better for having eaten it.

I looked across the street at my lighthouse. Betty was right. Beacon Harbor needed me, now more than ever. I was still shaken by the thought of Mia's death, but I wasn't about to take the fall for her murder. Not this street-savvy, New York City girl. I took a deep breath and stepped into the sunshine.

CHAPTER 17

"What's going on here?" I demanded, marching up to the first person in uniform I could find. The crime scene tape around the lawn was bad enough, but now a small team of hazmat-suited investigators had invaded my café. One man was snapping pictures while three others wandered the recently cleaned bakery looking for evidence. The officer I confronted was in traditional police blues and a cap, watching the proceedings with mild detachment while nibbling a cookie.

At the sound of my voice, the officer turned and raised the cookie in greeting. "Ms. Bakewell, I presume?"

I'd been expecting a man. The officer confronting me now was a middle-aged woman, thickset and slightly shorter than me. Her dyed-blond hair had been pulled off her face, revealing penetrating brown eyes under a fringe of wispy bangs. Her unsmiling face was highly intimidating.

Shocked, angered, and slightly confused, I pointed at the chocolate-chip cookie in her hand. "Aren't you afraid you'll be poisoned or something?"

"Interesting that you mentioned poison." The officer set her cookie on a napkin and hit me with a probing gaze. In that moment I was longing for the kind smile of Officer Tuck.

However, unwise as it might be, my Linds-itude flared. "I'm sorry, have we met?"

"Sergeant Stacy Murdock. No, we have not met. Haven't had a need to meet, until now."

If I had met Sergeant Murdock at a New York City gala, I would have been impressed as heck by her. Here was a woman in her forties with a tough-as-nails air who'd risen through the ranks of a very demanding profession. That takes a hefty combination of brains, brawn, and pluck. However, meeting her now—on the wrong side of the police crime scene tape—all I felt was a heart-pounding brand of dread. Women were tough, especially when annoyed by another woman. I had the feeling that Sergeant Stacy Murdock had been dragged away from a long-needed vacation on my account. And if that wasn't bad enough, she'd been eating one of my cookies. For the life of me I couldn't tell if she liked or hated it. I took a deep breath and tried another tactic.

"I'm sorry. This is all new to me. It was our opening day, and now I find my bakery is filled with. . . ." I waved a hand at the white-suited workers.

"This is called investigating the scene of the crime, Ms. Bakewell. A woman who was known to you was murdered on the premises this morning. You offered poison as a possible murder weapon. I find that very interesting."

Good job, Linds, I screamed at myself while consciously softening my tone. "I was being impertinent," I apologized. "I've just come from the police station, where I was questioned by Officer McAllister. He said that you were at the hospital talking to Jeffery Plank, Mia's . . . I mean, the victim's boyfriend. I also learned that the suspected cause of death was poison, most likely cyanide."

Sargent Murdock, guarded, calculating, tilted her head as she narrowed her gaze. "He told you all that, did he?"

"He did," I said defensively, thinking of the sweet, utterly scrumptious Officer Tuck. "Because he knows as well as I do that I didn't murder that woman."

"Really?" Her tone oozed cynical intrigue. "And what would bring him to that conclusion?"

"My honest plea of innocence as well as the fact that it would be a terrible business decision. The mere fact that I've sunk a lot of cash into this old lighthouse—have worked my tail off decorating, baking, hiring good people, and marketing for opening day—should tell you that I'd never sabotage my dream bakery by murdering one of my customers."

A corner of her unadorned mouth lifted slightly. "Does it? Rumor is, money's not really an issue with you. For all I know, this whole lighthouse bakery endeavor could be the perfect setup to murder your rival."

My jaw dropped. "Rival? That woman was hardly my rival."

"I'm well aware of your relationship with the deceased."

"Good!" I snapped. "Because if Jeffery didn't tell you

at the hospital, I'll tell you now. I moved here to wash my hands of them both."

Without creasing her deadpan face, Sergeant Murdock added, "Just like you washed away all the evidence from your bakery cases, floors, and counters?"

"*Wah, wah . . . what?*" I stuttered as my stomach quivered with a painful ache. I looked at my bakery. Earlier this morning, Mia and Fiona had done their utmost to trash it, smashing donuts against the cases and spilling coffee everywhere. Dylan and her nervous energy, bless her, had made it presentable again—in the hopes that we could reopen for lunch. Was that a crime? According to the look on the sergeant's face, it very well might be.

"Your bakery. It's been cleaned," she repeated. "Tampering with a crime scene is a federal offense."

"But . . . but we didn't know this was a crime scene when we straightened up the place. This is a bakery. Cleanliness is just as important to us as creating delectable baked goods. The café and bakery counters were filthy, thanks to Mia Long and her friends. Mia started it, but Fiona Dickel and her protesters were happy to jump in and lend a hand. They vandalized my bakery on opening day! This is a place of business, after all. Once Mia was whisked away by the ambulance, we thought we might be able to reopen for lunch," I explained.

"Really? Well, that is optimistic of you." Sergeant Murdock was obviously going to expound on that thought when she was pulled away by one of the men collecting evidence. A moment later she returned. "Your bakery's remarkably clean. We're going to be taking your trash as evidence. And since you live on the same premises as your place of business, we're going to need to search your home as well."

"Fine," I replied stoically. "I've nothing to hide. Anything else?"

"Actually, yes." She paused and held up her hand. "I want to know how you baked such a perfect cookie. The flavor's extraordinary, and you've managed to get the right amount of crunch and chewiness in every bite. I've heard that your donuts are good too."

"They are," I told her. "And I assure you, Mia Long didn't die from eating them."

"They need a warrant, Linds!" Kennedy, blocking the door with her body, glared at me. She was also blocking Wellington, who had no idea what the excitement was all about but felt he should jump in with a series of earth-shattering barks. "That's the law," she added above the noise.

"I know the law," I soothed, trying to calm her down. "But they don't need a warrant if I agree to let them search, which I am."

"Really? Do you think that's wise?" Kennedy eyed the sergeant and her team as if they were a band of pesky teenagers. "Without consulting a lawyer? They think you're a murderer!"

"But I'm not. Wellington, down!" With my dog under control, I stepped back, allowing Murdock access to my cozy lighthouse home.

Kennedy, Wellington, and I stayed outside while the police snooped around, looking for God only knew what. If they were indeed on the lookout for cyanide, they were going to be disappointed.

"What if someone is trying to frame you?" Kennedy offered, casting a nervous sideways glance at the lighthouse. "What if they planted a bottle of, you know, that poison stuff in your house?"

"Cyanide, you mean?" It was a troubling thought. "Very few people enter my house. Besides, if there was a bottle of cyanide, I doubt it would have my fingerprints on it. Without my fingerprints, they couldn't link me to the crime." As I spoke, I noticed the frightened way Kennedy was looking at me.

"How do you know so much about cyanide and crime scenes?" she asked. "You didn't . . . have anything to do with Mia's death, did you?"

"What?" I cried, looking at her. Wellington, hearing the excited tone of my voice, lifted his head. He'd been drinking lake water, which now dripped from his droopy jowls as he pranced back to where we stood. "You know I didn't kill Mia. Why would I?"

Behind the flawless tawny skin, I thought I saw her blanch. "Right," she was quick to add. "I was just making sure that you still despise Jeffery. I mean, if you still have feelings for him . . . ?"

"Stop right there." I held up a hand. I'd known Kennedy a long time. She wasn't one to beat around the bush, like she was doing now. I could tell there was something she wasn't telling me. I then recalled the way she had looked when she had burst into the bakery kitchen, running after Wellington with Officer Cutie Pie fast on her heels. She'd been upset; she was on the verge of an apology. The very memory caused a twinge of dread. "Look," I told her. "We need to talk. But not here, and not while scary Sergeant Murdock is searching my home for evidence."

CHAPTER 18

After a long morning of baking, the excitement of opening day, and the real sorrow and horror of murder, I was zonked. I wanted nothing more than to shower, crawl beneath my covers, and sleep for an entire day but couldn't. Kennedy had a secret to tell me, and we were going to talk.

Sergeant Murdock and her team had left the lighthouse after performing a thorough search of the bakery, living quarters, and grounds. The sergeant, far from being warm and friendly, said very little about her findings. What she did tell me was that I wasn't to leave town and that the bakery would remain closed until further notice. Before she left, however, she asked to purchase a dozen cookies.

"For my kids," she stated gruffly, taking the bag off the counter. "Not much of a baker myself."

"Because you're too busy fighting crime and busting up bodies in Beacon Harbor, right?"

Sergeant Murdock stared at me a moment with her un-smiling eyes, then left the bakery. I gave a slight shiver, locked the bakery door after her, and sought the comfort of my cozy lighthouse kitchen.

I had one more task left, and that was to play hardball with Kennedy, wooing her with a comforting meal and taking her off guard with a bottle of good wine. And I knew just the meal to make her. Wellington, a slave to his belly, was fed first, primarily to stop the drooling and the pleading eyes. Once he was happily gobbling his kibble, I opened my fridge and began pulling out my ammunition—a pound of fresh chicken breasts, a pound of large white mushrooms, butter, onion, garlic, potatoes, and a bottle of dry Marsala wine. I was going to make one of Kennedy's favorite meals, my dad's famous Chicken Marsala over garlic mashed red potatoes. It was one of the few meals Mom really went to town on at home, for-getting all her strict dietary rules and enjoying the deli-cious crispy chicken smothered with mushrooms sautéed in plenty of butter and Marsala wine sauce. As for the garlic mashed potatoes, they were simply to die for. Ken-nedy, who idolized my mom, shared her enthusiasm for the dish.

"Whatcha making?" she asked, sauntering into the kitchen in designer jeans and a cute billowy-sleeved top.

"Your favorite. While I get things ready, why don't you uncork that bottle of pinot grigio I picked up in Tra-verse City?"

"Chicken Marsala—and a bottle of pinot? It wasn't exactly a successful grand opening, but I'm willing to celebrate." Kennedy grabbed the corkscrew and grinned, totally misunderstanding the meaning of the meal, which was fine by me. "As a New Yorker from London," she began, uncorking the wine, "who vacations regularly in France, it's hard to admit, but these local wines are quite good." She poured two glasses and was about to plop down at my kitchen table when I stopped her.

"Before you get too comfortable, mind helping me with the mushrooms? It's been a long day, and I'd love the help."

"No problem. I'm famished. I'll do anything if it'll help get the food on the table faster."

As Kennedy washed and sliced mushrooms, I started on the tiny red potatoes, washing them, cutting them in half and putting them in a pot of salted water. While the potatoes were cooking on the stove, and a bulb of garlic was roasting in the oven, I turned my attention to the chicken breasts. The key to a delicious Chicken Marsala is a tender, crisp, flavorful chicken breast. For this I liked to cut the plump breasts in half, tenderize them a bit with a mallet, then season each thin cutlet with salt, pepper, and dried garlic. Before the breasts went into the hot pan with melted butter, I liberally sprinkled each with flour then shook off the excess. The frying chicken smelled heavenly. Once browned and perfectly cooked, I removed them to a warm oven and began sautéing the mushrooms Kennedy had prepared. As the mushrooms cooked, I added two cloves of roasted garlic, a tablespoon of finely chopped onion, a tablespoon of tomato paste, and a cup of Marsala wine. As the wine cooked off and the mushroom sauce began to reduce, I added the last few spices, oregano, and a little freshly chopped parsley. All that was left to do was to mash the potatoes using butter, half-and-half, another two cloves of roasted garlic, and salt and pepper.

"Smells amazing, Linds!" Kennedy exclaimed, waving the essence of the meal toward her nose. She was nearly drooling like my dog as her eyes held to the two plates of crisp chicken cutlets slathered in savory Marsala mushroom sauce over garlic mashed potatoes. I had no sooner placed them on the table than Wellington lifted his head. His silky black ears perked just before letting out an earth-shattering bark. Sensing the arrival of a friend, he rushed the door with his tail wagging like a flag.

"Am I interrupting?" Rory asked, walking into the kitchen. The look of concern on his face was genuine. I hadn't seen him since I'd been taken down to the police station for questioning.

"Please join us," I said, welcoming him to take a seat at the table. "Kennedy and I are just about to eat dinner. I've made plenty."

My plan had been to get Kennedy to tell me her secret. However, with Rory there I wasn't sure that was a great idea. It wasn't because I didn't trust Rory. In fact, I perhaps trusted him a bit too much. He was ex-military, had served his country, was totally hunky, and was a genuinely good guy. Sure, he was a bit reclusive and secretive about his comings and goings, but all this I chalked up to his writing process. I mean, the guy was working on a military spy thriller or something. I'm sure he needed his privacy. No, I trusted Rory. It was more the fact that he had seen Kennedy's working side—her pushy promoter persona—and he hadn't liked it one bit. He might judge her harshly were she to reveal that she might have goaded Mia and Jeffery the moment she'd spotted them outside the bakery. Or maybe she hadn't. I honestly didn't know what she had done.

Hungry, tired, exchanging pleasantries, we all attacked the food on our plates with zeal, each of us mindful of digging too deeply into the morning's debacle or the matter of murder. Then, having eaten half his meal, Rory suddenly set down his fork.

"I never imagined it would be so dangerous living next to you," he stated, looking squarely at me.

The moment the comment had been spoken, my mouth went instantly dry. I swallowed painfully before apologizing. "Again, I'm terribly sorry. But I really had nothing to do with Mia's death."

The intense look on Rory's face melted. "I know that. What I meant was, this meal. It's one of the top five meals I've ever had. Is everything you make delicious?"

"Pretty much," Kennedy answered, leaning on her elbows. "And please indulge us, what were the other four meals that topped this?"

Rory took the challenge. "The fresh-caught king salmon I landed and cooked on the banks of the Kenai River in Alaska. Steaks fresh from an elk I tracked for three days in the mountains of Wyoming. Walleye pulled from Lake Wabatongushi in Canada . . ."

"Good gracious!" Kennedy exclaimed. "Those are all wild meats—all animals you killed!"

Rory stared her down, ticking his fourth finger, while adding defiantly, "My mother's lasagna, and now Lindsey's chicken and mushroom dish."

"Chicken Marsala," Kennedy corrected, casting me a grin. "It's one of my very favorite meals. I know I came off a bit overreaching today, Rory dear, and I do apologize. Perhaps we can repair some of that damage out of our love for this meal."

"Great idea," I said, refilling their wineglasses. The meal had fortified my nerves, and I was feeling courageous. "We were all a bit on edge at the news of Mia's death. Which brings me to this afternoon—right at the point when we learned that Mia had died en route to the hospital. You came bursting into the kitchen, Kennedy, looking distraught and ready to apologize for something, but you never got the chance."

Kennedy, ready to take a sip of wine, stilled and set the glass back on the table. Her perfectly shaped eyebrows drew closer in consternation as her gaze held mine. "I, um . . . about that. I was probably overreacting."

"Undoubtedly." Rory shot her a stern, military look. "I've only just met you, but even I knew that you've been acting wonky all day. Your behavior, it's been suspicious from the start—the guerilla marketing routine, dressing up Wellington and parading him around the town under the guise of drumming up business."

"Because I *was* drumming up business!" Kennedy glared back at him.

"True, but you were also up to something else. Nobody acts so crass and pushy without being up to something."

"Kennedy does," I added, coming to her defense. I was shocked and a little disturbed that Rory was going after her. However, he had been there too. He had seen her burst into the kitchen looking panicked. I never thought he'd suspect her of foul play.

Taking matters into my own hands, I said very gently, "Kennedy, you know something about Mia's murder. We both know that you do, so now's the time to talk. Look, you're among friends here. We're not going to judge you, but we do need to know what you were going to tell me."

"He's going to judge me!" She jabbed an expensively manicured finger at Rory. "He's been judging me since I got here."

"Because you stick out like a sore thumb."

"She does too!" Kennedy tilted her head in my direction.

"In a good way!" Rory defended, continuing to stare her down like the poor elk he'd shot in Wyoming.

"Please, you two. We all stand out in this town—for our own reasons. But, Kennedy dear, I must agree with Rory. You knew something before you came here. What was it?"

After a minute of defiant silence, she finally relented. "Alright, fine," she erupted, and slapped down her napkin. "I knew you wouldn't forget about that little scene in the kitchen, just as I know you're not going to like what I have to tell you, Linds. I really should have told you sooner. I thought I could handle it. I mean, Rory's right. It's partly the reason I'm here."

Dread filled me. "What in the name of all that's holy did you do?" I uttered. "You didn't . . . you had nothing to do with Mia's death, right?" Rory, harboring the exact same suspicion, stared at my beautiful friend. There was nothing flirtatious about it.

"I didn't poison her," she declared. "But I did . . . tamper a bit."

"What do you mean by 'tamper'?" My stomach contracted painfully, which, after eating such a rich meal, wasn't a good thing. Kennedy looked largely unfazed as she said this, which made me even more suspicious and ill.

"Don't look at me like that," she chided. "I didn't kill her. But I did exact a measure of revenge—purely on your behalf, Linds. I mean, you're my best friend. You'd do the same for me."

"That depends on what you did."

Kennedy drained her wineglass, then continued with passion. "It all started a month after you caught Jeffery cheating with Mia—and on your birthday, no less! You were devastated, Linds, and I would have been, too, if I were in your shoes. The man is deplorable, and his little tart is no better. For heaven's sake, you quit your job and moved to Michigan. Michigan! Who in their right mind moves to Michigan? You left me alone in New York City!"

Kennedy was being dramatic. She had a fabulous career and tons of friends in the city. Sure, she was my best friend, but we talked daily. And she loved my lighthouse. Whatever she'd done, it must have been bad. Kennedy seldom backpedaled like she was doing now. I crossed my arms. "Go on," I insisted. "A month after I caught Jeffery and Mia, what did you do?"

She gave a forceful sigh. "It was really all his doing," she explained with a flip of her hand. "I was watching a morning talk show when they suddenly cut to a cooking segment featuring your ex." She rolled her eyes at the memory. "Jeffrey was his cocky old self, smiling at the cameras while shamelessly plugging his restaurant and new cookbook. Can you believe the title? *Plank It!*? I nearly vomited in the back of my throat when I saw it hovering before the cameras. The pretention! The nerve! The lack of imagination! Anyhow, I was about to turn it off when Jeffery made a crazy, politically incorrect remark about cows. He was cooking a couple of thick, juicy steaks for the hosts and jokingly remarked that cows were too stupid to live. He pushed it further by stating that their only real aspiration was to be slathered in butter and seared on obsidian rock or a hot slab of sea salt."

Rory, aghast, shook his head. "What a bastard," he remarked. "I'm a hunter. You might not understand this, but the code of the hunter is to honor the dignity of every animal, especially the ones who give up their lives during the hunt. Cows are no different."

"Interesting," Kennedy remarked with a touch of skepticism tainting her voice. "In general, I'm not a fan of shooting wild animals for meat, but your take on it is almost noble. Anyhow," she continued, returning to her story. "Jeffery's insensitive comments raised eyebrows on the show, but it was nothing compared to what the PETA people and the vegans were saying on Twitter. The whole thing was blowing up in Jeffery's face, and I couldn't resist the temptation to wield a little influence of my own."

"Oh no," I breathed. "What did you do?"

She combatted my fear with a breezy smile. "I'm an influencer, darling. I have the ear and minds of millions of people. How could I pass up the opportunity to destroy Jeffery Plank and his stupid cookbook? All I did was side with the PETA people. I might have organized a protest outside Sizzle as well. I might have even brought some adorable livestock with me. The cows, I'll have you know, took particularly strong umbrage. Then, because I could, I began trashing his new cookbook, *Plank It!*, on Twitter. I basically created a publicity nightmare, the likes of which he might never recover from. You'll be happy to know that *Plank It!* is tanking at the bookstores."

"Happy?" I cried, staring at my friend with incredulity. "I admit that when I found Jeffery and Mia together, I was heartbroken. But he did me a favor!" I looked at them both, making sure they understood. "I came here and started all this. I would never have had the courage if it wasn't for cheating Jeffery and that tart, Mia. But you?" I pointed accusingly at Kennedy. "You went after his livelihood." And then it hit me. My eyes flew wide as I inhaled sharply. "That's why he and Mia were here! Revenge. They came to ruin me just like you ruined him, only . . . only I had no idea that you ruined him!" My heart was pounding like a hammer in my chest. I was furious. Rory, following along, was puzzled and angered as well.

"That's why he kept calling me!" It suddenly made sense. "He called nearly every day, only I never took his call. I thought he was calling to apologize—or grovel. Oh, Kennedy, how could you? I didn't want you to ruin Jeffery—"

"He deserved it."

"Well, that may be. But you should have told me."

The publicity-warrior melted, and the real Kennedy Kapoor poked through. "I was going to, Linds, honestly. But I pushed it too far. I knew you'd be furious if you caught wind of my involvement in Jeffery's demise."

"Ya think?" Rory chimed in with a sobering dose of sarcasm. "Who would have thought a malicious tweet could destroy a man's business?"

"That's the power of the internet," I remarked, before turning my attention back to Kennedy. "Jeffery may be a cheating pig, but he worked hard to make Sizzle one of New York's top restaurants. And poor Mia. She was quite talented, you know. She didn't deserve to die because of . . . because of . . . Oh God!" I cried, and cradled my head with my hands. Tears threatened. It was really too much.

"That's part of the reason I came here," Kennedy softly admitted. "Of course, I was going to support Lindsey and help her make the best run at opening day of any lighthouse bakery. I was, admittedly, also afraid that Jeffery would catch wind of what you were doing and try to harm you. He thinks you hired me to destroy him."

"What?" I cried, drying my eyes.

"Well, look, he obviously does. I came here to set the record straight and to head off any trouble that might arise from my actions. As you can see, I failed on all accounts." She flung up her hands in defeat.

I was fuming, I was so mad. Kennedy's secret was a bombshell. I was honestly having a hard time trying to process what she was admitting to as well as all the ramifications it had on my opening day. That's when Rory piped up.

"Correct me if I'm wrong, but how is Mia's death linked with Kennedy sabotaging your ex-boyfriend's restaurant? It makes no sense. If what you're saying is true, Kennedy, and Mia was, in fact, poisoned, then Lindsey could hardly be the suspect. I can honestly attest to the fact that she had no idea you had tried to ruin Jeffery's reputation as a chef. Lindsey's not only surprised by your actions, she was also visibly surprised by the arrival of Mia and Jeffery at the bakeshop this morning. I was standing beside her. I saw the look on her face when Mia walked in. In my opinion, Lindsey has no reason—or means—of poisoning Mia. How could she when she had no idea they'd be there?"

"Good point," Kennedy said, casting him an appreciative look. "So that leaves us with the obvious fact that whoever poisoned her knew she'd be at your bakery."

"Which would be you," I pointed out, staring at my friend.

While Kennedy thought on this, Rory added, "Or Jeffery, or one of Mia's adoring friends. Think of it? They came in a group to ruin you, Lindsey. You and your bakery make the perfect foil. My bet is that one of them had a reason to want her dead."

"By heavens, I think you might be right." Kennedy held Rory in a near-loving gaze. She then shifted her attention to me. "You didn't know Mia was coming. I had a feeling she and Jeffery might show up, but couldn't really say for sure. However, they all knew. They all made the journey with her."

"And they all cheered her on as she destroyed my bakery." I shook my head, dismayed that my friend had commenced a campaign to destroy Jeffery's reputation as a chef, and yet happy she'd finally come clean about her deeds. "Thank you for being honest," I told her. "I now understand the motive that drove Mia to ruin my opening day. She'd been seeking revenge for her lover and his livelihood. The question is, what person in her entourage would want her dead?"

CHAPTER 19

Kennedy, guilt-ridden yet grateful to have finally come clean, took it upon herself to scrub down the kitchen and attend to the dishes while I left the lighthouse with Rory.

Wellington, of course, had come with us. He loved the attention Rory showered on him, and would, no doubt, accompany him home even if I didn't walk with them. But it was a cloudless night, and the lake looked so beautiful as it carried and caressed the light of the moon on its waves. I found the crisp air cleansing, its freshness like a balm to my nerves that Kennedy had nearly stripped bare.

"I don't remember if I ever got the chance to say it, but I will now. Thank you for helping at the bakery today. I honestly don't know what I would have done if you hadn't been there to stop the chaos and whisk Mia and her friends outside."

"Truthfully, I'm glad I was there. I was a little nervous about working the espresso machine, but I eventually got a handle on it. Also, I'm relieved to know that you're not a killer. Living next to a baker is hard enough, but a killer?" He shook his head.

Was he joking? It was hard to see his expression on the dark beach, but then the moon lit up his smile. He picked up a piece of driftwood and tossed it down the beach for Wellington to retrieve.

"You didn't really think that I . . . ?"

"I didn't know what to think when that young officer whisked you off to the station. I had half a mind to think he was just trying to get you alone. I saw the way he was looking at you."

Officer Tuck had been looking at me? I wasn't aware of that, but it gave me a little thrill to hear it. I noticed that Rory was still grinning. He was teasing me again. "Officer McAllister I can handle. He was a perfect gentleman down at the station. However, Sergeant Murdock is another story."

"Was he trying to hit on you too?" The look on Rory's face was anything but teasing.

"I doubt it, but I'm not much of an expert on those things."

Rory stopped walking. "You can't tell if a man's hitting on you? Well, that explains a lot."

I grabbed his hand and pulled him along. "I know when a man's hitting on me," I assured him. "But Sergeant Murdock's not a man."

"He's a woman?" He sounded confused.

"She's a woman," I corrected. "I'm surprised you didn't know."

"Why would I?" he replied. "I keep to myself and try to obey the law. Also, Betty never mentioned it. And you'd think she would, being the town gossip and all."

I smiled inwardly at the thought of Betty Vanhoosen and Sergeant Stacy Murdock chatting it up like besties at the local diner. Bright, bouncy Betty, and sour Sergeant Stacy had very little in common as far as I could see, besides the fact they both lived and worked in the same small town. "This may come as a shocker, but Sergeant Murdock is not the warm, friendly type."

"Let's just hope she's good at her job," he replied, standing before the steps of his wide back deck. The outdoor lights of the log home were on, casting the already-handsome man in a very favorable light. All thoughts of Officer Cutie Pie faded. He was a boy. Rory Campbell was all man. Suddenly, I was filled with the memory of his recent kiss. I wouldn't hate it if he tried again, I thought, and waited a beat too long for him to make his move. But he never did. Instead, Rory thanked me for dinner, gave Wellington a pat on the head, and made me promise that I'd call Sergeant Murdock in the morning with an update on the new information we'd learned from Kennedy.

The moment I returned to the lighthouse I flopped into bed and reached for my laptop. True, I was exhausted. But I was also flummoxed by the fact that Rory hadn't even tried to kiss me—after I'd made him dinner and walked him home, no less. In fact, he gave Wellington more affection tonight than he'd shown me. Begrudgingly, I acknowledged that murder could be a turnoff for him, or maybe he was just tired. Then there was the plaguing thought that he might possibly be afraid of becoming involved with me because of Kennedy. She was my dear friend, but the poor man had just learned what she'd done to the last man I'd been romantically involved with. Ruin and murder were enough to scare off any man.

I opened my laptop, contemplating the thought that revenge was an insatiable monster all its own. If all that Kennedy said was true, and after a quick Google search I saw that it was, then Jeffery and Mia had every right to be mad at me. They had come to the Beacon Bakeshop for revenge, but something had gone very, very wrong. Mia had died—had been poisoned, but why?

Searching for answers, I decided to start at the beginning and read about the demise of Sizzle and the tanking of Jeffery's book, *Plank It!* I even pulled up a YouTube video and watched his gawk-worthy performance on the morning show Kennedy had referred to. Yet just as the video was about to end, my laptop screen went blank.

"What?" I uttered, and began hitting buttons. I was panicking. I didn't think I could handle my computer dying too.

Wellington, having slipped into a peaceful puppy slumber, sprang awake at my outburst. He peered over the foot of my bed, his soft brown eyes foggy with sleep. Sensing my frustration, he leapt up and joined me.

"It's okay," I soothed, stroking the soft fur of his head. Although Wellington had his own bed, he relished any opportunity to join me in mine. And tonight, I wasn't about to shoo him away. "My computer just died," I told him. "Be thankful you're a dog. Technology is a real curse for us humans." I was just about to close my computer and snuggle in bed when the chilling words appeared on my screen.

She didn't like your donuts. She was lying. She was dying.

The hair on the back of my neck stood on end. I cast a

glance at Wellington and typed, *What? Who is this? How are you typing on my computer?*

Typing? Communicating. Reaching out to you, Lindsey Bakewell. Murder. Unfinished business.

I shook my head, but it was still tingling with fear. Whoever was messing with me knew my name. That creeped me out. *Who are you?* I typed again, then watched as the words appeared on my screen.

Lightkeeper.

There is no lightkeeper, I typed angrily.

There is a light, there is a keeper. You are a keeper of recipes. I am a keeper of light, Captain Willy Riggs.

"Am I going crazy?" I asked the room at large while staring at my screen. Wellington picked up his head. I gave him a gentle rub, setting him at ease as I wondered who the devil was hijacking my laptop. I wasn't born yesterday, and I didn't really believe in ghosts, but this idiot was doing his best to challenge that. I was about to pick up my phone and call the police. The thought of Sergeant Murdock's unsmiling face stopped me. I had half a mind to close my laptop when another thought struck me. Someone claiming to be the ghost of a dead lightkeeper was trying to contact me. They knew my name. They knew Mia had died. Damn me, but I was going to play along and see what else they knew.

Captain Willy Riggs? I typed, peevishly. *I do remember hearing that name. Tell me, what exactly are you the captain of?*

Former captain of the schooner Ellie Rose.

In what year?

Eighteen forty-five to eighteen fifty-eight

I rolled my eyes at the screen. *That's a long time ago.*

I'm surprised you know how to type on a computer. Gotcha, sucker!

Whoever it was waited a minute before replying, *Communicate. Trying to reach you.*

Well, damn his determined spirit energy! Not a bad answer, I thought, then probed further. *Why are you contacting me?*

Untimely death.

Who died? I asked, looking for something a little more specific.

Angry lady donut dunker, and me.

Now that was chilling. I stared at the screen a moment, drawing comfort from Wellington's warm, silky fur while I gathered my nerves. Was I really conversing with a ghost, or just a creeper?

Alright, if you are the Captain, prove it. When was the last time you were in the lightroom? As I typed the ridiculous words, I was trying to recall what Rory had told me about Captain Willy Riggs. Rory said that according to legend, Captain Riggs had been shot at an unknown location somewhere on the windswept beach. After being shot he had made his way to the lighthouse, climbed the tower stairs, and lit the lantern one last time before he died. But what year was that? Unfortunately, the answer that appeared on my screen was a little closer to home than I expected.

Last night.

I inhaled sharply, recalling the mysterious light emanating from the lightroom. As far as I knew, only Rory and I knew about that.

That light was you? What did it mean?

Danger. A storm approaching.

Although the night had been clear, I had a feeling I knew what he meant. *You were trying to warn me?* I typed.

Yes.

Could I have stopped Mia Long from being murdered? I asked, filling with colliding emotions.

No.

Then why warn me? What are you trying to do? If you're trying to frighten me, congratulations!

No. Do not be frightened. I am your friend. We are kindred spirits. I want you to find the woman's killer, and mine.

Was this ghost-creeper serious? *But I'm a baker,* I typed with growing frustration. *I don't know anything about investigating a murder. Where do I even start?*

With the boyfriend, of course.

I stared at the words and realized the Captain was undoubtedly correct. The screen blipped and suddenly came back to life, landing on the last page I'd been reading. Jeffery's pitiful interview on the morning talk show. Apparently, the Captain, or whoever it was that had hijacked my computer, was gone.

Could Jeffery be the one who killed Mia? Could he have used revenge on my bakery as a cover to divest himself of an embarrassing mistake, namely Mia Long? No doubt he'd been acting strangely. I recalled how he had lurked in the corner of the café, sampling a piece of my coffee cake as he left Mia to storm my counter and create chaos on his behalf. Jeffery wasn't even that upset when Mia collapsed. He never lifted a finger to help. Rory had been the one to escort her outside. Rory had been the one to start CPR when she wasn't breathing. Dear heavens, maybe the Captain was correct. Maybe Jeffery Plank had a reason to want Mia dead. But why?

That was the question I needed to ask him.

Chapter 20

The morning began with a clap of thunder. Fitting, I thought, as I threw on a robe and headed downstairs to the kitchen. My head ached, and I needed coffee. Wellington needed his morning romp around the lighthouse grounds followed by a cookie and a dental chew.

The moment I hit the landing, I was struck by the smell of brewing coffee. Why was coffee brewing so early? Although I always set up the coffeemaker the night before, I hadn't pressed the button. An unsettling feeling hit me then, and I thought, oh no, what if the ghostly captain had taken it upon himself to make me coffee? Could that be any weirder than the conversation I'd had last night on my computer? Had a ghostly entity really taken over my laptop, or was it just some hacker playing a trick on me? Maybe I had dreamt the whole thing? While my head was spinning, Wellington was unfazed by my problems and trotted down the stairs, heading for the door. If there was a ghost in my kitchen, Wellington didn't care. He had other pressing needs at the moment. I unbolted the lock, opened the door, and watched him bound out into the rain, happy as a duck in a puddle. I had half a mind to wait for him, but the pull of coffee was too strong. I crossed the short hallway and peered into the kitchen, half-expecting to see the old weathered ghost of the first lightkeeper at the table.

"Morning." At the sound, my heart nearly leapt out of my chest. It wasn't the ghostly voice of an old dead guy. It was Kennedy, which was equally as puzzling. Like ghostly entities and vampires, mornings weren't really her scene. She looked up from her iPad, set down her teacup, and smiled.

"What time is it?" I asked, thinking I had overslept.

"Early. I know. And before you offer a snappy remark about seeing me vertical before noon two days in a row, which, I admit, is a miracle, I want you to know that this is me trying to be a better friend. I even pushed the button on the coffeemaker for you. See? Coffee."

"That was you?" I said reflexively, when what I really should have done was thank her.

Kennedy rolled her eyes. "Well, it wasn't Wellington."

I pulled a mug from the cupboard and filled it with the freshly brewed coffee. I had to admit, it smelled heavenly. Resting against the counter, I took a sip, all the while thinking of how to tell her about the strange conversation I had last night through my computer. There was no eloquent way to broach the subject. After another fortifying sip, I blurted, "Something weird happened to me last night."

She arched a black brow. "Kissing a backwoods hottie? Not so weird considering where you live."

"What?"

"You and Sir Hunts-a-Lot. Maybe you're too busy frosting donuts to notice, but he's totally into you."

I shook my head. "No, I'm not talking about Rory. And . . . we didn't kiss."

This surprised her. "Pity. You were quick to walk out the door with him. Don't tell me you're just friends?"

"Honestly, I'm not quite sure what we are. But what I'm trying to tell you is that last night something took over my computer."

"What do you mean?"

"I was thinking about the murder," I told her, joining her at the table. "I wanted to understand the depths of your meddling and started Googling Jeffery Plank. I was in the middle of watching that video, the one where he makes that insensitive remark about cows on the morning show, when suddenly my computer went black. I thought it died, but then words started to appear."

Kennedy, abandoning her iPad and her tea, stared at me. "What kind of words?"

"Look," I said, feeling a bit foolish. "Don't judge me too harshly, but I think somebody took over my computer—somebody claiming to be the ghost of the first lightkeeper at this lighthouse."

"How . . . interesting," she remarked, looking at me as if I was a donut short of a baker's dozen.

Biting my lip, I asked, "Is it? Look, either somebody's hacking my computer and messing with me, or I'm conversing with a ghost. Truthfully, I don't know which one is worse." I raked my fingers though my thick hair and cast her a nervous look.

Kennedy, enthralled, leaned forward. "This conversation, was it erotic?"

"What? No! It was cryptic. It was about the murder of Mia Long."

"Cryptic yet not erotic? I'd say you're dealing with a ghost." She was annoyingly unfazed by this.

"Listen to yourself," I chided. "You're telling me I'm conversing with a ghost. Doesn't that sound crazy to you?" I stared at her, entirely forgetting my aching head and the coffee.

"Look, darling, if there's one thing I know, it's the internet. And my experience tells me that any hacker targeting you is obviously a pervert. You're a beautiful single woman with loads of cash. That makes you a target. But you say this hacker is talking about the murder of Mia Long? That just happened. It's only just made the news this morning." Kennedy turned her iPad to me. She'd been reading an article sensationally titled Donuts to Die For. Beneath the headline was a picture of my lighthouse bakery with its happy red awning above the door and the outside tables capped off with equally bright umbrellas. All the yellow police tape around the perimeter was like a sobering slap in the face.

I clutched my chest. "This is horrible," I uttered, heartbroken at the sight.

"Horrible?" Kennedy looked at me with a slight grin perking up her lips. "I'll admit that this picture's a bit of a downer. But look at that tagline! Nothing like a bit of sensational news to pique public interest."

"What does the article say?" My heart was pounding with dread. I didn't have the nerve to read it. The last thing I needed was bad publicity.

"Interestingly enough, just the facts as the reporter knew them. It states that a woman died outside your bakery yesterday after choking on a donut." Kennedy waved it off and shut her iPad. "What I find more interesting is that someone or something took the effort to contact you last night without using any of the accepted ways—like email or social media. Also, without you clicking on a bum link or something, I don't think it's possible to be hacked. It's called phishing. Then, here's another thought. Why you? You're not a detective. What can you do about the murder of your ex-boyfriend's tart?"

As she spooned out her convoluted logic, my heart began to pound with illogical fear. Kennedy did have a point. But a ghost? Did they really exist? And if so, was it usual for them to chat over a computer?

As if reading my thoughts, she added, "Look, I'm no expert on ghosts, so we should probably consult an authority . . . like a medium or an exorcist. But that would take time. For now, let's say it is a ghost." With her hands gripping her teacup, she tilted her head. "I am curious. What did it say?"

"Well, he calls himself the Captain, and he knew that a woman had been murdered at the lighthouse. Even stranger? He had tried to warn me the night before my grand opening."

Her dark eyes glittered with interest. "Really. How did he do that?"

"It was two nights ago. Remember I had just learned that I was going to be short a barista? I went over to ask Rory if he'd help at the bakery. I was standing on his back deck when we saw an odd light glowing in the lantern room. It was similar to a lighthouse light, only not as bright. It was around eleven o'clock. That wasn't you, was it?" I thought to ask.

A contemplative look crossed her face. "Definitely

not. I don't go up there alone. That place gives me the willies."

Her confession sent a little shiver up my spine. "Why didn't you tell me that?" I asked.

"Really? You just bought this place. You sank a lot of money into it. I didn't want to be the one to tell you that it's haunted."

I was about to press her further, asking how she knew it was haunted, when Wellington started barking at the door. "Hang on a moment," I said, and went to get Wellington. To my surprise my dog wasn't alone. Dylan was there as well, standing beneath a dripping umbrella.

I ushered her inside, took her umbrella, and dried Wellington off with a handful of towels. I then poured her a mug of coffee and sat her at the table next to Kennedy. While Kennedy brought her up to speed on my mysterious conversations with a ghost, I pulled a bag of carrot cake muffins out of the refrigerator. I had made them the morning before our grand opening, testing out a new recipe. The muffins were scrumptious, with all the flavor of a hearty carrot cake in a lighter, fluffier muffin batter. I planned on adding them to the bakery shelves but hadn't gotten around to calculating out the recipe for the larger batch. I warmed the muffins in the microwave, bringing them to a nearly just-baked temperature. As the girls chatted, I topped each muffin with a generous amount of the fluffy cream cheese frosting I had made to go with them.

"Dangit!" Dylan remarked, eyeing the frosted treats. "Are these mini carrot cakes? I really didn't come here to beg breakfast, but I can't resist. These look amazing."

"They are," Kennedy said with an air of nonchalance.

She picked one up, took a bite, and added, "I've learned to accept that everything Lindsey makes is amazing."

Wellington, settling for a hearty bowl of kibble instead of a carrot cake muffin, happily ate his breakfast as we sat at the kitchen table, enjoying the tasty baked goods while discussing the death of Mia Long.

"When I left here yesterday, you'd been taken to the police station for questioning," Dylan reminded us. "I had just sent the girls home with a fresh loaf of bread when Sergeant Murdock showed up and declared the bakery a crime scene. I was totally freaked out. You don't grow up in Beacon Harbor without having a healthy respect for that woman. I wasn't sure what to do, so I pulled all the cookies from the oven, shut everything down, and tried to clean up as best I could, but she just wanted me out of there. Murdock wouldn't tell me much. She asked Rory and me a few questions, then sent us on our way. I could hardly sleep last night I was so upset at the thought of this place being shut down. Then, about an hour ago, I got a call from Frank Peters."

"Oh no!" I exclaimed. Frank Peters was one of our suppliers. "I was so distraught yesterday that I forgot to call everyone and cancel all orders until further notice."

"No problem," Dylan said. "Got it all handled, boss. Unfortunately, the poor guy came out here early this morning and saw the yellow crime scene tape. Totally freaked him out. Had his truck parked behind the bakery and called me, checking to make sure everyone was okay. I gave him the scoop as far as I knew it. Told him I'd call him once everything gets resolved."

Dylan, who loved early mornings, had thankfully taken control of our deliveries. Her past bakery experience combined with her knowledge of locally sourced dairy and produce vendors had been invaluable to me, and I trusted her good judgment. I felt like an idiot having forgotten to call them.

"So," she began, her face holding a skeptical grimace after Kennedy had brought her up to speed, "you think you've made contact with the ghostly captain? Not surprising to me," she remarked with a knowing look. "You might not think it to look at me, but I was a bit of a delinquent when I was a kid." She challenged her statement with a grin while highlighting the piercings around her ears and pulling down the neck of her shirt to reveal a small howling wolf tattoo. "My spirit animal," she added.

"Cool," Kennedy remarked, staring at it. "My spirit animal is a pair of Louboutin shoes."

"Not an animal," Dylan told her with an eye roll. "Anyhow, Beacon Harbor was Boresville as a kid. For a little excitement we used to come here in high school, ya know, to sneak a beer or smoke a little weed. Back then we all knew that the lighthouse was supposed to be haunted. Heck"—she shrugged—"it was part of the attraction. We'd get high and then hear something that would spook us, like a tumbling brick, footsteps, or the sound of a door creaking on its hinges. Sometimes we would swear that we heard a man's voice in the wind. Anyhow, we were all a bunch of chickens." She laughed at the memory. "But one night, Mike actually broke in to the tower. It was always locked, ya know, for safety reasons. Mike brought a lock-cutter with him he'd stolen from his dad. He'd always wanted to climb the tower. I didn't. I had a healthy respect for the old building and the ghost who was rumored to live here. That's why he dragged me up there with him."

"What a jerk," I said, feeling frightened for her.

"He's totally a jerk," she agreed. "But he was my older cousin and like a brother to me. I've looked up to him all my life. That's why I went along with him up the tower stairs."

"And this is the reason I don't have a brother," Kennedy remarked in all seriousness. "My dear mother had more sense than to give me one."

Somehow both Dylan and I found this remark ridiculously funny.

"My late mother's not to blame either," Dylan added with a little grin. "It was my aunt's fault."

"The nerve!" I said, and we all laughed.

"Wait!" Dylan stifled her giggles with a sip of coffee. "I didn't tell you the scary part. Mike and I climbed the tower stairs. I remember it being dark. I also remember the odd smell, like smoke, only there wasn't any fire. Then, when Mike reached the lantern room, he stopped moving. Every muscle in his body went stiff. I shoved him aside and peered around him."

"Wha . . . what did you see?" I asked.

"Oh, I saw a ghost, alright—we both saw him, the Captain. He was just standing there, staring out the window dressed in old-timey clothes. The moment we came into the room, he turned to us."

My breath caught in my throat as my hand clutched my chest. "Then what?" I whispered. "What did he say?" I wanted to know if this specter could speak.

"Nothing," Dylan replied. "He just vanished. Gone, just like that. That's how we knew it was a ghost."

It was safe to say that Kennedy and I were both spooked.

Dylan, noting this, was quick to relieve our fears. "Don't worry, boss. Mike and I survived our ghost encounter without a scratch. Everyone knows this old place is haunted, and who are we to say that ghosts don't use computers? It's odd, but maybe they can."

"It is odd, isn't it," I agreed, staring at the half-eaten carrot cake muffin on my plate.

"Another odd thing," Dylan began, looking at me. "Scary Sergeant Murdock's claiming murder. Do we, in fact, know what killed that woman?" She leaned in, her fit, compact body and snapping brown eyes looking more curious than concerned.

"They suspect she died of cyanide poisoning."

"You've got to be joking!" Dylan slammed her mug down, looking offended. "How is that even possible?"

"They think one of the donuts she ate was laced with cyanide," I informed her.

"What?" she cried. "You and I were making the donuts. Why would we lace one with cyanide? More importantly, why would we try to kill that cuckoo-nut? I didn't know her, and you certainly didn't know she was going to show up . . . did you?"

We explained all we knew to Dylan, including the fact that the only one who had any inkling that Mia might show up was Kennedy, and that Kennedy was nowhere near the bakery counter when Mia supposedly had been poisoned.

"So, what are we going to do about it, ladies?" Dylan's brown eyes were not only probing, they were issuing a challenge. "We can't just sit here twiddling our thumbs all day."

I poured more coffee in her empty cup, refilled my own, and returned the pot to its burner. "*We're* not going to do anything. I'm going to drive over to the Harbor Hotel and pay Jeffery Plank a little visit before he skips town. He's the grieving boyfriend, supposedly. I thought he was acting suspicious yesterday, and last night I was convinced of it."

Kennedy leaned close to Dylan and whispered, "The ghost of Captain Willy Riggs. He suggested the name."

Kennedy was grinning. Her grin faded the moment I told her that I was taking her with me. "You need to set the record straight and tell Jeffery that I had nothing to do with his demise."

"Oh, no, no, no!" she cried. "I'm not confronting him—not without a bodyguard! If he sees me, there's going to be another body added to the list, namely mine."

"You're trying to be a better friend," I reminded her.

"Better—not dead," she corrected.

Dylan stood, walked over to my counter, and plucked my marble rolling pin off its decorative holder. "Since Lindsey needs to talk with the victim's boyfriend, and you need a bodyguard before you'll accompany her, looks like I'm coming too." She rapped the rolling pin against the palm of her empty hand. I had to admit, although it was farcical, Dylan almost looked intimidating.

"The job's yours!" I said, applauding her pluck. Shifting my attention to Kennedy, I added, "You and I are getting dressed. Then we're all going to drive over to the hotel to pay Jeffery boy a little visit."

CHAPTER 21

It was a small town. Dylan, thankfully, had a friend who worked behind the front desk of the Harbor Hotel who was willing to scribble Jeffery's room number on a scrap of paper and slip it to us.

"You didn't get this from me," the woman said, adding an arched brow for effect.

After locating Jeffery's room, the three of us stood before his door. I knocked loud enough to wake the dead, which seemed to do very little. Then, right before I was about to knock again, I heard a muffled voice on the other side asking after our identities.

"Room service," Kennedy offered. The devious nature of her grin was rewarded a moment later when Jeffery appeared, sleepy, bedraggled, and visibly angry.

"You're not . . . room service!" Fuming with indignation, he backed into his room like a crab scrambling for cover on an exposed beach. "And, God in heaven, what is *she* doing here?" While Jeffery might have expected me to come pounding on his door, and while the sight of Dylan holding a rolling pin behind me confused him—not recognizing her from the bakeshop—the effect Kennedy had on him was on another level. She, after all, had led a group of animal rights protesters in a march outside his trendy restaurant. Although sporting a youthful crop-top, fashionable wide-leg pants, a floppy-brimmed hat, and four-inch designer heels, hers, apparently, was the face of destruction.

"No, we are not room service, darling." Kennedy shot him a pitying look. "We're old friends who have a bone to pick with you."

"Yeah," Dylan chimed in, slapping the rolling pin against the palm of her hand. "Though I'm not your friend. I'm the muscle." Dylan was fit, but tiny. Jeffery might have smiled had his face not been so painfully contorted with incredulity.

"Mind if we come in?" I took the liberty of pushing past him before he could protest. Kennedy strode in behind me, her high heels clip-clopping on the hardwood floor of his pricy hotel room. Jeffery's business might be in trouble, but he still traveled in style. Dylan, comfortable in jeans, sweatshirt, and a rolling pin, brought up the rear.

"God, I need a cup of coffee," he uttered.

In a flash of compassion, I said, "We can make that happen. We may be angry, but we're not sadists. Dylan, would you mind popping down to the hotel restaurant for a coffee? Do you still take yours with cream?"

As Jeffery nodded, Dylan protested, "Do you think it

wise sending me away in the presence of a murderer?" As if wielding a sword, she pointed the rolling pin at Jeffery.

"Murderer?" he snapped. His arrogant gaze homed in on me. "Is that what this is about? You think I'm the murderer? You think I had something to do with . . . to do with . . . ?" His perpetual snobbery was swiftly toppled by destitution. "Oh God," he moaned and covered his face with his hands.

As Dylan went for coffee, we sat Jeffery down in one of the room's overstuffed chairs. He was clearly undone by Mia's death, sobbing into a tissue like a giant, blubbering baby. The word *murder* had opened the floodgates, so to speak. I was sorry to admit that his current display of emotion was more than he'd ever shown to me.

"I've already talked to that police lady," he whined, looking up from his tissue. "I don't need to talk to you. You're not the police. The only thing you have in common with Sergeant Whatsherface is that you both come on way too strong."

Way too strong . . . like Sergeant Murdock? Why did that remark irk me so? I didn't have time to give it much thought, however. Instead, I pulled up a chair and cast him a level gaze. "Look, we need to clear the air here."

"Clear the air? Are you freakin' kidding me?" His eyes blazed as spittle formed in the corners of his mouth. "It doesn't even make sense," he spat. "You accuse *me* of murder when she was eating one of *your* donuts!" While Jeffery and I stared one another down, Kennedy gingerly took a seat at the end of the king-sized bed, careful not to touch the rumpled sheets. Jeffery looked up from his soiled tissue.

"She was eating my donuts," I admitted. "But so was everyone else, for that matter. Besides, I couldn't have killed her. That's why I'm here. To tell you that I didn't even know you and Mia were in Beacon Harbor."

He sneered. "How typical of you, Lindsey! So smug in your own success that you can happily destroy the livelihood of others and sleep peacefully at night. Why wouldn't we come to Beacon Harbor? It's not like the whole world didn't know that after our relationship ended and after you destroyed my career, you left town to open a charming lighthouse bakery. 'Wall Street's Golden Girl Follows Her Dream'," he quoted. "How flipping fabulous for you! And how ignorant of you to think that we wouldn't be here to give you a little taste of your own medicine. But then"—he paused for a dramatic breath and gasped—"you had to kill my Mia!"

He was about to cry into his tissue again when Kennedy stopped him. "Man up, you sniveling dolt! Didn't you hear what Lindsey just said? She didn't know you were coming, therefore she couldn't have harmed Mia, even if she'd wanted to. Oh, sure, she could have come around the counter to strangle her. The way that crazy donut-smashing diva was acting, she deserved it. But our Lindsey showed an amazing amount of restraint, wouldn't you say?"

"But she destroyed me!" he accused, shifting his gaze between us.

"And that's what we've come to tell you," I replied. "I just learned last night what Kennedy had done to your business. I had no idea Sizzle was in trouble, Jeffery. If you'll remember, I blocked all your calls."

"And you expect me to believe that?"

"Believe whatever you like. It's the truth. When I caught you and Mia together, I was so angry and embarrassed that all I wanted to do was bury my head in the sand and run away. I was so sad for us both, Jeffery. I had no inkling that you were so unhappy in our relationship that you would turn to your . . . your pastry chef for love. I felt so betrayed. I felt like an idiot! But I never wanted to destroy you."

"She didn't," Kennedy added. "That was your own doing, Jeffery, boy, by making those insensitive remarks about cows on national television."

"She's right, I'm afraid. You started it."

"And I finished it." As Kennedy spoke, she elegantly crossed her legs. "You made two mistakes, darling. The first was that you broke my best friend's heart. The second was making a fool of yourself on national television. I can honestly tell you that Lindsey had no idea what I was doing to you on her behalf."

Jeffery sat in a near-catatonic state taking it all in. Then, suddenly, he snapped. Emitting a primal growl, he launched himself at Kennedy, aiming for her neck.

Thankfully, he never quite got ahold of his target. Kennedy, being a city girl, knew a thing or two about self-defense. I stood in stupefied horror watching as the two wrestled on the bed like some freakishly mismatched WWF spectacle—a fashion-forward influencer versus a metrosexual celebrity chef. I didn't know what to do. Quite frankly, I didn't feel that either one of them was capable of inflicting any real physical harm. Still, it was troubling. Kennedy was tenderizing Jeffery's face with her rapid-fire hands; Jeffery had resorted to pinching. Thankfully a knock at the door grabbed my attention. It was Dylan, coffee in one hand and rolling pin in the other.

"I knew this would happen." She shook her head while handing me the coffee. A moment later Jeffery was back in his chair holding on to the cup like a life raft, while Kennedy was safely back on the bed preening her rumpled ensemble like a caged tigress.

"Honestly," I began, looking at Jeffery, "we didn't come here to fight. We came here to question you about Mia's death. Someone who knew she was coming to the Beacon Bakeshop poisoned her, which makes you the most likely suspect."

"What about her?" Jeffery pointed an accusing finger at Kennedy.

"Poison, really?" she said, rolling her eyes. "I know I'm a woman, but that's a little too cliché for me."

I shot her a look imploring her to keep her mouth shut. Obviously, she ignored it.

"Besides," she continued, "if I was going to snuff that little tart out, I certainly wouldn't do it in my friend's bakery. That would look bad for Lindsey, and I want Lindsey to sparkle and shine. I want her to succeed, which leads us back to you."

"The vengeful ex-lover," Dylan added, because she couldn't resist. "Were you growing tired of Mia too—just like you did with Lindsey? Poisoning her in the bakeshop would be the perfect foil."

It was a moment before Jeffery's jaw engaged. When it did, he cried, "No, I didn't bump off my girlfriend! And why should I talk to you three? Clearly, you are all deranged."

"If I appear a little deranged, it's because somebody murdered Mia Long in my bakeshop, Jeffery, and I want answers!"

"And I want answers too. Your vicious friend ruined me, Lindsey! I'm bankrupt." He threw up his hands in defeat, and for the first time since barging into his hotel room, I felt truly sorry for him.

Having worked in the world of finance, I knew that bankruptcy was the death knell of any business. That was bad enough. I couldn't even imagine what it might mean for a rising celebrity chef. It would take a miracle to come back from such ruin. I suddenly realized that I just might be able to summon a little miracle of my own for him. I looked Jeffery square in the eye and asked, "Do you want a second chance?"

"A second chance? Ha! How can you offer me a second chance?"

"Not me," I said. "Kennedy. She has the power to fix the little problem that you and she caused."

"I do?" Apparently, in Kennedy's world, once her opinion was known, there were no takesie-backsies. But this was our best bargaining chip, and for the sake of my bakery, I was going to use it.

"You do, Kennedy, but only if Jeffery is willing to co-operate."

Jeffery offered a pathetic laugh. "Good try, but what can she do? Nobody is willing to touch me now. The damage has been done. Thanks to your friend, *Plank It!* is tanking at the bookstores. I'll never get another book deal. And because she made my restaurant the laughing-stock of New York City, I can't even give my meals away."

"Well, you should have thought of that before you started insulting cows on national television!" I admonished. "Cows are not only intelligent animals, but they're the darlings of the farmyard." Being a city girl, I didn't really know if this was true, but I didn't care. I was trying to make a point.

"Gentle giants of the prairie, they are, with kindly souls and heart-melting gazes." I looked to Dylan for support, thinking she'd know a bit more about cows than Kennedy or me. She nodded, urging me on. "They can't help it if they taste amazing," I continued. "And because they do, they should be treated with dignity and respect. Let's start there. You answer our questions about Mia, and Kennedy will do a podcast with you from my bakery."

Kennedy, embracing the idea, shot Jeffery a challenging look.

"You can humble yourself before millions on the internet," I added enticingly. "You can apologize for the insensitive things you've said about cows. Kennedy can even help you rebrand yourself as an animal advocate, championing small farms that treat their animals humanely, and using only organically raised meats in your restaurant. I'm giving you the chance to make amends with the public and save your business. All you have to do is answer our questions."

He took a sip of coffee and stared out the picture window. Although rain and wind tormented the dark lake, the view from his room was spectacular. He took another sip and said, "I tell you about Mia, and you fix my life? Fair enough." He shifted his gaze to me. "Let me start by saying that I didn't kill Mia. I loved her. We've been together eight years, ever since culinary school."

The word *love* struck me. "When you say 'together,' are you referring to your friendship?"

His laugh was chilling. "Friends? We were far more than that, Lindsey. We were partners, soul mates. You and I?" He shrugged. "She encouraged that. You were our plan for success."

CHAPTER 22

"Narcissistic pig!" I cried the moment we left the hotel room, purely to keep myself from falling to the ground in a puddle of rain and tears.

It had been the hardest ten minutes of my life, hearing how Jeffery's crazy, ambitious pastry chef girlfriend had encouraged him to date me, although they were already lovers and partners in the restaurant. I'd met Jeffery during the private cooking lessons Kennedy and two other friends had surprised me with for my thirty-second birthday. I'd been dating a wealthy day trader at the time and had dumped him for the psychopath who had been using me for my money and connections. The marriage that I had narrowly escaped, purely because the idiot couldn't keep his hands off crazy Mia, would have been a disaster. He nearly stole both my soul and my money! Thank goodness the pair had thwarted their own best efforts by being careless. I felt used and horrible. And yet, as terrible as the whole confession had been, I felt a little vindicated as well.

I had escaped.

I lived in Michigan and owned a historic lighthouse and bakeshop café. How ironic that one of my coveted connections, as Jeffery had termed them, had done her best to destroy him on my behalf! We hadn't even known the whole story then. Truthfully, I could have lived the rest of my life happily ignorant of their deceit. But Mia's death had changed all that. With the promise of redemption dangling before him, Jeffery had squealed like a cornered pig. He explained how Mia had pushed him to open Sizzle. Mia had created the menu. It had been Mia's idea to cook pricey cuts of meat on different surfaces. Mia had pushed for the book deal. Mia, apparently, had been the brains behind the celebrity chef. Although he swore that he hadn't slipped her a deadly dose of poison, I didn't believe him. Jeffery's star was falling. He was defeated and desperate. I could only imagine what that might do to a diva-tyrant like Mia Long.

We were nearly to my car when Kennedy took hold of my arm. "I just want to state for the record, Linds, that your taste in men is truly stupefying."

"If you mean terrible," Dylan quipped, "I agree."

"How could I have been so stupid?" I felt as if I had just stepped out of a pool of used fryer grease. All the hot water in Beacon Harbor couldn't wash the slime from me. "Of all the available men in New York City, why that idiot?"

"Maybe because he could cook," Dylan suggested matter-of-factly. "You're a baker, like me, so food is important to you. Finding a man who can cook is the equivalent of Prince Charming, am I right? We can't help it. It's sexy. My Carl can be a real jerk, too, sometimes, but he works a grill like a wizard uses his wand. I hate to admit it, but his slow-cooked brisket is like a happy pill. One bite and I forget why I was mad at him in the first place."

"His food was sublime," I admitted. "Jeffery had talent; he charmed me. Still . . ." I shook my head in dismay.

"Well, on the bright side, darlings, we just may have found our killer. Anyone mercenary enough to marry a woman they didn't love wouldn't have any problem bumping off another 'inconvenience.' The question now is, do I even follow through with the podcast? We could retract it on the grounds of deception and villainy."

"We made a promise," I reminded Kennedy. "Although he's a cheating, lying worm of a man, he did give us the names of Mia's friends. They accompanied her all the way to Michigan. They were helping her destroy my bakeshop. Although he said that they were all on good terms, as far as he knew, maybe one of them wasn't. Maybe one of them planned to bump her off in my bakeshop and put the blame on me?"

"There's only one way to find out," Dylan said. "We need to talk with them before they fly back to New York. Since they're all staying here, I say we pay them a little visit."

"Excellent idea. But before we go knocking on any more hotel room doors, I think it's best you lose the rolling pin."

The first name on our list was Mia's sister, Abby Long, whom we found in the hotel restaurant having breakfast with the rest of Mia's entourage. The women were sitting at a table by the window, sipping tea and picking at their pricey restaurant meals—eggs Benedict, gourmet omelets, French toast stuffed with apple, Belgian waffles smothered in berries and whipped cream. Although the food looked delicious, the mood was somber.

"Abby?" I addressed a young woman who shared a striking resemblance to the recently departed.

"I'm Lulu," the woman said and was about to point to the woman in question when she cried, "You're that baker woman! You killed my cousin! Police! Police!"

If I thought we could sneak into the dining room unnoticed, I was wrong. Lulu was throwing a fit; all heads turned, and a man came flying out of the kitchen.

"Ladies! Ladies, what's going on here?" The man, lean, tidy, and somewhere in his early forties, had the distinct look of a manager. His was about to handle the situation when he spied Dylan standing next to me. His face, already an unhealthy shade of red, flushed even darker. "Dilly?" he questioned. "What are you doing here?"

Dilly? Kennedy mouthed to me with delight. I ignored her.

"The to-go coffee was so good, Chad, I just had to come back for a refill." Dylan's voice was full of sarcasm as she challenged him with her eyes.

"I thought you were being helpful," he looked down on her in a belittling manner, "bringing a cup to a grieving man. But I cannot allow you and your friends to come into my dining room and bother our guests."

"They're murderers!" one of the women exclaimed.

"We are not murderers," I assured him in my sweetest voice. "Chad, is it? I don't believe we've met." I extended my hand to him. "I'm Lindsey Bakewell."

"You're the newcomer in town," he stated, as if my

identity had just dawned on him. "You're the owner of that lighthouse bakery."

"I am." I smiled and introduced Kennedy. Dylan, he already knew. "We're not here to cause trouble. These ladies came to my bakeshop yesterday. Their friend had an unfortunate accident. We've come to extend our condolences. In fact," I remarked, having a brain flash, "I'd be honored if these ladies let me pick up their bill."

"And while you're tallying it up, darling," Kennedy addressed the man as she placed a chair between two of Mia's grieving friends, "why don't you bring us a few of those coffees as well."

The table quieted. Chad, the manager, left, and six pairs of curious eyes, like lasers on a hostile target, held to me.

CHAPTER 23

"Why are you here, Lindsey Bakewell?" Mia's sister, Abby, asked. Although the resemblance to her sibling was there, it was more pronounced in Mia's two younger cousins, Lulu and Marilee Mann. The other three women were childhood friends.

"I didn't kill your sister," I told her sincerely. "I can see how you think that I might have motive to do so. I didn't like her, not after finding her with my fiancé. Their affair was the reason I left New York. I came here to start my own business. Imagine how shocked I was to see them both here, on the day of my opening. Your presence," I indicated to them all, "was very unexpected. Tell me, when would I have found the time to sprinkle cyanide on a donut? That's what she died of. If you'll recall, Mia wasn't buying any of my donuts. She was steal-

ing them from my paying customers and throwing them
at my bakery case."

Abby's eyes narrowed in thought.

"The poison had to come from somewhere, and clearly
it wasn't me. So, who else might have a reason to want
her dead?"

"Are you seriously thinking one of us did it?" Lulu
asked as tears of anger and sadness rolled down her
cheeks. "We loved her! We looked up to her."

"She's right," the woman named Kim said. "We're all
the daughters of immigrants. Our parents worked hard to
put food on our tables. The Longs ran a restaurant. That's
where Mia got her start. She worked in their restaurant
since the age of eight, peeling shrimp and chopping veg-
etables. Even at that age, she knew she didn't want to
spend the rest of her life cooking in a tiny mom-and-pop
shop in the suburbs of New York City. She was gifted.
She wanted to go to culinary school and spread her wings.
And she did. That's where her career really began to take
off. That's when she met Jeffery Plank."

The six women who knew Mia best told us about her
life, her dreams, and her relationship with Jeffery. The
revelation of Jeffery and Mia having a long history together was still so new to me that it was hard for me to
hear all the specifics of their relationship, but I did. Of
course, I was blamed for ruining Jeffery's reputation and
his restaurant. The moment the accusation was flung at
me, Kennedy piped up and set the record straight. But as
the women talked and reminisced, explained and accused, it became clear to me that none of them had a reason to murder their sister, cousin, friend.

"Ladies, I thank you for your time. As I said earlier,

breakfast is on me. Before I leave, however, I have one more question to ask. Were Jeffery and Mia fighting?"

A secretive look flitted around the table, passing from woman to woman. Then, at last, Lulu piped up, "Of course, they were fighting. Everything they had worked so hard for was crumbling at their feet, all because of an insensitive comment made by Jeffery, and Ms. Kapoor's relentless tweeting."

"His comment was a gift from heaven," Kennedy noted. "How could I not run with it?"

I flashed Kennedy a look to zip it. I then asked, "Whose idea was it to come to Beacon Harbor to sabotage my grand opening?"

"That would have been Mia's." Abby sat back and took a reflective sip of her breakfast tea. "She was irate," she added. "She needed an outlet for her anger. Jeffery had virtually collapsed after realizing he was bankrupt. He fell into a depression and didn't even have the heart to rise to Mia's many demands and challenges."

"She was a fighter," Merilee offered. "She was trying to save the business. Thanks to Ms. Kapoor, she learned about your bakery and the grand opening. She told us her plan."

"And we told her that we'd come along and support her," Kim said. She'd given up on the Belgian waffle five minutes ago. "She was Abby's sister, but she always treated us like family."

"And what did Jeffery think of all this?" Dylan asked, barely able to hide her anger. "Did he *want* to come destroy Lindsey's bakery, or was he forced to take part in your pitiful plan?"

"He came with us because Mia told him he had to—

that he had to man up and face the woman who ruined him."

What? Oooo, if that didn't make my inner New Yorker quake like a volcano about to blow. Abby and her companions might have been grieving for a sister, but I wanted to shout at them all. They were so certain that I had ruined Jeffery when, in fact, I had come uncomfortably close to utter ruin myself. The hypocrisy was nearly too much for me to bear, but bear it I did. Because these women had just revealed that Mia had quite possibly gotten under Jeffery's skin. The question was, had he been desperate enough to silence her? The thought, apparently, had never crossed their minds. All the suspicion had clung to me, which might have been Jeffery's plan all along—to take down two women in one fell swoop! The ladies had told us enough.

"Safe travels," I told them, and I meant it. I plucked the bill Chad had deposited next to my coffee. Dylan and Kennedy followed me to the register. It was there I glanced at the order, noted that the hotel restaurant was on par with New York City pricing, and stopped. Chad had scribbled his number on the docket next to the words *Call Me*.

"What a perv," Dylan quipped, noting the message. "That's the reason I stopped working here."

"Dilly," Kennedy chided. "What an adorable pet name. So that's how he knew you. Wasn't sure if he was a friend or a lover."

Dylan gave a pretend shiver. "Blagh! And only my friends get to call me Dilly. Chad's a class-A creeper. After the Downtown Bakery closed, I got a job working in the hotel kitchen under him. Thought it would be great, you know, to expand my culinary skills to include food prep and cooking as well as baking. But then Chad started in on me. He usually sticks to the rich, bored-silly summer ladies. But sometimes he shops local. And I wasn't buying, if you get my meaning."

"We do, Dilly," Kennedy said, hooking her arm through Dylan's. "One has to wonder which one of those grieving ladies has taken him up on the offer?"

"It's none of our business," I told them, heading for the car. "And I'll tell you something else. I'm glad you're at the Beacon with us, Dylan."

"Me too," Kennedy said with a grin. "Lindsey may be a tyrant to work for, but she's got a gold star in workplace sensitivity training from one of the largest financial establishments in the country. No sexual harassment from her. However, as we've witnessed this morning, she's not above having one of her lackeys use a rolling pin to draw out a confession or two."

CHAPTER 24

It had been a morning of revelations. Dylan had a pet name. Kennedy could wrestle like a champ. None of Mia's friends had been dieting, and I had been used by the man I had been engaged to. No wonder I had a splitting headache. And it really began to pound when I thought of my computer and the person, or ghost, who'd taken it over, pointing me in the direction of the killer. Because there was no doubt in my mind that Jeffery was to blame.

"Linds, I have to bounce," Kennedy said the moment we arrived back at the lighthouse. "This is a working vacation for me."

"How's this a vacation?" Dylan shot her a questioning look. "You've been promoting the bakeshop since you've arrived. And just a few minutes ago, we, very possibly, talked with a murderer."

"Quite right, Dilly. But I'm being paid an obscene amount to tweet about some adorable sandals an up-and-coming shoe manufacturer sent me before I left. The rain is clearing; the lake looks so wonderfully dramatic, and I thought I'd slip them on and stroll down the beach with my video camera rolling."

"Sounds like a plan," I said, and thanked her for her help. Since the bakery wouldn't be opening, there was no reason for Dylan to stay either. Besides, she'd already been a tremendous help.

"Keep me posted, okay?"

"Will do," I said.

She was about to walk out the door when another thought stopped her. "Hey, would you mind if I came in early tomorrow? I'll be honest. I'm a little strapped for cash. When I took this job, I didn't expect the bakeshop to close down on the day we were supposed to open."

"Neither did I. And don't worry. You'll be paid for this week as promised."

Her proud head bowed slightly. "Thanks," she said softly. "But I don't want your charity, Lindsey. I want to work. I was thinking that I could prep the piecrusts, roll them out and freeze them until needed. I could measure out dry ingredients for coffee cakes and cookie dough and put them in airtight containers. I could—"

I held up a hand to stop her. "You had me at frozen pie dough. That's a great idea. But I'd have to clear it with Sergeant Murdock first. She's made it perfectly clear that the bakery kitchen is part of the crime scene."

"Right." Dylan nodded. "Call me when she gives the all clear."

"Will do," I said, and watched her walk out the door.

Wellington was overjoyed to have me home. Although

all I wanted to do was pop a few Tylenol, lie down, and have a good cry, his beseeching eyes and wagging tail convinced me to grab his leash instead.

The leash was purely for appearances. As I walked along the beach in the opposite direction Kennedy had taken, Wellington romped through the surf, sand, and dune grass with abandon. His tail swished happily from side to side as he chased darting sand pipers and spooked gulls into the air. His tongue dangled with delight after eating wave after wave of spumy lake water. His happiness was contagious. It made me realize that our move to Michigan had been a blessing for us both. I had escaped Jeffery and a disastrous marriage; Wellington had escaped the dog walkers and the concrete jungle.

As we walked under clearing skies, I began to ruminate over the events of the morning. The truth was, any one of the women in Mia's entourage could have slipped her a dose of poison while she was busy destroying my donuts. But why? They all looked up to her. No one had a motive. No, it was that two-timing Jeffery who had my vote. He had cried and accused; he had lied and confessed. He'd been manipulated by Mia for years, going so far as proposing marriage to me to feed their ambition. But had she pushed him too far?

There was the motive. But how did he do it? Jeffery had stood aside and watched while Mia and her friends wreaked havoc in my bakeshop. He'd been eating a piece of my coffee cake. He'd been standing in the shadows. Could he have slipped her the poison before arriving at the Beacon? That had to be how he did it. But the truth was, I knew very little about cyanide poisoning. I'd have to know a bit more before jumping to any conclusions. Just as that thought popped into my mind, Rory's beautiful log home came into view. Wellington, as if reading my mind, looked at me with something akin to hope in his eyes. "Okay," I relented. "Get fish!" I told him. *Get fish* was code for Rory's house. I had no sooner uttered the words when I realized that Welly was already making a beeline for Rory's cabin.

At first, I thought he wasn't home. I had given a series of knocks that had gone unanswered. Welly sat at my feet, whining impatiently as I tried again. I was about to give up and walk away when the door suddenly opened.

"You're home," I remarked, looking at his disheveled clothing and mussed-up black hair. I wondered if he'd been sleeping and felt a twinge of guilt if he had. "I thought you might be out fishing or on one of your hunting adventures," I explained.

"Nothing that exciting," he remarked. "I've been up all night working on my novel."

"We've disturbed you. We should go."

"Nonsense. I've just brewed another pot of coffee. Come have a cup with me."

I took a seat at Rory's kitchen table as he busied himself in the kitchen. His log home was a modern, open concept design, where all the living and dining were done beneath a grand vaulted ceiling. The room, although covered in wood, was airy and light. This was due to the recessed lighting, a chandelier composed of antlers hanging from the ceiling, and a two-story wall of windows with a sliding glass door. Wellington, being wet and covered in sand, was on the other side of the windows, lounging on the deck while happily chewing a bone. "I've come to apologize," I told him.

"What for?" he asked, looking over his shoulder. He

replaced the coffeepot and walked around the kitchen island with two mugs in his hands.

"Last night. Kennedy's confession. I swear, I didn't know what she'd been up to. You must think that we're a pair of terrible women."

He took the seat opposite me and held me in his crystalline gaze. "Not a pair, just one terrible woman. Although I did find it touching that she went to such lengths to avenge you. That's friendship." He gave a slight, appreciative nod.

"Well, I felt just horrible about it last night. I'm sorry you had to witness that, but I have to tell you, today I'm actually glad she did her best to ruin Jeffery."

Rory nearly choked on his coffee. He set down his cup and stared at me from across the table. "Why?"

It was then I told him about our visit to the Harbor Hotel and all we had learned about Mia and Jeffery.

"Wait," he said, leaning forward, looking adorable in his tired, overworked state. "Are you telling me that your ex-fiancé was still romantically involved with his pastry chef while he was engaged to you?"

"Apparently, yes."

"And you had no idea?" The skepticism in his vibrant blue eyes was a little deflating.

"Don't look at me like that," I reprimanded. "Jeffery was very convincing in his role of devoted fiancé. He never let on. Kennedy had no idea either. Thank goodness he confessed to us this morning or I'd still be filled with guilt about what she'd done to his business and reputation."

"Clearly the man deserved it. But again, please explain to me why you went to his hotel room in the first place? If the man had poisoned his lover, he could be dangerous. He could have poisoned you. You should have called the authorities, Lindsey."

"Authorities? I don't have much faith in the authorities at the moment. They've already questioned him. He probably lied through his teeth."

"Then you should have called me." Apparently, to Rory Campbell, this was the next logical step. He didn't know Jeffery and he didn't like Kennedy, and yet I found his willingness to help adorable.

"You have a novel to write," I reminded him. "By the way, where's your computer?" I gave the room a once-over. For a bachelor he kept his house remarkably clean.

"I write in the loft," he said, pointing to the stairs and the balcony that overlooked the great room. "In the spare bedroom up there."

Although several people had mentioned to me that my lighthouse was haunted, Rory had been the most convincing. Whether he believed in ghosts or not, he'd seen the odd glowing light in the lantern room the night before Mia was murdered. He'd been the one to tell me about the meaning of it. Was it coincidence, or was my lighthouse haunted by the ghost of Captain Willy Riggs? I looked him square in the eyes, and said, "Right, well, the bakeshop's been shut down and I have some time on my hands. Besides, something odd happened to me last night. I was on my computer watching a video of Kennedy leading a protest outside Sizzle when suddenly my computer went blank."

"It died?" His face reflected concern.

"I thought it had, until I realized it had been taken over by the ghost of Captain Willy Riggs." There, it was out. I was curious to see what he would make of that.

I watched as concern morphed into a grin of pure mischief. "You think the Captain took over your computer last night? How much did you have to drink?"

"Why do you think this is alcohol related?" Honestly, I found that leap quite offensive.

He tried a disarming smile. "Look, Lindsey, I'm sorry. It's just that I don't think that's possible. Ghosts don't use technology."

"And how would you know? Are you an expert?"

"No, but it doesn't make sense. And anyhow, why do you think it was the Captain?"

"Because he told me."

Rory nearly laughed at this, until I told him about my odd conversation last night, including the fact that whoever it was typing with me had urged me to visit Jeffery Plank.

When I had told him everything, I took some comfort in the fact that he looked more worried than intrigued. Rory had been in the armed services. Although he never talked about his experiences, I knew he was an expert in the field of camouflage as well as a gifted marksman. The man could hunt like a pioneer, but I was curious if his skills included more technical knowledge, like computer espionage.

"I do know there are ways for someone to take over the computer of another, but the user has to give permission for remote desktop access. It can be a little complicated. Another way is to send a virus. Or, if someone is a very skilled hacker, it might be possible. You haven't clicked on any suspicious links, have you?"

I shook my head. I was pretty savvy about viruses and how to avoid them. Still, the thought that something had taken over my computer was unsettling. Even more unsettling? That person had pointed me in the direction of Jeffery Plank.

"So, it appears that somebody has taken over your computer and is urging you to find the killer. That sounds a little odd to me. I mean, what's in it for them?"

"Don't you see?" I leaned across the table. "Whoever it is that contacted me last night knew something. They directed me to Jeffery. He's obviously the killer, Rory. Think of it. Mia had been pushing him all along. She encouraged him to date me! How twisted is that? She was the one who dragged him and her friends all the way to Beacon Harbor in an attempt to sabotage me. Jeffery knew her plans. If you'll recall, he wasn't exactly a willing participant in the donut-smashing debacle. He was just standing there, eating my coffee cake as if he was waiting for something to happen. I think he meant to poison her in my bakeshop. Mia dying in my café on opening day would not only damage the reputation of my bakery, but he'd also be rid of what might have been a huge embarrassment. He had means and motive. All I have to figure out is how he slipped her the poison. Which reminds me. You wouldn't happen to know anything about cyanide poisoning, would you?"

Rory set down his empty mug and frowned. "Unfortunately, I do."

CHAPTER 25

It was late afternoon. Kennedy had borrowed my Jeep to drive around the countryside, scouting out the perfect location to snap a few pictures of herself sporting a pricey new designer handbag. The company that had hired her was marketing it to the equestrian set. It was supposed to resemble what a two-tone leather saddlebag might look like if it was a shoulder purse. To me it said *fancy leather wine pouch with extra buckles*, which was why I owned a bakery and not a trendy boutique, I supposed.

Kennedy promised to be back before dinnertime as she grabbed my keys. We decided to go out tonight, which was fine by me. Kennedy was working, and I needed time to think. I was sitting on the couch in the parlor with Wellington sprawled beside me, his giant head resting on the comfy leather arm. I was thinking of Mia. I was trying to make sense of her untimely murder when I suddenly had the desire to visit my bakeshop. I stood quietly, careful not to wake my dog. I tiptoed out of the parlor and slipped into the back hall, where I entered the café through my private door.

The yellow crime scene tape gave me a jolt, as did the empty bakery cases, the spotless counters, and the polished chrome of the kitchen. It wasn't natural. The ovens should be on; the mixers should be humming, the bakery cases should be overflowing with mouthwatering treats, and hungry customers should be seated at every quaint little café table. But they weren't. It suddenly dawned on me that Mia had indeed exacted her revenge.

Although I was itching to get into the kitchen and start baking, I refrained. I hadn't come here to bake. Baking was forbidden. The place was still a crime scene, although I doubted that the investigators had found much of anything. No, it was the menu board I was after. Across it in neon chalk were written the names of our opening day specials. On one half, my signature donuts were proudly displayed along with the daily coffee cake, muffins, and sweet rolls. On the other half were our drink specials, naming the few fancy coffee drinks Rory knew how to make. I took out a cloth and erased them all, wiping the board clean. I then picked up the bright green chalk marker and wrote the name *Jeffery Plank* at the top.

Understandably, he was my prime suspect. Beneath his name, in hunter orange, I wrote all the possible motives he might have had to want his longtime lover out of the way. Then I began to think of all the ways he could have done it. Thanks to Rory, I now knew everything I needed to know about cyanide and how it might be used as a weapon of murder.

His knowledge had been as thorough as it was disturbing. Because of his military background, he was particularly versed in all the horrific uses of cyanide in World War II and beyond. It was the preferred poison of the Nazis, he had told me, who not only used it in their gas chambers, but had also given it to high-ranking members of their party in the form of a suicide pill. Death, they believed, was better than facing capture and torture by the enemy. It was a chilling thought. There were many forms of cyanide too: liquid, powder, gas—it was all very lethal. And because it was, I was having a hard time figuring out how it had gotten into Mia's system while she was in my bakeshop.

Somewhere deep inside the folds of my brain, thoughts of adding another name to my *menu board of murder* began to surface. But for the life of me, I didn't know if I had the courage. He was my neighbor, after all. Wellington loved him. And last but not least, he was the hottest man in Beacon Harbor. Besides, what motive could Rory Campbell possibly have to want Mia Long dead? None, I reasoned, and banished the thought. After all, Jeffery Plank was the villain here.

I had just written beneath Jeffery's name, *men's room, paper towel soaked in cyanide* (I was brainstorming, adding anything that, literally, popped into my head), when I heard a voice from behind me.

"Either you're playing a strange game of Clue, or you're investigating a murder."

I spun around only to find Tuck McAllister in his police blues frowning at me. I'd been so busy pondering murder at my board that I hadn't heard him enter.

"Donut names," I blurted, standing in front of my neon scribbling. "They pop into my head all the time."

"Men's Room's not a good name for a donut, Lindsey." He was trying his hardest not to smile as he walked to the bakery counter. "We got a call from Abby Long earlier today. She filed a complaint, stating that you and your friends ambushed her while she was at breakfast. She said you were asking questions about her sister's death."

"What?" My inner New Yorker bristled at the thought of that woman tattling on us. "I paid for their breakfast!" I told him. "None of them seem to mind that. Had I known Abby was going to file a complaint with the police like a little crybaby, I wouldn't have been so generous."

"So, you're not denying that you went to talk with her?"

"Of course not. It was a logical step in the process. And you'll be happy to know that, aside from being a bunch of squealers, I don't think Abby, or any of Mia's other friends, is to blame. They all seemed genuinely saddened by her death."

Tuck stared at me through narrowed eyes. "Yeah, well, they should. Death is a sad matter. However, judging the measure of one's sadness is not a good way of proving someone's innocence. That's why we gather evidence. It's important to link the killer to the crime scene with something a little more substantial than grief. That's what we professionals strive to do, which is why I'm here. Don't take this the wrong way, Lindsey, but I'm going to insist that you leave this investigation to the professionals."

"I would, if I wasn't your prime suspect." I set down my chalk marker and moved to the front of the polished black granite bakery counter, standing across from him. "I'm doing what any self-respecting innocent person would do. I'm trying to take myself off your list, and I think I have. I think I've found Mia's killer."

"Really? So fast?" I detected a hint of mockery as he added, "And who, exactly, do you think did it?"

"Jeffery, of course. And I'll tell you why. He and Mia came here seeking revenge, but that had nothing to do with me."

As Tuck was trying to wrap his head around all I was telling him, particularly my conversation with Kennedy and the real reason Mia and Jeffery had come to Beacon Harbor, I asked him if it was okay to brew a pot of coffee.

"Fine with me," he said. "Although the bakery is still a crime scene, I believe all the evidence has been gathered."

"Is it okay to bake?" I asked.

"Not for public consumption," he clarified. "Your shop can't open until it's been cleared by the sergeant."

"Of course, but I hardly think she'll be mad if I grab a plate of cookies from the fridge." I smiled and popped into the kitchen to retrieve a few of the cherry-chocolate-chunk cookies Dylan had baked before we were officially a crime scene. With half a dozen of the delicious cookies on a plate, I headed for one of the café tables, indicating for Tuck to follow me.

Tuck took a seat. His eyes, I noticed, never left the plate of cookies. I got the feeling that the moment I had put them on the table I had lost him.

"Did you hear me?" I said, handing him a mug of steaming black coffee. "I honestly had no idea Kennedy had done so much damage to his livelihood. Therefore, his appearance here truly was a surprise, not to mention the fact that I don't own cyanide."

"These look delicious." With his eyes never leaving

the cookie in his hand, he removed his blue cap and set it beside him on the table. "Oatmeal, chunks of chocolate, toasted pecans, *and cherries*? Is that even legal?" He graced me with a heart-stopping smile before taking a bite.

Good heavens, I silently mused. Why couldn't he have been chubby and covered in acne? I consciously shut my mouth and sat across from him, trying not to smile like a brainless fangirl. "In my bakeshop," I told him, using a two-handed grip on my mug for support, "it's not only legal, it's the law."

I watched a moment longer as Tuck nibbled away on the cookie with something akin to euphoria. I should have been concentrating on the recent murder when, in fact, I was concentrating on his full, nicely shaped lips. I then reminded myself that he was still in his twenties, and that I was a murder suspect.

"Delicious." He looked up from his empty plate. "You know that I'm going to have to check your story, right?"

"Of course. I'll give you Kennedy's number. She'd be happy to tell you. She and Dylan came with me this morning when I went to apologize to Jeffery and set the record straight."

"Wait!" he said, narrowing his eyes at me. "You went to talk to Mr. Plank this morning as well?"

"Weren't you listening? He's the person we originally went to see. I thought I should apologize to him after learning what Kennedy had done. I even offered to have her reverse some of the damage by hosting a podcast for him at my bakeshop. All we asked in return was information on Mia's friends, thinking one of them might have had a motive to want her dead. That's when Jeffery told me—rather smugly, if you can believe it—that he and

Mia had always been *a thing* and that they had both used me for my money and connections. Our engagement was a sham. And I almost married him." Hard as I might have tried, I couldn't keep the anger from seeping into my voice. My hands, I noticed, were also trembling.

Tuck, with eyes the color of the lake under a cloudless sky, stared at me across his mug of steaming coffee. "Dear God, is that true?"

"Unfortunately, yes. That's what I was trying to tell you before you got distracted by my cookies." He didn't bother to deny it, so I pressed on. "Had I known this little fact one day earlier, I certainly would have had motive for murder. But Mia Long wouldn't have been my target."

He flashed a cautioning look. "You really shouldn't say things like that."

"Oh, I'm only joking." I waved an angry hand. "But my point is, I didn't poison anyone. I can also state with certainty that the crime scene unit didn't find any cyanide in my bakeshop. I don't have any. But I'll bet you a dozen cookies that Jeffery does. You, or your scary sergeant, need to talk to him again. He nearly married me for my money. He might have used cyanide on me too—to bump me off after the wedding. But he didn't get the chance, because I caught him cheating, got really drunk, and bought a lighthouse in Michigan—in that order."

"Jesus," he uttered and paused for a cautious sip. "I can't imagine any man cheating on you."

From any other man's lips, I would have thought it mindless flattery, but not from him. He was adorably sincere as he looked up from his mug. He's not *so* young, I reasoned, looking into his guileless blue eyes. I mean, history was full of women far older than thirty-five falling for men far younger than twenty-eight . . . right? Would it be so bad, I mused, dating a younger man? As I stared at him, my mind had crafted a fantasy of him running shirtless on the beach in the magical hour before sunset. I'd never seen him shirtless, but I imagined that under his trim-fitting uniform he had a six-pack. Tuck the shirtless runner was getting closer, smiling that glorious smile. I was about to smile back when my fantasy came to a crashing halt.

"But what motive does he have to want Mia dead?" Tuck, thankfully unaware of my inappropriate thoughts, pushed on with the demands of his profession. "You just said that they've been an item for years."

"Yes."

"Jeffery's engagement to you was a sham?"

"Yes."

"But not his relationship with the deceased?"

"No. But they were having problems."

"The sarge is convinced he genuinely cared for her. She interviewed him at the hospital."

"True, he might have cared for her. But I think she was driving him crazy."

He set down his mug. "You're just speculating. You have no proof of it."

"I have proof that she was crazy. Ask anyone who was in here when she stormed my counter and began stealing donuts off people's plates and throwing them on the floor. That's the definition of crazy, if you ask me. You could talk to Abby Long again, but I doubt she'd be objective."

Tuck nodded. "I'll consider it. But I also have some news for you. It's still confidential, but I thought I should tell you. The contents of the victim's stomach have been examined. You'll be happy to know that, according to

Doc Riggles, the medical examiner, your donuts were void of any trace of cyanide."

"Of course they were. Why on earth would I add cyanide to the mix?"

"Not so fast," he cautioned. "The cyanide wasn't delivered through a donut. It was in the coffee, a latte to be more exact. A person who ingests cyanide gives off a distinct almond odor on the breath. It's one of the telltale signs of cyanide poisoning. When I was helping perform CPR on Ms. Long, I smelled it. However, having never worked on anyone who's been poisoned before, I mistook the smell for almond flavoring that might have been used in her latte."

"We don't use almond flavoring," I told him. "We're not that advanced yet."

Tuck nodded in acknowledgment. "Anyhow, Mia ingested twice the lethal amount of cyanide through the little she drank. That's how the killer did it. And from what you, as well as others, have told me, Jeffery Plank wasn't anywhere near Mia when she collapsed. In fact, he wasn't near her the entire time she was in your bakeshop."

"That's true," I begrudgingly admitted, remembering how Jeffery had stood aside while Mia had stormed my counter. He was also nowhere near her when she collapsed on the lawn. "What if he slipped the poison in a cup of coffee he'd given her earlier? Maybe that's why he was standing off to the side? I thought he was just embarrassed by her behavior, but maybe he was waiting for the cyanide to take effect."

Tuck, having taken another sip of his own coffee, set down the mug. "Under normal circumstances, I'd say that's plausible. However, cyanide's highly lethal. The amount found in her stomach killed her nearly instantly.

Therefore, given what we know of his behavior and his distance from the victim, he couldn't have been our killer. Which brings me to the problem at hand. Who made Mia's coffee yesterday morning?"

The name, like a warning bell, kept appearing through the fog in my brain, and yet I strived to bury it deeper. There was only one person making coffee that day. I finally closed my eyes and uttered a painful, "Rory Campbell. But listen to me," I continued. "He wasn't supposed to be working yesterday morning. He's not even an employee. He did it as a favor to me. The young man I hired for the position broke his arm the day before. Rory jumped in at the last moment. What possible reason would he have to poison a perfect stranger?"

"That's the question. I tried to do a little background check on him this morning, but much of his personal information is classified. Did you know he's retired Special Ops? The guy served as a Navy SEAL and retired with the rank of captain. A man with that kind of training is capable of anything. How well do you know him, Lindsey?"

For once I found his probing blue eyes anything but adorable. "Umm, not very well. We're neighbors."

"He did you a favor in a pinch," Tuck reminded me. "You must know him pretty well to get him to stand behind an espresso machine all morning and make coffee on your bakery's opening day?"

"We've gone out to dinner," I begrudgingly admitted.

"Are you dating?" For some reason it sounded a little accusatory.

I stared back at him. "Well, no. I mean, I don't know. I don't think so. Truthfully, I know very little about him or his motives."

"And that's the problem. Nobody knows much about him or his motives." Tuck stood and picked up his cap. "I have a call in to one of his superior officers. Until I can confirm that he's not the killer, I'm going to insist, Lindsey, that you keep out of this investigation. I'm also going to suggest that you keep your distance from Rory Campbell."

CHAPTER 26

"This is where you want to eat?" Kennedy eyed the paneled room, frowning at the taxidermied wall art. "When you said you wanted to go out for dinner, I was thinking Traverse City chic and not some backwoods lovechild of a nineteen-fifties diner and Cabela's."

"It's called the Moose," I said, pulling her to the hostess station. "It's Rory's favorite restaurant."

Staring at the cold glass eyes of what was once undoubtedly a regal buck, Kennedy nodded. "Now, that I believe."

After a quick word with the hostess, we were seated in Karen's section, the frazzled waitress who seemed to know more about Rory Campbell than I did. After all, he'd been eating at the Moose long before I moved in.

Once seated at the faux-wood Formica–topped table, Kennedy leaned in. "So, let me get this straight. You think your current heartthrob purposely poisoned your cheating ex's lover having never met her? That's a stretch, even for him."

I leaned in as well and matched her near-whisper. "The cyanide was found in the coffee. He was making the coffee."

"I get all that, but doesn't a murderer usually have a motive?"

"Usually," I agreed, and rested my elbows on the table. "But Rory has a military background. He's a trained killer. We know he likes to hunt, but what if he . . . you know, has a taste for killing other things as well?"

"Like obnoxious donut-stealing divas?" Without much thought, Kennedy nodded. "I get it. She was obnoxious. She was destroying your opening day. Who *didn't* want to strangle her?"

"He was very calm about it all," I added, trying to recall the chaos of yesterday morning. "We were slammed. He had a lot of orders shouted at him—"

"Which I'm sure he was used to, being in the military," She rolled her eyes. "I doubt that set him over the edge."

"Yes, thank you. But he was working that espresso machine like a champ, pulling espresso for all the lattes, cappuccinos, mochas and Americanos people were ordering. He was also pouring coffee from the pots as well. You were outside, but behind the counter we were all pitching in, helping fill orders."

"And you think he saw Mia stomping up to the counter and stirred a little cyanide into her coffee—for the heck of it?"

I thought about that. It didn't seem right, but I had little time to ponder why. My train of thought was broken by a basket of rolls plopped between us, immediately followed by a curt, "Ladies."

At the sound of the voice, Kennedy and I sprang apart like a couple of note-passing teenagers. "Oh, hello, hon," waitress Karen said, recognizing me. "The jeans and T-shirt threw me off. Is it just you two tonight, or will you be expecting *another*?" The way she said "another" left little doubt as to whom she was referring to.

"Just us," I quickly assured her.

Karen gave a curt nod and took our drink order. She was just about to head to the next table when she stopped. "Hey, so what's going on with your lighthouse bakeshop? Heard some woman died there yesterday. That's a pretty bad omen for an opening day, if you ask me."

"She didn't ask you," Kennedy shot back, faster than a guard dog's bite. "And we don't believe in omens. The lady was *murdered*."

"What?" That got her attention. "No one said anything about murder."

"How did you know about my bakeshop?" I asked her.

"Gossip, hon. It's Memorial Day weekend. Everybody's out and about. And everybody talks. Heard Rory was behind the counter helping you out. Nice touch using a red-blooded, all-American hunk like him. Had I known about it earlier, I would have come to your bakeshop too. So, where is he tonight? You two have a falling-out or something?"

"Falling-out?" I questioned, blushing and scrunching my nose at the same time. "We're not . . . a thing. Just friends."

"Right. Next thing you'll be telling me is Ms. Glam over here shops at Walmart." It was meant as a joke, yet Kennedy rose to the remark like a challenged lioness.

"Two things, darling," she said, staring at our waitress. "First, nobody knows what Lindsey and Rory are, including them. They're still in the exploratory stage of their relationship. Secondly, I have been in a Walmart—during my college days. Where else could I get toilet paper, crisps, biscuits, and a stout pair of wellies in the same stop? Now Amazon Prime and Alexa handle the dirty work for me. I like you, Karen. So, tell us. Were you and Rory ever an item?"

Karen laughed with the force and vigor of a donkey. "I wish. Married, with three children, and a proud Walmart shopper to boot. I'll get the lemon water for Ms. Bakewell straightaway and see about that bottle of Chablis for you, hon."

The moment Karen left, I shot Kennedy a look. "You're scaring her. And did you have to order a whole bottle of wine? Don't you think you should cut back a little? We're working, after all."

"Thanks to you, I only have two vices left, blogging about fashion and wine. Leave me *something*," she dramatically proclaimed. Although Kennedy was mostly joking, we both knew she was referring to her former real addiction to shopping. Thankfully, with my help, she had slayed that demon before it destroyed her.

"I'm not having a glass," I told her, looking around the crowded dining room. It was Saturday night and the tables were filling fast. No wonder waitress Karen always looked a bit frazzled.

"Who are you?" she mocked, referring to my lack of will to drink a glass with her. "Beacon Harbor's changed you. In New York you were always in your Wall Street tower counting money. Now you're frying donuts, conversing with a ghost, and chasing after a backwoods enigma who just might be a closet poisoner. You picked a strange day to give up wine, Lindsey, darling."

"We don't know that Rory's a murderer. God, I hope he isn't. But the fact is, the cyanide was in the coffee."

"You said he's writing a book," Kennedy probed, then stared at the moose head prominently placed on the far wall. It was then I recalled my first visit to this restaurant. It had been my first date with Rory. He'd worn a jacket and jeans: I was wearing a dress by Chanel.

"Maybe there's a New York connection," I told her. "The first time I came here, Karen thought I was his agent."

"As in *literary agent*?" She laughed. "Do you even read?"

"Yes, I do. Although these days it's mostly recipe books. I've been busy baking." I mock-sneered in her direction and pressed on. "What if he really has an agent? What if he's been to New York City to meet with him or her? We know Rory likes meat. He's a hunter, after all. He could have dined in Jeffery's restaurant, Sizzle. That could be the connection!"

"Good heavens!" Kennedy arched a professionally shaped brow and picked up a roll. "There are twenty-four thousand restaurants in Manhattan alone, and you think he went to Sizzle?"

"It's a popular restaurant," I countered.

"*Was* popular," she corrected. "But let's say you're right. Let's say that he dines at Jeffery's restaurant. He'd have to be served a very gamy steak to exact a revenge like poison. And I say *very gamy* because the man's a hunter and he's obviously eaten plenty of gamy meat." Kennedy flipped her long black hair over her shoulder and took a bite of her roll.

"He'd ask for his money back," I offered logically. "And even if he did go to Sizzle, it's doubtful he'd ever see Mia. She was a pastry chef, not a server."

We both sat at the table nibbling rolls, pondering a possible connection between Rory and Mia, when Karen returned with our drinks. "It's a screw cap, hon," she slowly explained to Kennedy, pouring out a glass of Chablis from the bottle she'd ordered. "I'm leaving it with you so you can take the rest home." Kennedy had opened her mouth, a snarky comment sitting on her tongue just waiting to be launched, when I cut in with a question about Rory's agent.

"Oh, I don't know if he's got one. You just looked the part. I did know that he was writing a book. He liked to talk about it. He also liked asking questions about Beacon Harbor and the surrounding area."

"What kinds of questions did he ask?" I was curious to know.

"Local fishing hot spots, local history and legends, hunting, that sort of thing. Once, however, he did break from his usual friendly banter by asking about recreational drug use among the local population, particularly the teens. Told him we have our share of opioid overdoses up here as well. I think he was trying to escape that element, but there's no escaping it."

"Did he ever talk about cyanide, or inquire where to buy it?" I proposed the question as nonchalantly as placing a napkin on my lap.

A puzzled look crossed her face. "Don't think so. But you might want to ask him yourself. He's right over there." Karen pointed to the hostess station, where a throng of hungry diners had gathered. At the back of the crowd, poking a good six inches above the rest, was the unmistakable dark head of Rory Campbell.

The Moose was a popular place. Panicking, I ran a quick eye over the restaurant. There didn't appear to be any available tables. I chanced a look back at the crowd and locked eyes with Rory. He smiled and waved. Hope illuminated his face as he spotted our two empty chairs.

"He's coming to join us," I hiss-whispered. Kennedy, having spied him as well, had flipped into panic mode. She was scanning tables, looking for God only knew what.

"Bingo," she declared, and plucked the bottle of wine out of Karen's hand. She stood, picked up her glass, and grabbed my arm. "This table's available for the next lucky diner. We're heading over there."

I had no idea where *there* was. I might have protested leaving the comfort of our table if I hadn't spied Rory weaving his way toward us. I had to admit, he looked spectacularly handsome in his form-fitting Henley and faded jeans. His wavy dark hair had been meticulously combed into place, setting off his deep-set blue eyes to perfection. I hesitated.

Kennedy, sensing my weakness, tucked the wine bottle under her arm and tightened her grip on me. A moment later I found myself being propelled toward a middle-aged couple who were being led to a table near the back. To my utter surprise it was Betty Vanhoosen and a man of a similar age.

"We shouldn't," I whispered, trying to put on the breaks. "She's . . . on a date."

"She's your friend," Kennedy replied. "Friends don't let friends dine in danger. Now, smile and follow my lead."

CHAPTER 27

The hostess had no sooner plopped down two menus when Kennedy took a seat, surprising everybody. "Betty! What a surprise seeing you here. Mind if we join you?"

It was obvious that Betty had no idea we'd even been in the dining room. She'd been too absorbed with the man sitting across from her to notice much of anything. Although bald and bespectacled, he had a distinguished air about him. Betty Vanhoosen, I silently mused, you naughty, naughty girl.

"Lindsey, Kennedy, what are you two doing here?"

"We came for dinner. We were just about to order when we saw you. Wine, anyone?" Kennedy flashed her most charming smile and held up the bottle.

Betty and her gentleman were above all else polite and allowed us to join them. The waitress was hailed and sent to retrieve three more wineglasses. Betty was just about to introduce us to her friend, when Rory appeared. He looked miffed.

"Lindsey. Didn't you see me?" He was staring at me with an expression reminiscent of Wellington's whenever I had to leave him home alone. Rory, like Welly, oozed a heady mix of puzzlement and hurt. I didn't know what to say. Thankfully, Betty did.

"Why, Rory. What a pleasant surprise! You must join us too. I insist. Pull up a chair. I was just about to introduce a dear friend of mine. This is Bob Riggles. Bob's a widower," she felt inclined to inform us. "His wife and I used to be schoolmates." Betty leaned forward, her round face glowing with adoration as she stared at the man across from her. "You might be interested to know that Bob is the medical examiner for the county. And guess what? He spent yesterday afternoon digging around in that poor woman's body—"

"We prefer the term 'examined,'" Bob interjected kindly. "Just the standard procedures for an autopsy."

"Wait," Rory said. "You were the doctor who performed the autopsy on Mia Long?" Rory cast me a questioning look.

The older gentleman nodded. "That's generally what I do when foul play is suspected."

"And guess what he found?" Betty, not to be upstaged by the county medical examiner, was determined to reveal the findings. Unfortunately, Officer Tuck McAllister had already spilled the beans privately to me.

Kennedy, playing along, offered, "A whole lot of donuts?"

"Yes. But that's not all," Betty proudly informed us. "He found cyanide too, and coffee."

The gentleman across from Betty flushed a deep red. "Betty, dear, that's hardly appropriate information to be dishing out to the public, and over dinner, no less."

"They're not public, Bob. This is Lindsey Bakewell. The woman was murdered in her bakeshop. Rory and Kennedy were there too."

Bob, a more cautious man than Betty Vanhoosen, furrowed his bushy white brows as he took in the measure of us. "They were there, you say?" The wheels of his mind were spinning.

"Don't you see?" Betty said, grinning as if she was about to release some glorious form of magic into the world. "That's how the killer did it. The cyanide was put in the coffee. All that poor woman had to do was take a few sips, and *boom*. Dead as a doornail. Isn't that right, Bob?"

Bob hesitated. Staring levelly at the three of us, he answered, "Unfortunately, yes. All three of you were there at the time of that woman's death?" he asked again.

"It's my bakeshop," I offered plainly. "Kennedy's my friend from New York. She flew in to help me with my opening day."

Rory, sitting quietly in his chair while silently processing what Betty had divulged, offered, "I performed CPR on the victim. She collapsed on the lawn. Her heart had stopped, and she wasn't breathing."

"Interesting," Kennedy remarked, "since you were the one making all the coffee."

Although seemingly launched carelessly, the accusation hit its mark with force. The entire table fell silent and stared at Rory. Betty, taking it one step further, covered her gaping mouth with a hand. A plump, dark-haired waitress chose that moment to appear beside Bob. Smiling, she asked, "What are we having to drink tonight, folks?"

Kennedy, without looking at the waitress, raised her empty wine bottle. "Another bottle of this, please."

"A brandy old-fashioned for me," Bob added. Like Kennedy, he wasn't looking at the waitress. The rest of us remained quiet, causing the poor woman to scurry away.

Rory, fully aware that he was the center of attention, stared straight at me. "You seriously think that I had something to do with that woman's death?"

"You were making the coffee," Betty reminded him, her round, preternaturally pleasant face clouding with worry. She might, after all, be sitting across from a killer.

"As a favor to Lindsey," Rory defended. "She asked me to do it. You," he said, directing his rising anger at me. "You were avoiding me? You saw me coming and abandoned your table. You knew about the cyanide in the coffee, didn't you?"

"She might have," Kennedy coyly informed him.

His dark brows furrowed with anger. "That explains the reason you're here at the Moose. You're not here for the food, or the ambiance. You're checking up on me!"

"Actually, we were going to order something called fried perch. Lindsey insisted."

I shot Kennedy a look to zip it, and turned to Rory. "Officer McAllister came to the lighthouse this afternoon. He had a few more questions, which I answered. And, yes, he told me about the cyanide in the coffee. Look, a woman died in my bakeshop. I don't know what to think."

Rory, casting me a look that pierced my heart, slammed his napkin on the table and stood abruptly. Then, without another word, he left the restaurant.

Kennedy followed him with her eyes. The moment he was gone, she turned back to the table with a conspiratorial grin. "Well, that was awkward. So, darlings, are we still going to order this fried perch, or what?"

We didn't order the perch. I was upset, and Bob very likely believed that one of us had poisoned the poor woman on his autopsy table. Betty, realizing what she'd done by leaking the sensitive information, had grown upset as well, blubbering apologies and crying into her napkin. As for me, I was racked with guilt from all sides—Rory's haunting look of disgust, Betty's ruined date, and Bob's unconcealed suspicion. Kennedy was also unusually quiet, which, honestly, unnerved me even more. She remained at the table, seemingly mesmerized by the swirling Chablis in her glass. The night had been ruined. The promised fried perch suppers were just going to have to wait. I apologized to Betty and Bob, laid down enough money to cover the drinks, and left the table. Kennedy abandoned both her glass and her bottle, and followed me out of the restaurant.

We sat in the lantern room eating fast food burgers by candlelight. To our left the twinkling lights of the town and harbor danced along the waterfront. To our right was an endless expanse of darkness broken every now and again by a winking porchlight in the wooded hills. Rory's cabin, also located on this side, was now as indiscernible as the scalloped shoreline. Yet Kennedy and I preferred the view straight ahead, marveling how the lake seemed as vast as an ocean. It was a moonless night. The stars overhead sparkled like diamonds on an endless sea of black velvet, while the lake below had only a voice by which to recognize it. The measured sound of waves rolling on sand had become so familiar it was akin to a lullaby.

"He looked so hurt," I remarked for the tenth time, staring at the blackness beyond the windows.

Kennedy shoved a fry into her mouth and followed it with a sip of chocolate shake. "I harken back to my original question. What's his motive?"

"You were the one who practically accused him at the table," I reminded her.

"Well, yes. Somebody had to do it. We all couldn't just tiptoe around the elephant in the room, which was the fact that Sir Hunts-a-Lot down there"—she gestured out the window in Rory's direction—"had access to all the coffee. Don't you find it odd that he was the one who escorted Mia out of the café, only to perform CPR on her seconds later?"

"He was removing an annoyance," I said, then thought about it. Remembering something Officer Tuck had told me, I blurted, "The smell!"

"That's just the onions on my burger, Linds. Helps mask the fake-meat flavor."

"No, not that. The distinctive smell that cyanide gives off. Tuck said that victims of cyanide poisoning give off an unmistakable almond scent."

"We're on a first-name basis with Tuck, are we? And after only one day!"

"He insisted." I ignored her grin. "If Rory knew so much about cyanide, why didn't he detect it? The moment he started CPR he would have known, wouldn't he?"

She had finished her shake yet was still sucking on the straw, making an annoying milky gurgling sound as she stared at me. Finally letting go, she said, "That is troubling. Whether or not he poisoned her, he should have known the signs. And yet he kept at it and said nothing. Why is it that all the gorgeous men turn out to be psychopaths?"

I shook my head as my stomach churned with a sickening feeling, thinking how easily I had fallen under his spell. First Jeffery and now my uber-hot neighbor. I had taken the fact that Wellington liked him to be a good sign. Welly had always been a good judge of character. For instance, he'd always growled at Jeffery, but maybe my pup had finally sold out his guard dog instincts to his stomach. Fresh-caught fish had turned him. I shook my head as another sickening wave washed over me. "What we have to do now is link him to the crime scene."

"*We?*" Kennedy shot me a look. "Oh, no-no, Lindsey, dear. We've done more than our share already. We've learned that Jeffery's a wanker and that Mia's friends are sycophants. But Rory, he's way out of our league. He's been trained by the military to kill people."

"That may be, but he also knows a lot about cyanide. He was making the coffee and he was the person who escorted Mia out to the lawn, where she collapsed. He then started CPR, which he continued until the paramedics came. Those are the facts. What we don't know is how he brought the cyanide into the bakeshop—"

"Or why he'd want to kill a woman he's never met before." Kennedy grabbed her empty cup and wrappers and shoved them into the bag. "We're going around in circles here. All this talk of murder—and very likely that cheeseburger—is hurting my head. I say we sleep on it until morning. Then maybe we should consider paying Jeffery boy another visit. Maybe he knows of a connection between Rory and Mia?"

"Maybe he does," I agreed, and picked up my trash as well. Kennedy, turning on her cell phone flashlight, headed down the circular stairs. I had just blown out the candles when I noticed a light far across the water. I watched it for a minute, thinking it was a boat, but it didn't appear to be moving. Also, I had learned that boats at night ran with several lights clearly visible: a white stern light, a red port light, and a green starboard light. The light in the distance was only one hazy white light, and it seemed to have appeared out of nowhere. As I continued to stare at the lone point in the blackness, a cold burst of wind hit the back of my neck, while the faint smell of pipe smoke tickled my nose. My skin prickled of its own accord, giving me an unsettling feeling that perhaps I wasn't alone. That's when I noticed another dim light, bobbing far down the beach. I stared at it a moment and watched it disappear. The light on the horizon had also vanished. I blinked and stared again, thinking that maybe I had imagined it.

"Linds, are you coming?"

"Yes," I cried, and flipped on my phone light. Without looking back, I ran down the three flights of circular stairs as fast as my legs would carry me.

CHAPTER 28

Kennedy retired to her room without a care, which was fine by me. There was no reason to tell her about the unsettling feeling I'd had in the lantern room or the strange vanishing lights I thought I had seen. Even as Welly and I took our nightly walk down the beach, I was still trying to rationalize what I had experienced. Maybe it had just been my overactive imagination combined with the reflection of a particularly bright star. But as Wellington strained toward the lake at the end of his leash, I was forced to realize that my starlight theory was ridiculous. The stars overhead were too remote, and the waves crashed onshore with force. Welly didn't seem to care one way or the other. He loved the water almost as much as he loved chasing seagulls. He loved the way it drenched his thick fur, and that he could drink as much of it as he pleased, hence the reason our nightly walks were conducted on a leash.

After Welly was given his cookies and tucked into bed, I climbed into my own bed, but not to sleep. I was too keyed up and needed some answers. I leaned against the mound of pillows and opened my laptop instead, lulled into comfort by the gentle snoring of my dog. Last night someone claiming to be Captain Willy Riggs had contacted me via my computer. Whoever was typing with me, be it man or ghost, seemed to believe that Jeffery was a person of interest, which he turned out to be in more ways than one. Jeffery might not have been the one to slip Mia a deadly dose of poison, but he had revealed a very damaging truth to me. He had also pointed us in the direction of Mia's friends. Thanks to Officer Tuck and the medical examiner, Bob Riggles, we now knew more about the cyanide poisoning that had killed Mia. It had been delivered through the coffee she drank, which had caused us all to point a finger at Rory Campbell. Having access to the coffee, he seemed to be the obvious source of the poisoning. Yet deep down in my gut, I didn't believe it. And even more distressing to me was the disappointed look in his eyes as he left the Moose.

Maybe Captain Willy Riggs didn't believe it either. After all, if I believed in ghosts, I might be inclined to think that the first keeper of the Beacon Harbor Lighthouse had tried to contact me in the lantern room. And if he had tried to contact me there, it would only follow to reason that he'd pop into my computer and try to type a few lines to me as well. I was at least willing to entertain the thought.

I started out just as I had last night, by Googling things on the internet. The first thing that struck my curiosity was the Captain himself. I wanted to learn a little bit more about him as a man, not as a legend, and what might have happened on the night he died. I read up on the United States Lighthouse Board and soon landed on a database in the National Archives. To my amazement, the original logbook of the Beacon Harbor Lighthouse had been preserved, all the old pages digitized and available for me to peruse. After meandering down that rabbit hole for over an hour, and making what I thought was a notable discovery, I decided to turn my sights from Captain Willy and educate myself on ghosts. I wound up watching a slew of spooky videos on YouTube of ghostly encounters.

After watching about four of them, I began to catch a pattern. They were all shot in poor lighting, the actors (and I use the term loosely) were all overreacting to small noises or things the camera just happened to miss. And the ever-popular declarations of, "Oh my God, it just touched me!" could never be proven. My personal favorite was a video of a coffee mug sliding across the counter of some shabby kitchen in the UK. At one point I even spied the glint of what I believed to be fishing line that had been attached to the handle. Lame, I thought. All you ghosts are so lame.

I was about to fall asleep when the screen on my computer flashed brightly then went dark. Although I had been expecting it, the suddenness with which it happened sent my heart racing. "How on earth are you doing this?" I floated the question to the room at large and held my breath, waiting for the electronic words. A moment later they appeared.

Has the angry lady been avenged?

It was his opening salvo, and just like the night before I found it utterly chilling. I took a deep breath to steady my nerves, then typed, *Good evening, Captain. And the answer to your question is no. The angry lady has not been avenged.* Although I knew that whoever it was typing with me had meant Mia, I took the question a little more personally. I was, after all, an angry lady too. My bakery's opening day had been ruined. And I had not yet been avenged.

There was a slight pause and then the words: *Was it not the boyfriend?*

For some reason that question depressed me. If I was, in fact, conversing with a ghost, I would have thought he'd have better *insider* knowledge. After all, he was the one who suggested, and rather cryptically too, *the boyfriend*. I thought he was on to something. I thought, albeit wrongly, that ghosts could float around and get inside people's heads and learn the truth. I was either conversing with a totally lame ghost, or I wasn't conversing with a ghost at all.

Actually, I typed, *the boyfriend turned out to be a bust. He couldn't have done it. The "angry lady" drank coffee laced with cyanide. The boyfriend wasn't close enough to slip it into her coffee.* There! Take that, I thought.

She was poisoned?

I grimaced and shook my head as I replied, *I thought you knew that.*

She died an untimely death.

Yes, and the police still don't know who killed her.

You need to dig deeper, Lindsey Bakewell.

I gave a little grunt at this. Like I didn't know that already. I'd been racking my brain for two days trying to figure out who had murdered Mia Long, and why. *I am trying,* I told the Captain. Then confided, *Another name keeps popping up as well. It answers the question of how, but not why. And, truthfully, it makes me uncomfortable just to think about it.*

You are referring to the Hunter.

That sent a chill up my spine! There was only one hunter I knew, and his name was Rory Campbell. Unfortunately, he'd been on my mind all night. Whoever was typing with me was doing a good job of creeping me out yet again. I took a deep breath and called on my inner New Yorker to answer this one. *Can you please be a little more specific? This is Michigan, after all. Everybody hunts.*

A moment later I watched the words slowly appear on the screen: *The Hunter-Soldier.*

Do you mean Rory Campbell?

Yes.

Is he the killer? I hated myself for even typing those words, but I had to consider it.

The hunter-soldier has secrets.

I rolled my eyes at the computer screen. *Yes, I'm well aware. A real tall, dark, and silent type. But I was the one who asked him to make the coffee. I can't honestly think of a reason for him to poison a woman he didn't know.*

Then you must ask him.

I was about to counter this when the screen flashed, beeped, and sprang back to life, depositing me exactly where I'd left off. Another video of a lame ghost encounter was about to load. With my heart tripping loudly in my chest, I closed the screen and shut my laptop.

Rory Campbell, I thought . . . or the hunter-soldier, according to the thing messing with my computer. But whoever it was typing with me was correct. I needed to confront Rory. He deserved at least that much. Rory was the first real friend I'd made in Beacon Harbor. He'd shown me nothing but kindness since I'd arrived. For heaven's sake, I had kissed him and still harbored fantasies of doing a heck of a lot more than that. If Rory Campbell had a reason to poison Mia, maybe he'd share it with me. Whatever the case, I was going to pay him a visit in the morning.

I'd had no idea how long I'd been sleeping when I awoke to the sound of Wellington barking. I sprang up in bed, my heart pounding with fright as my dream swiftly faded from memory. Wellington was at the window. The curtains had been thrust aside, his giant head pressed to the screen. A light breeze fluttered through as he continued barking at something unseen on the lawn. I was about to cross the room and shut the window when I realized that my phone was also ringing. It was three thirty in the morning. I ordered Wellington to stop barking and grabbed my phone. I was half-expecting to see Mom's *Vogue* cover light up the screen. What I wasn't expecting was the name Betty Vanhoosen.

"Hello," I answered cautiously.

"Are you awake?" Betty sounded frightened.

"Honestly, not quite. What is it, Betty?"

"Lindsey, I'm so sorry," she blathered. "I shouldn't have called you at this hour. But . . . I just remembered something very important about, you know, *the murder*."

"Betty, what is it?" Although I was still wiping the sleep from my eyes, her tone had grabbed my full attention. "Are you okay? Do you need help?"

"I . . . I can't tell you over the phone. They might be listening. Can you meet me at my office tomorrow?"

"Who's listening, Betty?"

"Tomorrow. At my office. Don't say a word to anyone." There was no reply to that. Betty, having been spooked by something, ended the call.

I was about to go to the window and see what Wellington had been barking at when he turned suddenly and jumped up on the bed. I pulled him next to me and tried to fall back to sleep. Unfortunately, Betty's frantic call had chased the Sandman away.

CHAPTER 29

I awoke to the smell of frying bacon and realized I had overslept. It was nine o'clock in the morning. My bedroom door was open, and I prayed it was Kennedy making breakfast and not the cryptic entity that had a penchant for midnight conversations on my laptop. The moment my feet hit the floor, I remembered the call from Betty as well. It was the reason I had overslept. The sound of her voice had frightened me; her desire to meet me at her office had kicked my sleepy brain into high gear, imagining all types of horrific scenarios.

After a quick shower, I dressed and made my way down to the kitchen with the intention of heading out the door as soon as possible. However, seeing Kennedy at the stove plucking strips of charred bacon from a smoking pan stopped me in my tracks. She must have heard me coming. Because just as I had entered the kitchen, she turned from the smoking pan and grinned.

"Look. I'm cooking!" Although puzzled, I applauded her initiative. The fact that she hadn't started a grease fire was also impressive. "You need to go shopping," she informed me. "Your refrigerator is appallingly empty."

It really wasn't. She was merely complaining about the lack of ready-made foods.

"I didn't know what to eat, so I snuck into the bakery to see if you had anything good in there," she informed me. I came beside her and turned off the burner under the smoking pan. I reflexively moved the pan to a cooler spot while Kennedy picked up an egg. "Dilly was in there, hard at work in the bakery," she continued. "I suppose it's okay, since you told her it was. Looked like she had a rough night too. Anyhow, she's making cherry Danish. They looked delicious. She's bringing some out when they're done. In the meantime, she asked me to fry some bacon. Didn't have the heart to tell the poor dear that I don't do that. This"—she pointed to the plate of extra-, extra-crispy bacon—"is from your giant bakery refrigerator." As she spoke, she attempted to crack the egg into a bowl. Having no feel for the task, she came down on the rim with surprising force. The egg imploded in her hand. "Ahhh, bugger all!" she cried and ran to the sink with a handful of scrambled raw egg.

I picked up a sponge and attacked the mess while she attempted to wash the incident from her memory.

"Well, you did a good job with the bacon," I remarked, noting that my dog wasn't in the kitchen begging for a piece.

"Thanks," she replied, drying her hands. "I had a little help from the internet."

"Where's Wellington?"

"He was barking at the door, so I let him outside."

I nodded, poured a cup of coffee, and was about to head out the door to find him when Dylan popped into the kitchen from the parlor entrance carrying a tray of freshly baked, beautifully iced cherry Danish.

"Dylan!" I exclaimed in wonder, turning my attention from Welly and the door. "Those look amazing!"

She forced a smile and set the tray on the table. "It's been a weird week. Couldn't really sleep, so I popped in early and decided to try my hand at making Danish. I haven't made these in years. I wanted to see what you'd think."

There's nothing on earth to rival a freshly baked Danish. A lot of bakeries took shortcuts with laminated dough, often ordering it from suppliers because it's so tricky to get right, not to mention time-consuming. Laminated dough is the key to the most delicious pastries, like croissants, Danish, and every treat made with puff pastry. Lamination is essentially a process in which a slab of chilled butter is flattened, encased in a sweetened yeast dough envelope, rolled flat, and folded into a tri-fold rectangular shape. The dough is then chilled to stiffen the butter, and then rolled out again, where it's folded in a tri-fold rectangle once again. This process continues until the required layers are achieved. When I was in my private cooking class learning baking from Jeffery, he had told me that a proper Danish dough should have 243 buttered layers. That was meant to intimidate me, until I, being the number-cruncher that I am, pointed out that 243 is divisible by three, or three to the fifth power, which would require repeating the tri-fold process five times. He had kissed me for that. I quickly expunged the memory and focused on Dylan's Danish. One look and I knew she had worked hard on the multilayered, flaky, butter-laminated sweet dough.

Kennedy returned the carton of eggs to the fridge, poured another cup of coffee, and picked up the plate of bacon. "Executive decision. We're having bacon and Dilly's cherry Danish for breakfast."

"Dear heavens, what would my mother think?" I teased.

"Ellie already knows you're crazy, darling. You moved here." Her grin was sarcastic. "This," she continued, waving her mug at the tray of Danish, "is wantonly reckless. When you talk to her today, and you should," she reminded, "don't mention the Danish."

I hadn't talked with my parents since Mia's murder. I didn't want to frighten them, and I wasn't in the mood to field the load of questions I knew they'd ask. Instead, I put the impending phone call on my mental back burner and picked up a Danish. To my delight, it tasted even better than it looked. The dough itself practically melted in my mouth. Combined with the slightly tart cherry filling and sweet icing, it was like heaven. It would definitely be a star at the Beacon Bakeshop . . . if we were ever able to open our doors again.

"Amazing," I proclaimed, swallowing the last bite and getting up from the table. "Really, I'd love nothing more than to stay here all morning and chat with you two, but I have to find Wellington. Then I'm heading over to the real estate office."

Dylan, caressing her coffee mug, suddenly looked up. A troubled look crossed her face. "You're not thinking of selling the place, are you?"

"No. Betty called last night and asked me to meet her there this morning. She sounded pretty freaked out about something."

Kennedy grinned. "I'd be pretty freaked out too . . . if I was shagging a man who probed dead people for a living."

Dylan, after choking on a bite of Danish, stared at her. "What the heck are you talking about?"

"Betty's dating a man named Bob Riggles. He's the medical examiner. Isn't that just scandalous?"

"We don't know that they're dating." I shot Kennedy a cautioning look and picked up another Danish. "And don't spread any rumors. What we do know," I said, turning to Dylan, "is that it now looks as if the cyanide that killed Mia Long wasn't in one of my donuts. It was found in the coffee she drank."

Dylan covered her mouth. "Oh my God," she breathed, her troubled eyes shooting between Kennedy and me. "Rory was making the coffee. Do you think . . . ?"

"Oh, Dilly, we don't know what to think." Kennedy, serenely puzzled, shrugged with palms pointing skyward. "He could have easily done it, but the question is, why would he?"

Still shocked by the news, she shrugged. "If it's any consolation, I still think it's the boyfriend, or one of those snooty women."

"We can sit here and speculate all day." I plucked two pieces of bacon off the plate as I spoke. "But we shouldn't. I'll be back in a few minutes," I told them, and left the lighthouse. They knew that I was going to find my dog. What they didn't realize, and I did, was that my dog had gone for his morning visit to 'get fish' at Rory Campbell's cabin.

CHAPTER 30

"I owe you an apology," I said to the angry, albeit hot-looking man filling the doorway. "We found out the cyanide had been delivered through the coffee and jumped to the obvious conclusion. We were at the Moose trying to gather information on you. It was a shabby thing to do. My only excuse is that we were scared, and curious, and hungry. We thought that maybe you and Karen had dated."

"Jesus . . . H . . . Christ!" he slowly expostulated, his crystal-blue eyes boring into mine like a laser. Wellington picked that moment to shove his big, fluffy head around Rory's hip. He opened his mouth and stared at me too. "That has got to be the most stupidly honest thing I've ever heard. And *blagh!*" Rory spat with distaste. "How could you think Karen and I dated? She's a decade and a half older, not to mention married with three kids."

"Well, I didn't know that until last night, did I?" I held up the cherry Danish Dylan had made. "I've brought you a peace offering. The burnt bacon is for my dog. May I come in?"

Preparing for an uncomfortable conversation, I took a seat while Rory plated his Danish and poured two mugs of coffee. I took the one closest to me, grasped it with both hands, and was determined to be frank.

"Look, I'm not proud of suspecting you of murder. You've shown Welly and me nothing but kindness since we've arrived at the lighthouse, but I don't know much about you other than your passion for hunting, fried perch, and writing. You were making the coffee at my bakeshop; the medical examiner has stated that the cyanide was delivered through the coffee, not a donut as originally thought. You also know a lot about the stuff. You were the one who escorted Mia to the lawn when she started fake-choking. Only now we know that it might not have been fake after all. Do you see where I might be suspicious?"

Clenching his jaw, he tilted his head. "I appreciate your honesty, Bakewell, but your lack of perspective is astounding. All the same, it must have taken courage to come knocking on my door, especially since you think me capable of murdering a woman I've never met."

"You had my dog. You still hang your morning catch on your deck, knowing he can't resist. You knew I'd come here eventually."

"I tried to send him home, but he likes it here. I don't blame him. I think Kennedy scares him. Did it ever occur to you that she has a more logical connection to the victim than I do?"

"Of course. And Wellington loves Kennedy. She may

be a handful at times, but she's not a murderer. She doesn't know a thing about cyanide, nor was she near the coffee, whereas you know a lot about killing, being in the military, and you were making the coffee."

I'd never seen Rory go from calm to angry so fast. As if flipping a switch, his dark-lashed eyes narrowed to mere slits of icy blue as he growled, "*You* were desperate for a barista! *You* came knocking on *my* door in the middle of the night! I am not a barista. I can barely brew a pot of drinkable coffee, but I said yes. And do you want to know why? Not to poison a stranger, for God's sake, but because I admire you. I admire what you've done. I admire the fact that you left a comfortable, lucrative career to follow a dream that led you to an abandoned lighthouse on the shores of Lake Michigan. I admire your hard work and your awesome dog. In short, Bakewell, I said yes because I wanted to see you succeed. Crazy as it sounds, I wanted to support what you've worked so hard to create. I jumped behind the counter and did my best, and now you have the gall—no, the audacity—to think that I intentionally poisoned some crazy woman creating a scene? Did it escape your notice that I was the one who tried to save her life by administering CPR?" His face had gone red as he sucked in air with the intensity of an overweight runner.

He was angry, and flustered, and utterly adorable. The fact that he admitted to admiring me sent a wave of pure tingling happiness throughout my body. This handsome, hunky, dream of a man admired me, possibly even liked me, and yet my head was screaming a warning at my careening heart. Rory was kind, confident, and full of integrity, and yet I'd been fooled by men before. Therefore, very cautiously, I voiced my last concern.

"It hadn't escaped my notice that you tried to save Mia. But for a man who knows so much about cyanide, I do find it odd that you didn't detect the smell of it on her breath. Officer Tuck told me how victims of cyanide poisoning give off a very distinctive scent, and yet you said nothing."

His jaw dropped as he stared at me in disbelief. The silence, like his troubled look, stretched out a beat too long. My heart sank, realizing I had called his bluff. I should head for the door, I thought, and covertly reached for Wellington under the table. Unfortunately, my dog was sitting at Rory's feet.

"Come, Welly," I said and stood. I took a step from the table.

That move caused Rory to jump to his feet as well.

My heart exploded with fear. "I . . . I have to go—"

"Oh, for Christ's sake, Lindsey! Sit back down!"

"No. Gotta go." I sprinted for the door. Welly, thinking it some great game, sprang from under the table and bounded after me. So did Rory. I was just about to reach for the handle when Wellington jumped on me, causing me to stumble. I was about to hit the floor when a strong grip on my arm pulled me back on my feet. That's when I realized I was standing between Rory Campbell and the solid wood of the door.

He started to say something but fell on top of me instead.

"Wellington, stop!" he cried, his hard chest heaving against mine. I might have thought it erotic if he wasn't a murderer and Wellington wasn't trying to thrust his giant head between us for a salvo of excited puppy kisses. The untimely tongue had just nailed Rory on the cheek.

Rory offered another stern command and Welly stood down, yet Rory hadn't made a move to step away from me. "Lindsey, my God! Will you please listen to me? I am not a murderer. I mean, I have killed, but only bad people, and only in the name of my country. I don't poison innocent women."

"Was she a spy?" I asked, gasping for breath.

"What? No!" He looked closely into my eyes. Wellington, I noticed, had settled down and was now lying on the floor with his head between his paws. "And the reason I didn't detect the cyanide on her breath was because I can't. If you would have let me explain—instead of accusing me of covering up a murder before running for the door—I was about to tell you that not everyone has the gene necessary to detect cyanide on the breath. In fact, upwards of twenty-five percent of the population doesn't have it, including me. And even if I did, the almond odor could be masked by other smells . . . like the donut she was chewing before she collapsed. For the last time, Lindsey Bakewell, I did not poison Mia Long!"

"Do you swear it?" I asked, staring back at him.

"I do," he uttered, and further convinced me of it by bringing his lips to mine.

Rory Campbell kissed me with more passion than Jeffery Plank ever had. It was compulsive, erotic, and highly intoxicating. Time stood still, sandwiched between the door and Rory, kissing him back with a welling of need that surprised even me. I could have stayed like that all day, and he could have too, until a pestering thought finally broke through my sex-driven mind. With my hand firmly planted on Rory's chest, I tried to catch my breath.

Rory grinned. "I knew you were going to be trouble when you moved next door, Bakewell. Never thought you'd accuse me of murder, but at this very moment I don't even mind. My bedroom's over there." He pointed to a door down the hall. "I'd take you right here, but your dog is staring at us."

I'd never been with a man so utterly male and so utterly sexy as Rory Campbell. I'd been thinking of ways to seduce him ever since moving next door, but could never quite pin him down. And, quite frankly, I'd been too exhausted to try. Now, however, he was inviting me to his bedroom. I should have turned off my mind and gone with it—been more spontaneous, like Kennedy. But I couldn't. I was the responsible one.

He'd brought his lips over mine once again, ready to seal the deal, when I uttered, "Betty."

He didn't hear me. His passion had been ignited. He was a man on a mission, and it appeared as if nothing could deter him. He scooped me up in his arms and took a few steps toward that mysterious door at the end of the hallway. I repeated the name a little louder. "Betty Vanhoosen!"

Like nails on a chalkboard, the name had an instant effect. He stumbled, cursed, and nearly dropped me. "I'm sorry," he apologized, regaining his grip on me. "I just thought you said—"

"Betty Vanhoosen."

"Christ!" he uttered, and set me on my feet. "Is that your safe word? Am I moving too fast for you? I have to be honest. That name's a real passion deflator for me."

"I'm sorry. And please don't take this the wrong way. You're a magnificent kisser, but I just remembered something very important. Betty called me in the middle of the night. She woke me out of a dead sleep, but I could tell she was very frightened by something. She asked me to meet her at her office this morning. I've been so busy eating Danish and suspecting the worst of you when I should have been thinking of Betty. What if she's in trouble? I'm afraid I'm going to have to take a rain check on . . . the bedroom tour." I offered a sympathetic smile. "It might also be a good idea if we had a few more dates before we cross that bridge. A moment ago, I thought you capable of poisoning a woman with cyanide."

"And yet you were quick to forgive me," he added, taking my hand. "I'm coming with you. You can't drop a name like Betty Vanhoosen and expect me to sit at home twiddling my thumbs."

It was agreed that Welly would stay at Rory's cabin. We were just about to leave when Kennedy strolled across the deck carrying my rolling pin.

"Thank heavens," she cried, the moment Rory and I came out the door. "I had a feeling you were going to sneak over here. 'I'm going to get Wellington,'" she mocked and rolled her eyes. "You sure were taking your sweet time. The way you were dawdling I thought he might have gotten to you as well." She held Rory in a hooded gaze while gripping the rolling pin in the middle and wiggling it like an unhinged teeter-totter. Kennedy, a stranger in her own kitchen let alone mine, had no idea how to hold a rolling pin, making the move far more comical than menacing.

"He did . . . get to me," I told her, linking my arm through Rory's. "But not in the way you think. I'm soundly convinced he's innocent."

"Really? And may I remind you that money is your forte, not men?"

"Like your habitual gambler, I've had a string of bad luck. I'm not willing to retire the dice just yet. Now, put down that rolling pin. We're off to see Betty."

"Oh, I'm not putting this thing down, darlings. But I am coming with you."

CHAPTER 31

"Betty," I said, walking into the vast, brightly colored office. She'd been sitting at her desk, staring out the picture window behind her. She turned at the sound of my voice and frowned.

"I . . . I thought you'd come alone." Betty had always been brightly attired and pleasantly cheerful. Whatever had frightened her had not only taken the joy from her voice but had caused her to wear a dull, unflattering brown dress as well. Brown clearly wasn't her color. Maybe she thought it made her blend in, like the muddy-brown pelt of a deer in the autumn forest. Only, in her colorful office it had the opposite effect.

"I'm sorry," I said, continuing into the room with my friends. "But you didn't specify that when we talked."

And just like that dull-pelted deer caught foraging in a

rose garden, she turned her wide, unblinking gaze on Kennedy and Rory. At last she relented. "No? Well, maybe not. It doesn't much matter now. Come in, all of you, and shut the door. Last night I had a revelation, and I haven't slept since."

After we all took a seat around Betty's desk, she confided, "You were all at dinner last night, so I needn't tell you what a mess I made of it with Bob, blurting such sensitive information like that. He confided in me, and I blew it. My only excuse is that I was excited to have that little bit of information. I was trying to impress you all when, in fact, I really embarrassed Bob and likely made an enemy out of you, Rory. I told you all the source of the poisoning. Of course, you were making the coffee." She looked at Rory.

"True," he replied with a nod. "But why on earth would I poison one of Lindsey's customers?"

Her face was fraught with worry as she answered, "Well, that was the question that bothered me last night. After Bob dropped me off at home without even so much as a good-night kiss, I was trying to come up with a good reason as to why you might slip poison into that annoying woman's coffee. I was going through that terrible day in my head, trying to remember the details, when I suddenly remembered something that made my blood curdle."

We were all waiting for what that was when Kennedy leaned in, prompting, "And what was that, darling?"

Betty looked at us, her face blanching as her hands began to tremble. "The cup of coffee that killed that woman came from my hand."

Kennedy, without giving that statement deeper thought, chirped, "You poisoned Mia?"

"No," I corrected as the confusion of that day swirled in my head. "What she's saying, I think, is that Mia grabbed the cup of coffee out of her hand."

"Are you sure you're remembering it correctly?" Rory asked, concern darkening his face.

"Oh, I'm darn sure, my dears. I had come to the bake-shop with half the business owners of this town. We'd all been so excited to welcome your lighthouse bakery to Beacon Harbor. It's been years since we've had a real bakery here, and who would have thought the old light-house would ever get a second chance to shine. Sure, the light has gone out, but you've breathed new life into the old place. And we were so excited to try your baked goods. The girls behind the counter were working hard to get our donut orders correct. We had quite a large coffee order as well, which you were gallantly attempting to fill." She paused to smile at the man sitting across from her.

"That was about the time Mia came in with her posse," I added, recalling my shock at the sight of her.

"Yes," Betty said. "Fiona Dickel and her lot chose that moment to storm the counter as well. There was such a press of bodies reaching for the counter that it was hard to tell exactly what was happening. And you lot were all working your tails off. I remember that you, Lindsey, were helping Rory fill the coffee orders. Wendy, Eliza-beth, and Dylan were helping as well. I don't remember which one of you handed me my coffee, but I do remem-ber Fiona bumping into me. At one point she even reached over my shoulder to knock one of the drinks off the counter, splattering the lot of us. There was so much shoving and jostling. That Mia woman was making a ter-rible scene, drawing our attention. Then she grabbed the latte out of my hand—MY HAND! Don't you see? That woman wasn't the target. I was!"

"Oh my. . . ." I brought a hand over my gaping mouth. Somehow, until that very moment, I had never considered that Mia might not have been the target—that her death might have been an unfortunate accident. The thought sent a chill up my spine.

Rory, obviously never considering this either, stared at Betty in disbelief. He was also the first to ask, "But . . . who would want you dead?"

"Probably not you," she said, patting his hand. "Out of all the people behind the counter that day, you're the person I know the least, so naturally thoughts of you and a possible motive took up a good deal of my night. But then I came to the obvious conclusion. I gave you the deal of the century on that lakefront log home. Of course, you came at the right time, but I advised the previous owners to accept your lowball offer."

Rory, sneaking a covert sideways glance my way, countered, "It wasn't that low."

Betty ignored him. "I also gave you the heads-up on your newest neighbor."

For a moment the old Betty was back, flashing a coy smile as she attempted a wink. It came as no surprise that she had talked me up before I moved in. Betty, although a habitual gossip, quite possibly fancied herself a match-maker as well. And because she had planted that seed, Rory had plucked up the nerve to come barging through my kitchen door, albeit with a string of half-eaten fish. Unless Rory was hiding a dark secret, which I highly doubted, Betty had nothing to fear from him.

"There's no way on earth I'd poison you either," I added.

"I know that, dear. And Kennedy, you're off the hook as well. You weren't even behind the counter, but you were trying to warn us."

"I was trying to warn Lindsey that her former wanker of a fiancé and his obnoxious lover had come to the bakeshop. I should have told her sooner."

"Yes, but what's done is done." Betty sat back in her chair and exhaled loudly. "I'm afraid that leaves Dylan, Elizabeth, and Wendy."

"You can't possibly think one of them did it?" They were my employees and I was slightly horrified that she'd even consider them. But as quickly as I voiced my concern, Betty put me at my ease.

"I'm only mentioning them because they were behind the counter with you and Rory. Elizabeth and Wendy have just graduated from high school. I've known them since they were babies and would never have recommended them if I thought they were trouble, which they're not. Sweet girls and good students too. They're also hardworking."

"I agree. You also recommended Dylan, which as you know I'm eternally grateful for. I know she was a bit of a wild child in her youth, but surely you don't suspect her of tampering with your coffee?"

Betty shook her head. "No. Whatever demons that young lady has, she's committed to slaying them. We had a talk the other day. I wanted to see how Dylan was getting along. She told me how grateful she was to be working at your bakery. She loves the Beacon Bakeshop. I can honestly say that although you've just opened it's changed her life for the better." Here she paused as a wave of anger swept through her. "No, I'm afraid there is only one person who wants me dead, and her name is Fiona Dickel."

Although the name came as no surprise, what was surprising were the lengths Fiona had gone to in order to harass Betty. It all began when Betty, acting for the city, had the nerve to put the old crumbling lighthouse up for sale.

"I couldn't sleep last night I was so worked up by my discovery. I was going to call Sergeant Murdock, but I felt silly. I took a shower instead, got dressed, and came here."

"What time was that?" Rory asked.

"Two in the morning. That's why I didn't call the sergeant. Didn't want to wake her."

"But you were okay with waking me?" I cast her a probing look. "You called me at three in the morning, remember?"

"Your light was on, dear. I'd been going through my file of hate mail sent by Fiona and her smelly gang, when I saw the Oberland Dairy truck pull up at your back door. Dairymen are up early, but so are bakers. I assumed you were working in the kitchen."

"No," I said, thinking about that. "I was sound asleep when you called. Wait. That's not quite right. I awoke because Wellington was barking at something outside. You had called at the same time. I just assumed he got spooked by the phone ringing in the middle of the night."

"But somebody was already in the kitchen," Betty said. "The light was on."

"That was Dilly," Kennedy replied. "She was making Danish while Lindsey and I slept. And it was just about the most delicious thing I've eaten."

"It was," I agreed. "After learning that the police had declared the Beacon Bakeshop a crime scene, Dylan was concerned about her finances while we were closed. I told her she could continue her baking schedule as usual. She's also in charge of early deliveries."

"Either that," Betty quipped, "or she's having an affair with the Oberland Dairyman. Anyhow, dear, sorry I woke you up, but the revelation was shocking. Fiona has been in a private war with me for months, making death threats. I'd never taken them seriously until last night. And, to make matters worse, she stormed into my office a short while ago—just before you three arrived."

This was a shocker. "What did she want?"

Betty shook her head. "She made the usual threats, only this time she's determined to shut me down with a lawsuit, one that will jeopardize my Realtor's license. And just to be obnoxious about it, she stole my lunch. Hope she chokes on it too, the nasty witch."

"Have you called the police?" Rory asked.

Betty shook her head. "It was only lunch."

Rory stared at her a second too long, then closed his eyes while shaking his head. "No," he said, opening them again. "About Fiona's threats and the fact that you were holding the coffee laced with cyanide before it was ripped out of your hands by Mia Long."

"Oh that. Not yet. I wanted to tell Lindsey first. It's her bakeshop, after all." Betty leaned across her desk and took both my hands in hers. "I wanted you to know, dear, that the rude little woman's death had nothing to do with you. Fiona Dickel wanted to shut you down as well, and she saw her chance. However, fate intervened." After speaking these words, Betty looked up at her ceiling and crossed herself.

"It scares me to death to think that had I taken one sip of that latte I'd be dead. It would be my body on that dissecting table under Bob's knife and not that woman's!

I'm so angry I could march over to Fiona's house and strangle her myself."

"That's not a good idea." Rory left his chair and walked over to Betty. Resting a hand on her shoulder, he said, "You've suffered enough. Go home and get some rest, Betty. I think it's best if Lindsey calls Sergeant Murdock with this news. She'll want to speak with you as well."

Betty nodded, promising she'd go home, lock the doors, and take a nap.

The moment we were outside I took out my phone.

"What are you doing?" Rory asked.

"Calling the police. You said I should be the one to tell them the news."

He took the phone from my hand and ended the call. "Not yet. I'd like to have a word with Fiona Dickel first."

I was about to question that move when Kennedy chimed in, "That's the best idea you've had all day, Rory darling. I have the rolling pin; you have the muscle. Her sheer hatred of Lindsey should inspire a vitriolic tirade as well as a confession."

"Perfect," I said, shaking my head at them. "But if we're going to confront a deranged woman, shouldn't we first find out where she lives?"

"Already got it," Rory informed us as we headed for his truck. "It was printed on Betty's folder of hate mail. And since I have experience with hostiles, I'm going to insist that I do the talking."

Kennedy linked her arm through his, and smiled. "We'll see about that."

CHAPTER 32

Fiona lived a mile outside of town in a pricey development known as Pine Bluff Estates. Although far from the lakeshore, many of the homes in the neighborhood had a spectacular view of Lake Michigan from atop the bluff after which the development was named. Admittedly, I was shocked when Rory turned in the main entrance to the neighborhood and continued along the winding road, passing one executive home after another. Fiona hadn't struck me as the type of woman who'd buy in to such luxury, knowing the hefty environmental impact the neighborhood had cost to the surrounding forest. She struck me as more of the artsy type. I had pictured her living in one of the many charming midcentury cottages that made up the neighborhoods behind the town—the kind with overflowing flower boxes beneath the windows and hand-crafted garden sculptures frolicking amongst the well-maintained gardens.

The house Rory pulled up to wasn't even close to my vision. It was a large, two-story, brick-faced dwelling with a roof that sprouted off in at least six different angles and pitches. There were no gardens to speak of, and the lack of shrubbery—nay, landscaping—gave the large home a severe, almost institutional look. The only indication that Fiona lived there at all came from all the protest signs sprouting from the patchy lawn. There were dozens of them, ranging the gamut from local government officials she didn't like, to various climate and environmental causes, to two on gun control, and five dedicated to her personal pet project, the destruction of my lighthouse bakery. The one that chilled me to the bone, however, was a poster with Betty's face on it and the words: *This Realtor Sells Landmarks for Profit!* Thankfully, Fiona's house sat at the end of the road.

"Her car's here," Rory noted, parking his truck behind the moss-green Subaru.

"She better be, too," I said, getting my game face on.

"Looks like the house of a nutter," Kennedy added, ignoring our remarks while removing her sunglasses. "She's taken the time to plant protest signs, but they'll never grow bushy enough to block out that atrocity." She waved them at the house. "Money without taste is the real crime here."

"And possibly murder," I reminded her, pulling her up the steps with me. The knowledge that this woman could have tried to poison Betty Vanhoosen and, by sheer mistake, killed Mia Long instead inspired me to take action. I wanted answers, and Fiona Dickel was going to provide them.

What Fiona's home lacked in shrubbery, it more than made up for in home security. Two surveillance cameras sat under the eaves on each corner of the house along with floodlights. A video monitoring system guarded the door, which Rory addressed by pressing the button. It was the type of system that not only chimed through the house but also alerted a designated cell phone to the fact that someone was at the front door. Even if Fiona wasn't home, she'd still have the option to address us. The silence was unnerving.

"Do you think she's ignoring us on purpose?" I asked.

Rory shrugged and tried again, this time talking into the speaker on the security system. "Fiona, this is Rory Campbell. We'd like to discuss an important matter with you. Please open the door."

"*Please open the door*," Kennedy mocked in her proper English accent. "Like that's going to work. All the woman can see is your large, muscular frame and well-defined pecs. You're scaring her with your alpha male attitude. Let me take a crack at it." Kennedy, holding the rolling pin behind her back, nudged him aside and stood before the camera. She rang the bell and announced, "Ms. Dickel, Lilian Finch here from the global initiative on wildlife preservation and shrubbery protection act. Did you know that by planting just two small pieces of shrubbery near your house you could help feed the Borneo pygmy elephant for one month? I'd love the opportunity to show you how you can help save this endangered animal."

Rory, growing used to Kennedy's ways, was in danger of erupting with a case of the giggles. Apparently, the great hunter had never heard of the Borneo pygmy elephant and thought she had made it up.

"What?" she hiss-whispered. "They're *adorable*. If Fiona's home, she'll open that door."

But the door never opened. That's when Rory took matters into his own hands. He wasn't about to leave without speaking to Fiona. "I'm going to go around back and see if I can't find a point of entry."

"Why don't we try the door first?" Kennedy said.

"Right. With all this security she's going to leave her front door open? I don't think so."

Kennedy, unable to resist the urge, reached forward and grabbed the handle. To everyone's surprise, the door clicked open.

"Okay," I uttered, stepping into the stark, cavernous home behind Rory. "Now I'm creeped out."

"It's even worse than I thought," Kennedy said, coming beside me. "Ocher walls, funeral parlor furniture, plastic fruit in wooden bowls, it's as if she just stopped caring."

"Hush," I whispered, feeling strange for having entered the home of another without permission. "Fiona," I then called out, hoping for an answer.

It was agreed that Rory would take the upstairs while Kennedy and I split up and searched the main floor. The house was eerily silent. Although there was plenty of light streaming through the picture windows at the back, there was a brightness coming from what I thought might be the kitchen. As Kennedy headed for the great room and the deck, I walked through the formal dining room, noting that the décor wasn't as bad as Kennedy made it out to be. Stressful situations always brought out the snark in her. It was also part of her charm.

Although Fiona's style was eclectic, she had an undeniable passion for nature. Gracing her dining room wall was a stunning painting of the Sleeping Bear Dunes National Lakeshore, a pristine sixty-five-mile stretch of Lake Michigan guarded by towering dune-topped headlands that rose to over four hundred feet above the lake. The old Beacon Point Lighthouse I had purchased sat on the southern end of the protected lakeshore. The lighthouse had been built to help guard the dangerous passage between the mainland and the Manitou Islands. What was once a thriving farm community and timber shipping port was now the haven of naturalists and tourists. And I had bought a part of that history, restored it, and had turned it into a bakeshop café. If I was an idealistic environmentalist like Fiona, I might have hated me too. But the reality of the situation was quite different. It was either my lighthouse bakery or high-end vacation condos. The sad fact was that thanks to satellites and the global positioning system, lighthouses were a relic of the past.

With this disheartening thought, I turned the corner and entered the kitchen.

And then I screamed.

CHAPTER 33

Sirens blazed in the distance, getting ever closer as Rory knelt beside the body. I had gotten the shock of my life when I entered the kitchen and saw Fiona sprawled face down on the floor in a puddle of dark liquid, a mangled ham and Havarti sandwich clutched in her cold hand. There was no point in Rory even attempting CPR. Fiona had no pulse, and it was hard to tell how long she had been lying there, robbed of her life and dignity in soiled plaid shorts and tie-dyed tee.

"This is very bad," Kennedy remarked for the second time. Her hand waved in front of her face in agitated disgust. "And *EWOOOO!* Who wears plaid with tie-dye? Who jams their hairy legs into tube socks before jamming those into clunky Birkenstock sandals? It's so obvious what happened here. Bad fashion choices killed her."

"Are you kidding me?" Genuine anger seized Rory's face as he stood up from the body. "A woman is dead in her own kitchen, lying in a puddle of soda while holding a sandwich, and you think she was murdered because her clothes don't match?"

"She's not serious," I said, gently touching his arm while flashing Kennedy a cautionary look. "And we don't know that she was murdered."

Discovering the body had put us all on edge, yet clearly some of us were handling the situation better than others. Rory, for instance, had taken charge the moment he heard me scream. I was a trembling, blubbering mess, while Kennedy had chosen cattiness and delusion as her coping mechanisms. It might have been easier to believe that bad fashion choices had been Fiona's demise rather than acknowledging the truth . . . which was that another woman was dead and no amount of cattiness or quivering was going to bring her back.

"Are you sure calling the police was the right move?" I looked at Rory, noting that the sirens were close by. "What if they think we did this?"

"We couldn't leave her, Lindsey. But you're right. The three of us standing around the body of the one woman in Beacon Harbor who vocally wanted to shut you down, that's going to raise suspicion."

"But look at . . . look at the evidence." With my head averted, I waved at the splatter of sodden sandwich bits floating in the remains of the spilled drink. "She could have choked on the sandwich, or had a heart attack."

"Or she could have been poisoned, like Mia Long was. We won't know for sure until Doc Riggles performs an autopsy, which he's going to have to do." He then pointed to the white bakery bag on the counter. "And I'll bet my black truck on the fact that this was the lunch she took from Betty's office."

"You think someone poisoned that lunch—Betty's lunch?" The thought sent a shiver up my spine.

"Look, it's a long shot, but we could check." I didn't like the look on his face as he said this.

"How are we supposed to do that?" Kennedy snapped as wrinkles of disgust marred her lovely face. "If you want us to scoop up all those bits of chewed food, count me out. Also, I don't think the police will take too kindly if we tamper with the evidence."

"We're not going to touch a thing. You both know that I can't detect the smell of cyanide, but maybe one of you can. There are three of us, which means that the odds of one of us being able to detect cyanide on the breath are pretty good. If neither one of you can smell the bitter almond scent, then there's a good chance Fiona wasn't poisoned. Now, who wants to go first?"

There wasn't much time, and neither Kennedy nor I was excited by the prospect of smelling the mouth of a dead person. Rory, unafraid of corpses and having no such qualms himself, kneeled near the body, getting ready with his end of the bargain. He was going to tilt Fiona enough to expose her mouth.

Due to the blaring sirens, I could tell that the emergency vehicles had arrived. There wasn't much time. Kennedy, being the opportunistic friend she was, shoved me forward. "You go first."

"All right," I said, trying to fight back the urge to vomit as I gingerly got into position. It was nearly impossible not to look at Fiona's bluish face, or step in the puddle of soda.

On Rory's cue, he rolled the body while I sniffed

Fiona's mouth. It hit me like skunk spray on a dewy lawn. "Sour almonds! Sour almonds!" I cried, then I lost my cookies on the floor beside her.

We had no sooner jumped back to the safety of the kitchen island when Sergeant Murdock appeared with Officer Cutie Pie McAllister fast on her heels. Rory had reported the body, but the sight of Kennedy and me standing beside him in the kitchen caused both to suffer a swift bout of shock. While Tuck stared at me in speechless discomfort, Murdock schooled her emotions like a champ and focused instead on the body on the floor.

"Well, well, well," she said very softly, squatting beside Fiona Dickel. "What on earth happened here, do you suppose?" It was a rhetorical question, for as soon as she said this, she brushed aside a lock of long red hair from Fiona's neck and checked for a pulse.

"She doesn't have a pulse," Rory informed her. "We've already checked. And the vomit's not hers."

"Mine, I'm afraid." I raised my hand like a schoolgirl. Why, in God's name, did I feel compelled to do that? Vomiting was nothing to be proud of, and scary Sergeant Murdock was not amused. "I'm, ahh, not used to dead people."

A look of slight terror crossed Tuck's face as his boss made her way toward me. "And that raises the question, what were you three doing here, Ms. Bakewell? Surely you and Ms. Dickel were not friends."

"No," I agreed. "We came to talk with her. We saw that her car was here and rang the bell several times, but she never answered. We were going to leave when we decided to try the door. It was unlocked."

"And you just walked in?"

I nodded. Murdock's cold stare, as frightening as the face of a dead woman, induced me to spill the beans as well. Much to the surprise of Rory and Kennedy, I blurted, "She had threatened Betty Vanhoosen with a lawsuit for selling me the old Beacon Harbor Lighthouse. We also had reason to believe Fiona might have been the one who put the cyanide in the latte Mia Long drank. Betty told us—right before we came here—that Mia had taken the latte out of her hand. *Betty Vanhoosen* was holding the cup laced with cyanide, and she had a suspicion that Fiona had slipped her the dose of poison when she wasn't looking. Betty had forgotten about that, but suddenly remembered it in the middle of the night."

Both officers were soaking all this in when the EMTs arrived. Sergeant Murdock held them off and called in the crime scene unit instead. The moment she was finished, she turned to me. "For your own safety, Ms. Bakewell, if you have any information regarding the death of Mia Long, call the police and report it. You are not a professional. You should not be investigating this crime. Now, aside from the vomit, has anything else in this kitchen crime scene been compromised?"

"No," Rory answered for me. "We were all searching different parts of the house. Lindsey discovered the body. The moment she did, we called nine-one-one."

Murdock gave a curt nod. "Ms. Bakewell and Ms. Kapoor, I know. I don't believe we've met."

"Rory Campbell." He thrust out his hand. Murdock hesitated before she shook it.

"Ah, yes. You were also at the Beacon Bakeshop the day Mia Long was murdered. You spoke to Officer McAllister here. You were the one performing CPR on

Ms. Long, is that correct?" Rory nodded. "Very well. I'm going to ask you three to return to the lighthouse. Once there, I need you to call in every one of your employees who was working Friday morning when Mia Long was murdered. I think you'll appreciate that there is some new information on the case. The death of Fiona Dickel has complicated things, especially since there is suspicion of foul play. Officer McAllister will be around shortly to take new statements from each of you."

Fiona's kitchen was getting crowded with all the first responders flocking to the scene. Tuck was about to escort us out when Murdock, with a roll of yellow tape in hand, turned.

"One more thing. Did you come here with the intent of intimidating Fiona to withdraw the lawsuit?"

"No," I answered. "We came here because Fiona had stolen Betty's lunch."

"What?" For the first time Sergeant Murdock broke character. "Are you telling me the sandwich in Fiona's hand came from Betty's office?" Murdock locked eyes with Officer Tuck.

"We don't know that for sure," Rory answered. "But we suspect the white bakery bag on the counter was Betty's lunch. Betty told us that after Fiona threatened her with a lawsuit, she took the lunch off her desk and stormed out of her office."

"Well now," Sergeant Murdock breathed and shook her head, releasing several wispy strands of blond hair as she did so. "If that doesn't just open a whole new can of worms."

CHAPTER 34

"We came as soon as we could," Elizabeth said, walking through the lighthouse door with Wendy.

"We were having a cookout at my house," Wendy offered. "Mostly family. Dad's grilling, but some of our high school friends were there as well. We're minor celebrities, you know, having worked at a bakeshop where somebody's died."

Although Wendy was openly proud of this fact, my insides were cringing at the thought. "I'm truly sorry about all that," I said, ushering them into the parlor. Rory was already there, sitting in the armchair while sharing one of the armrests with Wellington's giant head. He was petting my dog with one hand while sipping a scotch on the rocks with the other. It had been a rough afternoon.

After giving my attention-loving pup a thorough round of hugs and smooches, the girls took a seat on the couch.

I took their drink orders and went to the kitchen, where Kennedy was helping me with the Margherita pizzas.

There was no doubt in my mind that when Officer Tuck arrived, there was going to be a stressful round of questioning. After summoning my three employees, I got to work on the nerve-soothing snack that had never failed me, namely the Margherita pizza. In my former life, after a tough week in the financial district, Kennedy and I would meet at our favorite pizzeria and order the classic pie that consisted of tomato sauce, soft mozzarella, and fresh basil on a chewy, perfectly fire-baked crust. They weren't too hard to make at home either. Forgoing a homemade pizza dough due to time restrictions, I had pulled out two cans of the refrigerated kind, rolled them out thin, and covered each with a layer of fresh tomato sauce, a drizzle of olive oil, fresh basil leaves, and fresh slices of soft mozzarella cheese. Once the oven was hot enough, I placed the pizzas on a baking stone and baked each one until the mozzarella was bubbly and the crust a nice golden brown. The first one had just come out of the oven and smelled divine. Kennedy was slicing it up with the pizza cutter while I poured the girls a tall glass of raspberry lemonade. We were still waiting for Dylan, who'd been out on the lake on her cousin's boat.

Driving from Fiona's house back to the lighthouse in Rory's truck, we had talked about the unsettling fact that I had detected the telltale sign of cyanide on Fiona's breath. It was the sharp scent of bitter almonds, only I had said sour almonds, because my stomach had been heaving with disgust. But the fact remained that the three of us believed Fiona had been poisoned and that poison could have only come from one place, the lunch Fiona had taken from Betty's office.

There were two troublesome scenarios to consider, knowing that. If the lunch had been tampered with, either someone who was not Fiona was still trying to poison Betty, or Betty had set a lethal trap for Fiona, perhaps even offering her the lunch. I liked Betty. It was hard for me to even consider her a murder suspect, but the fact was, Betty had been in the thick of things in my bakeshop. She and Fiona had been in a feud over the sale of the old Beacon Harbor Lighthouse long before I moved to Michigan. Betty had called me to her office to tell me that Mia had grabbed the coffee out of her hand—the poisoned coffee—but what if that coffee had been meant for Fiona? It was distasteful, but we had to consider it.

Another thought was that maybe one of Fiona's fellow protesters was the culprit. Fiona was an annoying person on a good day. It wasn't a huge stretch of the imagination to entertain the possibility that she had pushed one of her followers too far.

On a similar note, Betty might have had other enemies in town as well. She was a friendly person, gregarious and well-connected. She was the type of woman who liked to know what people were up to. And she hadn't come to my bakery alone, either. Could one of her friends or one of the business owners in town have a secret vendetta against her? Anything was possible. And because it was, it was making matters worse. The list of suspects seemed to be growing, not shrinking.

The one thing Kennedy, Rory, and I all agreed on was that Wendy and Elizabeth would be treated gently. The poor girls had been scared enough after Mia's death, so much so that Wendy had passed out. Fiona's unexpected death would have to be delivered tactfully. The only reason they were called in at all was because Murdock believed one of them might remember something important.

"I've just eaten a brat, but there's always room for pizza, especially one that smells as delicious as that." Elizabeth, tall, thin, self-composed, and pretty, reached out and grabbed a slice.

"Well, I just ate a giant plate of nachos." Wendy, not as tall as Elizabeth but just as lovely, rolled her big blue eyes. "Don't like the way my dad grills brats. He cooks 'em until they're crispy, but I'm going to have one of those too, although I might remove the green stuff."

"Basil," I said. "Not a problem. The Margherita pizza is as versatile as it is delicious."

Making sure Wendy was firmly seated on the couch, we told the girls of Fiona's death, leaving them a chance to ask questions before Tuck arrived to take another round of new statements.

"Do you think she was poisoned?" Elizabeth asked, eyes wide and nervously wringing her hands.

"There's a strong chance that she was, but we won't know for sure until the medical examiner's report comes back."

"Oh my God! Oh my God! Fiona Dickel's dead?" Wendy was starting to hyperventilate. "My mom's gonna freak. They were in the garden club together."

"What have I missed?" Dylan came through the door with her boyfriend, Carl, and her cousin, Mike. "Did you say Fiona Dickel's dead?" She shot me a troubled look. Carl and Mike were stunned as well.

"As a doornail, I'm afraid," Kennedy replied. "Have some pizza."

We quickly brought everyone up to speed on the situation. "The police wanted us all here so that they can take new statements," I informed them. "It appears that Betty suddenly remembered that Mia Long had grabbed the latte out of her hand, the one that was laced with cyanide. Fiona was at Betty's office earlier today and took her lunch when she stormed out. There's a strong suspicion that the lunch Fiona stole from Betty was also poisoned. Mike, Carl, you're welcome to stay. You were also at the bakeshop when Mia collapsed. Officer Tuck will be arriving soon to take new statements, hoping one of us will remember something important."

"Look," Dylan said, a slice of pizza in one hand and an Oberon in the other. "I know everyone's thinking it, but I'm going to come right out and say it. Fiona Dickel was a total stark-raving witch. I can't believe it took someone this long to bump her off. Not only was she crazy, she steamrolled every committee she was on. And you of all people should know, Lindsey. She wanted to destroy your bakeshop nearly as much as that woman Mia."

Although Dylan was more indignant than shocked, Mike was clearly struggling with the thought of another death in Beacon Harbor. "Look, I don't even want to say it, but has anyone considered that Betty might have something to do with this? Betty's like a mother to this community. She knows everyone's business and tries to help whenever she can. She never had kids of her own. Beacon Harbor is her child, and she'd protect it at all costs. Maybe Fiona had pushed her too far." Mike shrugged and took a swig of beer.

"We've thought of that as well," Rory said. "But if she did poison the latte she was holding, why didn't she give it to Fiona? Why didn't she swat it out of Mia Long's hand the moment she stole it from her? Betty might be a busybody, but she's not a murderer."

"As far as we know," Dylan added, her brows drawn in concern. "But there is another possibility. Maybe Fiona's secret lover tried to poison her?"

"That woman had a lover?" Kennedy, looking a bit bored with the discussion, suddenly perked up. "Whoever he is, he must be a color-blind masochist."

"It's a woman, actually," Dylan informed us. "One of her lighthouse-hating protesters. Cover your ears, girls." She grinned at Elizabeth and Wendy while pretending to cover her own ears. "I know this because I saw them pawing one another on the dunes. She's two-timing her artist-boyfriend, Perry Brockman."

We were about to discuss what this could possibly mean when Welly bounded for the door. Officer Tuck had arrived.

"I'm sorry to put you all through this again," he said, removing his cap and raking a hand through his hair. "Unfortunately, as you know, there's been another death. What I'd like to know is which one of you handed Betty Vanhoosen her coffee drink?"

Rory set down his scotch. "Not me, but I made it. I was making a lot of lattes that morning. I think Betty and all her friends ordered some type of latte."

"It could have been either Dylan or me," I answered honestly. "There was a press of hands at the counter. It was a madhouse."

Dylan looked at the young officer. "I just remembered something. Fiona was reaching for the counter too. She knocked off one of the lattes. She could have just as easily slipped poison into one of the drinks. Customers put on their own lid, if they want one."

"Yes," Tuck nodded. "Betty had the same observation."

Wendy, perking up, said, "I remember that too. Elizabeth and I were plating donuts and coffee cake as fast as people could shout their orders at us. But I remember Fiona shoving Betty. She was shoving a lot of people."

Tuck nodded and scribbled in his notebook. The moment he looked up, the floodgates opened, and we told him everything else we'd discussed, giving him plenty of information on Fiona; her lover, Perry Brockman; her other lover, an unknown lady; as well as our suspicions regarding Betty.

Tuck closed his notebook. "I appreciate everyone's information. We'll be looking into all of these leads." Tuck, all business and no dimples, gave a curt nod and placed the notebook back in his shirt pocket. "I wish I had better news, but the sergeant insists the bakeshop remain closed another day or two, until we have a further look into the matter of Fiona's death."

"Wait!" Dylan said, looking visibly put out. "Are we suspects in that one too? None of us were there. How can we be suspects?"

"I didn't say that you were, Ms. Dykstra. All I'm saying is that the bakeshop is to remain closed until further notice. Also, none of you are to leave town in case we have more questions."

It was a dour ending to a particularly hard day. The girls had been frightened at the thought of being murder suspects. Dylan, feisty to the core, was angry. Carl and Mike, having been far from the bakery counter during the fracas on Friday, were visibly frustrated with the lack of useful information they could give. When everyone had left the lighthouse, Kennedy, Rory, and I took the remaining pizza and beer up to the light room. Once the pizza was gone and every possible motive for murder exhausted, all that was left was a spectacular sunset.

As the sun kissed the watery horizon, throwing a palette of reds, oranges, blues, and purples across the sky, I suddenly thought of the Captain and wondered what he'd make of it all.

CHAPTER 35

It was nearly dark when we left the lighthouse to walk down the beach with Rory. I had insisted that Kennedy and I go with him. Wellington needed his nightly walk, and I needed to clear my head. As Kennedy and Rory chatted about murder and the new suspicion of Betty, I held on to Welly's leash, pulling him from the spume of the dark lake while lost in my own thoughts. Soon we were traveling down the crushed stone path through the pine trees that led to Rory's back deck. We climbed the few steps with him and said good night. He was just about to disappear through the door when I compulsively uttered, "Captain Willy Riggs."

Rory stopped in the doorway and turned back to look at me. "What about him?"

"I almost forgot."

Both Kennedy and Rory flashed me a quizzical look. "Forgot what?" Rory asked.

"The night before the grand opening, after we saw that odd light coming from the lantern room, you tried to pass off the legend of the Captain as just a ghost story. I nearly believed you, but I don't anymore. I hate to admit this, but I've been reading up on Captain Willy Riggs and the matter of his death."

Kennedy stared at me as if I'd just gone mad. "Fabulous, darling. But why in God's name are you banging on about that now? We've already established that your lighthouse is haunted by some old dead guy. Harmless enough. I, for one, don't want to talk about ghosts when we have to walk all the way back to your lighthouse in the dark."

"You have Wellington to protect you," Rory reminded her, and gave my drooling dog a pat on the head. He turned his attention back to me. "Look, Lindsey, I don't know for sure that your lighthouse is haunted. But it does have some pretty interesting history attached to it, the mysterious death of Captain Willy Riggs being the most sensational part of that history."

"Well, there's really not that much evidence regarding his death," I told them, thinking of the ghost I'd been communicating with. "What I've been concentrating on are the facts. Captain Riggs, like every lightkeeper, had sworn an oath to diligently and faithfully uphold the duties of his office, namely ensuring the safety of passing ships and protecting the coast. On the night he died, he was obviously upholding these duties. Every account I've read says that he most likely saw something taking place down on the beach that compelled him to leave his post in the lantern room." I pointed in the direction of my lighthouse. "It's commonly believed that he was shot during this altercation. It's also commonly believed that he made it back to the lantern room, where he valiantly kept the lantern going until sunup. The next piece of the story is a fact, which is that the body of Captain Riggs was found in the lantern room on May eighteenth, in the year eighteen ninety-two. Cause of death was a gunshot wound to the chest. A couple of men from the town went to investigate after a ship's captain complained to the harbormaster about the dark lighthouse on the point. It was the first time it had been mentioned. It had been speculated that the lighthouse had been dark for two days."

"Wow," Rory exclaimed. "You really have been reading up on him. However, regarding the ghost, I really don't think you have anything to—"

"I know that," I said before he could finish. "But if the ghost of the Captain is still lingering around, it's likely because he has unfinished business. Unfinished business seems to be a common thread in hauntings."

Kennedy, looking a bit spooked, crossed her arms as if to protect herself. "You're oddly focused on this old ghost, Linds, when you really should be focused on the fact that there's a murderer on the loose in Beacon Harbor."

"True. And I am. It's part of why I'm mentioning all this now." I looked at them to see if they were following. They weren't, so I pressed on. "I told you that I've been poking into the matter of the Captain's death, and last night I think I found something important, something that was overlooked."

Rory's dark brows furrowed. "Lindsey, I hardly think that's possible. I'm sure the matter was thoroughly looked into."

"One would think. But things were different back then. Beacon Harbor wasn't a tourist destination, it was a busy shipping port. And the law and forensics weren't what they are today. A lightkeeper back then was supposed to keep a meticulous log of his observations and his duties, including the names of every ship that passed within his view. He would have known all the local captains and the cargos they carried. Legend says that Captain Willy Riggs confronted an unknown party on the night he died, but I don't think he did. During his time at the lighthouse, there was a lifesaving station down the beach, somewhere in the vicinity of where your house now stands."

"Really?" Rory looked impressed. "I was unaware of that."

"It was demolished in the forties, after the Coast Guard took over. Anyhow, my point is that if the Captain did see an imperiled ship, or thought lives were in danger, he would have signaled the station, or at the very least roused some of the locals for help. That was standard procedure. But legend says that he went out alone. If this is true, I think he left the lighthouse to assist someone he knew."

"Wow, you really need another hobby. Googling a dead guy at night isn't healthy." Kennedy pulled her arms a little tighter around her body and fake-smiled at me. Rory, however, understood what I was saying.

"You think he was murdered by a friend? Are you just speculating, or do you have proof?"

I shrugged and pulled out my phone. "I found his lightkeeper's logbook in the National Archives data-base," I explained as I opened the PDF I was looking for. "I took a screenshot of the pages in question. Here are the pages for May, eighteen ninety-two. Do you see anything odd?"

They both looked at the screen of my phone, scrolling through the digitized yellow pages of the old logbook.

Kennedy looked up, her face underlit by the glow of the screen. "Is it odd that his handwriting is so small and that he's so focused on the weather? Total type A in my opinion."

"All the entries are pretty standard," Rory noted, ignoring Kennedy.

"They are," I agreed. "Nothing's out of the ordinary there. However, what is odd is the fact that there are several pages missing. See?" I scrolled through the document, pointing out the page numbers. "I didn't notice it at first until I checked it against the exact date the Captain's body was found. He was found on May eighteenth. The logbook stops on May fourteenth. The longest the Captain's body could have been in the lantern room is two days, possibly only one. If that's the case, at least two pages had been removed. No one ever reported that."

Rory's face, illuminated by phone and by porchlight, held something akin to wonder. "My God, you've been investigating two murders. You checked the logbook? I can't believe you found that."

"I couldn't believe it was available in the National Archives, but it was. Also, I'm used to looking for anomalies in numbers, so nonsequential page numbering jumped out at me like a rose sprouting from a patch of weeds."

"What does it mean?" Kennedy asked, interest piquing for the first time.

"I'm not sure, but this is where I'm speculating. I think Captain Riggs was blindsided by a friend. I think he saw something he wasn't supposed to. I think he was shot on the beach and carried back to the lighthouse by the man who shot him. The man would obviously know that all his maritime activity had been documented by the light-keeper. He put the deceased captain back in the light-room, filled up the lantern to buy more time, and tore out the most recent pages in the logbook. Then he slipped back into the night and got away with whatever it was he was doing."

"That's utterly diabolical," Kennedy remarked. "However, and I hate to be the Debbie Downer of lighthouse lore, but I have to remind you that it doesn't matter. The old dead captain's really dead, darlings, and nothing's going to change that. So, again, why bang on about this now?"

"Because the last time somebody died in the light-house was in May of eighteen ninety-two. Then, Friday morning, Mia dies. And now Fiona. Both women were in the lighthouse. I think these murders have pulled the Captain from his eternal rest. I think he's still protecting the lighthouse. Remember the story Dylan told us about how she and Mike snuck into the tower and went up the stairs? Dylan said she saw his ghost in the lantern room. I think he's still there. I think he's trying to tell us something."

"Like the fact that you're going crazy?" Kennedy held me in an admonishing look.

"I hope I'm not," I told them honestly. "But what if these murders are somehow connected? All three of these murders seem to revolve around the lighthouse. Mia was trying to ruin my bakery; Fiona was trying to shut me down for buying the lighthouse; and the Captain . . . ? Maybe someone was trying to shut him down too?"

"Or he made an enemy in the town," Rory added. "But you're right. Although it's highly unlikely there's a direct connection to Captain Riggs, there's definitely something going on in this town that's getting innocent women killed."

"Those two women were hardly innocent," Kennedy added. "They both wanted to destroy your bakeshop."

"And Betty might be the one protecting it, only I don't know why."

Rory, thinking on this, added, "You might be right. Betty Vanhoosen is a very popular woman in this town. Everyone knows her; everyone loves her. She puts on her friendly, bubbly blonde act, but what if she's really playing us all?"

"Like someone might have been playing Captain Willy."

Rory nodded. "She and her friends were at the center of the ruckus on Friday morning. Then, today we find out that she was holding the poisoned coffee that killed Mia. She was also the owner of the lunch that killed her fiercest rival, Fiona. No matter how you look at it, every road leads back to Betty Vanhoosen."

"Well, darlings, we need to keep a vigilant eye on her, then."

"And we need to find out what secret she's protecting."

Rory, taking Welly's leash out of my hand, agreed. "I'm walking you two back home. And from now on I think it's best we keep Officer Tuck in the loop. If Betty is behind all this, she's one dangerous woman. Who knows the lengths she'd go to in order to protect her secret?"

CHAPTER 36

I was dead tired by the time I climbed into bed. I hadn't even cracked my laptop or opened the cover on my iPad. The flame of my curiosity had been temporarily extinguished by the gruesome reality of murder and thoughts of Betty Vanhoosen possibly having deceived us all. We didn't know it for sure, but statistically speaking, it was always the ones you least expected who did the unthinkable. Welly, tuckered out as well from chasing the careful sounds of nocturnal animals rooting amongst the seagrass, curled up on his extra-large bed and fell asleep, his head resting on his teddy bear. I gave him a hug and jumped straight into my own bed, with every intention of sleeping.

And I did, until plagued by nightmares of a time long ago, on a headland shrouded in fog and a friendly face that hid a desperate secret. The friendly face, unrecognizable yet familiar, smiled at me, then turned sinister. There was a gun in his hand, a gun aimed straight toward me. I was going to die. The terror of that thought made me scream, but my throat was paralyzed. I couldn't produce a sound. Knowing the trigger was going to be pulled, I tried screaming again, and again, producing only a high-pitched squawk. I had never been so frightened in my life. I couldn't scream; I couldn't run; I was going to die. Me! But why? I stared at the shadowy face and felt a paralyzing hopelessness. It was too late, I thought. But I had questions. I knew they'd never be answered, and that realization was nearly as tormenting as the gun. It was about to go off, and that's when I felt something wet and warmly gooey on my cheek. I opened my eyes. Wellington was standing over me, softly whining while licking my face. I'd never been so happy to see him. I threw my arms around his fluffy neck and softly cried into his fur. Although a hundred and fifty pounds of shedding, drooling fluff, there was no better nightmare-chaser than Welly.

The nightmare, still fresh in my mind, haunted me. Although I'd never consciously admit it, I did have an odd feeling that it was somehow connected to the other entity that shared the lighthouse with me, namely Captain Willy Riggs. Could it have been a message from him? Could it have been his last memory? I didn't know what to think, and I certainly didn't want to dwell on it any longer. After an hour of trying to get back to sleep, I finally gave up and headed downstairs to the kitchen with Wellington trotting happily behind me.

I turned on the coffeemaker, then stepped outside into the cool predawn air. I stood on the dew-covered lawn in my bare feet, watching as Wellington vanished in the darkness on his morning task, his black fur indiscernible against land, sea, and sky. Knowing he wasn't far, I turned my ears to the therapeutic sound of waves rolling onto the beach. I felt at peace once again—the nightmare lifting off me like fog dissipating in the morning sun. Like an old friend whispering in my ear. The moment Welly appeared from the darkness, we left the solitude of the lake and headed for the kitchen.

"How does quiche sound?" I asked. Although I had my dog's undivided attention, the word floated over his fluffy head. I grinned and ruffled his ears. "How about a spinach and BACON quiche?" That did the trick. It's said that highly intelligent dogs recognize up to 260 words. Welly, although intelligent, was not at the top of the list. His adorable factor, however, was off the charts, and his favorite words seemed to revolve around his belly and the people who appeased that belly. The mere mention of bacon sent his tail wagging while his nose covertly scanned the countertop for the scent of his favorite snack. There wasn't any. He then accompanied me to the bakery refrigerator, where I pulled out a pound of thick-cut bacon. "Here it is. Has to be cooked first," I told him. He must have understood that word too, because he pranced out of the forbidden bakery kitchen and through the connecting door to our living quarters.

While the bacon was cooking in my private kitchen, I appeased Welly with a cookie and his daily dental chew. Not as good as bacon, but it did the trick. Then, with clean hands, I set to work on my favorite, flaky, tender, all-butter piecrust.

Opening day, we had offered mini quiches, although donuts had definitely been the star of the show. However, if the murders were ever solved and the bakery was ever up and running again (I was being self-indulgently pessimistic), I would highlight the savory, protein-packed egg dish. The fact that it came baked inside a piecrust was even better.

With the crust rolled out and waiting in the pie plate, and the thick-cut bacon strips (minus two for the furry taste tester!) crisped to perfection and chopped, I whisked five eggs into a cup of milk and added a quarter teaspoon of both salt and pepper. I set the egg mixture aside and layered all my savory elements on the bottom of the crust, starting with the cooked bacon. A cup of freshly shredded Swiss cheese went next, followed by a quarter cup of freshly shredded Parmesan cheese, a cup of chopped fresh baby spinach leaves, and a sprinkling of thinly chopped scallions. This was topped off with the egg mixture and a ring of foil around the exposed crust to protect it from overbaking in the hot oven. I always liked to remove the foil the last fifteen minutes of baking to achieve that nice golden-brown color.

After I put the quiche in the oven, I poured another cup of coffee and set to work on washing and slicing fresh fruit. Fruit, in my opinion, was always a nice complement to the richness of a quiche. And since it was summer, a berry-melon medley would be perfect. While I sliced strawberries and cut up cantaloupe, I turned my mind once again to the problem of Betty Vanhoosen.

Maybe we were overreacting, thinking Betty was somehow involved in the murders. I recalled her voice the night before, when she had awakened me from a dead sleep. There was a note of terror coming from her end that had given me chills. I knew she was a busybody, but was she a gifted actress as well? I'd have to investigate the possibility. Her confession of holding the cup of coffee that had poisoned Mia Long could be genuine, or she could have used her acting skills to throw us off the trail of her intended victim, Fiona Dickel. Either way, Rory had been correct when he had said that all roads seemed to lead back to Betty Vanhoosen, only we had no clue as to why, or what she might be involved in. Our suspicions, however, deserved to be noted. There was only one thing to do. As soon as the police station opened, I was going to call Tuck McAllister and voice our concerns.

While the quiche baked, and after all the fresh berries had been added to the berry-melon medley, I did a little poking around on the internet to see what I could learn about Betty.

Not surprisingly, she had a personal Facebook account. What was surprising was that her last post had been on Friday morning, featuring a picture of the Beacon Bakeshop and encouraging everyone to stop by and check it out. The thoughtful post touched me. It was a nice thing to do, and yet suspicion lurked in the back of my mind, wondering if she'd had an ulterior motive.

After perusing her Facebook page, I next went to the website for her real estate agency. It was a good site. The homepage featured a scrolling banner with all the new listings in the area with links for virtual tours. Since I wasn't in the market for a home, I went straight to the bios, clicking on Betty's. The first thing that struck me was that the Harbor Real Estate Agency had been started by her late husband, Peter Vanhoosen, who died of a sudden heart attack in his late forties. I felt a pang of remorse reading that. I didn't know that Betty had been married, and I had never thought to ask. After her husband's death, Betty had taken over the agency.

The couple, childhood sweethearts, never had children. In Betty's own words, *The real estate agency was*

*our baby; the town of Beacon Harbor our family; and
Peter and I have been honored to be able to serve this
wonderful community in so many ways.* Peter had served
as the town's mayor from 2000 until his death in 2008.
Betty was the current president of the Chamber of Commerce. In the early days of their marriage, they had saved
several of the historic buildings of the town from demolition, including their own, by purchasing them to preserve
the history of Beacon Harbor. Once renovated, space
would be leased to small businesses and the apartments
above rented out—or, in the case of the old Lundy Man-
sion, sold to a couple who had converted the house into a
charming bed-and-breakfast. Peter Vanhoosen had even
bought up huge tracts of the surrounding forests and
marshland in the late eighties with the intent to never sell.
It was his effort to stave off unwanted expansion and
commercialization of the town.

Although the Vanhoosens looked good on paper, my
own experience in finance told me that civic-minded en-
trepreneurs, operating under altruistic visions, often made
enemies of those they were trying to serve. Betty Vanhoosen was a wealthy woman. She was the sole owner of
her real estate company, a landlord to many of the businesses, and wielded a hefty amount of influence. She was
a woman who was obviously used to getting her way.
Fiona Dickel had crossed her and was now dead. I'd have
to ask Tuck if there were any other suspicious deaths surrounding Betty. Maybe there was a history there.

After shutting down my computer, I tossed a couple of
the Danish Dylan had made the day before into the oven to
perk them up. The quiche was nearly done, and it smelled
divine. Knowing that Kennedy would likely sleep in this
morning, I shot off a text to Rory, asking if he'd like to

join me for breakfast. I was eager to talk with someone about the Vanhoosens, yet after having sent the text, a pang of remorse shot through me. Why did I assume Rory would be awake so early? I didn't want to wake him, and I certainly didn't want him to think I was desperate for his company . . . which, truthfully, I was. I cringed at the thought. Visions of my mother, the beautiful Ellie Montague-Bakewell, shaking her finger at me popped into my head. "Never chase after a man, Lindsey," she always advised me. "It makes you look desperate."

I had a habit of ignoring Mom's advice, and where did it get me? Alone in a lighthouse in the hinterlands of Michigan. I had also ignored her calls for the last few days and thought maybe it was time I gave her a ring and told her about the calamity of my opening day. Mom had warned me against coming here, and had warned me against opening a bakery. Although she'd be sympathetically horrified at the death of Mia Long in my bakeshop, as well as the death of Fiona (whom she didn't know) two days later, my pride was still too raw to give her the satisfaction that she might have been right all along. The logical part of me knew that I'd have to call her sooner or later. I took a deep breath and stroked Welly's soft fur for moral support. I was just about to press her number when my phone buzzed in my hand.

It was a text from Rory. *Be over in a few.*

I set down my phone and breathed a sigh of relief. "Crisis momentarily averted!" I smiled at Welly and gave him a kiss on the head. "Rory's coming for breakfast. We'll call Ellie later."

The moment I released my grip on my dog, he started barking and ran for the door. My heart leapt when I real-

ized Rory was already here, knocking softly on the other
side.

"What took you so long?" I teased, flinging open the
door. Wellington continued barking. To my utter surprise,
it wasn't Rory on my doorstep, but Tuck McAllister. And
he wasn't smiling.

Startled, I pulled Wellington back inside and motioned
for Tuck to do the same. "What are you doing here so
early? Well, good timing at any rate. I wanted to talk to
you, and I'm just about to pull a bacon and spinach
quiche out of the oven."

Tuck flinched. "Lindsey Bakewell, I'm placing you
under arrest for the murder of Fiona Dickel, the murder
of Mia Long, and the intent to do harm to Betty Vanhoosen. You have the right to remain—"

I held up a hand. "Hold on a minute." I was not in the
mood for games, especially when my oven timer was
buzzing. I left Tuck standing in the hallway and dashed
into the kitchen. "Look, I appreciate a good prank like
everyone clsc, but shame on you for bad timing."

"Lindsey, this isn't a prank." Tuck had followed me,
the tone of his voice stopping me in my tracks. "I'm taking you in."

I turned off the oven, removed the Danish and the
quiche, and turned to face him. "You can't be serious!
What evidence do you have to accuse me of those terrible
things?"

"I'm sorry, Lindsey, but that's for Sergeant Murdock
to explain."

CHAPTER 37

The bear had been poked. My inner New Yorker was beyond piqued, and I was reeling with indignation. "This is bollocks!" I cried again, using one of Kennedy's favorite expletives as I paced the small interrogation room waiting for Sergeant Murdock to arrive. The woman was taking her sweet time. Fearing that I might be difficult and resist arrest, Tuck had put me in handcuffs before stuffing me into the back of his squad car. It had all happened so fast. He'd accused me of murder; I'd left Wellington in the kitchen with a cooling quiche; and Rory was on his way. I was doubtful the quiche would even be there by the time he arrived. It would just be Wellington, an empty pie plate, a bowl of untouched fruit, and no me! I hadn't even been given the chance to shoot off a quick text alerting Rory and Kennedy to the fact that I'd just been charged with the murders of Mia Long and Fiona Dickel. That was double bollocks!

I was just about to knock on the door again and demand that I be let out when Sergeant Murdock appeared.

"Ms. Bakewell, please take a seat." Murdock shot me a commanding stare from under her wispy blond bangs. She had the posture and attitude of an alpha dog, reminding me that, sure, I could step out of line, but I'd be bitten in the process. I decided to curb my inner New Yorker and took a seat at the bare wooden table.

"Look," I began, the moment she sat opposite me. "There's been some mistake. I had nothing to do with the deaths of those two women. We tried to save Mia's life, and we were the ones who found Fiona Dickel."

"We understand all that. Do you know what Fiona Dickel died of?" The question was delivered with a tilt of her head and the narrowing of her brown eyes.

I began to sweat, thinking of what to say. Sure, I knew. I had smelled the telltale bitter almond scent on Fiona's breath. But she wasn't supposed to know that. I held her gaze and shrugged. "No. Not really."

Her small mouth stretched into a misleading smile. "Care to take a guess?"

"Cyanide," I said. "Either that or a heart attack."

She sat forward, her eyes locking onto mine. "As a matter of a fact, it was cyanide. Care to guess how it was delivered?"

"Obviously something she ate. Look," I said, getting angry, "I'm sorry Fiona was poisoned, but what I don't understand is how you can make a giant, unfounded leap and blame me for that! My friends and I went to talk with her. We suspected Fiona of trying to poison Betty. We never expected to find her dead."

"Because you expected Betty to die," she offered smugly.

"What? No!"

"After leaving the crime scene, I went to speak with Betty at her office. You mentioned that Fiona had taken Betty's lunch. You indicated that the lunch on the counter had come from Betty's office. Is that correct?"

"Yes." I stared at her, wondering where she was going with this.

"When Betty learned of Fiona's death, she was, naturally, shocked. However, when I told her the cause of death, and that the source of the poisoning had come from the lunch Fiona had taken from her office, Betty turned a shade of white only possible in redheads and fresh corpses. Do you want to know why?"

My throat had suddenly gone as dry as a desert. I swallowed painfully and nodded.

Murdock's smile faded. She was all business once again. "Because you were the one who sent her that lunch. The lunch laced with cyanide was meant for Betty, not Fiona."

"Wha . . . wha . . . what?" It was a shocking allegation. At the mention of the lunch and Betty, my thoughts began to swirl as my rapidly rising pulse pounded in my ears.

"Betty told me how you were supposed to visit her that morning. As noon approached and there was still no word from you, she said that Paige, her office manager, rang her with the message that you had sent over lunch. Shortly thereafter, Fiona arrived with her threat of a lawsuit. The two women had words and Fiona stormed out, taking the lunch with her. She ate the lunch. The cyanide was in the Coke."

"But . . . I didn't send Betty that lunch!" I cried, thinking of Betty and how brilliantly she'd played me. My God, I'd walked right into her trap. She had called me with the revelation that she'd been holding the coffee that killed Mia Long. I had believed her. I had even suspected Rory of slipping the cyanide into the coffee, when she obviously had done the deed herself—possibly with the intent of giving it to Fiona. Now she was accusing me of trying to murder her. I was going to take the fall for Betty Vanhoosen! That thought kicked me into the red zone.

I grabbed Murdock's unsuspecting hands. "That lunch wasn't from me!" I told her, hearing the desperation in my voice. She yanked her hands out of my grip, and I continued. "I saw that lunch bag. It was white. Red's the color I'd use, and I would never put a sandwich in a bag! It would be boxed up with a side of fresh-cut veggies and dip, and a cookie. A delicious cookie," I added pointedly. "And that sandwich in Fiona's hand was a ham and Havarti on marbled rye. I don't even have marbled rye. Also, we don't serve fountain drinks. There's no way that lunch came from me!"

The sergeant wasn't pleased. "Are you finished? Did I say that you made it? We know it didn't come from the Beacon Bakeshop. You're supposed to be shut down until further notice, remember? The sandwich came from Harbor Hoagies. We've already spoken with them and confirmed it."

"Well, that's a relief!" I stared at the sergeant. My game face was on and ready to win. "Because I've never been inside that deli. And if the order was phoned in, it could have come from anybody. The fact that Harbor

Hoagies delivered it to Betty's office should tell you that either someone who works there is trying to poison Betty, or Betty put that poison in the Coke herself knowing that Fiona would come by and take it. Or," I added, another thought occurring to me, "Betty could have just offered it to Fiona herself. That's right. We can't ask Fiona, because she's dead!"

"Ms. Bakewell, if the order had been phoned in, we would have checked the phone records. But it wasn't. We have an eyewitness who said that a woman came into the restaurant, stated her name was Lindsey Bakewell, ordered the sandwich with a drink, paid for it with cash, and left."

I closed my eyes tightly and shook my head. When I opened them again, I repeated the fact that I had never set foot in Harbor Hoagies, and that the person behind the counter had obviously been mistaken. Then I had another thought. Betty had connections in the town. Maybe she had coerced Paige into lying for her.

"Paige didn't say that you delivered the lunch," Murdock corrected. "She told us a boy had delivered it. The delivery boy said it came from you."

"How convenient," I snarled. "And I don't suppose we know who this boy is?"

Murdock shook her head. "We're trying to find him. We will."

"Great. Officer Cutie Pie—I mean, McAllister—cuffed me and brought me in because I've been charged with murder. That was negligent. And you've been negligent as well, embracing Betty's story like that without bothering to check my alibi or to state a possible motive for wanting to murder Betty Vanhoosen . . . or Mia Long, for that matter." I stared at her, sucking in air like a fish out of water. For the first time, Sergeant Murdock looked flustered.

"I have lawyers," I told her. "Bloodsucking lawyers at my beck and call." Okay, that might have been an exaggeration. My dad had a buddy who was a reputable corporate lawyer and family friend, but Murdock didn't need to know that. "And if you don't want me bringing them here, I suggest you call Kennedy Kapoor, Dylan Dykstra, and Rory Campbell. Every one of them will attest to the fact that I wasn't anywhere near Harbor Hoagies yesterday. I was at the lighthouse all morning. Then I took my dog with me as I made a brief visit to the home of Rory Campbell before visiting Betty at her office. Once you've talked with them, you might want to ask yourself why I would want Betty Vanhoosen dead. She's my friend, or she was until she threw me under the bus."

I watched as Murdock scribbled down the names of my friends. When she was done, she looked up once again. "Officer McAllister was acting under my orders. And you are correct. We haven't thoroughly checked out your alibi for yesterday morning. I was acting on the statement of an eyewitness—"

"Of a person who's never before met me!" I slammed my fist on the table to make my point. "Also, do you have a copy of the receipt? It should have been time-stamped. I'd like to see it. And I'd like to know how much I supposedly paid for a ham and Havarti on marbled rye."

Puzzled, Murdock looked at me. "Why does that matter?"

"I'd like to know how to price my sandwiches. To combat the taint of murder, I'm going to have to use savvy marketing and favorable price points to get the ball rolling again. The folks at Harbor Hoagies might think they know me now, but they're really going to be cursing my name when I reopen with my Beachgoers' Boxed Lunch Specials, starting at a dollar below the competition."

That almost made Sergeant Murdock smile. "I like you, Bakewell. And your chocolate-chip cookies passed the Murdock test. My kids loved 'em. But I'm afraid we're going to have to keep you at the police station awhile longer. Let's just hope your friends can corroborate your whereabouts yesterday morning."

CHAPTER 38

Just like in the movies, I was granted one phone call, yet for some reason I thought it would be a good idea to call Mom instead of a lawyer. The moment she answered the phone, I realized my mistake.

"Lindsey! Why haven't you been answering your phone? Dad and I are just dying to know how your opening day went. I know you're busy, dear, but he's been on pins and needles. You know he grew up in a bakery around those parts. Although he claims he's glad to have left that life behind, I'm skeptical. Friday morning, he baked a dozen blueberry muffins in honor of you. Saturday it was bran with raisins. Sunday it was cinnamon-swirl crumble top. I've been giving them to the neighbors. Today he's making a pie. Perhaps if you had called—"

"Mom," I cut her off. "I'm sorry, but I don't have much time. I'm in jail." The phone call degraded from there. I quickly filled Mom in on the two deaths and why I was now being held at the police station.

"Things like this didn't happen to you in Manhattan. I still can't get over the fact that your cheating ex brought his lover to your bakery. What was Jeffery thinking?"

"Again, Mom, he was trying to ruin me. We can chat about this later. I might need a lawyer."

"I'll ask your father. He knows plenty. Are they sure Mia's dead?" Mom was having a hard time digesting the fact that my bakery was currently shut down, and that Jeffery and Mia had come all the way to Michigan. "And why would you kill a woman you've only just met?" She was referring to Fiona.

"I didn't, Mom." I clutched the phone closer to my lips and whispered, "I think I'm being set up. Is Dad there?"

"He went to the market early this morning to get fresh berries for his pie. We're playing golf with the Bingfords then heading over to Roger Steel's place for his annual Memorial Day cookout."

"Sounds fun," I said with a blatant lack of enthusiasm. "Have Dad call me when he gets back."

Shortly after my disastrous call to Mom, my friends arrived.

"Lindsey!" Kennedy ran to me the moment I entered the waiting room. She acted as if we'd been separated for years by the horrors of incarceration, and not the three hours it had actually been. Murdock, momentarily taken aback, shot her a steely-eyed gaze, but to no effect. Kennedy was immune to intimidation.

I was happy to see Rory and Dylan as well. They represented the only real friends I had left in Beacon Harbor, and the fact they were gripped with concern caused me to feel both grateful and ashamed. Since Mia's death in the bakeshop, things had gone from bad to terrible-on-steroids. I'd been accused of two murders and an attempted one. Statistically speaking, the crime-ridden streets of New York City had been far safer for me than the quiet vacation village of Beacon Harbor. Thanks to the signed statements of Kennedy, Rory, and Dylan, swearing that I was nowhere near Harbor Hoagies at the time the sandwich had been purchased, I was now a free woman.

The entire situation had puzzled Murdock. In fact, in order to be certain my friends weren't lying on my behalf, the eyewitness from Harbor Hoagies was brought down to the station. The young man was then asked to pick me out of a lineup of five other random women, two of whom worked at the police station, two from the township offices, and one officer's wife. The kid stared at us for ten whole minutes before finally stating that none of us fit the description of the woman he saw. That woman, he said, had been wearing a long coat; a scarf over her hair, neck, and chin; a wide-brimmed hat over that; and round sunglasses. In short, he had no idea what she looked like. Sergeant Murdock, finally satisfied, apologized to me and promised to look into the possibility that Betty Vanhoosen might be behind the whole thing.

"You just vanished from the lighthouse without a word!" Kennedy stated, giving Murdock her haughtiest glare. "Would have been nice to know what had happened instead of being shaken awake by Sir Hunts-a-Lot over here, who, apparently, was promised quiche."

Rory, clearly not a fan of Kennedy's nickname for him, explained. "I knew something was wrong the moment I arrived," he said. "I've never seen an empty pie plate on your kitchen floor before, and I've never seen Welly so guilt-ridden. I thought maybe you drove off somewhere, but your Jeep was still in the garage. When I couldn't find you, I thought maybe you'd been kidnapped."

"That's when he woke me up," Kennedy interjected. "And that's when we called the police. Imagine our surprise when they told us you'd been charged with murder."

"I came as soon as I heard," Dylan said, adding her part of the story. I felt a pang of guilt, realizing my arrest had pulled her from her morning workout. Her hair was in a ponytail, and she was in shorts and a *Tough Mudder* T-shirt. "Talk about incompetent investigating." This was said loudly, causing Murdock and Officer Cutie Pie, who'd just appeared in the waiting room, to flinch. "Lindsey Bakewell charged with murder? Ha! Her only crime is fixing up a derelict lighthouse and tempting this town with delicious baked goods. I'll have you know that Lindsey's the kindest person I've ever met!" Dylan looped her arm through mine. "Let's get out of here. Police stations give me the creeps."

Tired, hungry, and badly in need of a caffeine buzz, I suggested we grab a bite to eat. Thanks to Wellington, quiche was out of the question. Although normally a model of canine obedience, unguarded food always got the best of him.

Since Kennedy had taken Rory to the police station in my Jeep, and Dylan had driven separately, we decided to meet at Hoot's Diner. It was three miles out of town near the highway, a safe distance from the police station and a place we could put our heads together over the matter of murder. Built in the seventies and remodeled in the nineties without ever changing the woodsy owl theme, there was a certain Up North nostalgia that clung to its pine-paneled walls. It was a family favorite, and why not? Breakfast was served all day, and the coffee, though not strong, was hot and good.

We sat at a booth near the back of the diner. While waiting for our food, I shot Mom a quick text stating that I wouldn't be needing a lawyer after all. Then, as our food arrived, I regaled my friends with the story of my arrest.

"Wait!" Kennedy leaned forward, her eyes wide with intrigue. "Officer Tuck threw you in handcuffs? Isn't that like"—she chanced a look at Rory and lowered her voice—"one of your fantasies?"

"What? No," I was quick to admonish, although my cheeks burned with embarrassment as Rory stared at me. "He thought I was resisting arrest," I explained. "Which I might have been doing."

Rory looked troubled. "The bigger problem here is that Betty claimed you sent her that lunch. Either she's trying to cover up the murder of Fiona Dickel by making you take the fall, or someone really might be trying to kill her."

"Betty and Paige might be in it together," Dylan offered, taking a sip of her coffee. A thoughtful look crossed her face as she set down the mug. "We know that whoever ordered the lunch at Harbor Hoagies was a woman. Betty could have thrown on a disguise, ordered the lunch herself, and paid some kid to deliver it. She could have snuck back to her office before the sandwich was delivered. I know Paige," Dylan added with a grim set to her lips. "Went to high school with her. She's worked for Betty since graduating. Paige Winston's been a brownnoser since kindergarten, but it obviously paid off. Betty saw something in her, took her under her wing, and has given her a steady job with good benefits. She's as loyal to that woman as Wellington is to you, Lindsey."

"Are you suggesting that if Paige knew what Betty was up to, she'd lie for her?"

Dylan nodded.

"Or," Rory began, ready to play devil's advocate, "Paige could be the one trying to poison Betty." Apparently, Dylan wasn't buying that one. "Before you ignore the possibility, remember that Betty's never had children. What if she's leaving everything to Paige, including Harbor Realty? Maybe Paige is getting greedy and wants Betty out of the picture?"

"I like where you're going with this, Rory, darling," Kennedy added, setting down her fork. "But that doesn't explain how the cyanide got into Betty's latte the morning of Mia's murder. Was this Paige person even at the bakeshop that morning? Could she have slipped her the poison?"

"She wasn't there," I said, recalling my conversation with Paige after my first visit to the police station. "She was manning the front desk at Betty's office. But the Betty/Paige angle is worth looking into. On the other hand, if Betty is the target, I'd feel truly terrible if we overlooked something. Someone might still be trying to kill her, and we don't know why. Last night I did a little snooping on Betty. Along with Harbor Realty, she owns several of the buildings in town. I was unaware of that fact when I moved here. I've met most of the business owners of this town, but I wasn't aware that many of them don't own the buildings their businesses are in. It makes them Betty's tenants. She could have very easily ticked one of them off somehow."

"Or maybe she's blackmailing someone?" Dylan added thoughtfully.

We all thought about this a moment. "That's a good point," Rory added.

"We already know that a woman disguised herself, purchased the sandwich, and poisoned the Coke," I told them. "It stands to reason that if Betty's not the murderer, then some other woman is behind this. Who did she tick off? Who is she blackmailing? I say we concentrate on those who rent from her, paying close attention to business owners who might be in the Chamber of Commerce as well."

"Good plan." As Rory complimented me, I blushed under the heat of his gaze, remembering his kiss all too well. If I was a betting woman, I'd say he was remembering it too. It caused him to clear his throat, adding, "Betty also owns quite a bit of land around the town."

Dylan, shocked, asked, "How do you know that?"

"Apparently, Dilly, Lindsey's not the only one here who knows how to use Google." Kennedy winked at Rory.

"For once, Kennedy's right." Rory tipped a pretend hat in her direction, invoking a smile. "I've looked into Betty too," he continued. "I honestly don't know what's going on here either. On that note, I say we do a little poking around to see if anyone can tell us something that might shed some light on the matter of Betty Vanhoosen. Is she more angel, or is she more devil? And if she's a devil, is she capable of murder? You ladies start in town. I'm going to grab my truck and pay a visit to the Department of Natural Resources in Traverse City. Betty's land is privately owned, but a good deal of it is bog, which is protected by state ordinance. I thought I'd check with the boys of the DNR and see if they have anything interesting to tell me."

"Sounds like an excuse to go hunting," Kennedy quipped.

"Any excuse is a good excuse," Rory replied with a grin.

Stuffed with blueberry pancakes, caffeinated, and with a new plan, I addressed my friends. "Alright, sounds like we have a long day cut out for us. While Rory heads to the hinterlands, with or without his hunting rifle, we're going to snoop around the town and talk with Betty's tenants. Hopefully something will come to light from all of this, because orange isn't my color. I can't go to prison."

With a gentle smile, Kennedy placed her hand over mine. "I won't let that happen to you, Lindsey, darling, because . . . UCK!" She made a face. "Orange! Should be a crime to wear that color. Secondly, you're not a killer, you're a baker. Let's take Welly with us just in case we run into trouble."

Kennedy was under the impression that Welly was a guard dog. My gentle boy didn't have a mean bone in his body, but I nodded all the same. "The heathen ate my quiche," I stated. "He owes me. I suppose if his beseeching eyes and adorable fluffiness don't get people talking, we could always threaten drool."

Dylan flashed a smile that didn't quite reach her eyes, and slid out of the booth. "Guys, this all sounds like fun, and I'd love to join you, but I'm afraid I have to bounce. I've kind of committed myself to cleaning Mike's boat. We had a bit of a party on it yesterday, and he's got a big charter tomorrow."

"Of course," I said, feeling a bit stupid. She was part of this town and had a life other than my bakery. The fact it was still shut down made me feel incredibly guilty. I slid out of the booth and gave her a big hug. "Thanks for coming down to the police station this morning. Once again, I'm so sorry that all this drama is surrounding my bakery. Don't know what I'd do without you. Say hi to Mike and Carl for me. And if they can think of anyone who might have a bone to pick with Betty, give me a call."

"Will do, boss. And keep me posted. For the record, I'm placing my money on 'Betty the Devil.'"

CHAPTER 39

"Well," I began, walking out of Harbor Scoops with a waffle cone buckling under the weight of an obscene amount of butter pecan ice cream and a dish of vanilla for Welly. The ice cream was heavenly. Welly, waiting patiently outside, worked his busy tail with excitement. Kennedy, a step behind me, was carrying a cone of equal proportion to mine, only hers had been dipped in chocolate, rolled in nuts, and loaded with rocky road. "Seems like Dylan's backing the wrong Betty," I said. "Either she really is an angel, or her halo is all smoke and mirrors."

Kennedy licked her cone to stop it from dripping, and nodded. "Stand here. We need a selfie in front of this place. This town is positively charming. I thought we had stepped into a Hallmark holiday movie when we entered that Swiss chalet and found a year-round Christmas shop, but this darling little ice cream parlor speaks to the child in me, and we both know I'm virtually a huge child." With the expertise of a professional, Kennedy whipped out her phone. "Ready?"

I knew the drill. I lifted Wellington's head from his dish and got into place. Kennedy snapped the picture as we pressed our heads to my dog's and pretended to lick our cones. The red-and-pink-striped storefront topped with a bright red awning was the perfect background. Unfortunately, as Kennedy took her picture, Wellington took a shot at her cone with his tongue.

I laughed. "Looks like he made contact. I want a copy of that."

She handed me her cone and worked the mini keyboard with both thumbs. "It's going up right now. I'm tagging you in the photo. And shame on you, Wellington. That nice lady gave you your own ice cream."

After posting her picture, Kennedy put her phone back in her purse and took back her cone. She gingerly ran a napkin down the compromised side and took a lick. Wellington looked up from his empty dish with hopeful anticipation.

"Ginger Brooks, owner of Scoops, was the last person on the list," I said, putting a line through her name.

I had made a list of all Betty's renters and friends, starting at the head of the town with the Tannenbaum Christmas Shoppe, the first shop in Beacon Harbor that tourists saw when entering the town. Kennedy had never been inside the Swiss chalet that not only looked like Santa's workshop on steroids, but smelled inside like the essence of Christmas. Felicity Stewart, the owner, had been at my bakeshop on opening day. Although she owned the Swiss chalet and was not a renter, I knew she was one of Betty's friends. And just like Felicity, Ginger Brooks had nothing but good things to say about Betty.

I looked at Kennedy and shrugged. "She's clearly a Betty Vanhoosen fangirl as well."

"I would be too if I was two months behind on my rent and my landlord reduced it by half until I could catch up. That's downright neighborly!" This was said in Kennedy's best shot at an American cowboy accent.

We continued down Main Street with Wellington prancing at the end of his leash, his luxurious black fur glistening under the late afternoon sun with the healthy sheen of one who's eaten a spinach and bacon quiche and a dish of hand-scooped vanilla. I supposed he earned it, melting hearts and making friends of all the business owners and their pooches. Welly had a particular fondness for Libby, a golden retriever who resided in the Book Nook bookstore with her owners, Ali and Jack Johnson.

The Book Nook had been our second stop after the year-round Christmas shop, Tannenbaum. Kennedy was correct. Beacon Harbor was a very charming town, and the Book Nook seemed to tie the community together, not only by offering a wonderful and carefully selected offering of books, but because of the owners, Ali and Jack Johnson. Ali and Jack had also been at my bakeshop on opening day. The Johnsons, like me, had moved to Beacon Harbor with a dream—theirs was the dream of opening a charming bookstore. In a world where bookstores seemed to be closing due to online shopping, the Book Nook was a breath of fresh air. And although I had talked with Ali and Jack many times, I had no idea the impact Betty Vanhoosen had on their dream. According to Ali, Betty, who owned the building, had wanted their bookstore so badly in Beacon Harbor that she reduced her their rent to half of what she was originally asking.

"As far as landlords go," Ali explained as Welly and Libby sniffed one another with tail-wagging delight, "Betty's tops. She's friendly, understanding, and works nearly as hard at promoting our bookstore as she does selling houses. But you already know that. There was no bigger advocate for your lighthouse bakery than Betty." Ali smiled. She was a handsome woman in her early sixties with lovely white hair and a serene countenance. She was a very likable person, as was her husband, Jack. I could see why Betty wanted this couple to succeed. They were the type of people who would add value to any town.

I had to agree she was correct. "Betty's been very supportive of my bakery. But can you think of anyone who might wish to cause her harm?"

Ali's pretty face clouded. "Fiona Dickel," she whispered, and crossed herself. Because Ali, like everyone else in town, knew that Fiona had been found dead yesterday in her home. Thankfully, the details of her death hadn't been released yet. A troubled look passed between husband and wife.

"Surely Betty had nothing to do with that," Jack added with confidence. He'd been playing with the dogs. Welly, loving the attention, poured on the charm. He sat and offered his giant paw.

"We've been admiring your dog since you moved in. Have you ever thought of adding a dog treat or two to the menu?"

"I have plans for that," I replied, and thanked them for their time. "And please, bring Libby down to the Beacon Bakeshop once we've been given the okay to open again.

There's a budding romance going on here, and Welly could use a friend. She's welcome anytime, as are you."

It was pretty much how the rest of the day went, as Kennedy, Wellington, and I walked from shop to shop, trying to find that one person who deviated from the "Angel Betty" narrative. Although many joked about her nosy nature and chattiness, the general consensus was that Betty was not only generous with her time and money, but she was a very good person. It had been my experience with her as well, and yet two suspicious murders had made me doubt it.

We'd been walking toward the lighthouse in near silence as we ate our ice cream. Then, thinking about Betty, I suddenly stopped. Harbor Realty was just across the street. I looked at Kennedy, who was in mid-lick, and said, "We need to talk with Betty. All we've learned is that Fiona Dickel was the only thorn in her side, which we already knew. She didn't see eye to eye with everyone, but there's been no real motive for murder. And from all we've learned of Betty, I just don't think she's capable of it. If all Betty's saying is true, somebody really is trying to poison her. Only Betty can tell us who has the most to gain from her death."

"And you think she's going to talk with you? She thinks you tried to poison her, hence the reason you were recently charged with attempted murder"—she waved her hand in the air—"and murder. Another observation. Looks like the realty office is closed for business."

Kennedy was correct. We crossed the street and checked the door. It was locked.

"Poor thing's probably scared to death," I offered. "Let's take Wellington home and drive out to her house. With any luck we'll find her there."

* * *

Betty lived on the other side of town, down a private road that hugged the scalloped shoreline. Unlike Fiona's sprawling spectacle of new construction, Betty's house was of another generation, one that prided itself on workmanship and detail. It was a charming two-story home of tan fieldstone, steeply pitched roofs, bay windows, and brown shutters. It had the look of a cozy English cottage surrounded by stunning gardens and lush greenery. However, the charm of the home was not to be outdone by the spectacular back lawn rolling down to the lake. Without doubt, Betty's house was the jewel of Beacon Harbor.

"Get behind the bushes," Kennedy whispered, and rang the bell. She wanted me out of sight, and I agreed. I was probably the last person Betty wanted to see, but I was here to convince her otherwise.

When a few minutes had passed and there was still no answer, Kennedy rang the bell again. That's when an overwhelming feeling of dread hit me.

I poked my head out of the bushes. "What if they got to her? What if somebody actually succeeded in bumping her off?"

"I was thinking the same thing. But before we freak out, I'm going to abuse doorbell privileges and give this little noisemaker the ringy-dingy to end all ringy-dingys. If she doesn't come running or call the police herself, we're going in." She took a deep breath, faced the door, and attacked the bell like a woodpecker on crack.

It worked like a charm. A cry of "I'm coming! I'm coming!" wafted through the door, followed by a rush of heavy footsteps. The door flew open and Betty gasped. "Kennedy!"

"Hi, Betty." Kennedy moved to block the door at the same moment I popped out of the bush.

"Lindsey!" Betty shrieked, her voice two clicks below a full-out scream. "I'm not talking to you!" Betty went to slam the door, but Kennedy's foot was in the way.

"Ouch! Betty, stop!"

But Betty didn't stop. She abandoned the door and darted down the hall as fast as her chubby legs could carry her, disappearing inside the house.

"I got her!" I said, and ran after her as Kennedy hopped on one foot behind me.

After a short chase, a slight struggle, and a lot of pleading on my part, I finally convinced Betty that I wasn't trying to kill her. To make my point, I let her sit in a chair with her cell phone poised to dial Sergeant Murdock should she feel threatened. I then began to explain my side of the story, namely that I hadn't sent the lunch that had killed Fiona Dickel.

A volley of *Oh! Oh! Oh!* left her mouth in relief as she finally believed me. "I didn't really believe you had it in you, dear, but one never knows—and Paige did say that you were the one who dropped off the lunch in the first place. I mean, not physically you. It was a boy, but he said you paid him to deliver it, or Paige told me that's how it went. At any rate, I thought you sent the lunch because you were running late." Betty paused for a breath. "When Tucker came to deliver the news that Fiona was dead and that she'd been poisoned by the lunch, I"—she waved a hand above her head with nervous excitement— "I thought you were the one trying to do me in! I mean, my latte killed that annoying woman, and then my lunch killed Fiona. You must understand how that might look bad for you. The coffee came from your bakeshop; the lunch had your name associated with it, and all I did was put two and two together." Betty's round blue eyes still held a note of suspicion as she looked at me.

"Betty, I'm a numbers' person by trade, and believe me, I did the math on that one too. In most cases two and two does equal four, but that's only when no other variables are taken into account. The first variable is the fact that I like you. I have no reason to wish you harm. Then there's the fact that there were five of us behind the counter that day and at least thirty people in the bakeshop proper, most of them rushing the counter. Mia Long and her bad behavior is yet another factor. Mia went to great lengths to draw attention to herself. Any one of us behind the counter, or near you, could have slipped you the cyanide when you weren't looking."

Betty nodded. "True, but the lunch delivery from you sealed the deal."

Kennedy jumped to my defense. "That's because whoever is out to get you is trying to frame Lindsey for the deed. Look at her." She gestured to me with a gracious sweep of her hand. "Beautiful, gullible, and filthy rich. Lindsey's an easy target."

I rolled my eyes at Kennedy, and continued. "If I was the only person you told about Mia grabbing the poisoned cup of coffee out of your hand and I wanted you dead, it would stand to reason that I might try it again by sending you a lunch with a poisoned Coke. You called me in the middle of the night to tell me, but I can't be the only one who knew. Who else did you tell?"

Betty blanched and covered her mouth. "I might have told Paige," she admitted. Kennedy and I were thinking the same thing when Betty added, "And Chad, who manages the restaurant at the Harbor Hotel—"

"You told Chad?" Kennedy and I cried in unison.

"It just sort of slipped out," Betty said defensively. "I was very upset."

"What did Chad want?" I asked, thinking of the opportunistic restaurant manager who had scribbled his number on the breakfast receipt.

Betty shrugged it off. "He came by to chat. He was voicing his concern about a mutual friend of ours, as he often does. Nothing out of the ordinary there. Oh dear," she suddenly cried. "I'm afraid he may have spilled the beans about my poisoned coffee to your ex, or that Mia woman's friends. They're still at the hotel, you know, and the fact she took the coffee from me would exonerate them all. Like your bakeshop, Lindsey, those poor people haven't been cleared to resume their normal lives."

Kennedy's black eyes narrowed in disgust. "What if that wanker is trying to blackmail you for real this time? He could have had any one of Mia's friends purchase the lunch, poison the Coke, and deliver it to Betty under the guise that you sent it. It would link Mia's murder to hers, and both back to you. That little stunt would be sure to shut you down for good!"

I thought about that for a moment, ran the possibilities through my head, and shrugged. "Honestly, it's not likely, but it deserves to be looked into. The trouble is, Jeffery didn't poison Mia. She was an unfortunate victim of a more devious plot to poison Betty. I strongly doubt Jeffery would jump on that bandwagon just to ruin me. However, Betty, that does bring to mind Paige, or anyone else whom you might have offended."

The thought visibly depressed Betty. "You think that Paige could be behind the poisonings?"

"Have you offended her? Does she have anything to gain by your death?"

"Certainly, I could have offended her." Betty sat back in her chair and mindlessly caressed the vase on the decorative table next to her as she considered this. "She's a young woman, and I'm her boss. I'm also a bit of a perfectionist. Are you asking if she inherits anything from me?"

"I read your bio on your realty website. Your husband passed away, and you don't have any children."

Betty pursed her lips. "Well, my estate is complicated. I may not have children of my own, but I do have two godchildren as well as a niece and nephew. They'll each get a little something. Then there's some land that my deceased husband has put into a trust. I have control of it now, but it will eventually go to the town. The land is intended for a wetland preserve. It will never be developed. Mike Skinner, our local jack-of-all-trades, keeps an eye on it for me in exchange for hunting rights. I let him and a few other young men of the town hunt on that property. They must have the proper licenses, of course. I don't want poachers there, but taking down a healthy buck in the fall really helps these families through the winter."

"That's really kind of you," I said, growing more impressed with Betty by the minute. I then thought to ask, "Does Rory hunt on your land?"

"Not that I know of. He's never asked, but if he did, I'd grant him permission. Mr. Campbell has always displayed good judgment, though I'm afraid the same can't be said about me. I'm so embarrassed that I thought he might have tried to poison me."

"You weren't the only one," Kennedy added and gave her a reassuring pat on the hand.

Betty gave a sympathetic nod and continued. "Most of my wealth will go to the town in the form of a charitable trust," she explained, "and to other various charities. However, I have thought about leaving my business to Paige Winston, but that's not stated in my will."

"Then there's no motive," I said, deflated.

"Not an obvious one," Betty concurred. "But, my dears, unless I'm the unluckiest person in the world, it doesn't change the fact that somebody *is* trying to kill me."

CHAPTER 40

We left Betty's house with more questions than answers, which was disappointing. Although Jeffery might have learned from Chad, the chatty manager of the hotel restaurant, that Betty Vanhoosen had been the target of the poison that killed his lover, I doubted he'd be stupid enough to pick up the torch and try to finish the job in order to frame me. Kennedy suggested we drive over and talk with him, but I wasn't in the mood.

The matter of Paige Winston deserved to be investigated. I didn't know Paige very well, but I was willing to talk to her. Betty didn't like that idea one bit and called Officer Tuck herself with the lead. "Leave it to the professionals," she had told us. "May I remind you that the last time you two meddled, someone died?"

It was true, but I wasn't ready to head home just yet. Indulging my curiosity, Kennedy and I drove out to the

Benzie Area Historical Society Museum so that I could investigate another matter.

"Is this about the dead captain who haunts your lighthouse?"

"Maybe," I said. "I'm curious about some of the families that might have lived in the area during the time my lighthouse was built. As I told you, I don't think the Captain was murdered by a stranger."

"Oh, I get it. Because Paige Winston is off the table and you don't feel like confronting Jeffery again, you're going to try to solve the murder of Captain Willy Riggs?"

"Nobody was ever charged with his murder, because there were no witnesses. It's similar to this case in the fact that we have a person who likes to drop poison into drinks, but no motive and no witness. Basically, I've failed with the one, so I'm going to concentrate on the other."

"Oh, that's logical," she remarked sarcastically. "Well, while you talk with the docent, I'll be over here looking at pictures old dead people. Holler if you crack the case, darling."

I'd been in the archives for an hour, copying records of family names and a few articles of interest, when Rory sent me a text.

Dinner at my house tonight. I've got steaks, a grill, and plenty of beer. You bring the dessert and Welly.

I'm on it, I texted back. *See you in a few*, and went to get Kennedy.

Back at the lighthouse, while Kennedy prepared romaine lettuce for a simple Caesar salad—there was no mention of veggies in Rory's text—I set to work on a traditional cherry pie, my personal favorite of all the fruit pies. Thank goodness I had purchased a large bag of frozen Montmorency cherries from one of the cherry orchards outside of town before opening my bakery. Traverse City was the cherry-growing capital of the world, producing 40 percent of the world's cherries. I was excited to use the pert red fruit in future baked goods, but tonight I would wow Rory with my dad's own amazing recipe for cherry pie.

Taking out a large saucepan, I filled it with six cups of frozen tart cherries, sprinkled a tablespoon of fresh lemon juice on top of them, and gave it a good stir. I then covered the pot and warmed the cherries on medium heat, inducing them to thaw and release their tart juices. While the cherries worked their magic, I took out a small bowl and mixed one and a quarter cup of sugar with four tablespoons of cornstarch.

After a few minutes thawing on the stove, I turned off the burner and let the cherries rest. Then I jumped to the bakery kitchen to nab one of the premade piecrusts Dylan had stored there.

Dylan and I had discussed piecrusts ad nauseam. While I had championed the all-butter crust for flavor, she championed a crust with vegetable shortening for the flaky texture. We had finally settled on a crust that combined the best of both, one and a half sticks of unsalted butter for flavor, and one-third cup of shortening for texture. This was cut into three cups of all-purpose flour, with a pinch of salt and a tablespoon of sugar added for good measure. Once all the butter and shortening had been cut into the dry ingredients to the size of peas, it was then blended with half a cup of ice water and a teaspoon of cider vinegar to achieve that perfect rolling texture.

The cider vinegar had been Dylan's addition. It was another ingredient that would add to her perfect flaky crust obsession.

With two piecrusts rolled out and one sitting in a pretty ceramic pie plate, I turned on the burner and stirred the sugar mixture into the juicy cherries. I continued to stir until the cherries were thick and bubbly. Once I was satisfied with the taste and thickness of the filling, I stirred in three tablespoons of butter for silkiness and poured the mixture into the waiting crust. I had actually contemplated topping the pie with snazzy latticework or a cute braided edge, but I didn't have time. I still needed to shower and change. Therefore, a traditional top crust is what I went with. Having a little extra dough, I rolled it out and made a couple of decorative cherries. These I placed in the center of the pie. I then brushed the crust with milk and sprinkled it with finishing sugar before sending it into the oven.

While the pie baked, I showered, got dressed, and met Kennedy downstairs in time to remove the pie. It smelled wonderful, confirming my long-held belief that there was nothing better than a freshly baked cherry pie. Although it was piping hot, it would firm up and cool nicely by the time we ate it. I packed up the pie, the salad, and set out for Rory's house with Kennedy and Wellington.

Although my day had started out on a terrible note, the crisp air of late spring, coupled with the beginnings of what was sure to be a spectacular sunset, had brought it full circle. I was out of jail and having dinner with friends on a deck overlooking Lake Michigan. It was about as perfect as it could get. Rory's thick steaks were perfectly grilled, and Kennedy's yummy Caesar salad more than made up for the fact that Wellington had eaten my entire breakfast quiche. Just to prove the point that his belly was, in fact, a bottomless pit, he had wolfed down the T-bone that Rory had made for him in mere seconds, and was now hyper-focused on the bone.

"I'm a bit disturbed to hear that Betty doesn't have any enemies other than the recently deceased Fiona," Rory remarked before taking a swig of his beer.

"She obviously has an enemy," I countered, "a subtle one that her positive personality and rosy outlook fail to acknowledge. I'm stumped. Fiona was so vocal about her dislike for Betty that anyone else by comparison might seem harmless."

"We're looking for a needle in a haystack, darlings." Kennedy paused to take her last bite of the delicious pie. Waving her empty fork, she added, "And speaking of needles in haystacks, were the heroes in beige able to help you?"

Rory chuckled. "The DNR officers didn't know much about Betty's land, since it's privately owned. Betty doesn't hunt, but they did say that a couple of local men have permission to hunt there. The DNR makes regular visits during deer season to make sure that anyone hunting on the property has the proper licensing and is abiding by the laws, but beyond that they didn't have much to say. After my visit there, I thought I'd hike around the Vanhoosen forest myself."

I was taking a bite of pie when I looked at him. "Betty did mention that she let a couple of men hunt on her land. Can't imagine they'd be upset with her."

"Did she mention their names?" For some reason this interested him.

"No. You'd have to call her and ask. Did you find anything?"

He drained the beer he'd been drinking and set the empty bottle on the table. Grimacing slightly, he answered, "I'm not sure."

"What does that mean?" Kennedy wrinkled her nose at him.

Rory, rising to the challenge, leaned forward. "Betty owns a lot of land. To use your own analogy, it's just a haystack if I don't know what I'm looking for."

"Well, here's another observation, Sir Hunts-a-Lot. If you don't know what you're looking for, then it's just a waste of time." Kennedy, to make her point, plucked a rogue crouton from the near-empty salad bowl and shoved it in her mouth, giving a dramatic crunch. That made me laugh. Rory did too, and all talk of Betty and murder faded away with the setting sun.

"Welly and I will be waiting just over there," Kennedy said, as we were about to take our leave. It had been an enjoyable night, and we had lingered too long. Kennedy had assumed, like the observant friend she was, that I wanted a moment alone with Rory, should he try to kiss me again. I was entirely open to the possibility.

"This wasn't the date I promised you," he said, standing very close. "Unless you plan to bring your friend on all our dates. In that case, this is date number one."

"Funny," I said, and smiled. "She'll head back to New York once the murderer is caught and the bakeshop opens again."

"God, that can't happen soon enough." He bent his head for a kiss. Like a fine glass of wine, it radiated throughout my body, warm and tantalizing. And, like said wine, I wanted to keep drinking. Therefore, it took some effort to pull away.

"Speaking of that," I said, taking a deep breath. "You found something in the woods, didn't you?"

"I may have." He grinned and bent to kiss me again.

"Wait." With both my hands on his very firm chest, I pushed him back a hair. "What? You have to tell me what you found."

His handsome face, like the flip of a coin, turned from playful to grim. "No, Lindsey. Not yet. Leave this one to me."

His tone was convincing, and although New York Lindsey would have pushed him to his limits, the new Lindsey bowed out with grace. "I trust you," I said. "And I'll trust you to tell me when you're ready."

CHAPTER 41

It was a fact that Rory had earned my trust, but that didn't mean I could just turn off my insatiable curiosity like a light switch and go to bed. Kennedy, having eaten too much cherry pie, was done for. During her sugar rush, we chatted, watched an episode of *Jane the Virgin* on Netflix, and drank a cup of herbal tea. Then, while I brushed Wellington—a necessary half hour if I didn't want dog fur all over my lighthouse—Kennedy made a few social media posts and checked her email. "I'm out!" she declared at midnight, and went up to bed.

I was tired too, but made another cup of tea instead. Then, leaving Wellington curled up on the carpet, I took my tea and climbed up the light tower stairs.

I didn't know what I was looking for, and that had been part of my plan. Sitting in the lightroom, staring in the direction of the lake was a darkness so complete that only the stars in the heavens were visible. Looking toward the town of Beacon Harbor, it was another matter. Soft lights lined the streets, and fainter ones twinkled down the shoreline and up the wooded hillsides where homes and cabins stood. But it was the lake that held my interest. As I stared out at the nothingness, part of me understood how Captain Willy Riggs must have felt that first night when he climbed the three flights of stairs to the lantern room to light the great beacon, and the allure of such an existence. Danger was part of the job, but not murder. And yet I couldn't help but feel a stab of sadness to think that's what had ended his career.

After a long while of staring at the blackness, sipping herbal tea and yawning in turns, I decided to turn on my flashlight and read the list of family names I had copied during my visit to the Benzie Area Historical Society Museum. I had found the census for the year Captain Riggs had died. I didn't know what I was hoping to find, but thought that maybe a name would spark a memory of one of the articles I had read of the Captain's death, or maybe there'd be a name connecting to a family still living here. However, after perusing the list, I realized that I probably should have had a copy of the current White Pages for reference. I was a newcomer to the town and didn't know much of the history or the family names. Also, reading such a list in the dead of night was akin to looking through columns of large numbers. My eyes were drooping as tiredness was finally catching up with me. The papers slipped out of my hand and dropped to the floor, scattering all over. I slapped my face, drained the last dregs of tea, and began gathering up the copies.

As I knelt on the floor with the papers, one of them

caught my eye. I'd been so focused on the old list of family names that I had forgotten all about the articles I'd copied. Although this article was dated two years after the Captain's death, a docent at the museum had pointed it out to me as one of interest. Apparently, it was quite the scandal of the day. How it related to my lighthouse or the Captain's death I didn't yet know, but I decided to give it a quick read.

The article was lengthy and the type small. I yawned more than a few times trying to read it. The gist of it was that a prominent captain in the town had been accused of a crime. The man's name was Captain Edmond Cuthbert. The captain owned his ship and had been a longtime resident of the town. He was partially responsible for petitioning the state to give Beacon Harbor town status. Although revered as a pillar of the community, Captain Cuthbert had been found out to be a ringleader for a band of thugs. Although he touted himself a lumber baron, transporting milled lumber across the Great Lakes, he was, in fact, a smuggler of stolen paintings, jewelry, alcohol, and gold. I turned off my flashlight.

"Smuggling," I said to the glittering stars. "Smuggling," I uttered again as if it was somehow important, and closed my eyes.

I awoke to the sound of my name as the sweet smell of pipe smoke tickled my nose. An instant later, my eyes flew open, yet all I saw was darkness. Momentary panic struck, as I realized I was not in my room, not in my bed. Yet as the gossamer web of dreams faded, it suddenly hit me. I had fallen asleep in the lantern room, and although my skin prickled as ephemeral impressions of an older man in a dark blue uniform smoking a pipe receded into the darkness, I knew I was alone.

I took a deep gulp of air. The moment I did, a thunderous bark echoed up the tower stairs. Wellington! What time was it? I sat up higher in the chair and glanced at my iPhone. Three o'clock, it said. Dammit, I thought. Some lightkeeper I'd be, falling asleep on the job.

Wellington let out a string of agitated barks.

I leapt from my chair. "Welly, I'm coming!" And I had every intention of doing just that, until I saw the lights.

They were not coming from the lake like they had the other night. This light, happening in two short bursts, had come from the marina. I picked up the pair of binoculars I kept in the tower and tried to see where the light had come from, but it was too dark. Then, unbelievably, the sound of a diesel engine starting up pulled my attention a little closer to home.

Although lantern rooms were traditionally surrounded in glass, mine, because it hovered just above roof level and had been built on a point, had a dark shield that prevented the beacon from shining directly on the lighthouse and the land behind it. Historically speaking, when the great lantern was lit, it would rotate, casting its beam across the lake in a sweeping arc that touched land on both sides of the point. However, as the beam rotated over the lighthouse, the shield blocked it from flooding the town with an unwanted roving light. For this reason, I had to peek around the shield to see what was happening on the lighthouse grounds. My jaw dropped when I saw the white sides of the Oberland Dairy truck pass under my garage lights. I ran around to the other side of the dark panel and watched it pull out of my driveway and turn down Lakeshore Drive, heading for the marina.

"Just a minute, Welly," I cooed down the stairwell, hoping to calm my dog. "I'll be down in a second. Be a good puppy." Wellington continued to whine as I picked up the binoculars once again and followed the Oberland Dairy truck to the marina.

My heart was pounding as I kept telling myself that there wasn't anything suspicious about an early morning delivery—even though I was certain we didn't have one scheduled, being that we were closed and not using copious amounts of butter, eggs, cheese, milk, and cream at the moment—or the fact that the truck was now backing up on one of the long cement docks. Two beams of light appeared this time, both making their way toward the vehicle. The driver got out and opened the rear doors. Then he began unloading what looked to be sacks of flour.

I got a good glimpse of one of the men from the marina. "Uber driver Mike!" I shook my head in dismay. "What the devil are you doing with so much flour in a dairy truck at three in the morning?" My inner voice promptly answered, *Nothing good*. Then, the words from the old article came flooding back to me: smuggling. In that moment it all clicked. Captain Willy Riggs had seen smugglers on that night long ago. The thought kicked my inner New Yorker into the red zone. Blood pulsed behind my eardrums, but not from fear. It was pure, unadulterated outrage.

Obviously, whoever else was on the docks had no idea I'd been watching them. I had the element of surprise, and I was going to use it. With a head exploding from indignation, and a heart demanding answers, I grabbed my flashlight and cell phone, and descended the tower stairs as swiftly as I could.

"Come on, Welly," I whispered, pulling him into the cool darkness with me. We left the lighthouse grounds and made our way onto the beach. It was then that I realized that Mike was loading all the sacks of flour onto his boat. And I caught a glimpse of the other man.

Anger consumed me, spurring me to run faster across the beach. Because, once again, I realized that I had been used. When I hit the halfway mark, I also realized that I was in the remotest point on the long stretch of beach. The lighthouse was far behind me; the marina loomed in the distance. Then, suddenly, Wellington stopped. I took another step or two until his booming bark broke the silence.

A frisson of fear shot through me at the same moment a beam of a light broke the darkness, casting my shadow on the beach before me. I spun around. Momentarily blinded by the light, I grabbed Wellington by the collar and brought my arm up to shield my eyes. In one painful clench, all the blood drained from my heart.

"Dylan," I said, and stared at the gun in her hand.

CHAPTER 42

"Where ya going, Lindsey?" Her tone was conversational, but I was too stunned to speak, and she knew it. Wellington, normally greeting her with wagging tail, was clearly agitated by her sudden appearance. He emitted a low growl as she added, "You should be asleep, safely tucked in bed. Him too."

"I haven't been sleeping very well, not with the bakery being shut down."

"Well, that is a pity." Her pretty face clouded as if she meant it, but then her eyes hardened again.

Wellington, sensing my fear, let out a series of earth-shattering barks.

"My God, the barking! Barking! Barking! Barking!" she mocked. "Stop the barking, Lindsey, or I'll have to stop it myself." She flipped her dark ponytail behind her back and aimed her gun at my dog.

Dylan had officially snapped, and it broke my heart. I'd thought we were friends; she had gone out of her way to help me, and she'd been a dream of an employee. What the heck had she gotten herself into? Wellington was straining against his collar as he barked at her. He was a big dog, and strong. I held on for dear life. "Dylan," I pleaded, "I don't know what this is all about, but please put down the gun and let's talk. You're scaring Welly. He doesn't like guns pointed in his face."

"Not my fault," she said, holding her gun steady.

"Okay. Okay, don't shoot. Let me send him away."

"I swear, if he comes toward me, I'm putting a bullet in him."

I'd never been so scared in my life. Welly was more than a dog. He was my best friend, a constant companion, a calming presence in a world of chaos. I needed to send him to safety, but I wasn't sure he would go. I knelt in the sand beside him and gave him a long hug, thinking I might never get the chance to feel his soft fur again. Fighting back tears, I took a deep breath, tried to smile, and held his giant head between my hands. "Wellington, go home." Then, with forced excitement in my voice, I commanded, "Get fish. Get fish!" and pointed down the beach, hoping he would know what that meant. Slightly confused, he took two steps toward Dylan. She lowered the gun at the same time I sternly commanded, "Get fish!"

Welly lifted his head and looked at me. I fought hard to remain calm and prayed that all his obedience training would override his natural instincts. Apparently, it did. He turned and disappeared into the darkness.

"'Get fish'? That's your command? No wonder he's a muddleheaded nuisance." Flashing mean-girl attitude, she picked up a rock and threw it as hard as she could in Wellington's direction.

I flinched and was infinitely grateful when I heard it hit the sand. Angry, she swung her light down the beach. The rock was where she had thrown it; Wellington had disappeared. She might have wanted to investigate that further but knew that the longer her attention was on my dog, the more time I had to subvert her efforts. I was about to make my move when the gun, and the light, swung back to me.

"Give me your phone!" Angry, she snatched it from my hand. She looked at the unsent text and shook her head. "Tuck? As in Officer Tuck McAllister?"

"He's a policeman."

"He's an idiot. Shame on you!" She cast me a look of extreme annoyance as she erased the text. She then shoved my phone in her pocket.

Welly was gone and now my phone. I felt extremely vulnerable.

"Stupid move, Lindsey," she warned. "You must know by now that I can't let you live. You saw us, and now it's over."

"I saw something," I agreed. "But I'm still unclear as to what this is all about."

"It's about our little side business, one we've been conducting right under your nose."

Although her answer caused another wave of prickling fear, it was nothing compared to the barrel of the gun she was pointing at me. Unsure of what to do next, she brought out her phone and dialed a number. "Hey, babe," she addressed the voice on the other end. "Lindsey's seen us. I have her. What do you want me to do with her?" She gave a curt nod and ended the call.

"Really?" I said, and gave her my best *girl, you're crazy* look.

The one thing my inner New Yorker loathed was the feeling of vulnerability. Like a suit of protective armor, it came up around me, unleashing my no-nonsense city-girl attitude with a vengeance. Dylan had been conducting some kind of illegal business at my lighthouse; she had threatened to shoot my dog, and now she had my cell phone. It was time to go on the attack!

"You're taking advice from a man?" I poked. "That's so nineteen-fifties. Wait, you were talking to Carl, right?" I gave a disparaging shake of my head. "That's even worse, considering he's probably taking orders from Mike, which means you're basically shackled to the patriarchy. You're their puppet, Dylan; their tool. And if you're planning on using that gun on me, you might as well just flush your girl-power card down the toilet with your dignity."

"Stop it," she spat. I had gotten under her skin.

I wasn't exactly a modern feminist. I was a confident woman who loved working with other confident people and, for better or worse, loved men. I also believed that women needed the support of other women, unless they were holding a gun to your head. In that case, the gloves were off. "Dylan, as your friend and your boss, here's the truth. You don't need to be involved in your boyfriend and cousin's illicit dealings, whatever they may be. You're better than that. You're a gifted baker."

Illuminated by the flashlight, her face contorted as if battling an inner demon. "I sometimes think that's true, but it's not. I make bad choices, Lindsey. I can't help it. I just do." I was about to counter this when she poked the gun at me, indicating that I walk down the beach with her.

"I like baking," she admitted. "It calms me. And I liked working with you. But I knew from the very start that things were not going to end well." Her voice broke a little as she added, "I thought about turning them in, but I hardly know you, and Mike and Carl are all I have. Mike's taken care of me all my life. Carl can be a mean son of a gun, but Mike trusts him, and I know he has my back. Mike and I, we don't come from the best family, ya know. No silver spoons in our mouths. We've had to work for everything we've had. We're survivors, and we can't say no to easy money."

I took a deep breath. It was quite a confession, but I still believed I could reason with her.

"Well, for obvious reasons," I began, trying to ignore the gun in my back as I walked, "I'm not going to offer advice on men, but I do know a little about money. And here's the truth: There's no such thing as easy money. The trouble with money is that there are always strings attached. Take a loan from the bank and you'll be paying interest for the term of that loan; take a monetary gift from a friend and morally you'll owe them something of equal value in return; steal money and you'll be paying it off in prison. The best kind of money, Dylan, is the kind you earn yourself through hard work, perseverance, and smart choices. Just like you were doing at the Beacon."

"Aren't you listening to me?" she seethed, growing truly angry. "I wasn't making smart choices, or I wouldn't be here now. And here's the truth of it, Lindsey. You should have stayed in New York with your fancy job, your douchey boyfriend, and your easy life. This is a small town. We have our secrets." She shoved me forward again, causing me to stumble in the sand.

"Maybe I should have," I admitted, thinking of my

safe and secure life in the Big Apple. "But I needed a change. I honestly never thought I'd buy a lighthouse, Dylan, but the moment I saw the Beacon Harbor Lighthouse for sale on the internet, I had the feeling that I was meant to be here."

"Well, that was your mistake."

"Look, whatever you're involved in here, I can help you. Just please, put down the gun," I pleaded.

"It's too late, Lindsey. I killed that woman. I poisoned her coffee. It was supposed to be Betty, but I can't even get that right."

The moment Dylan had pulled the gun on me, I assumed she was connected to the murders, but hearing her admit it induced a whole new level of fear in me. "What? That was you? Why? Betty believes in you. She cares about you. She was so happy that you were working at my bakery."

"Poor Betty. She was happy to sell the old lighthouse the moment she knew it would be a bakery. She knew I could bake and wanted to give me the opportunity to use my skills again."

"But that's wonderful," I said, thinking that Betty was the closest thing Dylan had to a guardian angel. That she should try to kill her was unthinkable.

"Wonderful?" she spat. "It's a lot of pressure to live under. You don't know this, but Betty is my godmother. All my life she's been trying to help me, and all my life I've been disappointing her. Do you know how that feels—having a mother who doesn't care about you and a nosy do-gooder of the town who goes out of her way, trying to save your ass at every turn? I'm a screwup, Lindsey. I'm a constant disappointment, and she knows it!"

"Easy," I said, feeling the gun poking in my back with

her anger. "Betty is a charitable woman, and you're lucky to have her in your life. What I don't understand is why you tried to poison her with cyanide."

She grunted. "Because Mike told me I had to."

"What? And you listened to him?"

"I had to. Betty was a threat to our little side business. You see, Mike is also Betty's godchild. She adores him, always has, and would never believe he'd do anything to hurt the town. You may not know this, but before you bought the lighthouse, Mike was the caretaker of the property, making sure it didn't get too run-down. Betty helped get him appointed to the job. Thought he could use the extra money to supplement his fishing charter and Uber driving business. I told you that we used to hang out at the old lighthouse as kids, getting into trouble, remember? Well, once Mike got the keys to the lighthouse, our old habits kicked up again. You see, Mike has charm, and Betty trusts him completely."

"Again, why did you try to kill her? It makes no sense!"

"Because Betty was about to ruin everything. And you were going to provide us with the perfect means to keep our little operation going. Mike gave me the cyanide. Told me to slip it in Betty's drink when she came in on opening day, as we all knew she would. Having Betty die in your bakeshop would solve two problems. It would get rid of the nosy do-gooder, while giving Mike near total control of her property. And you'd be the one to blame for her death. With the bakery in a tailspin, I'd step in and offer to keep it going while you were in jail. In a few months we'd have enough money to buy it from you. I'd run the bakery, and Mike and Carl would have the means to run their business."

I stared at her in disbelief. "You've been using me and my lighthouse from the start! I don't know who's worse, you three or my cheating pig of an ex-fiancé."

"But Betty didn't die," she continued, ignoring my outburst. "How was I to know that you had pissed off a crazy little diva? And I certainly wasn't prepared for her anger. Imagine my surprise when I saw her rip that cyanide-laced latte from Betty's hand."

"You watched her do it!" I said. "You knew she was going to die, and yet you said nothing."

"Really? What was I supposed to say? Hey, don't drink that, it's laced it with poison? Not likely. And anyhow, it created the distraction we needed. Your bakery was shut down and you were suspect number one. When I asked to keep working, it wasn't really about the money. I needed to be there to handle things."

"But you were baking," I reasoned. "You were also helping us solve the murder."

"I was with you," she explained, "because you might have gotten suspicious if I wasn't. It was a good plan. After that little diva died, Mike got spooked and backed off Betty, hoping the murder would distract her long enough for us to finish what we started. But then Betty remembered that it was her latte that killed your friend."

"Wait. I'm confused," I admitted. "You're smuggling bags of flour out of my lighthouse and were trying to kill Betty because she cares about you?"

"Haven't you figured it out yet?" Dylan's voice held a tinge of disbelief. "Dear Lord, even nosy Betty was figuring it out, and that was the problem. She was watching it happen right under her nose. She has a perfect view of the lighthouse from her office window, and yet she didn't want to believe such illicit dealings could happen in her precious town, or that Mike and I were the masterminds behind it."

Dylan stopped talking long enough to shove me behind a tall outcropping of rocks. I realized too late that she had taken me to the most secluded spot on the beach. The hair on the back of my neck prickled as an image floated in my mind. Somehow, I knew with every fiber of my being that Captain Willy Riggs had stood in this same spot long ago. And on this same spot he had died. I thought it a bizarre twist in a surreal tale, because if Dylan had her way, I would die here too.

"We needed to get rid of Betty," she continued, knowing her confession wouldn't matter. "Betty was growing suspicious. She pulled me aside before the bakery opened, asking a lot of questions about the Oberland Dairy deliveries."

"So, Frank Peters wasn't really delivering our dairy products?" I asked, wanting to keep her talking.

"Frank Peters doesn't work for Oberland Dairy. He painted his truck to look like he does. Josh Cramer is the real delivery guy. He came last Wednesday at nine a.m. Betty knows the difference. She saw him as well as the other delivery truck Frank uses. She asked me if I was having a fling with the Oberland Dairyman because he's at the lighthouse so often. We all knew she was growing suspicious, and we couldn't take the chance."

"You were the one who ordered the sandwich at Harbor Hoagies," I stated, realizing how it all made sense.

"I did, and hired a kid off the street to deliver it to Betty's office. Saying it was from you was a nice touch, don't you think? You were the prime suspect in Mia Long's death. Blaming you for Betty's death would connect the two. You'd be behind bars, and I'd keep the bakery running. But it didn't work out that way."

"Only by the sheer grace of God," I added. "But why flour?" As I kept her talking, I realized Mike's boat had been loaded. Frank Peters in his dairy truck was leaving the marina. That's when I noticed a man making his way toward us on the beach. It was Carl.

"Flour?" she repeated, and gave an unhinged croak of a laugh. "You really are the most gullible big city girl I've met. Think more expensive, and far more addictive."

"Cocaine?" I asked, horrified. "Oh my God, you haven't been storing cocaine in my bakery?"

"Not cocaine. Heroin. Used to be pot, but now that it's legal everyone's growing it. We were too, on Betty's land that Mike has unprecedented access to. We have quite the production going on out there. But we've branched out. Heroin's the new drug of choice. Mike picks the load up from his supplier out on the lake in the dead of night. Frank in the Oberland truck picks it up from the dock and delivers it to our secret cabin on Betty's land. There we process it, hiding it in sacks of flour."

"That's what you're storing in my bakery? Heroin hidden in sacks of flour?" I was beyond outraged.

"Yep. There it waits, sitting harmlessly in storage until it's time to deliver it to our buyer. That happens on the lake too. And that's where we're going now, to meet up with him. From there the seemingly harmless sacks of flour are taken up to Canada and delivered to another storage unit run by the cartels. Pretty ingenious, isn't it?"

"No!" I seethed. "It's utterly despicable."

"Yeah, well, nobody suspects a sleepy little town like Beacon Harbor of being a link in the drug chain, and that's why it works. And it'll keep working, once you and Betty are out of the way."

The fact that she could talk so plainly about murder and her role in moving one of the most heinous drugs in history—using my bakeshop as a front, no less—pushed me over the edge.

"You're not a puppet of the patriarchy," I cried. "You're a parasitic drug mule!" Before she had time to react to that, I kicked her as hard as I could in the shin. She dropped the gun and moaned. Seizing my opening, I shoved her with all my might into the rocks. Dylan fell. I dashed around her, aiming for the open beach and my lighthouse, but I had underestimated her strength. I might have had the advantage of height, but Dylan was built like a tenacious woman wrestler. With the speed of a striking viper, her hand shot out, grabbing my ankle and twisting it. I fell to the ground beside her. We then both scrambled for the gun.

I wasn't proud of it, but I was officially in a girl fight. As Dylan pummeled me like a lump of overworked dough, I slapped, clawed, and elbowed my way through the sand, searching for the gun. "Ouch," I cried. She was on my back and had ripped a lock of my hair from my scalp. It burned. "Dammit!" I elbowed her with all my might in the thigh.

Dylan growled and wrapped her hands around my neck, trying to choke me instead. She was doing a good job of it too. I couldn't breathe. I was growing light-headed. I was close to passing out when my fingers touched cold metal. I pushed myself to the limit of my ability and reached for the gun. My fingers were nearly around it when I was suddenly yanked off the ground. The gun fell to the sand again.

"Kill her, already," Carl ordered. "We're wasting time." He flung me around and shoved my back against the rock. He then picked up the gun and handed it to Dylan.

With Dylan I'd had a small chance, but now it was two against one. My head suddenly filled with wispy images of another struggle long ago—another fruitless struggle. It was a premonition that I was going to die.

As Dylan walked over to me holding the gun, I rested my back against the rock and stared out at the dark lake. Tears came to my eyes as I thought of Wellington, Kennedy, and my parents. "Shooting me won't solve your problems," I uttered through a sob.

Dylan raised the gun and pointed it at my head.

"She's right," Carl mused, and took a step toward me. I kept my focus on the lake, the calming lake. I thought I was hallucinating when I saw a dark figure rise out of the waves behind Carl, dripping water like a neoprene monster. It moved stealthily onto the beach. I thought I was hallucinating until a sudden flash of clarity made me realize what was happening.

"We should bring her aboard the boat and drown her. That way no one would find the body." It was the last thing Carl said before dropping to the sand with a dull thud. The man stood tall behind him, staring at me.

Dylan screamed. Fear gripped me anew as she aimed her gun. She was going to shoot the diver!

My inner New Yorker sprang into action. With the speed of an angry prize fighter, I sucker punched her as hard as I could in the face. "Not on my watch!" I cried, as the gun flew from her hand and her limp body dropped to the ground beside her boyfriend.

The diver, wasting no time, zip-tied their hands behind their backs. He then lifted his mask. "The beach is secure," he said into the military-grade speaker near his mouth before removing it altogether.

Floodlights appeared, illuminating the darkness as the roar of boat motors sprang to life. The identity of the diver, my rescuer, was no longer a mystery.

"You're mighty brave for a baker," said Rory Campbell, and wrapped his cold, wet arms around me.

CHAPTER 43

I was still stunned and shaking as the beach burst to life with a hive of activity. Coast Guard boats were on the water. Police sirens blared as squad cars raced across the sand to assist us. Carl and Dylan were beginning to stir as Mike, aboard his fishing charter now loaded with drugs, was making a run for it. He wasn't going to get far.

"I've never been so scared in my life," I admitted, resting my head against Rory's wetsuit as Sergeant Murdock and Officer Tuck jumped from their cars. "I feel so stupid. I never saw it coming." Then, looking up at him, I asked, "How did you know where to find me?"

"Welly came howling at my door at three in the morning, covered in sand. He was in such a state of agitation that I knew something was wrong. The fact that you weren't with him set off all my alarm bells. I left him in my cabin and ran to the lighthouse. When I found it unlocked and the door to the tower open, I climbed to the lantern room. Once there I saw the flashlight on the beach as well as the activity at the marina. I had a pretty good idea of what was going on." Rory gave me another life-affirming hug and released me. Still close, he looked into my eyes. "Lindsey, I haven't been totally honest with you. I have a lot to tell you, but let me start with this. I am a retired Navy SEAL, but I've been working undercover for the Coast Guard for the last six months—"

"Was news to us, too," Murdock interjected as she bent to pull Dylan from the sand. She then broke character completely and graced us with a smile. Dylan, still wobbly from my epic punch, glared at me. "Got to hand it to you, Bakewell," Murdock continued. "For a baker you're one tough cookie. And Campbell, glad you're on our side. Welcome to Beacon Harbor." She turned and walked Dylan to her squad car. Tuck and another police officer had taken control of Carl. That's when Kennedy suddenly appeared, marching toward us through the sand in designer silk pajamas and panting from exertion.

"What is going on here?" she demanded, looking slightly unkempt. "The beach is lit up like a music festival, only there's no music, just—Oh my God! Dilly?"

Dylan, embarrassed, looked away as Kennedy stomped over to her. Always ready for a photo op, she pulled out her phone and began snapping pictures. "I can't believe it. I feel so betrayed. You're the murderer? You were the one poisoning people with cyanide? You shut down Lindsey's bakery? Why on earth would you do something like that?"

"Drugs," I answered for her. "Apparently, Dylan was storing them in our bakery before they could be smuggled out."

"What?" Kennedy found the news just as outrageous as the rest of us. She then turned to Sergeant Murdock. "You searched Lindsey's bakery for hours. How does something like drugs escape your notice?"

"Because we hid them in the sacks of flour, the ones with red lettering," Carl bragged as he was shoved into the back seat of Tuck's squad car. He stuck his head out and continued talking. "The sacks of flour with the blue lettering is really flour. Those were the only ones Dylan opened for the bakery, and you never knew it. Ha!"

"The jokes on you, Carl. You'll be wearing felon-orange for the rest of your life. Nothing screams pathetic loser as loud as felon-orange." Kennedy shut the car door on him before he could reply. She then turned her attention to Rory. She looked him up and down from head to toe. "I don't even want to know what's going on here, but you're dripping all over my friend."

"He saved my life is what he did," I told her. "I thought I was going to die. Dylan was going to shoot me because I'd finally realized what was going on. I was up in the light tower researching the Captain's death when I saw the dairy truck leave the lighthouse and drive to the marina. It was three in the morning. I knew something wasn't right. I left the lighthouse with Wellington and went to investigate. Dylan must have been in the bakery. She followed us across the beach and pulled a gun on us. She was going to shoot Welly because he was barking. I . . . I was so scared."

"Oh, poor darling," she cried, and hugged me as if her life depended on it. "I can't even imagine. What a she-devil; what a pack of wankers. Oh, and look at your face!" She gasped, turning me toward the headlights to get a better look. "It's getting all puffy, and . . . is that a black eye?"

"I was in a girl fight too," I blubbered, fighting back tears of embarrassment. "A girl fight! Imagine what Ellie would say if she ever found out?"

Kennedy smiled. "Ellie Montague-Bakewell would be as proud of you as I am. You caught the murderer and exposed a drug ring." Then, as if it suddenly dawned on her, she asked, "Is . . . Wellington okay?"

"He's fine," Rory said, setting her at ease. "He's also quite the hero. Wellington and his frantic barking set the whole takedown in action. I was aware that something illegal was going on in Beacon Harbor and have been trying to put the pieces together. Wellington's arrival in the middle of the night sent me running to the lighthouse. From there I was able to see that something was going on down the beach. I alerted the authorities, coordinated my plan with the Coast Guard, then suited up for a night mission. I left Welly at my place, for obvious reasons, and got in my boat. The moment I rounded the point, I got into place, reported my location, and slipped into the water. And then I swam like the devil toward shore, and Lindsey."

I looked at him. "My goodness, you really do have secrets, don't you?"

Kennedy smiled at him as well. "Don't let this go to your head, Hunts-a-Lot, but you really are my hero. Thank you, my friend." I believe she would have given him a big hug if he wasn't still dripping all over the sand in his diving gear. The water would have wreaked havoc on her silk pajamas. Instead she shook his hand.

"And you, my friend," she began with an air of resignation, "you solved the mystery and saved your bakery. I suppose this means I'm going to have to honor my word and do a podcast with Jeffery."

Wellington, having been separated from me for the remainder of the night, sprang on my bed at ten in the morning and attacked me with his joyful tongue. Although tired after six hours of restless sleep, I was overjoyed to see him as well. I was acutely aware that if it hadn't been for Wellington and his faithful obedience to me, he might have gotten shot, and I might have been Dylan's third victim.

Welly's presence also meant that Rory was downstairs. My dog had spent the night with him. Rory had promised to bring him back in the morning. I got out of bed, washed my swollen face, ran a comb through my sand-infested hair, and threw on a pair of jeans. I then left my room to meet him.

Kennedy was in the kitchen making coffee. There was no sign of Rory.

"He stopped by a few minutes ago to drop off Welly," she informed me. "I practically pulled him inside, but he refused to come in. Said he was in a hurry, but he wanted me to give you this." She handed me a note.

> *Lindsey,*
> *Had to leave town to finish the business started last night. Dylan, Carl, and Mike are to be transferred into federal custody and officially charged with their crimes. Won't bother you with the details, but I want you to know that I'm happy you and Wellington are safe. We need to talk, but not over the phone. Please bear with me until I return.*
> *Rory*

"Is it a love note?" Kennedy set a cup of coffee on the table and leaned over my shoulder. "Umm, not a love note," she remarked, unable to resist the temptation of reading the message. "Or maybe it is. We are talking about Sir Hunts-a-Lot, after all."

"I can only imagine what other secrets he's been hiding from me." I folded the note and gripped the mug of coffee with both hands, allowing its warmth to seep through me. I was in desperate need of caffeination, just as I was desperately trying to come to terms with the drama of last night. I had almost died at the hands of a woman I'd considered a friend; my dog had saved my life; and Rory Campbell was a flipping badass military special-ops hero. If it hadn't been for Rory and his impeccable timing . . . but I didn't want to think of that now. I took a sip of coffee and remarked, "I respect the undercover work, but I don't think I could handle learning he's already married with kids. Do you think he's married?" It was the only reason I could think why he wouldn't want to talk with me over the phone.

"If he is, he's going to live to regret it." Kennedy arched a menacing brow, causing me to smile.

"Whatever his secrets, the fact that I'm sitting here this morning, and the Beacon Harbor murderer has been caught, pretty much guarantees that I'll forgive him nearly anything."

"Smart man," she said, and raised her coffee mug to him.

I was just about to whip up a quick batch of blueberry muffins when Betty stopped by. She had come bearing flowers and a bakery bag from the local grocery store.

"Until your wonderful bakeshop came along, this was all we had." She placed the bag on the table and pulled out what looked like a coffee cake, only it wasn't. The rectangular cake had a crumble top sprinkled with powdered sugar and was filled with a layer of fluffy buttercream and strawberry jam. I'd never seen anything like it before, but it looked utterly sinful.

"It's a Swedish Flop," she proclaimed. "Although I'm not sure it's really Swedish. Not many have heard of it outside of Chicagoland, and since many of our vacationers come from the region, the owners of the grocery store decided to carry it. It's unusual but delicious, and after the trauma of last night"—her eyes began to tear up as she said this—"I thought you could use a treat."

"Oh, Betty, that's so thoughtful of you." As Kennedy went to find a vase for the flowers, I pulled three plates from the cupboard, three forks from cutlery drawer, and poured another cup of coffee for Betty. "This treat of yours looks like the perfect complement to a cup of hot black coffee."

Kennedy put the vase of flowers on the table as I began to cut and plate slices of the decadent coffee cake. I placed one in front of Betty and thought she was going to burst out in tears.

"I'm so sorry, dear," she said, dabbing her watery eyes with a napkin. "I honestly thought you were trying to murder me. Will you ever forgive me?"

"Betty, you've been nothing but kindness to me since I've moved here. And I must confess something to you as well. We thought that maybe you were behind the poisonings. We soon realized how wrong we were to suspect you."

"Well, dear," she said, placing a comforting hand over mine, "with two deaths in this quiet little town, we were all growing suspicious of everyone. But I must say, I never suspected that Dylan and Mike were behind everything."

"If it makes you feel any better," Kennedy began, the first bite of Swedish Flop balancing on her fork, "I didn't either. I was really beginning to like Dilly, too." She no sooner placed the Flop in her mouth than her whole face lit up with pleasure. "Not your granny's spotted dick, that's for certain! Never heard of Swedish Flop before, but it's now at the top of my list of favorite things."

Kennedy wasn't far off the mark. I'd have to look into adding Swedish Flop to the bakery cases. The first challenge would be finding a good recipe.

"I told you that I had two godchildren, but I never mentioned their names. I've always been so careful with Dylan and Mike," Betty explained, still trying to process the fact that they were caught up in a drug-smuggling ring that had been taking place on her private land and my lighthouse bakery. "They had a rough start of it, you know. A long history of felons in the family, and parents who didn't set the best example. My dear Peter wanted to make a difference. I did too. We convinced their parents to have the children baptized in the church, stating that Peter and I would be honored to be their godparents. You see, we thought we could make a difference in their lives. Peter and I took our vows seriously. We always tried to be a positive influence. When Peter passed, I continued to uphold our promise. I really believed that I could redirect their talents and energy. There is good in them," she proclaimed like the forgiving soul she was. I wasn't so ready to forgive. "Sampling Dylan's baked goods is proof of that. I really thought they had changed."

"She was a good actress," Kennedy said. "You have to

remember, Betty, she did her best to poison you. By my count, you should have died twice."

Betty shivered at the thought.

"You're a good person for trying to help them," I told her. "Maybe that's why Dylan never succeeded in poisoning you. I thought about that last night as I was trying to fall asleep. What are the odds that two angry, albeit innocent, women subverted her efforts by stealing something from you? Mia took your cyanide-laced coffee, and Fiona your cyanide-laced Coke. I guess what I'm getting at is that you have one heck of a vigilant angel watching over you."

"It's my Peter," she said, looking up at my ceiling with fondness. "I've always felt he's my guardian angel. Maybe while I was blindly trying to protect Dylan and Mike, he was, in fact, protecting me from them."

"It's a comforting thought," I told her, thinking it just might be true.

Betty and I chatted awhile longer. Through her I found out that Chad, the manager of the Harbor Hotel, had scribbled his phone number on the receipt not to ask me out on a date, as I had been led to believe, but to warn me about Dylan's history. She'd lost her job at the hotel when she was found stealing from the cash register. Chad, having a fondness for Dylan as well, never pressed charges. He also never suspected Dylan in any wrong-doing regarding Mia's death. He was simply trying to give me a heads-up, and Dylan likely knew it. Then, as we were finishing our coffee, I thought to ask her about a name that had piqued my curiosity the night before.

"You've lived in Beacon Harbor your whole life. Have you ever heard of a man by the name of Captain Edmond Cuthbert?"

"How odd that you should mention that name. I've never heard of Captain Edmond Cuthbert, but a man named Carson Cuthbert was Dylan and Mike's grand-father. Molly and Carson had two daughters, Carol and Cathy. We all went to the same high school." Betty's gaze grew distant with the memory.

"Lovely girls, but there was always something quite tragic about them. Their father was an alcoholic, you see. Unfortunately, both Carol and Cathy ended up marrying men of very weak characters as well. It's a long story. I'll spare you the sordid details because you already know the ending. But if you're interested in learning about the family history, you should go to the archives in the library."

After Betty left, Officer Cutie Pie stopped by. He needed a signed statement of the proceedings of the night before, which I was happy to give him. He then told me that once all the evidence of drug smuggling had been removed from the bakeshop, it would be cleared to open once again.

Kennedy and I cheered and celebrated the news. We pulled a bottle of champagne from the refrigerator and popped the cork. Then we made Tuck drink a glass with us.

"Come on," I prodded. "I'm now on Murdock's good side. She likes me. I caught the Beacon Harbor murderer red-handed."

"Besides, darling," Kennedy said, putting a glass of bubbly in his hand, "what happens at the Beacon, stays at the Beacon." She graced him with a flirty grin.

No man could resist that, including Tuck.

We were laughing, chatting, and making ridiculous toasts, when another knock came at the door. Wellington barked.

"I'll get it. I'll get it," I said, setting my glass of champagne on the coffee table before following Welly to the door. I opened it and got the shock of my life.

"Mom! Dad!" I cried, and ran into their waiting arms.

"After your call yesterday morning from the police station, how could we not drop everything and come to your rescue? We called Kennedy. She filled us in on the details. We had just arrived at the airport to catch our flight when Kennedy called again and told us how you were almost shot on the beach by your baker." Tears sprang to Mom's eyes as she talked. "We're so thankful you're alive, Lindsey." Mom gave me another hug and sauntered into the lighthouse with her two little white West Highland terriers, Brinkley and Ireland, prancing behind her like the supermodels they'd been named after. "Oooo, and isn't this just darling? I was expecting rustic, not this cozy little lakeside haven."

"Hope you don't mind we brought the dogs," Dad said, and smiled sheepishly. Wellington, for one, was overjoyed. "I'm so glad you're safe, my dear, although I heard you lost your assistant baker." Dad grinned. "I decided to come out of retirement and lend you a hand."

"Oh, Dad," I cried, and hugged him again.

CHAPTER 44

"Hi, friends, welcome to another edition of my podcast, Kennedy's Crusades, where we learn about all things hot, fabulous, and trendy, with me, your host, Kennedy Kapoor. Speaking of hot, fabulous, and trendy, we're coming to you live today from everybody's favorite lighthouse bakery, the Beacon Bakeshop Café in Beacon Harbor, Michigan. It's no secret that it's the brainchild of my bestie, Lindsey Bakewell, who will blow your mind with her delicious baked goods tomorrow, when she launches Opening Day 2.0. We hope to see you there. Another matter that's not so secret is that a few months ago, I took umbrage with Lindsey's cheating ex-fiancé, rising celebrity chef Jeffery Plank, over his insensitive statements about cows. Well, friends, as fate would have it, Jeffery and this fashionista have crossed paths once again, and I've had another chance to talk with the celebrity chef. After the recent death of his longtime love, renowned pastry chef Mia Long, it appears that Jeffery's ready to clear the air about many things, including his philandering ways, his derogatory remarks about cows, and his new personal crusade to champion responsibly raised meats. Ladies and gentlemen, it's my great pleasure to introduce my special guest today, Jeffery Plank."

"I'm so proud of you girls," Mom said in a soft voice, leaning on her elbows as she watched Kennedy conduct her podcast from across the bakery counter. Kennedy had set up her microphone and cameras at a secluded table under the wall of lighthouse memorabilia. It provided her and Jeffery enough privacy to conduct their interview, with the added benefit of having a live audience, namely Mom and me.

Mom and Dad had been a godsend from the moment they appeared on my doorstep, helping me get the bakeshop and café ready for what we were now calling our grand opening 2.0. I had high hopes for round number two, especially since Dad had been in the kitchen for two straight days, baking like a fiend. He'd been overjoyed to find he still had some mad baking skills since his days working at his parents' bakery in Traverse City. Mom had abandoned her disinfectant cloth to watch Kennedy in action.

"Look at her," she remarked softly, gesturing toward Kennedy with an elegant wave of her hand. I gestured to Mom to follow me to the kitchen so we wouldn't disturb Kennedy's live interview. Mom continued. "She's created a fashion marketing empire by blogging and tweeting. I don't understand it, but it's remarkable. In my day we didn't control the camera or the narrative. We simply put on our clothes and smiled."

I looked at her, wondering when the tables had turned. Kennedy had idolized my mom since the day they'd met, and now Mom was the one full of admiration.

"You were a model, Mom," I reminded her. "Kennedy's an influencer. We'll get her to explain it to you."

"And you," she said, shifting her focus to me. "I've been bursting with pride since the moment I entered this lighthouse. When you told me that you were quitting your job on Wall Street and moving to a lighthouse in the middle of nowhere, I cried. I cried, Lindsey, because I thought that my beautiful, talented daughter had given up on life, but now I understand. This is your dream, and you had the courage to follow it. I've always known that you were gifted in so many ways, but seeing this place brings it all home for me. You're a gifted baker with a head for business, just like your dad, only you have far better taste in decorating. I swear, Linds, I'm going to sample everything that comes out of that kitchen."

I was blushing with happiness. "Thanks, Mom, but you don't have to eat anything here. I won't be offended in the least. You're a model; it's part of the model's code: no butter, sugar, or yummy breads."

She gave me her cover-girl smile. "That was the old me," she confided. "The new me is practicing yoga and mindful meditation."

"Mom, that's great. But yoga doesn't burn the cals like cross-training."

"Oh, this isn't about calories, dear. Those are important, but not as important as you are. Yoga and meditation have taught me to be more mindful of the things that really matter. Truthfully, your father was driving me crazy when he retired. I needed better coping mechanisms, hence the yoga. And I want to sample everything you make as a celebration of your art and all your hard work. You are my daughter, and I'm so proud of you."

I stared at her, thinking she'd been abducted by aliens and replaced with a calmer, gentler, carb-eating clone. Then, however, the real Ellie Montague-Bakewell emerged.

"Of course, I'm not eating everything at once," she cautioned with a flip of her long, perfectly colored and styled ash-blond hair. "I have one of the world's most enviable wardrobes and I'd be a fool to throw it all away on warm, crusty, chocolaty, fruit-filled gluttony, but I am willing to dip my toe in moderation."

"Mom!" I teased. "You're living on the edge. But maybe it's time to let go of the old wardrobe and start a new one."

"Stretchy waistbands and long, billowy tops?"

I nodded. "I hate to break this to you, Mom, but you're getting older. Why not embrace it and start your own line of clothing for . . ." I didn't want to come out and say *old ladies*. Mom was in her midsixties and still looked great. I didn't want to offend her, so I settled on, "women of a certain age."

"I'll think about it." She grinned and opened the kitchen door. We went back to the bakery counter, leaning against it as we watched Kennedy's interview.

You know," Mom whispered, "I was never a fan of Jeffery's. I never thought he deserved you."

Jeffery, somehow hearing this, broke his concentration and stared at Mom. She smiled and waved.

"Oh, he didn't," I agreed, waving at him as well. Kennedy asked her question again, demanding his focus. "But I do feel bad about Mia. Jeffery's a talented chef. I won't ever date him again, but I will go to his restaurant. And I think others will too. He deserves a second chance, and I think he'll get it. Say what you will, but Americans are very forgiving people."

"That's very nice of you. And it was nice of you to let your father help in the kitchen. I haven't seen him this happy in a long time. Have you tasted this?" She held up a slice of Dad's apple-cinnamon bread, fresh out of the oven. "It's positively scrumptious . . . And speaking of scrumptious, who's that?" Mom wiggled her bread at the bakery doors. Outside, a handsome man was making his way to the bakery, his progress hindered by a small herd of dogs who'd been frolicking on the lighthouse grounds until he appeared.

"That's Rory," I said, waving at him through the windows. I smiled as he waved back.

"That's Rory?" Mom cast me a look while arching a pencil-enhanced brow. "I had pictured him as thicker, hairier, and with a sloping brow. That man out there is *gorgeous*."

I took off my apron and laid it on the counter. "He wears a lot of flannel and camo," I confided, watching him greet his canine friends.

"It doesn't matter what he wears with those shoulders and trim waist." Mom flashed me a suggestive grin and picked up her washcloth.

CHAPTER 45

I left the bakeshop and walked with Rory and the dogs to a little spot on the beach beneath the lighthouse. "What's this?" I asked, spying the blanket and the little wicker picnic basket.

"The beginnings of an apology." His smile was earnest as he offered me a seat on the plaid blanket. Welly was just about to sit down beside me when I shooed him away, making room for Rory. Brinkley, wearing her signature pink diamond collar, and Ireland, wearing an identical one in emerald—it was the only way I could tell them apart—were both clamoring for a space on my lap. Welly, eyeing the lapdogs with envy, opted for a corner of the blanket beside Rory. I ruffled his big head and watched with pleasure as Rory began unpacking homemade sandwiches, a tray of sliced melon and strawberries, a bag of potato chips, and a bottle of wine. "I'm better with a grill," he confessed, handing me a kaiser roll filled with so much roast beef and cheese, I almost laughed.

"These look delicious," I told him honestly. "But before I take a bite, I have to ask: Are you married?"

"What?" He looked at me as if I'd gone mad. "No."

"Any kids?"

He shook his head.

"Good. You said you had secrets. I won't have a picnic with you if you're hiding a wife and kids. It might not look like it at times, but I do have standards." Overestimating my abilities, I took a bite of the ridiculously large sandwich. The bun slid back; meat, cheese, and a fringe of lettuce squirted out the sides. I felt like a toddler eating a Big Mac for the first time, and, in all likelihood, looked the part. Covering quickly, I mumbled, "Really good," while covertly picking up the scraps before the dogs attacked them. But, like blood in the water, the dogs sensed weakness and dove in.

Rory, acting quickly, pulled out a strip of roast beef from his own sandwich and lured Wellington to his side while I brought the models under control.

"I've never lied to you, Lindsey," he said, nudging Welly's curious nose away while attempting to pour a glass of white wine. Achieving success, he handed me the glass and poured one for himself. "But I have omitted the truth from time to time. I am trying to write a book, and I do hunt when it's the right season, but my real focus has been to stop drug trafficking across the Canadian border. When Mia Long was murdered at your bakery, I felt that maybe somehow you were involved in the drug ring. But the more I've gotten to know you, the more I realized what an idiot notion that was. However, I did suspect a connection to your bakery. Your friend Kennedy set off all kinds of warning bells for me, but the more I investigated her, the more I realized she's exactly what she claims to be. The woman posts literally everything she does on social media. Unless you're into clothes and makeup, it's not very interesting."

I was in the process of taking another bite of the sandwich before his confession. I set it down and stared at him. "You thought I was smuggling drugs?" I found the notion more than a little insulting. "That's why you've been keeping tabs on me?"

"Yes and no. It's not that simple. I was contacted by Captain Miller of the Coast Guard shortly before you moved in. He and his men have been tasked with many things, but the illegal shipping of drugs across our northern border has been a particular thorn in his side. His intel suggested activity along this stretch of coast, and since he knew I had recently moved into the area, he contacted me. Then, shortly thereafter, you bought the lighthouse and a whole flurry of activity began."

"The place was a dump! I was in the midst of renovations! You . . . you were spying on me?" I nearly spilt my wine.

"I came to be neighborly," he said with a wan smile. "I met Wellington first, if you'll remember. And I had gotten the lowdown on you from Betty. Welly was the perfect icebreaker. And, in all honesty, you've been the best neighbor I've ever had."

His look, like his beach-picnic romantic gesture, was sincere. "Thanks, I think."

"It's a compliment, Lindsey, which is why I have to confess another misdeed of mine. You see, I really did plant the notion that your lighthouse was haunted."

"But it is haunted," I countered in all seriousness. "All my life I thought ghost stories were just that, stories. I've never believed in ghosts, but I do now." He was looking at me with something akin to pity. I narrowed my eyes and confessed, "I've felt the Captain, Rory. Captain Willy Riggs really did die in this lighthouse. Well, he died on the beach, then was brought back to the lighthouse. We've been through that."

He nodded. "That's history. History is real, but ghosts aren't. Take, for example, that night before your grand opening. We both saw a light in the lighthouse. I told you it was a ghost light, a portent of danger. I was a little spooked by it as well, but now I believe it was Dylan who was up there signaling the delivery boat."

"But you don't know that for sure, do you?" I cast him a look and popped a strawberry into my mouth.

"No, but it stands to reason. Given what we now know, I do believe it was her."

"I've read the articles, Rory. The ghost lights of Beacon Harbor were happening long before Dylan and Mike started their drug trafficking ring. And you went up there, remember? You said you didn't see anything."

"I didn't, but I did do something that I'm not proud of. I saw your computer up there and planted some military-grade software on it that enabled me to contact you directly and covertly."

I was about to attempt another bite of the huge sandwich when he said this. Warning bells exploded in my head as anger crept into my throat. "That was you? You pretended to be the ghost of Captain Willy?" I was outraged.

"I told you that I didn't know what was happening at the lighthouse. I wanted to keep an eye on you. Then, when Mia Long died, I grew suspicious. I thought it best to engage you directly and see if you'd get involved. I'm sorry to have scared you. I wanted you to think that you were conversing with a ghost."

"Well, mission accomplished! But I liked talking to Captain Willy. Once I got over the fact that he was a ghost, I rather liked him. We were connecting."

Rory stared at me. "Yes, but . . . that was me." He gave me an odd look as he repeated, "I was the one talking to you, not a ghost. Lindsey, if you'll bring me your laptop, I'll remove the software."

With the help of the dogs, I had managed to eat half the sandwich. The wine, however, I had no problem with. I emptied my glass and stood up from the blanket. "Nah, I'm good."

"No. Really, I should remove it."

"I like the Captain," I repeated again, staring at him with a straight face. "He really got me, you know? It's been a long time since anyone's talked to me like that in bed."

Rory began to understand what I was saying. "Interesting," he said. "Did you know that I'm a captain too?" Welly picked that moment to sit up and lick him in the face.

"I didn't know that," I said, impressed to hear it. "But here's an even more puzzling question." I lowered my voice conspiratorially. "Do you think ghosts know about sexting?"

His blue eyes twinkled at the thought. Playing along, he shrugged. "Not sure. But I think you should definitely give it a try."

"I agree. And I will, but right now I've got a bakery to get ready. Tomorrow is Opening Day 2.0."

Rory stood with his back to the lake. Welly and the models stood as well. "Need a barista?" he asked, a hopeful look on his face.

"Thanks, but I've actually got that covered. I've also figured out what happened to Captain Willy Riggs on the night he died. In an odd sort of way, I believe his story has come full circle. Did you know that Mike and Dylan were related to the man most likely to have shot him?"

Rory, looking impressed, shook his head.

"I'm still digging out the details. Anyhow, I was planning on telling the Captain all about it tonight at, oh, say, ten o'clock? That's a little early for the Captain, but it's better for me. I have to be up very early."

"I'll bet." He smiled.

"Thanks for the lunch, Rory. And I accept your apology. See you at the bakeshop tomorrow."

"Wouldn't miss it for the world."

I cast him a smile and headed back to the lighthouse with three rambunctious dogs leading the way.

CHAPTER 46

I had butterflies in my stomach, I was so nervous. I had prepared for this day for so long, and I was undoubtedly ready. Still, thoughts of murder and mayhem lingered. Ten minutes until the bakery was officially open again. It was Opening Day 2.0. Why was I so nervous?

It was a sunny, blue-sky morning on the lake. That should have been a good omen, right? On the other side of the door, a crowd was gathering. Murdock, Tuck McAllister, and two more officers I recognized, due to my short stint in the slammer, were first in line, all dressed in their police blues. Murdock and Tuck were chatting with Kennedy. She had insisted on parading Wellington outside on the bakeshop lawn again, something I was a little uncomfortable with. The last time she had used such tactics, it hadn't gone well. "Oh, do have a little confidence, Lindsey," she had chided. "Welly's the town hero. Do you think he'd let another sniveling drug smuggler through these doors?"

She had a point.

Behind the police officers, I spied Ginger Brooks and Felicity Stewart. The women were chatting amicably with Carol Hoggins from You Had Me In Stitches and Christy Parks from the Bayside Boutique. Next the Johnsons arrived with their dog, Libby. Bill Morgan appeared as well. All four women turned and waved at the new arrivals, reminding me that Beacon Harbor really was a close-knit community.

Wellington, spying Libby, was so excited he slipped from Kennedy's grasp to welcome his furry friend. Kennedy chased after him as more people came up the walkway, spilling onto the lawn and milling around the outdoor tables and under the bright red umbrellas.

Where was Betty?

"Dear?" I took a deep breath and faced the bakery cases. "What do you think?"

Mom was behind the counter proudly wearing her red apron over a designer black blouse and black jeans. With the exception of her signature, age-defying bangs, her hair was swept off her face and tied into a thick ponytail. She smiled, batted her long eyelashes, and spun around. Wendy and Elizabeth giggled. "Now it's your turn, girls."

The moment Wendy and Elizabeth met my mother, they immediately recognized her. I honestly thought they were too young to know who Ellie Montague-Bakewell was, but the internet is a strange thing. I cringed to think that Mom might possibly have been made into a meme. I'd have to check. Like Kennedy, the girls had instantly fallen in love with Mom, and now regarded the Beacon Bakeshop as officially the coolest place in the county to work. As the girls put on their camera-ready smiles and twirled in their aprons, mimicking Mom, Dad burst through the kitchen door holding a tray loaded with donuts. He nearly crashed into the girls, but skillfully lifted the tray, avoiding disaster.

"Sorry," he said. I heaved a sigh of relief. "Here you go, Linds, one last bit of pastry to fill out your beautiful cases."

"Dad, these look amazing," I uttered, stunned. The entire tray of donuts had been frosted in bright, beachy colors—cherry red, vibrant raspberry, delicate orchid pink, lemon yellow, blueberry blue, white vanilla, and decadent chocolate. Some were cake, some raised, but all were covered in decorative sprinkles. I'd never seen anything so eye-catchingly delicious before. "I thought we weren't going to make donuts," I reminded him. Dad slid the tray into the last vacant spot in the bakery case and wiped his hands on his apron.

"Well, dear, that would be a mistake. The donuts you made sounded truly delicious, they did, and I understand your hesitancy to make them again. But this is a bakery, and you need donuts. I snuck these beauties in after we made the apple and cherry Danish and the three coffee cakes."

"But what if they bring bad luck?"

"Luck?" Dad shot me a disapproving look. "You're a Bakewell, Lindsey. Haven't I always told you that we Bakewells don't count on luck? We work hard and forge our own destiny. Sure, there are bumps along the way, but they're just bumps. Besides, your mother and I are now here. What can possibly go wrong?"

The moment Dad said this, the lighthouse door burst open and Wellington, Brinkley, and Ireland ran into the awaiting café. The models yapped excitedly. Rory appeared a beat later, chasing after them.

"Sorry," he said, trying to get control of the three dogs. "I found Wellington running around by the light tower on his leash. I figured he got away from Kennedy. These two ambushed me in the living room."

I was relieved to see Rory. I was afraid he might not show up at all, but had pushed that thought aside. After wrangling the dogs and putting them safely on the other side of the lighthouse door, I wrapped my arms around him and gave him a kiss. "I'm so glad you're here." I whispered.

"Me too," he said, and smiled. After greeting Mom, Dad, and the girls, he asked, "Would anyone mind if I jumped behind the counter and helped Elizabeth with the coffee drinks? I know you've been training hard on the espresso machine," he said to her. "But there's quite a crowed out there. It's always good to have reinforcements behind the line."

"I'm good with it," Elizabeth said, nodding. Like Mom, both girls had their long hair tied back in a ponytail.

I handed Rory an apron. "Looks like you're in. I think you two are going to make a great team."

"Without a doubt," he said and high-fived both Elizabeth and Wendy as he walked behind the counter. For the first time all morning, the butterflies were settling.

"Hey," I addressed him. "When you were outside, did you happen to see Betty?"

Rory, peering at me from over the espresso machine, shook his head.

"I hope she's okay," I said, and meant it. No one had seen much of Betty since the incident. The thought of Mike and Dylan's duplicity had depressed her, but I prayed it hadn't crushed her spirit. Beacon Harbor just wouldn't be the same without Betty Vanhoosen.

"Two minutes to go," Mom announced. "Everyone, to your stations."

I took a deep breath and said a silent prayer. The moment I did, the faint smell of pipe smoke tickled my nose. As the familiar scent registered, the bakery lights flickered. I knew without a doubt it was the Captain. How odd that I should believe in ghosts. New York Lindsey would never have entertained the thought. That's because New York Lindsey had never lived in a haunted lighthouse before. I smiled at the thought, knowing that the Captain was still in residence. And I believed he was letting me know that he was ready too.

Dad, staring at the lights that had gone momentarily haywire, cried, "What the heck?"

"It's an old building, Dad. Nothing to worry about."

Before Dad could reply, Wendy's face flashed surprise as she pointed at the door. "Look," she commanded.

I spun around in time to see the crowd outside parting like Moses commanding the Red Sea. But it wasn't Moses at the helm. It was Betty Vanhoosen. Dressed in a blue-and-white-striped shirt, smart navy blazer, and red capri pants, she resembled the captain of a party boat ready to set sail as she marched along, greeting her friends. Kennedy stood before the door, waving her to the front. The moment Betty arrived, she knocked on the glass and smiled at me. That was my cue.

"Everybody ready?" I asked. I looked at the five remarkable people standing behind the counter: Elizabeth, Wendy, Mom, Dad, and Rory. The butterflies were completely gone, replaced by a welling of pride, gratitude, and happiness. "Here we go, Opening Day 2.0," I said, and unlocked the door.

The bakery was soon filled with my new friends and plenty of kind strangers. Having Mom behind the counter was a smart move. If her smile could sell designer clothing and pricey perfume, it could do wonders with reasonably priced baked goods. People loved her, and Mom enjoyed the attention. Wendy worked seamlessly beside her, filling orders, chatting with customers, and having a ball doing so. Dad preferred to stay in the kitchen, where he readied the next group of trays to go into the bakery cases. Rory and Elizabeth, working on the other side of the cash register, combined their talents and worked the espresso machine as if they'd been doing it for years. Quiches, coffee cakes, and donuts appeared on plates as drink orders were called out by name and placed in the hand that had ordered it. When Betty received her latte, the crowd fell silent.

A flash of panic seized me as Betty stood there, staring at the frothy drink in her hand.

She took a tentative sip. Waiting the space of a few heartbeats, she shrugged and took another. "Delicious," she finally declared, and flashed Rory a wink.

"I'll have what she's drinking," exclaimed Sergeant Murdock, wiggling her finger at Rory.

"Make mine a double," Kennedy added, squeezing between Murdock and Officer Cutie Pie. She placed her arms around their shoulders. Laughter bubbled through the room. I was laughing too. This was the moment I had dreamed of the night I had made that chancy internet purchase, and it had finally arrived.

The Beacon Bakeshop was open for business.

RECIPES FROM
THE BEACON BAKESHOP

Feel like trying some delicious donuts at home? Here are
some tried-and-true recipes that will have your friends
and family raving!

Delicious Raised Donuts

Prep time: 8 hours. Cook time: 3 minutes a batch. Makes 18 raised donuts.

Hint: Make the dough the night before and let it rise in the fridge overnight.

Ingredients:

1 cup plus 2 tablespoons of whole milk, warmed to 105 degrees

¼ cup sugar

One package active dry yeast (2½ teaspoons)

10 tablespoons butter (1¼ sticks), melted

2 eggs, lightly beaten

4 cups all-purpose flour

¼ teaspoon salt

Oil for frying (using a neutral flavored oil will get better results, like corn, safflower, peanut, or canola)

Directions:

Warm the milk in a small saucepan until it reaches 105 degrees, or is warm to the touch. Stir in sugar. Next, add the yeast and stir until dissolved. Let yeast mixture sit for 5 minutes until the yeast starts to bubble on the surface. Pour into the bowl of mixer.

Add melted butter and beaten eggs. Using the paddle attachment, beat ingredients together.

With mixer on slow, add the flour and salt, stirring until the dough comes together. Mix for five more minutes to activate the yeast.

Turn sticky dough into a lightly oiled bowl and turn once to coat both sides. Cover with plastic wrap and place in the refrigerator for at least 8 hours.

Remove dough from the fridge and turn out onto a lightly floured surface. Roll dough out until it is ½-inch thick. Using a 3-inch donut cutter, cut out the donuts. Line baking sheets with parchment paper. Lightly spray the parchment paper with oil to keep donuts from sticking. Place donuts and holes on parchment paper, cover, and let rise in a warm place until doubled in size, about one hour. Donuts will be very light and delicate.

Line a baking sheet with paper towels. This is where the fried donuts will go immediately after the fryer to absorb the excess grease. Keep plenty of paper towels on hand for replacements!

To fry the donuts: Using a deep pot, Dutch oven, or home fryer, heat two to three inches of oil to 375 degrees. Use a thermometer to hit the right temperature. Carefully add the donuts to the hot oil in small batches, usually three at a time. Once donuts reach a nice golden brown (about 1½ minutes), turn over and cook the other side. I use chopsticks for this part, but you can use a slotted spoon. When donuts are a beautiful light brown, remove from fryer and place on paper towels. Cool slightly, then dip in your favorite donut glaze. *See Donut Glazes below.

Easy Cake Donuts

Prep time: 30 minutes. Cook time: 3 minutes per batch.
Makes 16 classic cake donuts.

Ingredients:
3 cups all-purpose flour
1 tablespoon baking powder
½ teaspoon salt
½ teaspoon freshly grated nutmeg (optional)
2 large eggs, room temperature
¾ cup sugar
2 teaspoons vanilla extract
3 tablespoons unsalted butter, melted and cooled
½ cup buttermilk (or whole milk), room temperature
Oil for frying

Directions:
In large bowl, mix flour, baking powder, salt, and nutmeg. Set aside.

In the bowl of an electric mixer using the paddle attachment, beat the eggs and sugar until thick and pale, about 5 minutes. Beat in the vanilla extract. On low speed add flour mixture, cooled butter, and buttermilk, alternating each one in turn until a nice soft dough forms. Cover bowl with plastic wrap and let sit at room temperature for 30 minutes, or until dough is firm enough to handle.

Turn dough onto a floured work surface. Roll out to ¼-inch thickness and cut with a donut cutter or 3-inch biscuit cutter. Place donuts on lightly floured parchment paper and let rest 10 minutes.

Line a baking sheet with paper towels. This is where

the fried donuts will go immediately after the fryer to absorb the excess grease. Keep plenty of paper towels on hand for replacements!

In a large, heavy pot, Dutch oven, or deep fryer, heat 2–3 inches of oil to 350 degrees. Use a thermometer! Place a few donuts at a time in hot oil and cook on each side until the donuts are a nice golden-brown color, about $1\frac{1}{2}$ minutes per side. Immediately drain on paper towels. Cool slightly, then dip in your favorite donut glaze.

Donut Glazes

Decadent Chocolate

This is the perfect glaze for a homemade cake donut.

Ingredients:
1 stick unsalted butter
¼ cup whole milk
1 tablespoon light corn syrup
1 teaspoon vanilla extract
½ cup of semi-sweet chocolate chips
2 cups sifted powdered sugar

Directions:
Place butter, milk, corn syrup, and vanilla in a medium saucepan. Gently heat ingredients until melted. Remove from heat and add chocolate, stirring until melted. Add powdered sugar and whisk until smooth. Immediately dip cooled donuts into glaze, then place on a cooling rack. Let donuts rest 30 minutes until glaze is set, then enjoy!

Vanilla Glaze

If you like Krispy Kreme donuts, you'll love this glaze. It's the perfect complement to a freshly made raised donut.

Ingredients:
3 cups powdered sugar
1 teaspoon vanilla

4 tablespoons salted butter, melted
½ cup whole milk, room temperature

Directions:

Place powdered sugar in a medium mixing bowl, add the vanilla and melted butter. Slowly whisk in milk until glaze is smooth and the perfect texture. This glaze should be a bit runny. Dip warm donut in glaze and set on a cooling rack until glaze is set.

Hint: For brightly colored donuts, add less milk to the recipe above to make a thicker glaze, then experiment with your favorite food coloring. Add brightly colored sprinkles for that extra wow factor!

Hog Heaven Donut Glaze

This decadent glaze works on either type of donut and makes the perfect breakfast treat.

Ingredients:
1/4 cup butter
1/2 cup brown sugar
3 tablespoons whole milk
1 tablespoon light corn syrup
2 teaspoons maple extract
2 cups powdered sugar
4 to 6 strips thick-cut bacon, cooked, drained, and
    chopped into 1/4-inch-thick bits

Directions:
In small saucepan, combine butter and brown sugar. Heat on medium heat. Slowly whisk in milk and continue to heat for five minutes, stirring often until butter is melted and sugar is dissolved. Remove from heat. Add corn syrup and maple extract. Whisk in the powdered sugar until smooth. Dip donuts in icing then place on cooling rack. Immediately sprinkle with bacon before glaze sets. Enjoy!

Traverse City Cherry Delight Donut Glaze

This glaze works best on raised donuts.

Ingredients:
4 tablespoons tart cherry juice
½ cup tart cherries, canned or frozen
2½ cups powdered sugar

Directions:
Place cherry juice and the tart cherries in a blender. Blend well. Add cherry mixture to the powdered sugar and stir. Add more tart cherry juice until desired thickness. Dip donut in glaze and place on a cooling rack until glaze is set.

Chicken Marsala

Prep time: 15 minutes. Cook time: 30 minutes. Makes 4 servings.

Ingredients:
3 tablespoons all-purpose flour
Salt
Freshly ground pepper
4 large (about 1½ pounds) boneless, skinless chicken
    breasts, pounded to ½-inch thick
4 tablespoons unsalted butter
3 cloves garlic, minced
1 (8 oz) package button mushrooms, sliced
2 tablespoons shallots, finely chopped
⅔ cup dry Marsala wine
⅔ cup chicken broth
⅔ cup heavy cream
2 tablespoons chopped fresh thyme

Directions:
    In a large zip-lock bag, place flour, 1 teaspoon of salt, and ½ teaspoon of pepper. Add the chicken, seal the bag, and shake well, until chicken is evenly coated. Set aside.

    In a large skillet over medium heat, melt 2 tablespoons of butter. Place the flour-dusted chicken in the buttered pan and cook until chicken is golden brown on both sides, about 6 minutes. Transfer chicken to a plate and store in a 200-degree oven to keep warm.

    Put remaining butter in the hot skillet. Add the garlic and cook one minute. Next, add the mushrooms and cook, stirring frequently, until the mushrooms release their juices and begin to brown, about 4 minutes. Next add the shallots and ½ teaspoon of salt. Cook for 2 more minutes.

Add the wine, broth, heavy cream, and thyme to the hot pan. Stir well, scraping any brown bits from the pan into the liquid. Bring to a boil, then reduce heat, allowing the sauce to simmer for 10 to 15 minutes. Sauce will thicken and become darker in color.

When sauce has thickened, add chicken and any remaining juices back to the pan. Reduce heat to low and simmer 2 to 3 more minutes until chicken is warmed through. Enjoy!

Hint: This dish is delicious on its own, but it becomes amazing when served with Decadent Garlic Mashed Potatoes!

Decadent Garlic Mashed Potatoes

Prep time: 10 minutes. Cook time: 20 minutes. Makes 10 servings.

Ingredients:
3 pounds russet potatoes
2 tablespoons kosher salt
1 stick butter
6 cloves garlic, crushed
1 cup half-and-half
1 cup grated Parmesan cheese

Directions:

Peel and dice potatoes. Put potato cubes in a large pot and cover with water. Add the kosher salt, cover pot, and bring to a rolling boil. Reduce heat while maintaining a boil to simmer. Cook potatoes until they are very tender, about 12 minutes.

In smaller saucepan, combine butter, garlic, and cream. Heat over medium heat until butter is melted and sauce simmers. Remove from heat and set aside.

When potatoes are done, remove from heat and drain off the water. With potato masher, mash warm potatoes in the pot. Stir in garlic cream mixture. Potatoes will become light and creamy. Next, stir in the grated Parmesan cheese. Let mixture rest a few minutes before serving.

Carrot-Raisin Muffins with Cream Cheese Frosting

Prep time: 20 minutes. Bake time: 25 minutes. Makes 12 muffins.

Ingredients:
1½ cups all-purpose flour
1 tablespoon baking powder
½ teaspoon cinnamon
¼ teaspoon salt
2 large eggs
½ cup brown sugar
¾ cup milk
¼ cup (½ stick) butter, melted
1 cup peeled and grated carrots
½ cup raisins
½ cup coarsely chopped walnuts (optional)

Directions:
Heat oven to 375 degrees. Grease muffin cups or use paper baking cups. In a medium bowl, combine flour, baking powder, cinnamon, and salt.

In bowl of electric mixer, mix eggs and brown sugar until smooth. Add milk and melted butter and continue mixing. Add flour mixture and blend well. Stir in carrots, raisins, and nuts.

Scoop batter into muffin cups and bake for 20 to 25 minutes. Let cool and frost with cream cheese frosting.

Cream Cheese Frosting

Ingredients:
1 stick butter, softened
1 8 oz package cream cheese, softened
4 cups powdered sugar
2 teaspoons vanilla extract

Directions:
In bowl of electric mixer, beat butter and cream cheese until fluffy. Add the powdered sugar one cup at a time, blending well. Add in the vanilla extract. Beat until frosting has a light, fluffy texture, about 5 minutes.

Bacon and Spinach Quiche

Prep time: 15 minutes. Cook time: 35 to 40 minutes. Makes 6 servings.

Ingredients:
1 piecrust (use your favorite premade or homemade crust)
1 cup milk
5 large eggs
½ teaspoon salt
¼ teaspoon pepper
4 slices bacon, cooked and chopped into little pieces
1 cup shredded Swiss cheese
¼ cup grated Parmesan cheese
1 cup fresh baby spinach leaves, chopped
2 scallions, thinly sliced

Directions:
Preheat oven to 425 degrees. Line a 9-inch pie plate with crust and crimp the edges.

In medium bowl whisk milk, eggs, salt, and pepper and set aside.

On bottom of piecrust, layer cooked bacon, Swiss cheese, Parmesan cheese, chopped spinach, and scallions. Pour egg mixture over the top and bake 15 minutes. Then reduce the oven temperature to 325 degrees and continue to bake for another 20 to 25 minutes, or until knife inserted in the middle comes out clean. Remove from oven and let rest 10 minutes before serving.

Cherry-Chocolate-Chunk Cookies

Prep time: 20 minutes. Cook time: 13 to 15 minutes per batch. Makes 2 dozen cookies.

Ingredients:
1 cup pecans, toasted then chopped
1¼ cups (2¼ sticks) butter
¾ cup brown sugar
¾ cup sugar
1 egg
2 teaspoons vanilla extract
1½ cups all-purpose flour
3 cups old-fashioned oats
1 teaspoon baking soda
1 teaspoon ground cinnamon
½ teaspoon salt
1 cup dried tart cherries
1 cup semi-sweet chocolate chips (can be made with white chocolate chips, or dark chocolate chips as well)

Directions:
Preheat oven to 350 degrees.

Put pecans on a cookie sheet and bake in the oven for 10 minutes, or until lightly toasted. Remove from oven and let cool before chopping.

In large mixing bowl with paddle attachment, cream butter and both sugars together until fluffy. Add the egg and vanilla and beat until blended. In a large bowl, combine the flour, oats, baking soda, cinnamon, and salt. Add this mixture to the butter-sugar mixture one cup at a time until dough is well blended. Add cherries, chocolate chips, and pecans.

On a parchment-lined baking sheet, drop ¼ cup cookie dough, placing each cookie 3 inches apart. Bake in oven for 13 to 15 minutes, or until cookies are a nice golden brown. Remove from oven and let cool on the baking sheet a few minutes before serving.